TWISTED VOICES

TWISTED VOICES

STORIES FROM ELLERY QUEEN'S MYSTERY MAGAZINE

EDITED BY
JANET HUTCHINGS
JACKIE SHERBOW

LEVEL
SHORT

Contents

Acknowledgements

Thanks to Abigail Browning and Carol Demont for helping to make this project possible, to Kevin Wheeler for assistance in preparing the manuscript, and to Martin Edwards for providing the title for the collection.

Grateful acknowledgement is made to the following authors for permission to reprint their copyrighted material. All stories first appeared in *Ellery Queen's Mystery Magazine*.

- "The Belgian" by Doug Allyn, copyright © 2017 by Doug Allyn, reprinted by permission of the author.
- "A Complicated History" by Daniel C. Bartlett, copyright © 2022 by Daniel C. Bartlett, reprinted by permission of the author.
- "Never Enough" by Liza Cody, copyright © 2023 by Liza Cody, reprinted by permission of the author.
- "Shall I Be Murder?" by Mat Coward, copyright © 2018 by Mat Coward, reprinted by permission of the author.
- "Hedge Hog" by Hilary Davidson, copyright © 2011 by Hilary Davidson, reprinted by permission of the author.
- "No Peace for the Wicked" by Martin Edwards, copyright © 2022 by Martin Edwards, reprinted by permission of the author.
- "Three Calendars" by Angelique Fawns, copyright © 2019 by Angelique Fawns, reprinted by permission of the author.
- "Dear Emily Etiquette" by Barb Goffman, copyright © 2020 by Barb Goffman, reprinted by permission of the author.
- "Tradition" by Ed Gorman, copyright © 2010 by Ed Gorman, reprinted by permission of the author's estate.
- "Best Served Cold" by Alice Hatcher, copyright © 2021 by Alice Hatcher,

Introduction

Most often in fiction a first-person narrator is also a central character (if not *the* central character) in the story being told, someone whose personal observations, thoughts, feelings, and acts are at the heart of matters. That's not always the case in the mystery field, where we are very familiar with first-person narrators who serve primarily as reporters of events rather than as primary participants in them—most of the "Watsons" of crime fiction fall into this category. When first-person narration is employed in a classical whodunit, the point of view is usually not deeply personal, it's more often objective and reportorial, and it's easy to see why. If a writer wants to challenge readers to solve a mystery, it's important not to have all of the thoughts that flow through the sleuth's mind accessible to the reader at the moment they occur.

One of the things that sets this anthology of stories from *Ellery Queen's Mystery Magazine* apart from all of our previous collections is that the stories we have included here are all told in the first person. But there is a slant to our theme. As the book's title suggests, there are no truly objective narrators here. The voices heard in these stories are all "twisted" in one respect or another. That doesn't necessarily mean they aren't truthful, but it does mean readers are unlikely, for one reason or another, to trust entirely in what they say. For that reason, the "fair-play" whodunit—in which what the reader is told can, for the most part, be depended upon—does not appear in these pages. Nor, for that matter, does the traditional private-eye story.

It's true that many of the most revered works of the private-eye genre have a first-person narrator who is also the story's main character, and part of the appeal of the form is that readers are allowed inside the head of the protagonist—seeing and feeling what the P.I. sees and feels as events unfold. The immediacy of this point of view appeals to many readers, and it also provides an opportunity for the writer to tell the story in a voice that belongs to an unusual character—often an eccentric and memorable voice. But the fictional private eye is also traditionally equipped with a strong moral compass, and although often flawed, with perceptions distorted at times by personal dilemmas, the character is almost always of sound as well as incorruptible mind.

The same cannot be said for many of the characters who people these pages. The concept of the "unreliable narrator" comes closest to capturing the sorts of voices that conform to our theme—although in some of our selections it's an illusion that the narrator is unreliable; it turns out instead that it's the assumptions of the reader that are way off the mark. In others, the narrator may appear perfectly trustworthy until the final twist at the end. It was remarkable to us as we started assembling the contents of this book that even without drawing from the classical whodunit or private-eye genres we ended up with a broad range of stories. There are caper stories and humorous stories, noir offerings and supernatural tales, stories with a literary bent and experimental stories, bizarre situations and heart-wrenching ones. Where these stories differ most, however, is in the types of "twisted" perspectives each of their characters brings to the book. Contributions by Joyce Carol Oates and O.A. Tynan take us into the minds of characters too young to see the world objectively. Martin Edwards's distorting (or clarifying?) lens is life after death. In tales by Doug Allyn and Angelique Fawns we have points of view contorted, respectively, by war and dementia, and in LaToya Jovena's offering a life and mind altered by COVID. Ordinary people whose perceptions warp humorously as events unfold feature in light-hearted stories by Tom Tolnay and Barb Goffman, while there's a much darker turn ahead for those whose willful misperceptions send them in criminal directions in pieces by Andrew Klavan and Ed Gorman.

Sometimes it's by the guiding hand of crazed narrators that readers must unravel the plot, as in Mat Coward's and William Burton McCormick's contributions. And then there are stories by Gary Phillips, Ian Rankin, and S. J. Rozan in which the narrators are career criminals, with points of view that permanently diverge from that of the law-abiding.

Extreme self-absorption may result in the most corrupt perception of all, as seen in tales by Liza Cody and Hilary Davidson. But guilt comes in a close second, as stories by Alice Hatcher and Daniel C. Bartlett reveal.

The last story in the book, by Mike McHone, is told in what is sometimes called the "deep third person," but with a difference. Its central character's mental makeup involves hearing voices—two in particular in addition to her own. With three personalities rolled into one, the story could hardly have been told in the first person without marginalizing the other two voices. Nevertheless, the narration *feels* like first-person, and the voices are certainly twisted in the sense of presenting a point of view (or points of view) outside the norm. The story supplies the outer limit to a collection that covers a lot of ground and that we hope will supply readers with many satisfying twists and turns as they try to figure out what can and cannot be believed.

—Janet Hutchings

The Belgian

by Doug Allyn

Have you ever wondered if your parents lay awake in the dark, regretting the paths they chose? The roads not taken? Because they had children?

Because they had us?

I used to chew on that sometimes, on long stakeouts, waiting for a target to show. But now? I mostly wonder…at the end of things…in the last desperate moments of his life…

If my father hated me.

God knows, he had cause. At eighteen, I was a handful, having trouble in school, petty scrapes with the law. Pop had to bail me out of juvie lockup to attend my mother's funeral. The last chance of peace between us died with her.

I enlisted the same week. Army.

Basic training in Texas, MP school in Fort Leonard Wood, then off to Afghanistan. Poured my anger and frustration into the job, turned out to be a natural at it. Maybe too good.

After three long tours in the mountains, hunting jihadis who couldn't find America on a map, I saw the world very differently than I had at eighteen. Saw my father differently too.

But I never told him. The few times I came home on leave, he was out on the road, long-haul trucking. Avoiding me, maybe.

I didn't blame him. Didn't worry about it overmuch either. When you're young, you think you have forever to set things right.

But our time was already up. It was four days too late before I even got the word.

That was the lag time, between the Tuesday night my father died in a blazing wreck on a northern Michigan highway and the Friday morning the news caught up with me.

I was in a sniper hide on a rocky hilltop overlooking some raggedy-ass village in Helmand Province. Waiting to cap a Taliban chief whose name I can't recall.

It was the luckiest day of that sucker's life. Not so lucky for me.

A 914, *return to base, ASAP* text usually means an immediate redeployment. A higher-priority target has popped up and needs to be taken out yesterday.

But not this time. My first sergeant was waiting outside my hooch, and from his face, I knew the news was bad.

But at first, I couldn't understand *how* bad it really was. He had to say it three different ways. It wasn't till he used the term "expired" that it finally registered.

He was telling me my father had been killed.

I couldn't make it compute. People don't die in America. They die in the Sandbox, in Kabul or Peshawar, killed by car bombs, or RPGs, or even freakin' friendly fire. I've sent more than a few off myself. But my dad wasn't in the 'Stan, he was...

Back home. In the world. Where it's supposed to be *safe*. That's why my unit's in these mountains, for chrissake. To keep our homefolks safe....But...

Okay. Finally, it sank in. I *got* the message. More from my first sergeant's eyes, I think, than his words.

Evil crap happens, even back home. The jihadis call it kismet. Fate. Bad luck. Doom. By whatever name, it had taken my father.

He'd cracked up his rig on a north-country road, and died in the crash. My sergeant, an old-time Green Beret named Wojowski, showed me a newspaper clipping. A picture of a burned-out truck sprawled on its side.

It was a tough swallow, but I got it down.

I thanked him, shook his hand, then ducked into my hooch to restock my pack. My target usually showed in his home village in the dark of the moon to bang his wives and grab up supplies. He was due in two days and I needed to be set up, waiting for him.

Wojowski followed me in, frowning at me the way my teachers used to, back in high school.

Wojo'd fought on three different continents. In some ways he was like a father to me. And I guess the job was open, since my father had…*expired*. I couldn't help smiling, remembering that word Wojo used. *Expired*. Like Pop's time had run out on some great parking meter in the sky.

Wojo saw that smile, and spun me around hard. He put both hands on my shoulders, looked me straight in the eye. And told me I had to go home. To see to…whatever the hell needed seeing to. It's what a son does, at a time like this.

I had no idea what he was talking about. What I *needed* to do was get back to my mountain stakeout before my target showed up. Besides, I could *think* up there. Make sense of what happened—

But Wojo wouldn't have it.

"This ain't up for negotiation, Beaumont. I've already replaced you on the line. Pack a bag, stud, you're going stateside, ready or not. I'll see you in a month. Or never, if you're half smart."

So. My father was dead, and I had orders to go home. And see to things. Whatever that meant.

Fine. I packed a bag.

Circling the world seemed to take no time at all. From Bagram to Ramstein, Germany, then on to Delaware, then Detroit. The planes were so clean and brightly lit it made me edgy. I kept waiting for groundfire to lance up at us. Which was nuts. We were at 35,000 feet, flying over water most of the time. Still, we didn't *need* running lights, so why make it easy?

A stewardess in a hijab served us Bud Light in paper cups. The beer tasted odd to me. Cold. And American.

The plane had a wide-screen TV up front. A newswoman was talking about some earthquake in India. A thousand dead, she said. I tried to remember if Michigan had earthquakes. Couldn't rightly recall.

I scarcely recognized my hometown airport. Algoma Municipal had doubled in size since my last rotation. Busy as an anthill now. I'd ridden the last leg of my journey in a commuter prop plane jammed with rednecks headed north for the November deer season.

I'd e-mailed my sister that I was on my way, thought she might meet me. She wasn't there. I didn't see anyone I knew.

But someone knew me. A slim woman, dark suit, dark hair, dark glasses, tossed her newspaper aside and rose when she spotted me coming up the ramp.

"Sergeant Beaumont? I'm Beverly Danvers," she said, offering her hand. "I'm with the personnel section at Camp Maynard. We're very sorry for your loss. Did you check any luggage?"

"No, just a carry-on." I patted my shoulder pack. "What are you doing here?"

"In cases of bereavement, aides are assigned to returning soldiers now," she said, falling into step with me. "It's standard procedure. But I'm afraid some other issues have come up since you left the field."

"What issues?"

"Your father's death was initially reported as an accident. Now it appears to have been a robbery gone wrong. The police may have questions for you."

"I've got a pretty good alibi."

"I'm sure they don't—oh," she said quickly, "that was a joke. In any case, you're coming home to an unhappy situation, Sergeant. I'm here to help in any way I can."

"Help what?"

She seemed surprised at the question. "Why, dealing with grief, of course. The death of a parent—"

"Look, lady, I haven't talked to my dad in years. I was ordered home for his funeral, so I'm here, but I'll probably head straight back afterward. I don't need a babysitter."

"But you do need a driver. You've served back-to-back tours overseas, Sergeant. Your license expired last year. You can't rent a car and your father's funeral starts within the hour. Would you like to change clothes?"

"What for?"

"Perhaps something…more appropriate?" There was that look again. She was dressed for mourning, a black skirt and jacket. I was dressed for the road, a leather jacket, jeans, and jump boots.

"My old man was a trucker, lady. It won't be a black-tie affair."

Algoma, Michigan, has two funeral homes, one for each side of the Vale River. Pawluk's Mortuary serves the north side, the low-rent side.

Our side.

My dad was there, or at least I assume it was him. The casket was closed. It could have been anybody. I rested my hand on the box, waiting to feel some…tremor of mortality. Some connection. But there was nothing, except a faint scent of barbeque. And maybe I imagined that.

An older, heavyset guy in a dark suit and loud tie moved up beside me, draping a beefy arm around my shoulders.

"How are you holdin' up, son? You probably don't remember me."

He was right.

"Sid Kelso, from the Brotherhood of Teamsters," he said, offering his hand. "I used to pick up your dad for meetings sometimes. Before you went in the service."

"I remember," I lied.

"Then you've got a good memory. Which is a shame, in a way."

"Why's that?"

"Because it'll go a lot easier on local folks if you forget a few things. Like what your old man told you he was into, the last few months. He wanted those drug runs for the hazardous-cargo pay."

"Drug runs?"

"C'mon, Josh, you been overseas, but you was born and raised in the north and know the score. It's been slim pickin's up here since the copper played out. All we got goin' is scrub timber and salvage that falls off the trucks along the Canuck border."

I nodded. He took it for agreement, and in a way, it was. In Michigan's Upper Peninsula, most of the Canadian border is an imaginary line drawn across the bottom of a lake. Inland, there are a hundred ways to jump the fence that don't involve checkpoints or paperwork.

"Was Pop working the border?" I asked, keeping my tone neutral.

He almost answered, then grinned and clapped a meaty paw on my shoulder. "That's exactly the right answer, son. If the law leans on you, you know from nothing, right?"

"Absolutely," I said. Which was the truth when I said it. I didn't know squat about what Pop was into. But I intended to find out. Kelso moved off to glad-hand his cronies. A couple of them glanced at me as they spoke. Memorizing my face, though I had no idea why.

I took up a post at the back of the room, looking over the crowd. The turnout was respectable. Thirty, forty people, working stiffs in flannel shirts and jeans, a few older guys in ill-fitting suits. Women in thrift-shop dresses, with runny-nosed kids in their arms, or clinging to their skirts. I recognized a few, but most were strangers. Truckers lead footloose lives.

Not many remembered me, or if they did, they knew of the troubles between me and my dad. A few came over to shake my hand and offer their sympathies, but nobody lingered to chat. Which was best, since I had only the vaguest recollection of who they were. I've felt more at home at tribal weddings in Peshawar.

"Josh?" a young woman separated herself from the crowd. It took a moment for her face to register. A younger, prettier version of my mom.

"Jolene," I said, gathering her in a clumsy embrace. "How are you, sis?"

"I'm okay. I'm glad you could make it. And a little surprised. It's been a long time. Is this your wife?"

"A coworker," Danvers said, offering her hand. "Beverly Danvers, from Camp Maynard. I'm so sorry for your loss."

"More than my brother is, I'm guessing," Jolene said, reading my face. "You didn't even recognize me, did you?"

"It's been...awhile, Jo," I acknowledged. "You're all grown up."

"It's been something like four years since we've heard a word from you, Josh. I'm married now, we have two kids. I wrote to you—"

"I got your letter. I sent a check—"

"And I sent a thank-you note. It came back address unknown."

"It's not uncommon for mail to be misrouted in that part of the world," Danvers put in.

"Are you sure you two aren't married?" Jolene asked. "You seem to be talking for my brother, and I have no idea who or what—sorry," she added, waving off Danvers's apology. "I'm a bit on edge. Can we talk for a minute, Josh? Away from all this?"

"There's a chapel just off the foyer," Danvers said. "It's this way."

We followed her down the hall to the next doorway. A quiet room, six pews, and a rostrum up front. A cross and a star of David. A uni-god chapel the way bus-station johns are unisex. No moon of Islam, I noticed. Or at least, not yet.

"Is something funny, Josh?" Jolene asked.

I wiped the smile off my face. Hadn't realized it was there.

"Sorry," I said. "It's been awhile since I was in a church."

"It's been awhile since you were *anywhere* I knew of," Jolene agreed, "and since it'll probably be even longer till the next time, let's get this done." She took a booklet out of her purse and handed it to me.

I opened it. It was a bank book. Sixty grand and change.

"What's this?"

"Pop's savings," Jolene replied. "He kept every dime you ever sent home, Josh. He was saving it for you. For when you came home."

"Damn it, Jo, I sent him the money to make your lives better, for your tuition and—"

"—and to rub it in just a little that you were making more in a month than Pop made in six? We didn't need your money, Josh. A letter home would have meant a lot more than a check. And for the record? I won a full-ride scholarship to Michigan State. Graduated with honors two years ago. Which you'd know, if you'd bothered to stay in touch."

"Your brother's duties often take him to remote areas where communications are difficult," Danvers put in.

"Communicating with my brother is difficult when we're in the same damn room," Jolene snapped. "And since you obviously don't know him well, kindly butt out and let us finish this. How long since you've seen Pop, Josh?"

I had to think. "It's been…quite some time," I admitted.

Actually it had been six years. I'd shown up out of the blue just as he was leaving on a week-long run up to Montreal. I don't remember what we said. Things were still edgy between us. Couldn't remember if we shook hands or not. I know we didn't hug.

"Have you written to Pop at all in the past few years? Or sent him a goddamn get-well card? He was dying, did you know that?"

I shook my head.

"Pancreatic cancer. Stage four. So maybe going out the way he did suited him better. The road was really where he lived. Where do you live, Josh? Really."

Her eyes were swimming. I was so baffled I almost went with the truth, that I belonged in the mountains, half a world away. Hunting holy warriors.

I put the book in her hand instead, and folded her fingers around it.

"I didn't send this to be saved, Jolene. I sent it to help out the family."

"We aren't family, Josh. Families stay in touch, families talk, families…give a damn about each other. Our last family tie is in that coffin in the next room. I'll hold this money till the next time I see you. Or until your lady friend here shows up to tell me you got killed somewhere with…poor communications. Where are you staying?"

"I thought I'd crash at the house."

"You'll have to check with the police first. They've got it taped off, Josh. They ransacked it, top to bottom. It's a mess."

"Why? What were they looking for?"

"I don't know." She sighed. "Evidence, I suppose. Can I ask you a favor?"

"Of course."

"Can you deal with the fallout here? Talk to the police and whatever else needs doing? My husband's out of town for a week, I had to stash my kids with a neighbor and I ahm—"

She broke off, her voice quivering. I reached out to comfort her, but didn't. Wasn't sure how she'd react.

"We'll take care of things," Danvers said quickly. "Go home, Jolene. Be with your children."

"Thank you, I guess," Jolene said, eyeing me, shaking her head. "When this is over, you should stop by and meet my Jerry and your nephews, Josh. We're all you have now. Does that matter to you at all?"

"Sure it does," I said. "Look, sis, I know this is a tough time—"

"Oh, please," she said, smiling in spite of herself. "I'm sure you mean well, but even as a kid, I always knew you were faking it."

"Faking what?"

"Giving a damn about me or anybody else. Keep trying, though, you're a better actor than you used to be." She kissed me quickly on the cheek, pressing a business card into my hand. "My new address is on my card, and my number. Call us sometime."

"I will. I promise."

"Right." She sighed, giving me a wan smile as she turned away. "I'll wait by the phone."

She hurried out of the chapel, brushing past two cops who'd just stepped in. Both men were in tan uniforms, with full-rig weapons belts, baseball caps. The older one was pushing fifty, with a face like a bloodhound, sad and surly. The younger one was tall, hawk-faced and slender, with dark hair. First Nation, maybe. He held the door for Jolene.

"Mr. Beaumont?" the older one said. "I'm Captain Snider, Algoma P.D. This is Corporal Blackthorne. I know our timing's lousy, but we need a word."

"About what?"

"Your dad, and his situation—"

"And his bank account," the younger one put in.

"If you could come down to the station with us?" Snider asked. "It'll only take a few minutes—"

"That's out of the question," Danvers said, stepping between us. "Sergeant Beaumont is a serving member of the U.S. military. As such, he's entitled to legal counsel before any questioning by civil authorities—"

"Come on, lady, there's no need to drag the MPs into this—"

"That's *Major* to you, *Captain*," Danvers snapped, flashing a military ID folder. *"Major* Beverly Danvers, army C.I.D. Sergeant Beaumont is home on humanitarian leave and—"

"Hold it!" I said.

"I've got this, Sergeant," Danvers said.

"No, you haven't. This isn't army business and I'm not in your chain of command. I'll answer your questions, Snider, but not for free. We'll trade. You tell me exactly what happened to my dad, then I'll tell you everything I know about it. I'll even give up my right to counsel," I added, waving Danvers off before she could object.

"Fair enough." Snider nodded. "What have you been told?"

"In the 'Stan, they said my dad was killed in an accident, but the major here said it may have been a robbery. What the hell actually happened?"

"A county Mountie was first on the scene, called it in as an accident," Snider said. "It was in the back country. Looked like a dead tree had dropped across the road, your dad swerved to avoid it and lost control. Crashed and burned."

"Where was this?"

"About forty miles north of Algoma, near the county line."

"Up near the border?"

"Not far," he admitted.

"Was he driving his own rig? An International ProStar, 'ninety-one?"

"That's right. Why?"

I waved off the question. "What was the load?"

Snider hesitated. "Pharmaceuticals."

"But not aspirin, right? You mean hard drugs. What kind?"

"Oxycontin," Snider admitted, curious now. "Hydrocodone, a few others in the same class."

"Did the load go up with the truck?"

"We aren't sure yet," Snider said warily. "Your dad's rig burned down to the frame. The state police are running a chemical analysis of the ashes. Why?"

"And my Pops?" I asked carefully. "Was he alive when it burned?"

The two cops exchanged a quick look.

"We haven't released that information yet," Snider said. "It stays between us, right?"

"That depends—" Danvers began.

"Stay out of this, Major," I snapped. "It's personal!"

I half expected Danvers to pull rank, rip me a new one. But she didn't. Given my mood, it was the right move.

"Your father was dead before the truck burned," Snider said. "Somebody shot up his rig pretty good, and your dad...um. He took a round through the temple, son. Killed him instantly. I'm sorry."

"There are worse ways to go," I said. "Like burning alive in a truck. How many rounds were fired?"

"I—I'm not sure. A dozen or so."

"Really? What caliber?"

"Two twenty-three. Full metal jacket."

"Military rounds?" I said, surprised.

"Definitely," Blackthorne put in. "From an M-16. We recovered the weapon near the scene. And I believe it's your turn, Sergeant."

"Fair enough." I nodded. "This is what I know, guys. I haven't been stateside in four years. Haven't spoken to my father in nearly six, and that was a quick hello/goodbye as he went out the door. That's it. Every damn thing I know."

"You can't help us at all?" Blackthorne frowned.

"I didn't say that. Where I've been, hijacking is a national sport, right up there with soccer and buzkashi."

"Buz—?" Blackthorne echoed.

"Buzkashi. It's like polo, but instead of whacking a ball, the horsemen fight over a dead goat. And quit blowing smoke. When a truck carrying a load of oxy cracks up twenty miles from the border, that load was in Canada an hour later and you both know it. What else aren't you telling me?"

"Your dad was a trucker with sixty large in the bank," Snider said. "Any idea where he got that kind of money?"

"I know exactly where he got it. It was a wire transfer from a blind trust in the Caymans. My unit set it up for me."

"Why a blind trust?" Snider asked.

"When I sent him cashier's checks he sent them back. So if you're wondering if he was paid off? If maybe he was in on this? He wasn't. Bottom line? He didn't need to take a bribe and wouldn't have anyway. Which is probably why he's dead."

"How did you manage a Caymans bank account?" Snider pressed. "What kind of unit are you in?"

"The sergeant is assigned to Special Operations," Danvers said. "And any information beyond that requires a security clearance above your pay grade, gentlemen. Do you have any more information to share? Or are we done here?"

Snider and Blackthorne exchanged a look. Snider shrugged, then Blackthorne turned to me.

"There's just one thing more, Sergeant. We have a suspect in custody. Spec/Six. Leach, Richard R. Does the name ring a bell?"

"Why would it?"

"He came back from the 'Stan six months ago. Maybe you knew him over there?"

"Sure. A hundred thousand grunts served there. We all hook up at Starbucks every Saturday for green tea. Asia's a big place, Captain. Where was this Leach stationed?"

"He won't say."

"But you think he had something to do with my dad's death?" I thought my tone was absolutely flat, but Danvers caught the edge in it and stepped in front of me, blocking my path.

"You need to back away from this now, Sergeant. It's a police matter. Leave it to the authorities."

"I'm cool, Major. But I'm also curious. What's Leach's story, Captain?"

"He's a hophead, been living on the streets or in shelters for months," Snider said. "Seemed harmless enough, but maybe he had a flashback or something. The night of the hijack we found him in a wrecked car a few miles from the scene. Had an assault weapon in the vehicle, pills from the hijack scattered around. He apparently tried some of the stolen dope, got buzzed, and rolled his getaway car. He was banged up some in the crash, maybe concussed. We were hoping he'd give it up when he came out of the fog."

"And did he?" I asked.

"Only his name, rank, and serial number," Snider said. "Used his phone call to ring up Camp Maynard, ask for an army lawyer. Whoever he talked to told him to dummy up, and they're taking their sweet time verifying his identity. Probably just another head case."

"What do you mean, another one?" I echoed.

"Camp Maynard is a hospital base now, run by the VA," Snider explained. "A rehab facility for wounded vets and others that are just…well. You know."

"Head cases." I nodded. "Maybe he's crazy enough to talk to me."

"Why would he?"

"Like you said, we're both fresh back from the Sandbox, Captain. You know the type. Head cases."

The Algoma cop shop was in the basement of the county courthouse. Concrete walls and floors painted battleship gray, a few battered metal desks. Four cages against the back wall facing each other across a narrow aisle. Stainless-steel toilets, drains in the floor of each cell to make hosing them down easier. Basically drunk tanks. I couldn't help smiling as I looked around.

Danvers was looking at me oddly. Again.

"I spent a week in this jail once," I explained. "Minor in possession of alcohol. Home sweet home, eh?"

Two cells were occupied. One was a businessman in a blue suit with puke down the front. Haggard, sick, and scared, he had a serious case of the shakes. Probably a DUI. I wondered if he'd killed anyone.

The cell across the aisle from him held my guy. Jeans and a denim jacket. Buzz cut. His face was swollen, sporting serious bruises, two gashes stitched shut, a third above his right eye, closed with a butterfly bandage.

He looked up at me as I approached. An empty gaze, and a familiar one. I see it in the mirror sometimes. I walked slowly down to his cell.

"That's far enough," Snider cautioned. "Stay behind the yellow line, Sergeant. No physical contact, and speak up, please. We want to hear anything he says."

"No problem," I said. "What did he tell you his name was?"

"Leach, Richard R." Blackthorne said. "I've got his serial number if you want."

"We won't need that," I said, facing the battered stud in the cell. "So? What should I call you, pal? Because you're definitely not Leach, Richard R. They give us that alias in training. What do your Special Ops buds call you?"

Nothing. It was like talking to the wall. But his eyes were locked on mine. I had his attention.

"Okay, don't talk, Leach, Richard R., just listen. You're in a world of crap, brother. It's hip deep to a giraffe and rising fast. When you finally wise up, and realize you *have* to talk to save yourself? Nobody will believe you. But I will. We've both worked Special Ops, so you know I can keep a secret. Just tell me what happened."

He shook his head curtly, then winced, realizing he'd just broken protocol by answering me at all, even if the answer was no. Which told a lot about him, and told him something about me as well.

"Last chance, pal," I said. "Give me something. Anything. I swear to you I'll run with it."

He cocked his head, eyeing me curiously, like a bird. And I knew he was in full lockdown. He wouldn't talk to me, or anyone else. He'd die first.

Damn. I turned away.

"Woof?" he murmured. Barely above a whisper.

I turned back, met his eyes a moment, then gave him a curt nod.

"What was that?" Snider demanded, hustling over. "What did he say?"

"I didn't hear anything," I said. "What about you, Leach, Richard R.? Did you say anything?"

But he was looking past me. Frowning. At Danvers.

"Major?" he called.

"You want to talk to the major?" Snider demanded. "We can arrange that."

But Leach was already backing away from the bars. Sitting on the edge of his bunk in a lotus position, he laid his open palms on his thighs and began humming to himself. He didn't look up when we turned away.

"What did he say to you?" Snider asked again.

"Not a word," I said.

"Shall we go back to the funeral home?" Danvers asked. We were in her car, pulling out of the Algoma station parking lot.

"What for?"

"The service will begin in a few minutes—"

"Nobody will miss me there, Pop least of all. Do you know where it happened? The crash, I mean?"

"I—yes, I know the place."

"Good. Take me there."

"To the crime scene? Why?"

I didn't bother to answer. Watched her instead. She caught me at it.

"Is something wrong, Sergeant?"

"Leach called out to you."

"He's clearly unstable."

"How old are you, Major?"

"I beg your pardon?"

"It's not a tough question."

"It's not a polite one either."

"Somebody shot my pops in the head, lady. We're way past polite. I'd guess you're thirty at the outside, young for command rank. So you didn't climb up the ladder from lieutenant. You had an advanced degree when you signed on, didn't you? In what?"

She considered her answer. Deciding whether to lie to me. Or not.

"I'm a doctor," she admitted.

"An M.D.?"

"A Ph.D. In psychology. I'm a forensic psychologist, Sergeant, specializing in PTSD. Post-traumatic stress disorder."

"I know what PTSD is, Doc. Guys in my unit do mandatory interviews with a shrink every thirty days. He asks how we feel, checks our reflexes, scouting for symptoms of combat stress. I've always been cleared for duty straightaway. I don't have PTSD. And I'm guessing you knew that before I got here."

Again, she hesitated. "I have seen your records, Sergeant. Which are exemplary, I might add. Your captain says you're the best fighter in his command. But you're coming home to a high-stress situation—"

"Sad," I amended, "but not stressful. Baggin' up a dead friend under fire? That's stress. All boxed up in a shiny new coffin, with soft music, family and friends gathered around? We should all be so lucky."

"The death of a parent—"

"Is a tough break," I said, cutting her off. "But you're in civvies, Major, and Leach called you by your rank, so quit jerking me around. He freakin' knew you. Is he a patient?"

"He—was, for a time," she admitted. "He walked away from the facility several months ago."

"And you just let him go?"

"It's a clinic, Josh, not a jail. Some returnees have difficulty adjusting to civilian life."

"Leach has adjusted himself into a jail cell, Doc. And his injuries weren't from a car crash. I've seen guys beaten like that, I've done it myself. Somebody worked him over."

"The police?"

"Not likely. There were no bruises or defensive wounds on his hands or arms. Even if he'd been restrained with cuffs or flex ties, there'd be marks. I'm guessing he was unconscious when he was beaten. So there's no way in hell he could have driven that getaway car. More likely somebody slipped him a hotshot, roughed him around, then dumped him near the crash scene. He's a patsy, Major. A fall guy. "

"Then why doesn't he say so?"

"Because he's been trained to resist interrogation, and believe me, Special Ops training is a lot tougher than that cell. Was he in Special Ops?"

She just stared.

"Come on, Major, we're on the same side here. Was he Special Ops or not?"

"Yes," she nodded. Reluctantly.

"What's his real name?"

"That's classified."

"It doesn't matter anyway. He wakes up in a cage, thinks he's in enemy hands, and falls back on his training. He's given up all he's going to."

"Not quite," Danvers said. "He said something to you back there. What was it?"

"He didn't say a word."

"It wasn't a word. He...barked at you, or something like it."

"He...woofed," I admitted.

"Like a dog, you mean? Why would he do that?"

"It's a running joke with guys who serve extended tours. We're like the Belgians..." I broke off, mulling that one over. Then swiveled in my seat to stare at her.

"Sweet Jesus," I said softly. "That's why you're here, isn't it? You're afraid I might go Belgian."

"Belgian? What on earth are you talking about?"

"The dogs of war, Doc. Like in Shakespeare? 'Cry havoc? Let slip the dogs of war?' Our K-9 Corps uses Belgians, mostly. Malinois. Attack dogs, trackers, bomb sniffers. They're smart, and aggressive. But once they've tasted blood? Chewed up an intruder or tackled a runner? They change. Here," I said, tapping my temple. "After that, you have to treat them like loaded weapons. Keep 'em leashed around strangers, especially kids. If little Junior accidentally pokes a Belgian in the eye, he might lose his little hand."

"I—still don't get the 'woof' thing," she said. "What's the joke?"

"Thing is, when a dog handler's tour is up, he rotates home, back to the states. But his dog doesn't. His Belgian retrains with a new handler, then goes right back to the war. Over and over. Until we're too crazy to trust anymore. Is that why you're here? Worried I've gone Belgian?"

"You're not a dog, Sergeant."

"Wish I was, sometimes. Their eyes are sharper, hearing's a hundred times better. If Belgians could shoot, we could all stay home, watch TV in our bunny slippers."

"You don't own bunny slippers."

"Nope. And the army doesn't waste a major with a Ph.D. on…what did you call yourself? A bereavement aide? If you've seen my checkups, you know I haven't wigged out. So why exactly did they sic you on me?"

"It's protocol now. In World War Two, most soldiers we call the Greatest Generation saw combat for eighteen months or less. Your unit's been operating in a combat zone for ten years. Battle fatigue is epidemic, substance abuse, domestic violence, even suicides. We have rigorous procedures in place for returnees now. Debriefing, decompression, counseling, medication when indicated. By coming home on emergency leave, you bypassed all the safeguards, Josh. And given your father's violent death—?"

"So you're a dog handler? Is that it?"

"Of course not. I'm only—"

"—here to help with my bereavement. Got it. How am I doing, so far?"

She didn't bother to answer. Concentrated on driving instead. I stared out the side window, watching the trees flash past, and the occasional billboard. Now and then I risked a quick glance at the major.

A handsome woman, I thought. Smart, empathetic. Hot, too, if you like the ice-queen type. And who doesn't? It was a pity, really.

I've conducted some brutal interrogations in the field. And I've seen hajji women spend a long damn day working over a prisoner, after a raid on their home village.

Bottom line? You can actually beat a person to death, break their bones, drain every last drop of their blood, without being certain that they're telling you the truth, the whole truth, and nothing but.

But you can get pretty damn good at knowing when they're not.

And I was dead certain the major was lying to me. About something important. But I had no idea what it was. And she was a shrink, a trained interrogator herself. Spent every working day asking questions, parsing the answers. She was probably better at it than I was.

So short of dangling her off a roof by her ankles—

I smiled at the thought.

"Is something funny?" she asked.

"Are there any really tall buildings nearby?"

"I—can't think of any. Why?"

"Count your blessings," I said. "It's your lucky day." Easing back in my seat, I closed my eyes.

Tactics 101. When you're overmatched, you withdraw, regroup, attack from a new direction.…I drifted off.

But not for long.

The car was slowing down. I sat up. We were on a back-country road, two-lane blacktop with twenty-foot berms on both sides of the road. Up ahead, I could see a scorched tree trunk in the ditch, and a savage scar gouged in the hillside, forty, fifty yards long. It was one I'd seen before. In the photo with the news article about my dad's death.

"Whoa! Stop right here!" I was already piling out of the car as she pulled over. I dogtrotted along the shoulder, reading signs, scouting the ground. I was wired up at full alert, feeling at home for the first time since I'd stepped off the plane. If I *were* a Belgian, my tail would have been wagging.

Until I got to the torn end of the tree stump and saw the shards of safety glass on the ground.

And I slowed my pace, then stopped, as I realized I was standing at the place where it happened.

Right here, a few feet away at most, was the exact spot where my father had been killed. Murdered. I waited for the tidal wave, the tsunami of grief and loss that would sweep me under, crush me beneath its weight.

I've seen grief up close, seen hard-ass lifers cry like babies over a dead friend. Seen hajji women wail their pain to the sky, cut themselves, or claw at their own eyes.

I waited to feel…anything. At all.

But all I felt were my hunting instincts kicking in. I realized I was already scanning the scene. Scoping it out, gauging the distances involved. I dropped to my knees and ran my fingers through the dry grass. Came up with a few bits of safety glass.

"Are you all right?" Danvers asked, hurrying over to me. "What are you doing?"

"Scouting the ground. This was a neat job. They wired up a dead tree at the top of that berm with C-4. Had a lookout with binoculars posted on high ground. When he spotted the old man's truck, they blew the tree, dropping it across the two lane, then one of them trotted along its length, wetting it down with gasoline, and lit it up. A quick, efficient roadblock.

"Pop should have stopped, he couldn't see beyond the smoke and flames. Instead, he veered off onto the shoulder here, trying to climb partway up the berm, hoping to squeeze past the fallen tree. But they were ready for that. At which point…"

I swiveled to look across the scorched blacktop, taking a moment to figure the trajectories in reverse, scanning the berm on the far side of the road.

"Up there," I said, pointing at a cluster of brush stacked against the tree line. "That's the hide where the shooter waited. That pile of brush ahead of us? A second gunman was staked out there, in case the first shooter missed. But he didn't."

"How do you know all this?"

I held out my open palm, showing her the glittering shards I'd collected.

"The police techs collected most of the glass, but there are enough pieces here to make out the pattern. It's a single spider web. One round. Military, two twenty-three. Probably killed him instantly, because the truck kept on climbing the berm, where the ground's all torn up. If he'd been conscious, he'd have swung it around, headed back down. Instead, it toppled over onto its side."

"And caught fire?"

"No. Not then. Diesel fuel is basically kerosene. It'll burn, but it doesn't spontaneously combust like gasoline. First they transferred the load, probably into some kind of work truck—TV repair, plumber, maybe a bogus log hauler. A truck with Canadian registration that could cross to the Canuck side of the border without arousing curiosity. Then they torched Pop's truck and dumped poor, stoned Leach, Robert R. a few miles away in a wrecked vehicle to take the fall for it all."

"The police think he was part of it. Everything you've described sounds like a military operation."

"That's the problem. They used C-4 to blow the tree. A chainsaw would have been simpler and safer. They used a traceable military weapon and ammo when you can buy a hot, anonymous hunting rifle in any backwoods bar in the north. They lit up the truck to draw the local law away from the border, and finally, left Leach behind to misdirect the hunt."

"But how do you *know* he wasn't—"

"Because Leach was Special Ops. He'd know better than to use gear that would point back to him. He'd leave straw hats and buggy tracks behind, blame it on the Amish."

"Amish?" She was staring at me.

"That was a joke."

"A joke about your father's murder?"

"I guess. What's your point?"

For a split second, I thought she might actually tell me…whatever she was holding back. But she shook her head without answering.

"The key to this thing isn't Leach, or the military tactics," I went on, "it's the cargo. Drug companies don't advertise shipments like this and Leach is fresh back from the 'Stan. He'd have no way of knowing which trucks were hauling what, or where to jump the border afterwards, or what kind of vehicle would go unnoticed on the Canadian side. Only locals with inside information about routes and cargo could pull this off."

"And you think you know who they might be?"

"I know who to ask. A slob named Sid Kelso, Pop's union rep. He's been wired into the trucking business along the border forever. Nothing happens he doesn't know about or get a piece of. If he didn't plan the raid, he knows who did."

Frowning, Danvers took a cell phone from inside her jacket.

"What are you doing?"

"Calling Captain Snider—"

"No!" I said, snatching the phone out of her hand. "You're not." I crushed the phone in my fist, underscoring my fury. She took an involuntary step back, but only one.

"Josh, the police—"

"If the cops grab Kelso, he'll lawyer up, warn his crew, and they'll jump to Canada. They'll lay low till this blows over, and in six months, they'll be back in business. But if *I* talk to Kelso? He'll tell me their names, and where I can find them, and he won't be warning anybody afterward. I'll run them down, and…settle up for this." My gesture took in the torn berm, the scorched tree. And my father's ghost.

"This is America, Sergeant. You can't just kill people."

"We took an oath to defend our country against all enemies, foreign and domestic. This bunch is domestic. They're fair game."

"It's not that simple."

"It is to me, Doc. It's what they trained me for. And I'm not one of your patients."

"Actually, you are. You've been closely monitored by the medical corps for the past eight years. Monthly checkups. You told me so yourself."

"For battle fatigue. I don't have it."

"And you never will. *Ever.* You won't have PTSD, or feel love, or hate, or even fear. You lack the capacity to feel emotions to any real depth."

It was my turn to stare. "Slow down. What are you saying? That I've gone Belgian?"

"That's not a term I would use."

"Then what's the word for it, Doc? Canine something?"

"The medical term is high-functioning sociopath, Josh. Your dysfunction was first noted during your Special Operations training."

"That's bull! I aced that training! Top of my class! If I was messed up, why didn't they flunk me out—?" I broke off, staring. Because I've got a good ear for liars. And she wasn't one.

And I realized, I had just answered my own question.

"This…condition? Going Belgian or high-functioning whatever you call it? It isn't a problem in the mountains, is it? It makes us better…dogs of war. And that's what we are, isn't it? Dogs of war. We really are Belgians. That can shoot."

"I'm sorry, Sergeant, I—"

"No, it's okay," I said, waving off her apology. "It's…almost a relief. To finally hear the truth. I've always known I was different. I had trouble in school, trouble with the law. But…" I broke off, remembering.

"What is it?"

"A few months ago, I'm in an NCO club, yukking it up with a couple of buds fresh out of the bush. And Bobby Gonzales was telling about this hajji he clipped, a lookout on a ridge. Eleven, twelve hundred yards across a valley. Helluva shot. But Bobby makes it. And the guy he capped tumbles over the edge. And it's a long ways down, half a mile, maybe. But he doesn't scream or flail around. Instead, he spreads his arms out wide. Like he's already an angel. Like he can fly. Turned out he couldn't."

I waited. Usually that punch line gets a smile. Not this time.

"And?" she asked.

"A guy at the next table overhears us laughing. And he's a chaplain, Catholic, I think. And he comes over, all misted up. Says Bobby's been in the mountains too long. That he was going Belgian, losing his soul. He had to go home."

"And did he go home?"

"Nah, they sent the chaplain home. Captain said he was bad for unit morale. But after? I chewed over what he said. About going Belgian? He was wrong to blame it on the mountains. Up high, it's…beyond beautiful. You can see forever. I'm at home there."

"No," she said firmly, grasping my arm. "America is your home, Josh. The northern town where you grew up? Is your home. You need to take a long leave, see what you've been fighting for all this time. And when you're ready, you can be helped. *I* can help you. With counseling, medication, you can adjust. You can have a normal life again."

"The mountains *are* my normal life, Doc."

"Josh—"

"But maybe you're right about the trip," I said quickly. "I have a few weeks' leave coming. I'll call Snider tomorrow, tell him what I think happened. Let them handle it."

"It's the right thing to do," she said, clearly relieved. "Here at home, it's his job, not ours."

"Copy that, Major. You're right, I get that. But for now, if you wouldn't mind? I'd like to be alone out here awhile. To spend some time…with my dad."

"I can't just leave you here—"

"Sure you can. I'll be fine. I'll call a high-school buddy to pick me up, we'll hit a few bars, make a night of it. I'm home now, Major, stateside. I don't need a babysitter."

"I know that, but…" She hesitated, reading my face. "Are you sure you'll be okay?"

"I'm good, Doc, but I do want to thank you. For looking out for me, and for telling me the truth. About the kind of dog I am."

"You're not a dog—" she began.

"Jeez, lady, I'm just kidding. You need to lighten up. Thanks again for everything." I snapped her a quick salute. She returned it, on reflex, probably. Then turned and strode off to her car. She gave me one last long, measuring look before she pulled out. I have no idea what it meant.

I waited till she was out of sight, then dialed up Uber for a ride back to town. To the funeral parlor.

Kelso will likely hang around the wake as long as there's a hand to shake. And he'll be wondering what the police asked me. And I'll tell him. In private, of course. And as soon as we're alone…?

He'll give up every damn thing he knows about the hijack, the crew that pulled it, and where I can find them. He'll talk, to save his life.

But it won't.

After I've settled with him and his bunch? It might be wise to take that road trip the major talked about. Disappear into the country I've been fighting for. And if I happen to notice a few things that need to be set right?

I'm good at that. Exemplary, the doc said.

She's a nice lady, and she meant well.

She was afraid the truth would devastate me. But she had that exactly backwards.

The *truth* has set me free.

I am Joshua Devlin Beaumont, and in my twenty-eighth year, I finally know *exactly* what I am.

I am a Belgian. I am a dog of war.

And now that I've slipped my leash?

Somebody really should cry…

Havoc.

Hey, Dad

by Joyce Carol Oates

Almost wouldn't recognize you. And you wouldn't recognize *me*. Your face is gaunter than your photo-face. Your eyes are hidden by dark-tinted glasses. The goatee looks like Brillo wires pasted on your jaws.

Hey Dad: Congratulations!

Hey Dad: Me.

I'm in the third row. I'm the face with the smile.

Hey Dad this is *coincidence*.

You are one of five Honorary Doctorate awardees.

I am one of two hundred twenty-three Bachelor of Arts awardees.

You are sixty-two years old. I am twenty-one years old.

We both look ridiculous don't we Dad? You in the black academic gown on this sweltering-hot day in May, in New England. Me in the black academic gown on this sweltering-hot day in May, in New England.

You in shiny black leather shoes, proper black silk socks.

Me in black leather sandals, sockless.

You in a folding chair on the commencement platform. First row of the select—President's party.

Me in the third row of two hundred twenty-three graduating seniors. Seated on the hard hard stone of the quasi-Greek amphitheater.

One of a small sea of black-robed kids. Some of us in T-shirts and swim trunks beneath the black robes 'cause it's God damn hot in mid May on our little Colonial-college campus in New England.

Some of us hungover from last night's partying. Some of us high.

Some of us God damn sober.

Confronting the rest-of-our-lives, God damn sober.

But hey Dad: It's cool.

Don't worry that I will make a scene. That I will confront you.

Though I will be crossing the commencement platform twice: the first time, to be honored as the single Rhodes scholar this year from our college, and the second time, less dramatically, in a long stream of B.A. candidates, to have my hand shaken (again) by the (smiling) President as the B.A. degree is "conferred" upon us.

Though I will be crossing the platform in my black academic robe and mortar-board cap passing within eighteen inches of your knees.

Though I seem to be, if your biographies are accurate, your only son.

That is, biographies indicate that you are the father of two daughters, from your first, long-ago marriage.

Biographies of M__ V__ are respectful. Mostly noting your *controversial work in ethics, political commentary*. Briefly noting your several marriages. And no record of your numerous *liaisons*.

Hey Dad relax: I'm not the type to confront, or to confound. I have never been the type, I think.

(For instance, I have not sought out my half-sisters. Not yet.)

You have not shied away from public pronouncements that have caused dissension, controversy. Your books on the "ethics of killing"—war, abortion, euthanasia—that made your early reputation. Your books on "American imperialism" in the Third World, your scathing attacks on "colonization in new forms."

You are the egalitarian, the friend of the oppressed. You speak for those in the Third World who can't speak for themselves.

You would not "colonize" anyone—of course.

Your (thinning, graying-coppery) hair is still long, in the style of the 1960s. Signaling to youth in the audience that, for all his academic distinction, and the Brillo goatee threaded with gray, M__ V__ is one *cool dude*.

Already when my mom knew M__ V__ in the long-ago, you were a person of distinction. And, for sure, one *cool dude*.

Not that Mom talked about you. Never.

Not that Mom thought about you. In recent years.

Not that my stepfather knew (much) about you.

Hey Dad this isn't about them. This is about *me*.

And this is about you.

This is about *coincidence*.

What a brainteaser to calculate the odds: not just M__ V__ receiving an honorary doctorate at his (unacknowledged, unknown?) son's commencement but the son *existing*.

For that hadn't been your intention, hey Dad?

It isn't an operation, it isn't surgery. It's a medical procedure. It's commonplace as going to the dentist.

And, later, losing patience: *Don't be ridiculous. There is nothing to be frightened of.*

I've been through this before. More than once.

Mom did not tell me any of this—of course. Mom is not the sort of person to burden others with bad memories of hers; Mom is precisely the sort of person who protects people from bad memories. And so, Mom did not ever tell me about you. When Mom spoke of her life of long ago when she'd been a graduate student at the distinguished Ivy League university in which you've been on the faculty for thirty years it was of the "intellectual ferment" of the time—the "exciting atmosphere"—"politically involved faculty." Surely she was thinking of *you* and yet—she did not speak of *you*.

And there *you* sit—having slid your watch to a position on your wrist, where the heavy black sleeve of your robe has fallen back, so that you can see the time: slow slow passing of time until *your name* is spoken by the President, and *you* will rise from your seat to be honored.

No other reason for *you* to be here today. Of course.

Blinding sunshine! Heat.

The quasi-Greek amphitheater looks like it has been hacked out of stone in some primitive time of public ritual, sacrifice.

In a lurid TV melodrama I would have brought a weapon with me to commencement. A weapon hidden beneath the ridiculous black robe.

But this is not TV, and it is not melodrama. The mood is too measured, stately, and *slow* for melodrama.

Or so you would think—hey Dad?

"Pomp and Circumstance" played by the college orchestra. Loud, brassy, militant. Pompous old music but hey Dad, your mean old heart quickens, I bet!

Your picture in the papers, your squinting-smiling photo-face.

Maybe the face is wearing out, a little. Corroding from within.

Decades now you've been winning awards. Decades you've been *a known figure*.

Graduate students and post-docs and interns and assistants. And young untenured professors. You are their General. They do your bidding.

Hey Dad it's a strain, isn't it: listening to other people speaking.

But hey, no one is going to confront you here.

No one is going to accuse you.

She hadn't accused you. Maybe by the standards of that long-ago era you hadn't violated university policy. Maybe there were no rules governing the (sexual, moral) behavior of faculty members and their students in those days.

It just isn't going to happen—that we can be together. Not just now.

I will pay for the procedure. I can't accompany you for obvious reasons but I will pay and I suggest that you make arrangements to have it done out of town and not here; and I will pay for your accommodations there of course.

Which you did not, Dad. Because Mom refused.

Which pissed you off considerably, Dad. Because Mom refused.

Because Mom wanted *me*. If it meant pissing you off considerably, and losing you—still, Mom wanted *me*.

Hey Dad guess how I know this? Reading Mom's journal.

Mom's journal—journals—she's been keeping since 1986 when she was a freshman at the university first enrolled in your famous lecture course.

More than three hundred students in that legendary course.

The Ethics of Politics. From Plato to Mao.

But it was later, Mom met you. When Mom was a graduate student in your seminar. And Mom became your dissertation advisee—a coup for the twenty-three-year-old since it's known that M__ V__ chooses few students to work closely with him.

Hey Dad we know: you've forgotten Mom's name.

Or if you haven't forgotten the name exactly, you've forgotten Mom.

For there were so many of them, in your life. Available/vulnerable women.

Though Mom went on to teach in universities herself. Mom became a professor of American history and politics at a good state university and Mom has a career not so distinguished as yours but Mom too has published articles, reviews, and books.

Has, or had. Mom isn't working now, Mom is pretty sick.

Mom has been pretty sick for a while. *Struggling* as they say.

Determined to beat it as they say.

And maybe she will. Odds are a little better than fifty-fifty she can make it.

Which is why Mom isn't here this morning. Mom and my stepdad. Why I am alone here this morning.

With my friends here at college, I'm a popular guy. Girls like me pretty much, too.

Maybe I resemble you, in some ways. Raffish-good-looking and thick wavy hair—the way you once looked, Dad.

The way you once attracted girls and women with that "kindly" smile.

But no more. You're old now, Dad. Eyeing girls like any old-man lecher.

But mostly I'm not like you—in any way. Mostly I'm alone. My truest self is alone.

Of course Mom doesn't know that I've been reading her journals. Handwritten notebooks kept on a high shelf in her study. They are not for anyone's eyes except Mom's, it seems.

And if Mom dies—maybe my stepdad will read them. Or maybe Mom will have destroyed them.

Mom isn't famous or distinguished enough for the journals to be published, I think.

So you don't have to worry, Dad. Not that you're worried.

And not much chance is there, Dad?—you're going to peruse the columns of names of the class of 2012 in the commencement program you've been given. For no name listed there could interest M__ V__ in the slightest.

Even my name with its little red asterisk to indicate *summa cum laude*.

Hey Dad here's a question: If you had known *me*, if you'd foreseen *me*, including the *summa cum laude* and the Rhodes scholarship for next year at Oxford, would you have insisted upon the procedure, just the same?

No? Yes?

"The ethics of killing." Did you ever wonder what it feels like to be *the killed*—hey Dad?

I have planned my strategy carefully this morning. The first time I'm called to the platform, I will shake the President's hand and pass by you without glancing at M__ V___ or any of the other honorary doctorates.

(Politely, you will clap for me. Without glancing at me. As politely, a glaze of boredom on your face, you will clap for other graduates singled out for such honors.)

But then, the second time, when I pass within eighteen inches of M__ V__ on the platform maybe I will pause, for just a moment—a "dramatic" moment.

In the phosphorescent heat of the sun. Nearing noon, the sun will be overhead. Even the shade beneath the stage canopy will be hot, humid. Perspiration will run in little trickles down your face, Dad. Inside your clothes, Dad.

You aren't a young man any longer. You may notice a shortness of breath, climbing stairs. A shimmering wave of vertigo at the top of the stairs. A dark place in your heart opening—*I have been a shit. My life is shit. Whatever terrible death awaits me, I deserve.*

I have rehearsed. I will leave nothing to chance. This is a "procedure"—a matter of strategy and execution.

After the President shakes my hand and the dean hands me my diploma and I am crossing the platform in a slow steady stream of Bachelor of Arts awardees all in ridiculous black robes flapping about our ankles and I pass no more than eighteen inches from M__ V___ in dark-tinted glasses and goatee I will stop, I will turn to you, and I will approach you, and among the buzz and hum of this part of commencement not many will notice. At first.

Whatever I may be carrying inside my black robe, I will have shifted in such a way that I can grip its handle. Tight.

And I will say—*Hey Dad it's me*.

No Peace for the Wicked

by Martin Edwards

At first I don't realise that I am dead, let alone that someone has murdered me.

The truth begins to dawn after I wake. I feel lightheaded and glance at the time. Five o'clock! Sun streams in through the patio windows. I'm lying on the living-room settee, not my bed. I'm a poor sleeper at the best of times, but for once I've dozed off in midafternoon.

I have a vague memory of a mysterious dream, of melancholy paramedics carrying a body on a stretcher out through my own front door. They have thrown a sheet over the deceased, but I recognise the floral slippers peeping out from beneath the makeshift shroud. They are identical to a pair which were an unwanted present from my nephew, Malcolm. I wear them around the house when I can't be bothered to put on anything nicer.

Surely that corpse can't be mine? What are strangers doing in my home? There are laws about trespass. I should know; I used to be a bailiff.

An English widow's bungalow is her castle. Especially in Autumn Shades. It's not so much a retirement village as a rural idyll populated—at least in the brochure and online video tour—by friendly, vibrant, and unusually attractive senior citizens enjoying undisturbed tranquillity.

The marketing guff waxes lyrical about the restaurant, bistro, vitality pool, putting green, steam room and sauna, hair and beauty salon, craft room, cinema, and gym complete with cardio wall. All the talk is of independence, community, and exciting new friendships. Not an intimation of mortality to be found, provided you overlook the sinister references to peace of mind coming from the availability of support and personal care 24/7 "as your needs change."

My late husband Dave was a builder. After he fell off a ladder—trying to fix the roof while the sun was shining, a pastime advocated by politicians but dangerous with a broken rung—I sold our house and moved here, to the end of a cul-de-sac called Sylvan Fields. I didn't see it as a one-way ticket to the grave. Plenty of life in the old girl yet.

Now, though, I feel dizzy, and somehow not myself.

A key rattles in the lock, and I go into the hall. A large mirror hangs on the wall and, out of habit, I check to see that my hair is tidy and see…

Nothing.

I'm simply not there. Surely I'm not still dreaming?

I'm not one to panic, but I tremble as the front door opens. Val, my next-door neighbour and closest friend, marches in. Why didn't she ring the bell?

"Hey, Val, don't mind me!" I say, unable to resist a touch of sarcasm.

She doesn't mind me at all. In fact, she ignores me altogether and heads straight for the kitchen. She goes to the wall cupboard and grabs from a top shelf the jar of homemade chutney that she brought last weekend. I haven't touched it, because, to be honest, I can't bear the jams, marmalades, and assorted preserves she constantly foists on me. Her heart is in the right place, but Waitrose do these things so much better. I donate Val's offerings to the food bank. One has to do one's bit for those less fortunate than oneself.

She presses the jar to her formidable bosom like a film star clutching an undeserved Academy Award. Her relief is as plain as the nose on her face. It's a large, curving nose which reminds me of the eagle in *The Muppet Show*. Once I upset her by asking if she'd considered surgery. Pardonable curiosity between friends, but she took it badly.

"What's up?" My tone is provocative. She's never had the nerve to say so, but I know she hates it when I poke fun at her. Like the little boy in *Alice*, I only do it to annoy, because I know it teases. "Don't tell me you were afraid you'd poisoned me!"

Again she takes no notice, as if she hasn't heard. I need to make sense of what is happening, so I block her exit from the kitchen.

She walks straight through me.

It takes a lot to shock me, but I defy anyone not to be shaken by the discovery that they no longer exist in human form.

A tentative knock on the door. Val stops in her tracks. A look of panic crosses her excessively powdered face. She tries to stuff the jar of chutney up her jumper, before wisely thinking better of it. Buxom is all very well, but there are limits.

Again a key sounds in the lock. This time Trevor comes in.

Trevor, my other next-door neighbour, who also has a key to the bungalow, "just in case." Trevor, whose proposal of marriage I turned down forty-eight hours ago. A retired pharmacist, he dispenses nuggets of homespun wisdom as liberally as he once dished out antibiotics. As well as plenty of other pills, according to malicious gossip.

How bitterly I regret pretending to be interested in his views on politics, climate change, religion, foreign travel, sport, and everything else under the sun. He interpreted civility as fawning adoration. The prospect of an eternity of listening to him drone on is as enticing as a lifetime of penal servitude in North Korea. He takes rejection badly, since he labours under the delusion that he is quite a catch. I suspect he had an eye on my nest egg. Dave suffered from a chronic phobia about paying tax, and he left me very comfortably off.

I put my hands on my hips and stick out my tongue.

"Trevor, what's wrong?" Val demands.

He shakes his head. "For a moment, it was like Polly was there, standing right next to you. Gave me quite a turn. Ever so spooky."

He says this without irony. I groan, but neither of them hears.

"Oh, Trevor, don't upset yourself!" Brazenly, she squeezes his hand. "You need time to grieve. It's not surprising that…your mind plays tricks."

"I thought I smelled her perfume."

The eagle nose wrinkles. "That awful scent of hers was so strong, traces are bound to linger, even now they have…taken her away."

Trevor makes a sobbing noise, but his heart isn't in it. His eyes are dry. They glint with calculation.

"That jar of chutney."

"Oh, this?" She looks at the jar with its cellophane covering as if startled to find it in her free hand. "It's freshly made. It…seems a shame to waste it."

He looks at her thoughtfully, and Val releases his hand.

"So what brings you here?"

"As a matter of fact, I'm on a similar errand." He coughs. "I gave Polly some stuff for the garden."

Her eyes narrow. "Some kind of pest killer?"

"Actually, yes. She was having trouble with wasps."

This is the first I've heard of it.

Val says, "I see."

"In the circumstances, I thought…"

"Yes, of course." They look into each other's eyes. "We don't want any misunderstandings. People getting the wrong end of the stick."

It's bad enough to discover that I'm dead, but I'm rapidly coming to the conclusion that I'm the victim of foul play. Never mind the aches and pains of age, I've always been as fit as a flea. If I'm destined for an early grave, it's because someone decided to send me there.

Trevor puts his hand on her shoulder. "It must have been dreadful for you, coming in and finding her like that. I know you two were very close."

Val dabs at the corner of her eye. "Such a terrible shock! I thought she'd died in her sleep. Mind you, she didn't look at peace. Not that she ever did. I don't wish to speak ill of the dead…"

"Perish the thought!" Trevor says hastily.

". . . but she did have a hide like a rhinoceros."

I feel my temper rising. Perhaps I am thick-skinned, but you need to be robust if you work as a bailiff and you're married to a tiresome philanderer like Dave.

"I hate to admit it," Trevor says, "but you're not far off the mark. Polly was a…character."

"You can say that again. When I rang that nephew of hers to break the news, he couldn't believe she'd gone. He thought she'd outlast us all."

The two of them giggle like conspirators. Malcolm is my late sister's son. Both his parents died in a plane crash last year, leaving him as my only close relative. He had a spell in the police, but that didn't work out. Since then he's drifted from job to job. I fell out with him when he didn't pay back some money he'd borrowed, but a few weeks ago he finally paid up. Since then he's made quite a fuss of me. Says he regrets his previous "poor choices," and mixing with "the wrong crowd." The truth is, I've always had a soft spot for him. In some ways, he reminds me of myself.

Val purses her lips. "I suppose he is her heir."

"I expect so." Trevor sounds forlorn.

"Of course," she adds, "it would have been different if the two of you had got married."

"Oh," Trevor says. "There was never any chance of that."

This is a shameful lie, and I let out a shriek of rage. Trevor twitches with anxiety. He claims to be a sensitive soul; unlikely as it seems, perhaps there is something in it. He seems aware of my presence in a way that Val does not.

"Seriously?" She can't help smiling. "I thought the two of you were about to name the day."

He shakes his head. "I was happy to help Polly out in the garden, but that's all there was to it as far as I was concerned. She became possessive. Read too much into simple acts of generosity."

Val peers at him like a quizmaster awaiting an answer to the million-pound question. "When you took her to that cottage for the weekend, I was certain…"

"I'm partial to the Cotswolds," he says defensively. "I simply mentioned that a spot of company was always welcome, and she invited herself. She really was rather bumptious. Not to mention demanding."

Outrageous! He begged me to go along. As for *demanding*, I don't recall any complaints, except when he thought the neighbours were eavesdropping. I was only trying to boost his morale. He'd paid for the trip, after all, and he isn't one to put his hand in his own pocket. I was simply fulfilling my side of an unspoken bargain. Paying my dues. With hindsight, I reckon he saw that weekend as investing for the future. He talked a lot about investments, actually. Interrogating me about what I did with my money. Recommending this fund and that. His favourite motto is: "You have to speculate to accumulate."

"That's not the way Polly told it," Val says.

"Polly! She looked after number one." He bites his lip. "Very different from you, if I may say so. I always admired the way you put up with her rudeness and bad temper."

Val lowers her eyelashes and murmurs, "She wasn't easy, God rest her soul."

"You can say that again." He swallows. "She treated you like dirt. Accepted your generous gifts and then sneered at you behind your back."

"She did?"

He sighs. "When I pleaded with her to treat you with the respect you deserve, she lashed me with that sharp tongue of hers."

"Polly never appreciated you. I used to tell her, he's a highly educated man, a walking encyclopaedia. Any woman would be thrilled to find such a soul mate," Val simpers. "Especially at her age."

Disgraceful. She's barely twelve months younger than me. And though I say it myself, she's worn much less well. Too much homemade jam, if you ask me.

"You're very kind," he says. "You're…all the things she never was."

Including *alive*, I reflect.

Val grabs both his hands. "You poor love. You need someone who appreciates you."

He treats her to what I'm sure he believes is a soulful gaze, but before he can declare undying devotion, there is a knock on the door. Guilty as sin, they spring apart.

"Hello?" says a muffled voice through the letter box.

"The nephew?" Trevor whispers.

Val calls out in a bright tone, "Come in!"

As Malcolm crosses the threshold, he finds himself in an embrace that knocks the breath out of him.

"I'm so sorry, dear!"

Val's voice quivers with emotion. She really is a first-rate actress. I had no idea.

"Thanks." Malcolm frees himself from her grasp. He's pale, but he gives Trevor a knowing look. "Nice to see you again, matey."

Trevor looks uncomfortable, which I find puzzling. I didn't even realise they were acquainted. Neither of them has ever mentioned the other to me.

As they tuck into tea and biscuits, I loiter by the patio window. To say I'm inconspicuous is an understatement. Even Trevor seems oblivious to my presence.

"How do they think she died?" Malcolm asks.

"An overdose of some kind," Trevor says authoritatively.

I'm appalled, but Val merely nods.

"Heartbreaking," she moans. "I'm devastated. Truly devastated."

"You're not suggesting…?" Malcolm begins.

Trevor interrupts. "I'm sure it was an accident. Polly had great trouble in sleeping. She must have taken something by mistake."

Val nods. "She was very careless. And hopelessly untidy. The state of that kitchen!"

"I suppose she got confused. Easily done."

"She was getting extremely forgetful, poor pet," Val says.

"Is that so?" Malcolm asks.

"I'd swear to it!" Val launches into a wildly exaggerated anecdote: "Only the other day…"

Disgusting! I refuse to listen. There's nothing wrong with my memory. Occasionally it suits me to feign amnesia about a shopping trip or an afternoon out, when I can't bear to spend any more time in her company. But to elevate a handful of excuses and white lies into some kind of incipient dementia is positively slanderous.

"There will need to be an inquest," Malcolm says.

"Formality," Trevor assures him. "Box-ticking bureaucracy. I play golf with the coroner, he hates stirring up trouble. Too hurtful for those left behind to mourn. What happened to Polly is sad, but perfectly straightforward."

"A tragic mishap," Val says.

"To err is human," Trevor pronounces, "but unfortunately it can have fatal consequences."

Malcolm rubs his eyes, prompting Val to touch his hand in a gesture of sympathy.

"Don't upset yourself, dear."

"Polly was a remarkable woman." Trevor has a faraway look in his eyes, as if he's composing a eulogy.

"Bubbly and fun-loving," Val chips in.

Trevor outbids her. "Heart of gold."

"She knew her own mind," Malcolm says with masterly understatement. "She had bags of spirit."

And now I *am* a spirit! Helpless and invisible. Is there nothing I can do?

I think rapidly. At least I can solve my own murder.

The work of a bailiff wins you few friends, but it teaches you a thing or two about getting to the truth. Seeing through hard-luck stories, concentrating on what really counts. And I believe in people paying their debts.

The snag is that I have no memory of my last waking hours. I can't believe I suffered an accident. And I'd never take my own life. No question, someone helped me along the path to kingdom come.

But who?

Malcolm watches the others. He must wonder what they are doing here, but is there more to it? Does he suspect either of them of hastening my end?

Val asks, "What will you do with the bungalow, dear?"

He feigns indifference. "Oh, I don't know. It's too soon. Can't live in a retirement village, can I? This place will have to be sold."

"Makes sense," Trevor says. Why does he look pleased?

Time is short, I'm convinced. When Trevor first walked in, my presence definitely made an impression on him, but I'm fading fast. If I'm not quick, I'll go to my grave without knowing who killed me. I must find out and make sure they get their just deserts.

Who had a motive?

The prime suspects are drinking my tea and scoffing my custard creams.

Val detested me, and was jealous because Trevor hoped to marry me. She wants him for herself.

Trevor was furious when I turned him down. But is there more to his anger than simple pique?

His reference to an overdose makes me wonder about drugs. When Malcolm was in the police, did he hear those whispers about Trevor supplying addicts? Given his taste for risky speculation, perhaps he needed the money. And it's interesting that he's dimly aware of my presence—is this a sign of a guilty conscience?

What about the murder method?

I've never made a secret of my insomnia, or that I take lots of stuff to help me sleep. To cover up a murder, why not suggest I took an overdose? Either deliberately—the grieving widow who never settled in her new home—or by mistake—the disorganised old bat with a memory like a sieve.

Val might have seasoned the chutney with something toxic. Trevor may have found a way to introduce pest killer into my diet.

Malcolm coughs. "Excuse me a minute. Tummy trouble. Must be the shock of hearing the news."

He dashes out of the room, and I follow. One advantage of my phantom state is that locking the bathroom door doesn't keep me out. As soon as we are both inside, he opens the large cabinet on the wall, where I keep my medicines. Like most residents in Autumn Shades, I have a formidable list of repeat prescriptions, and the shelves overflow with packets and bottles. He takes a bottle of my sleeping pills off the shelf and replaces it with an identical bottle from his pocket.

Breathing hard, Malcolm looks in the mirror. I'm at his side, purple with anger and a sense of betrayal. In the glass, I see only his crooked mouth, forming in a grin of triumph.

We return to the living room, to find Trevor enveloped in the capacious folds of Val's embrace.

"The poor chap has lost the love of his life!" she says to excuse herself. "He needs a hug. The simple warmth of human contact. The pain must be almost too much to bear."

I scream and try to give her the human contact she deserves by pulling her hair. But it's impossible. She can't see me or feel the touch of my fingers.

Whodunit?

Chances are, they're not sure themselves, but Malcolm's jiggery-pokery with the medicine bottle is the most practical method. Has he dabbled in illicit drugs? If he owes Trevor money, the proceeds of the bungalow sale would come in handy. Especially if Trevor himself is in hock to local drug barons.

Inheriting my house and money would solve Malcolm's problems. He had to move fast, in case I married Trevor.

I'm so glad now that I never got round to changing my will in my nephew's favour. Before he tried to worm his way back into my good books, I bequeathed everything to the food bank. It was the least I could do, after inflicting Val's rubbish on them.

Trevor stirs himself. "I don't mind saying, I'm rather peckish."

"You need a decent meal," Val advises. "Do you good. Shall we go for a bite together?"

"The bistro?" he suggests.

"Let's try that gourmet restaurant in town. Push the boat out. It's a sad day, but life goes on. We can toast Polly. It's what she would have wanted."

Nothing of the kind! But I can't see myself becoming a spectre at the feast. I feel dreadfully weak.

"I'll get on my way," Malcolm says.

"Can I offer you a lift?" Trevor says.

"Cheers." They exchange glances and I guess they intend to talk about money. The repayment of a debt.

I follow them outside. Trevor's car is in the drive, and they all jump in.

As he switches the engine on, I understand the truth.

They all set out to kill me. Only Malcolm succeeded, but morally each of them is a murderer.

They ought to pay.

I step out into the road, in front of the car, my hand raised.

Horror flashes into Trevor's eyes. He's seen me!

Or at least something.

He swerves and the car crashes into a spreading oak, centrepiece of Autumn Shades's environmentally friendly planting scheme.

As the car explodes into flames, I feel myself slipping away into nothingness.

The death of a ghost.

I've collected my last debt, and my conscience is deplorably clear. It's simply not true that there's no peace for the wicked. I won't be tormented by their spirits. Just as Dave never haunted me after I sawed through that rung of his ladder.

What Kind of Criminal?

by LaToya Jovena

People often describe handcuffs as cold. In truth they only start out that way. Eventually they warmed to the temperature of your wrists, but that didn't mean they were comfortable.

I preferred the satiny lining of my white faux-fur coat and the colorful walls of my new apartment. Instead I was in a bland room and forced to keep company with a detective that matched.

Bald. Medium brown. Medium height. Medium build.

Gray walls. Blue industrial carpet.

"I didn't defraud anyone. They got paintings. I got money. Things are bought and sold like that every day."

"You're right." His gaze lingered on my accessories. "Fakes and knockoffs are sold every day. The difference is the people buying them and the people selling them both know they're fake. They also both know they're committing a crime."

I looked at my Prada sunglasses and my fuchsia Birkin bag. Could they be fake? I'd gotten them through a stylist contact of someone at the auction house. They had worked with the stylist, but they had also worked with me.

I pushed the detective's insinuation out of my mind. If they were knock-offs they were indistinguishable from the real thing.

"It began as a mistake," I said finally. I really hadn't done anything wrong. I just had to explain that to him.

The detective smirked. "So you accidentally sold seven fake paintings for more than twenty million dollars?"

Well, when he said it that way it did indeed sound ridiculous, but that didn't mean it wasn't true.

February 2020

I was wearing a pressed white shirt, black slacks, an apron, and ballet-flat Crocs. L'Ambassadrice was opening in an hour. The scent of baking bread was so strong I could almost taste it. Almost. My stomach grumbled. I ignored it, tied my curly hair back with an amber-colored scarf, and started taking the chairs down off the tables they'd been stacked on the night before.

"Hi, Tasha," said Alma. She was carrying a basketful of cloth napkins and silverware to put on my now chairless tabletops.

"Hi, Alma." I reached for the napkins in her basket. "Did you get into anything fun on your day off?"

"Shep had a work thing in New York. I tagged along but I didn't see him much. I got a ton of great pics, though. My Instagram is going to look like a dream for at least two weeks."

I smiled.

There was no doubt in my mind that Alma was right. She was petite, with long wavy hair, and sort of exotic-looking, but you couldn't quite place where. What was this fun-loving beauty doing with boring K Street junior partner Shep?

Tagging along on his trips and spending his money.

"Have you heard about this COVID thing?" asked Alma. "They say it may be in the U.S. now."

"I've heard about it. Just like I heard all about Ebola in two thousand fourteen."

"Doors open in fifteen minutes," shouted a manager.

Thirty minutes later, my favorite part of the week walked in. Her tall, thin frame was painted in Alexander Wang athleisure. She stepped lightly to her table in Christian Louboutin hightops. Money made people wonder who you were, so she hid hers where only people with money would see it.

Shannon Ames, African-American painter of vibrantly colored portraits showing gray-skinned people doing everyday things. Her paintings were subtle, political, and inspiring; so was she. Subtly showing wealth. Quietly meeting with lobbyists. Casually exhibiting her life on Instagram.

Fridays were her cheat day and the reason I worked at L'Ambassadrice. I knew from her feed she spent time there downing cheeseburger americains and champagne. When I got the job, I learned she finger-painted on her iPad during *le binge*. I always snuck a peek at what she was working on and went home energized to paint something that never sold on my website.

Just being near her was enough. She practically radiated creativity. But of course, I wanted more. I wanted to become her peer. I wanted her to see my work. I wanted to meet her in the proper art setting and tell her how much her work meant to me, then have her ask why I looked so familiar.

But before any of that could happen, everything changed.

The bland detective looked at me sternly. "Were you finding it hard to stay away from Miss Ames?"

I rolled my eyes. "I wasn't stalking her. I followed her on Instagram, like millions of other people, and I waited on her when she came to the restaurant, which was my job. As a painter, I admired her talent. As a Black woman, I admired her hustle. That's it."

"Let's just get to the fake paintings."

March 2020

COVID was all everyone was talking about, but outside of a few canceled reservations, my life marched on.

Work.

Eat as much of the completely untouched throwaways as I could at work, so I didn't have to buy food.

Put money away for next month's rent.

Buy art supplies.

Try to sell my art.

Dow Jones dropped. COVID cases climbed. Flights became dirt cheap.

The cheap flights had the second-biggest impact on my life. They weren't cheap enough for me to go anywhere, but I overheard Shannon Ames talking on the phone at the restaurant. First-class tickets to Marrakesh were going for a song, and Shannon Ames was singing along.

The next day she posted a selfie by a pool.

A week later all nonessential businesses closed, leaving me out of work. I stole a five-pound bag of flour on the way out and applied for unemployment.

"What are you going to do?" asked Alma.

I was sitting in her beautifully messy apartment, full of furniture she'd gotten heavily discounted for the promise of promoting it on her Instagram. There were clothes strewn everywhere. Fashion Nova dresses. Pretty Little Thing activewear. The pair of giant Air Max 97s in Olympic gold in the corner had to belong to her K Street boyfriend.

"Well, there's a moratorium on evictions, so I guess I won't waste my unemployment on rent," I said.

"You already got your unemployment?"

"Not quite."

In fact, not only had I not received it, I had no idea when it would be coming. I called daily. The answer was always the same.

We received your application, but due to a large influx of applicants, we don't know when we will get to you.

I'd been eating peanut-butter-and-jelly sandwiches on freshly baked, stolen-flour baguettes for a week, but there was a more pressing issue.

I was running out of paint.

I had no way to buy more because my paintings weren't selling.

"What are you going to do?" I asked.

"My mom wants me to move to Manassas." Alma used her phone's camera to apply lip gloss with the precision of a surgeon. "It's so boring, though. Shep has been asking me to move in. I just don't know if we're that serious. Like if I don't slow this down, we'll end up married. Maybe it won't be so bad. I can't make it on unemployment." Alma made kissy faces at her phone.

Mommy and Manassas and marriage. Oh my.

I didn't have the love of people with money, but I did have talent. Lots of artists had dealt with poverty on their way to fame and fortune. Jean-Michel Basquiat, Amy Sherald, and my favorite customer, Shannon Ames, who'd been a waitress until she was thirty-eight. I just needed my talent to pay last month's electric bill.

April 2020

"I just need help getting everything from my closet into these boxes Shep had sent over," said Alma.

Her apartment was now devoid of furniture. She didn't need any of it at Shep's place. Apparently, she'd made a tidy profit unloading it all.

"Our job opened for takeout. Are you going back?" asked Alma.

"Not yet."

"Then what will you do?"

The answer was earn more at home on unemployment, eat from the food bank, and spend all my money on paint supplies.

Weeks of painting all day, showering the paint off, sleeping, then waking up to do it all over again had changed me. I was getting better. I recognized immaturity in my previous works.

I'd even sold a painting. A portrait of me as a child eating a peanut-butter-and-jelly baguette. The buyer thought it was *très chic.* I let them think whatever they wanted, paid my electric bill, and bought a steak dinner. *Très chic* indeed.

I couldn't go back to carrying Negronis around. At least not yet. But that's not what I said.

"Stay home so I don't get sick," was what I said instead. "It's not like we had health insurance."

"You know that lady who used to sit in your section every Friday? She's stuck in Morocco. They closed the borders. Shep's firm is trying to get her home...."

I tried to act natural. I continued folding the clingy-fabric dress in my hands and placed it gently in the box in front of me. My head was spinning, though.

". . . She's been crying about all the art supplies she can't get and how much she misses her home studio. I bet her studio is an influencer's dream. She lives in a row house on Corcoran."

"How do you know where she lives?" I asked, as nonchalantly as I possibly could.

"She got wasted at the Christmas party Shep's firm had. We had to drop her off."

More questions were forming in my mind, but I let Alma talk. Maybe I should have listened to her more often, she practically gushed information.

". . . It explains a lot. Artists are crazy, right? When Shep offered to help her get in the door she told us that she never carries keys. She opens her door with a magnet.

"I was pretty wasted too, so I didn't see it. I watched her climb the spiral staircase to her back door, and then she was gone."

Alma started talking about Shep, their apartment, his Peloton, and maybe getting a dog.

I left her apartment in a daze. I had missed so much. I had been so busy painting and promoting my own work that I hadn't logged into Instagram in nearly a month.

Shannon Ames had posted almost daily, just as she always had. I saw the villa she was staying in. It came with a butler, and she joked about how grateful she was for him because she was terrible with keys. She'd enjoyed the private chef and getting massages by the pool.

Then the tone shifted. She couldn't wait to create. She had so many ideas. She couldn't get home. She couldn't get supplies. She couldn't hug her mom. She couldn't kiss her nieces. She was sick of tagine and wanted a burger americain. She posted lots of pictures of wine.

The next morning, I climbed the spiral staircase to her back door. There was nothing high tech, just a tiny five-dollar box containing a key, with a magnet that attached to the bottom of her top step.

Calling her home beautiful was almost an understatement. The Kimpton George was beautiful, but it was trendy and worked too hard to remind you that you were in Washington, D.C. Shannon Ames's house was like being transported into a painting. Her furniture was muted. Mostly grays, some blacks and browns. There were heavy white ceramic vases on every tablelike surface and intricate chandeliers hanging in almost every room. Then there were the walls.

Every wall was painted a color straight out of a Shannon Ames portrait. Egyptian blue. Saffron. Emerald and fuchsia.

Her closet was stuffed to the gills with expensive shoes and clothing, all arranged by color. There was even a real safe for her jewelry.

Finally, there was her studio. Pristine. Not a drop of paint anywhere. Light flooded the room from all directions.

There was a row of four-foot-tall rolling tool chests completely lining one wall. Inside the tool chests I found exactly what I'd come for.

Seemingly endless tubes of Michael Harding paints, an incredible find because their most expensive hues could go for a hundred dollars per 1.35-ounce tube.

There were also stacks of Princeton paintbrushes still in their original packaging.

I filled my backpack to the point I could barely carry it. My goal was to prolong the length of time I could stay home to paint. If I didn't need to buy art supplies I could spend my money on utilities and toiletries, thus not needing to go back to work.

I was on my way out. I swear I was. Then I thought about canvases. Not the small ones I could afford, but the giant ones Shannon Ames used. I found the canvases, but it was in their pursuit that I found what had the biggest impact on my life.

"Are you going to tell me the paintings aren't fakes? That you broke and entered, then stole them?" interrupted the detective.

"I didn't break in. I had a key. It was more like trespassing," I said.

"It's starting to sound a lot like grand larceny."

"You keep trying to reduce what happened to a single brush stroke, but it's not that simple. It's multicolored and complex. Has anyone even complained about the paintings?"

"Shannon Ames's agent complained about his missing commissions."

The auction house had told me all about Shannon Ames's agent. The convertible-driving crybaby con-man. He'd called them. His attorney had called them. There was even a court date scheduled, but there still wasn't a commission for Shannon Ames's agent.

"He didn't sell the paintings," I explained. "The auction house only dealt with me. If he wants a commission for not doing anything, shouldn't he sue me?"

"Shouldn't you have found a job to pay for your hobby?"

I shut my eyes and took a deep breath, calming myself. I couldn't believe what he had just said.

"Art is not a hobby. Art is who I am. Art is what I am."

"What you are is a criminal, so tell me the rest of the story so I can determine exactly what kind."

The studio's closet was so stuffed with canvases I had a hard time understanding how she got the door closed. I pulled out a few of them before realizing I had no way to get them home. I started going through the rest of the closets in her house. I was hoping to find a furniture dolly; what I found instead was a basket truck, basically a giant plastic box with wheels on the bottom. It wasn't empty, though. There were two paintings inside it.

I have always felt a connection to Shannon Ames's work. Yes, she was a Black woman, like me. She was from D.C., like me. She had once been a waitress, like me. But to see her paintings, in her home where she had created them, was more intimate than sleeping in her bed. I knew what it was like to create something in private, to hide it away from prying eyes, and to only show it when you were absolutely ready to share it with others.

I stared at those paintings for what felt like hours. I'd never seen her work that close up before. In fact, most of her work I'd only seen on my phone. So being close enough to touch these paintings was like finding a key to Fort Knox, and touch them I did.

I could feel the brush strokes under my fingertips. I'd seen her studio. I'd rummaged through her paints and brushes. When I closed my eyes, I could see her painting the portraits.

It got dark out, which was a good time for me to head home. Fewer people would see me. But first I wanted to take a picture of the paintings. Who knew if I would ever see them again. I took out my phone, and saw I had an Instagram notification; without thinking I touched it.

Tears began creeping out the corners of my eyes.

"She was dead. Shannon Ames had drowned in the pool of her villa. In a bout of denial, I turned one of her TVs to CNN. It was true. What happened next is a bit of a blur."

I dabbed my eyes with my faux-fur jacket sleeve.

"I woke up on the floor of the studio with five paintings. Paint was splattered everywhere, including on me. Dirty brushes had been discarded to the floor where the paint had dried and they had stuck. My phone had died. I had no idea how long I had been asleep, but the paintings were dry.

"I panicked, put all seven paintings in the box truck, covered them with a blanket, then pushed them home. I plugged my phone in and took a shower. Then all I could think about was how hungry I was.

"I had no idea how I had made it through the previous four days, but I was suddenly so weak I could barely see my phone to order a pizza. When it arrived, I ate it in its entirety on the floor, leaning against the front door of my apartment."

May 2020

"I named her Tulum." Alma was referring to the giant beige rat she was carrying in her Louis Vuitton tote. "She's a chihuahua."

"Hi, Tulum," I greeted the dog. "Do you want something to drink?" I asked Alma. "All I have is water."

"I have wine." Alma pulled a giant bottle of Malbec out of her tote.

She reminded me of Mary Poppins. I wondered what else was in that bag as I retrieved two water glasses from my kitchen.

"What have you been up to?" asked Alma.

"Painting a bit. How about you?"

"I've gained a ton of new followers. They love Tulum and seeing my Peloton workouts. Some of my followers are into art. Can I post some of your paintings?"

Her words hit me like a slap upside the head. Why hadn't I ever asked Alma to share my work? I knew she was an influencer.

"I'd love that," I answered.

"Alma posted one of the paintings from Shannon Ames's house. Then she tagged me. The next day all of the art for sale on my website had been sold. I had thousands of new followers and at least a hundred messages. One of those messages was from the auction house."

"And you sold them the paintings as if the real ones belonged to you and the ones you painted were created by Miss Ames?" asked the detective.

"Isn't possession nine-tenths of the law? I possessed all the paintings. They were mine to sell."

"You're not the first criminal who thought they were the smartest guy in the room," the detective smirked. "Did the auction house know that two of the paintings were stolen?"

"They didn't ask. I didn't tell."

"I'm guessing that's the same approach you took with the fakes."

"What makes something fake?" I looked at my bag and glasses. "I used her brushes, her paints, her easels, her studio, and even her techniques. She could have painted the exact same thing."

"But she didn't, which is what makes them fake."

"Has anyone complained about the pieces?" I asked. "Other than her agent, whose only concern is that he didn't get a cut. Would he even be complaining if he had gotten paid?"

"You stole two priceless paintings. I'm sure someone is complaining about that."

"Her estate got a healthy cut. If there were complaints I would have heard about them."

"You broke into her house. Every item used to create the fakes was stolen. Paint. Brushes. Even the canvases themselves." The detective counted on his fingers as he rattled off the alleged stolen items.

I looked down at the handcuffs on my wrists. They were annoying me now. The room was devoid of sunlight. In fact, the light was downright inhumane.

I had two commissions to finish and I wanted to get gas before it got dark. Plus, I had promised Alma I would do a dance with her for her TikTok. I didn't have any more time to talk to the detective.

"Are there complaining witnesses about these supposed stolen supplies?"

"Why don't you give me a list of exactly what you stole," said the detective, sliding a notepad and a gnawed-on pen across the table at me.

"Why don't you tell me exactly what I'm charged with," I said, sliding the notepad back. I didn't dare touch the pen. We were still in a pandemic, after all.

The bland detective's eyes widened. He could stare all he wanted. I was done talking.

"Charge me or let me go," I said.

"Which of the seven paintings are the fakes, and which are the ones you stole?" His voice was an octave deeper, as if he had been taught that deeper voices would be taken more seriously.

He was still trying to intimidate me, but he had made a mistake. A big one. He hadn't known for sure some of the paintings were fake until I told him. All he seemed to know was that the agent didn't get his commission.

I stood up. "Charge me or let me go."

"You don't give orders. Sit back down. I'll tell you what you're charged with when you tell me which paintings are fake."

I stood in place and held out my wrists. "If I'm not under arrest, then handcuffs off. If I am under arrest, then I want my phone call."

He stood up, just a little below my height in my Louboutins. "Which paintings are fakes?"

I looked down slightly and saw him clearly.

Shannon Ames's agent had heard about the sale of the late artist's final works just like the rest of the world, on the Internet. He had done everything he could to get himself paid. When that failed he'd done everything he could to stop the sale of the paintings. He'd failed there too. If I had to guess he'd then tried everything he could to pursue criminal charges. But there wasn't a crime, exactly.

The only other person who could say for sure which paintings were fake, or stolen, was dead. That was the case for countless paintings. Museums, galleries, and auction houses were flooded with fake, or dubiously acquired, works. It didn't matter if the works were real or not, it mattered what people believed, and they believed in my paintings. Honestly knowing two of the works were stolen would actually increase their price. Nothing sells like a great story.

Eventually the agent found his way to this bland detective. A detective willing to waste time on his wild claims. A detective who came to me with no evidence. No video footage or fingerprints. He hadn't even Mirandized me. All he had was the story of one person, against me, a person he thought he was smarter than.

And now I knew that he knew nothing.

I fought to hold in my smile, unsuccessfully.

"Which paintings are fake?" the detective repeated.

"You're the detective. You tell me."

My Shopping Day

by Ian Rankin

Two things about being a good-looking guy who dresses well: one, you tend to get noticed; two, nobody thinks you capable of a naughty deed. In my line of work—necessarily peripatetic—there's a trade-off between the two. I'm hoping people will be looking at my face and not my hands. And I'm hoping they'll wander off in blissful ignorance afterwards.

I'm a pickpocket, only the term has lost its meaning—fine for Oliver Twist, but not for the 1990s. We're dippers, lifters. I specialise in handbags, shopping bags, carriers. I'm not a weightlifter or a big dipper—a little but often, that's me. I saw a stage act once, he could have the wrist watch off your hand, the belt off your trousers, and you wouldn't notice. He'd have your wallet, your glasses, your wife, your kids, and you'd take a look around and be naked and shivering in a dark alley.

He was that good. I'm not. But I look better than he did; I take care of myself. I went backstage after the show and he was pouring whisky into a glass that wasn't too clean. I got him to go through a couple of moves, thinking I could maybe incorporate them into my act, but nothing came of it. I asked him why, when he could make a fortune in train stations, airports, and cinema foyers, he was wasting his time on the stage of a working-men's club in Leven. He said the problem was he needed to show off. He had this gift, and he couldn't keep it quiet. He knew damned well that if he lifted a wallet, he'd want the victim to know about it.

Theatrical types; I've met a few.

I'm a bit of an actor myself, of course; have to be. My face is smiling, giving a come-on, and my mouth is saying all this pardon-me-all-my-fault stuff, but my mind is on what my hands are doing, slipping in and out of bags and baskets, palming the purse or the wallet or whatever of value happens to be lying there in plain view or just beyond. I wear expensive aftershave—not that cloying crap you see shagged to death on TV just before Christmas—and when I get close they get a good waft of it. It all helps to keep them occupied—preoccupied—during the performance. That was one lesson the old stooge in Leven taught me: preoccupation. Persuade them they're part of a certain scenario and they'll go along with it. Simple, really.

I frequent the big supermarkets and shopping centres. I see young women clicking their heels and holding clipboards, ready to collar some brain-fried shopper into taking part in their "consumer survey." Right, only what they're really doing is easing you into a pitch for double glazing, new kitchen, conservatory. And people keep taking the bait. I want to scream at them: "Come *on!* Wakey-wakey!" But what use would it do? A trawl up and down those aisles and your head is mush. I know shopping centres don't want you doing it, but just walk in some day and position yourself the safe side of the checkouts. Now stand there and watch the show. Watch a shopper breeze into the shop with head held high, trolley buzzing. Then watch them at the checkout, watch them as they leave. Their skin's turned gray, eyes dark. They frown, their jaw moves, there's almost drool there at the corners. Shoulders slumped, head sagging. These people have been beaten, pummelled. They've been hijacked, gagged, throttled, stymied, shaken, and stirred. On the way home, they'll be argumentative, downright rude, and once home they'll collapse, fight with spouse and kids, maybe have a little weep in the privacy of the toilet. And inside their head will be some shocking refrain, something they can't seem to shrug off without the aid of hard drink. It'll be some synthesized, sanitised, la-la-la singalong hit from the sixties or seventies. The music they shopped to, music you don't so much hear as ingest. While you're standing at the checkout, watching the sorry parade, you might want to try *listening* to that music. Believe me, it's hard to do; the music doesn't want you to listen to it. It wants you to feel it, which is a different thing altogether.

Okay, so you're thinking: The best time to lift those purses and wallets is when the shoppers come stumbling out with their trolleys laden, right? Wrong: I take them *inside* the shop, while their minds are at the same time filling with junk and jangling with a mental shopping list. They are seeing novelties they didn't know they needed— chocolate-flavoured pasta; canned caffeine with a free colour-change straw—and almost forgetting washing-up liquid and the kids' dinner. Boom: That's when I bump into them. That's when I brush against their cheap coats as I lean past for that perfect tomato towards the back of the display. That's when I half turn my head, give them the smile, and say something about how crowded the shop is today. Caught a little off guard, they're open to the full effect: dental work, jawline, groomed hair, expensive clothes, sweetened breath, and aftershave. My blue eyes sparkle with the same drops TV presenters use. The hand I've reached past their own wears a Breitling wrist watch, all bells and whistles and 2k of Swiss whatever. I'm working now. See, I don't just have to hold this woman—nearly always a woman—in thrall; I have at the same time to hide what my other hand is doing from other shoppers in the vicinity, some of whom, attracted to the show, will be watching me, watching her, and thinking they'd like to be over by the tomatoes right now instead.

It can take ten or fifteen minutes to size up the punter. They need to be a certain type—that goes without saying—and there has to be something worth nicking from them. I have to make sure nobody knows I'm shadowing them as I pass down the aisles with my handbasket (one or two items in it which I'll ditch later: I don't want to be standing in a checkout queue while my victim finds out she's missing cash and credit cards). So many variables; it's a juggling act, really. And I have to be a good psychologist. And I have to get away.

So you can see, it's not easy money when all's said and done.

But it beats clerical work, no?

Edinburgh had produced a good haul that Saturday. I'd hit three edge-of-town superstores. Saturday afternoons in those places are like hell on earth. Plus, they're either shrewd or tight-fisted on the east coast: no really easy pickings. They keep their money close to them and are suspicious of any stranger—*any* stranger. I blame those market researchers: You never know who's going to turn out to be one. Best-looking man I've ever seen came to my door…with the old clipboard and pen. Turned out he was trying to sell carpets. Looked like he was wearing one, too.

That Saturday morning, just to show you I'm not a bad bloke, I'd rejected a wallet which had been held out to me on a plate. There was a blind guy in the first shopping centre, walking the marbled and mirrored halls with confidence and a guide dog. The guide dog was a beauty of a Labrador: I love dogs, always have done. It was early in the day and I was just limbering up, sizing the place and its level of security. So I asked the old guy if I could pat his dog, gave me a chance to take a surreptitious look around. Gorgeous dog it was, come-hither eyes, all that. Nice and solid with a good coat. Liked to be stroked, too. So me and the old guy got talking. He was wearing some tatty old tweed jacket with greasy elbows—mind, I can see that smartness of appearance is problematical when you're blind. Anyway, the jacket was all baggy and worn, and when it swung open as the man leaned down to stroke his Lab, I saw his wallet inside, swinging from a loose pocket. And I could have had it, but he was blind, for Christ's sake, and maybe I just wasn't ready. So I decided to leave it alone. And guess what? He leaned a bit further down and the bloody thing slipped out onto the floor. He didn't seem to have heard it, too busy murmuring sweet nothings to the dog, whose name was Sabre. I picked up the wallet, gave its contents a once-over. Sabre's eyes were on me, but he wasn't saying anything. Seemed like he was on my side.

"You dropped this," I told the old fellow, wedging the wallet into his hand.

Temptation is a terrible thing, though….

Anyway, afternoon shift over, I'd returned to my car and driven it to the furthest corner of the car park to count my haul. I always choose the quietest corner, usually round by the loading bays. Saturday afternoons these aren't usually in use, unless someone's bought a bed or a bike and has driven round to load it into the car. Today, there was a transit van parked nearby, but nobody was in it, and when I looked around I didn't see anyone. So I spread the stuff on the passenger seat and got to work.

There was a guy I knew once called Playtex, partnered him a couple of times. He was called Playtex because he could lift and separate—as in lift people's money and separate them from it. Anyway, his advice was to get away from the scene pronto. But then one day while driving out of the car park, he smacked into a disabled car. There was a cop nearby, and of course Playtex didn't just have cash and plastic in his own car, he had the purses and wallets too, spread all over the place after the impact. Now me, I like to take my time, not panic. Go through everything then and there, that way I can ditch the unnecessaries as soon as possible. The purses and wallets go into a bottle bank if there is one; stick them in a bin and they might be found too soon. ID cards, photo-cards, that sort of thing—same place. Cash and credit cards, cash cards, stuff like that I keep, plus any little things like stamps. These days, of course, nobody's supposed to carry cash, but you'd be surprised. First thing a lot of people do before they start their shopping is visit the bank or the machine: They might need cash for a restaurant, a cup of coffee or a double gin, a taxi home, the TV papers....I get a lot of nice fresh tens and twenties. The plastic I offload to a guy I meet three times a week in a pub in Glasgow. It's a hassle, meeting him this often, but he says we have to "strike while the iron is hot." In other words, he needs the cards before they get too old. Some people, so he tells me, will wait up to a week before reporting missing cards, on the chance that they might turn up. Or they simply won't notice they're missing. But all the same, he needs them pronto, so he can maximise their shelf life. He can use cash cards too, though I don't know how. He bypasses the code or something; works a couple of times, then you throw the card away or the machine swallows it.

I'd made not too bad a showing that afternoon. The bottle bank was about ten yards away, so I got out of the car and walked over to it, pushing the leatherware inside. I could smell sour wine and beer slops, and knew I'd be drinking better than either that evening. I was just getting back into my car when I heard the squeal. It was coming from the transit. I heard it again. There was no one in the front of the van, so the sound had to be coming from the back. No windows, so I couldn't be sure. But yes: The whole van rocked suddenly and I heard a thudding sound. Then a voice—definitely a voice this time—a man's, hissing something that sounded very much like, "You won't do that again, you bitch!"

I got back into my car and just sat there, hands resting on the steering wheel. Then I put my window down. I didn't hear anything else. The van was white, mostly, but with a black roof. It looked like a respray. The front grille was crimson and the wing-mirror nearest me was missing. There was a partition behind the seats, blocking off the back. I licked my lips, wondering what was happening in there, wondering what to do about it. This last was easy to answer: nothing. Get the hell away from there and forget about it. I started my engine and slipped into first, crawling from the scene. I'd got as far as the bottle bank when, eyes on the rearview, I saw the transit's back doors swing open. I couldn't see inside; the van had been backed close to a wall. I watched a man jump down and slam the doors shut. He wiped his mouth with the back of his hand, then put his wrist to his mouth and sucked on it. He was over six feet, black T-shirt, black denims, and a black leather waistcoat. He looked in his forties, long hair thinning badly. When he looked up, he saw my car and seemed interested in it. I started off again, hoping he'd think I'd been paying a visit to the bottle-bank—which, after all, was the truth.

I circled the car park, but ignored the arrows to the exit, instead coming back round to where, from a safe distance, I could again see the transit. The man was moving now, walking towards the superstore's front entrance. He had an awkward, gangling gait, arms swinging low. He reminded me of a guy I'd known years back who'd been the roadie with a third-rate rock band. Same straggly brown hair and overdone sideburns, same sleepless eyes. It wasn't him, it just looked like him.

He disappeared through the automatic doors. I stared towards the van. From this distance, I couldn't see any movement, couldn't hear anything. But I knew there was someone in there, some woman. I didn't like to think about what she was doing there. Had he locked the doors after him? I could hare over there and maybe let her out....

If he didn't come back out and find me there. He'd seen me by the bottle-bank. Maybe he was standing in the shop doorway, waiting for me to make a move. A car was moving slowly towards the bottle-bank. It was a shiny black BMW, tinted windows. It didn't stop at the bottle-bank; it made for the van, stopped dead in front of it.

Christ, now what?

A man got out. He wore a cream-coloured suit, well-cut, and a pink polo shirt, plus sunglasses—and I'd bet they were Ray-Bans. His hair was light brown, neatly trimmed, and his jaw made chewing motions. He walked to the back of the transit and, without hesitating, pulled open the doors and jumped in. The doors closed after him.

I sat there frowning, conjuring innocent scenarios. The only one that seemed even remotely feasible was that the roadie-lookalike was a pimp, the BMW a punter, and the woman in the back a prossie. But in all honesty I didn't believe that, not for one minute.

Then the doors of the superstore opened, and this time it was a security guard who came out, two-way held to his mouth. He seemed to be scanning the car park. I knew the score: He wasn't looking for anyone in a transit van; chances were, he was looking for *me.* This time, I followed the exit arrows.

I was staying in a Bed & Breakfast, nicely anonymous on the Dalkeith Road. The front garden had been paved over to create three parking spaces, but mine was the only car there. It was out of season. I'd been asked if I was in town on business, and had answered that I was, the proprietor not seeming to notice that the weekend was a funny time to be conducting business.

There was a bathroom along the hall, and I soaked in a bath for half an hour, eyes closed. My jacket hung from a hook on the back of the door, its inside pocket padded with cash. The plastic was in a brown A4 envelope—sealed—beneath my car's passenger seat. Hotel and B&B rooms were public property, you never knew who'd come traipsing through, or how curious they'd be, so I preferred to keep the stuff in my locked car. The car itself was not worth stealing, not even worth breaking into. There was a yawning gap where a radio should be, and the upholstery was torn and frayed. There were times when it paid not to be showy.

I was reasoning with myself: There was nothing you could do; it would have been too risky; what if there'd been some innocent explanation? Do you want to see yourself in the clink? There was nothing you could do.

I kept coming back to that, trying to convince myself. *You won't do that again, you bitch!* And he'd come out of the van wiping his mouth and sucking his wrist. Had he tried something and she'd bitten him? The squeal I'd heard had been the sound of someone in pain. Maybe the man. Maybe her.

Probably her.

The bath was cold before I got out.

That evening, I tried eating Indian, but couldn't summon up an appetite. Instead I drove through the city, wishing I had a radio, something that might take my mind off things. A radio would have been cheap at the price. I found myself back at the "retail park." It looked different at night, eerie, otherworldly. The interiors of the buildings were well-lit, so you could see a lot of merchandise, only no one was buying. The car park was empty, sodium lights overhead deterring ne'er-do-wells. But I drove into the car park anyway. These places used private security firms, but they'd be tucked up inside the stores, and probably wouldn't venture out except in the direst emergency. I saw that there was a single car parked in the car park, a nice-looking Volvo, surrounded by a sea of spaces and the occasional island of metal trolleys. But there was no transit van. I stopped my car in front of where it had been and, headlights full-beam, got out to examine the ground.

I didn't know what I was doing, what I was looking for. Clues? Clues to what? Something that might put my mind at rest, perhaps, but I wasn't sure what would do that. There was nothing, of course, not the least sign that any vehicle had ever been there. Just a wad of gum lying next to the wall. I remembered the man in the BMW had been chewing something; this was probably his. Could I take it to the police? Look at this valuable piece of evidence, Officers! Can you test the saliva for DNA? Will it lead you to a house of slaughter, an evil trade in sex slaves?

Thank you, sir, and could we have your name and profession…?

What was I doing? There had been a noise from a van. A man had yelled something and come out of the van. Another man had gone into the van. So what? I would be leaving town the following day. By tomorrow night, it would all be forgotten. I got back into my car and reversed from the scene.

But as I passed the solitary Volvo, I slowed, then stopped. If someone had been in that van against their will, then maybe they'd been abducted. Abducted from where? From this very car park, perhaps. Which meant their car would still be here, unclaimed at the end of the day. I got out of my car once more and walked around the Volvo. Could have been dumped by joyriders, of course, except how many joyriders opted for Volvos? Again, I didn't know what I was looking for. I glanced around, saw nobody, and took a closer look at the car. No keys in the ignition. Something lying on the passenger seat. What was it? Looked like a letter. I tried to read the name on the envelope, but couldn't. Then I did something crazy—I tried the driver's door. And it wasn't locked. It opened with a soft click, no alarm. An unlocked Volvo: Now I knew something was wrong. I took out the envelope and held it under lamplight. There was a man's name on it—Mr. Roger Masson—but no address.

The woman's husband? The car didn't seem about to yield any other clues. I heard a lorry revving, and closed the door to the Volvo, heading back to my own car. I was behind the steering wheel before the lorry came into view. It seemed to be collecting rubbish from one of the other shops. I was driving out of the car park before I realised I still had the envelope in my hand.

I stopped at a pub on Corstorphine Road and asked for the phone book. Saturday night—the place was mobbed. Plenty of good-looking young women, a few giving me interested looks as I stood at the bar. Under normal circumstances, I'd have stayed for a drink, flashed around a bit of money. Maybe I'd have found someone for the night. But tonight, all I wanted was an address. Roger Masson: Barnton Avenue West. Back in my car I checked my A-Z, found the street, and drove there.

Ask me why. Go on, do it. I couldn't give you an answer now, couldn't have done then. It just seemed…it seemed a thing to do; maybe not *the* thing to do—certainly not the *sensible* thing to do—but *a* thing to do. And I did it.

Big houses next to a golf course. Very big houses, actually, detached, modern, big gardens. Very nice, and completely silent. It wasn't the sort of street where you'd nip next door for the loan of some coffee; you'd phone the stuff in instead. I stopped the car at the bottom of the drive. The gates were open, and I could see the house clearly. There were lights on inside. Someone walked across a window: a man. He looked worried. He was holding a portable phone to his ear. He held it away from his ear and broke the connection, then rubbed at his forehead. A very worried man. He let his shoulders slump. It was hard to tell from a distance, but he looked in his fifties, if well-preserved. Nice greying hair, open-necked shirt. He seemed to be staring into space, but I realised finally that he wasn't. He was looking out of the window.

He was looking at me.

He turned and walked from the room. The anxious husband, wondering where his wife was. What could I tell him? Nothing. All he'd done was satisfy me that something was wrong. And now that I'd seen his home, I had the feeling maybe the reason why Mrs. Masson had taken her Volvo to the shops this afternoon and not come back was that she'd been unavoidably detained.

By kidnappers.

I watched the front door open, and Masson come running out. He didn't have anything but socks on his feet, and consequently ran on tiptoe down the gravel drive.

"Hey, you!" he was shouting. "I want to talk to you!"

I started the car and moved off.

"Wait a minute! Help, somebody! Help!"

I tore away from there like I had something to fear. Up onto Queensferry Road and back towards town, missing at least one red light in the process and decidedly ignoring the speed limit.

Which is why the cops caught me.

Flashing blue lights in my rearview, and headlamps flicking to full-beam to tell me to pull over. So what else could I do? I pulled over, easing two wheels up onto the pavement to make room for passing traffic—ever the courteous driver.

I can wing this, I thought. I've not been drinking, and I've no unpaid fines. I can wing this.

"Step out of the car, please, sir."

I stepped out of the car. There were two of them, uniformed, one—the elder—talking to me, the other walking around the car like I was planning to sell it.

"Something wrong, Officers?" The elder blinked at me like I'd been watching too many films.

"Does a red light mean 'go faster'?" he asked, while his partner smirked. I tried a shy grin.

"It was on me before I saw it."

"Been drinking this evening, sir?"

"Not a drop." The younger cop was peering in through the front passenger window. I was all too aware of the plastic in the envelope under the seat. But the envelope was *sealed*: They couldn't open it even if they found it, not without reasonable suspicion. That might not stop them opening it, of course, but at least my lawyer would have a stick to beat them with.

"No?"

I shook my head, breathed out hard, remembered I'd tried eating a curry.

"Was that a madras or a vindaloo?" the older cop asked, not bothering to wait for an answer. His car had a computer on board; a lot of them do these days. Depends where you are; whether the regional force has had enough money in the kitty. He could go and put my licence plate through his machine: It would come up clean. Never buy a dodgy car.

"Just wait there," the youngster said, going to join his partner. So I stood by my car, arms folded, trying not to look guilty as a parade of motorists slowed to watch. The old guy was on his radio. I had a sudden thought: *Masson has called a 999 with my description.* Would he do that? No telling what a man will do when he's desperate. The cops were looking at me through their windscreen, maybe trying to sweat me, get me to run for it. No way, not with the envelope under the passenger seat.

So I stood and waited, and at last they came back, both of them.

"We'd like you to come down to the station," the elder said.

"What? Am I being arrested?"

"Just a routine matter."

"For not stopping at a red light?"

"Routine, sir. If you'll come with us."

I tried to look disgruntled, appalled—it wasn't hard. "What about my car?"

"My colleague will drive it, sir. If you'll come with me…"

I sat mute in the passenger seat all the way to the cop shop.

Police stations are not designed to make you feel like the driven snow, even if the worst thing you've done in your life is try peeping at your sister while she was in the bath. They are like black holes. Once you're in there, to the outside world you've ceased to exist, and the outside world itself ceases to have meaning for you.

That can be frightening. It can loosen tongues. Suddenly you remember about your sister, and blurt it out, dredging up a memory from ten or twenty years ago. You'd tell them anything, these quiet listeners, these stone faces. You'd tell them you once waded through her underwear drawer too, even if this were a downright lie.

I don't have a sister. I wasn't about to tell them anything.

The CID office was big and needed a lick of paint. There were large cracks snaking across the ceiling towards the flickering lengths of centred striplighting. There were six desks, big old bulky things, like school surplus from the Billy Bunter era. And there were detectives, wearing suits and ties and looking like they couldn't wait to knock off. I was seated in front of one of the tables. There was no one sitting across from me. I'd been asked if I wanted a cup of coffee. I'd declined. They didn't want to breath-test me, that much was clear. Nothing else was.

Then the detective came and sat down, pulling his chair in inch by inch till he was happy with the arrangement. He lined three ballpoint pens in a row in front of him. There was a clean pad of paper below the pens.

"Do you know why we've asked you here, Mr.…" He looked at a slip of paper in his paw. "Mr. Croft?"

He was not especially tall, but had bulk and confidence. His temples were turning grey; the rest of his hair looked like it would follow soon enough. His eyes were dark, sceptical. He watched me shake my head, then searched his in-tray, at last pulling out a sheet of paper.

" 'Six feet one or two,' " he read, " 'dark hair, well-groomed, well-dressed, blue eyes, squarish face, good teeth. A nice manner.' " He looked up. "Sound familiar, Mr. Croft?"

"I might know a few women like that."

He allowed a smile. "It could be you, Mr. Croft."

"Could be a lot of people, Sergeant."

"It's Inspector. Inspector Rebus."

"Look," I sat forward, "what is this all about?"

"It's about someone lifting purses out of bags, Mr. Croft."

"Ridiculous." I half laughed. "Good God, where's this supposed to have happened?"

"All over the city. You live here, Mr. Croft?"

"Visiting."

"When did you arrive?"

"Yesterday evening."

The detective nodded to himself. "Two women came up with this description, Mr. Croft. Two women in two different supermarkets, two different areas of the city."

"I did go to *one* supermarket this afternoon."

"Which one?"

I shrugged. "Cameron Toll, was that it? Somewhere near my hotel."

"Foot of Dalkeith Road?"

I nodded.

"What did you want?"

"Razors, deodorant…" I lowered my voice. "Contraceptives."

He ignored my man-to-man admission. "Got the receipt, by any chance?"

I laughed again. "Threw it away."

"What line of work are you in?"

"I'm a photographer." I am too: There's an SLR in the boot of my car. One thing about travelling around the country, I get to take some wonderful photographs. Twice now I've won my camera club's annual prize.

"For a company?"

I shook my head. "Freelance. I can show you my portfolio."

"Don't be disgusting," someone called from across the room. The inspector smiled at that, and I smiled, too. We were beginning to get along just fine.

"There's been some sort of mistake," I said. "Check my hotel room, my car." I gave him my most honest look, dewy eyes and all.

"Why were you in such a rush?"

"Sorry?"

"On Queensferry Road."

"I wasn't in any hurry. But when that road's quiet…you can build up a head of steam without noticing."

"Lucky you," the same voice called.

"So you've no objections to us searching your hotel room or your car?"

"None."

He nodded again. "So where's the stuff stashed?"

Bluff! my brain yelled. I stared him out, made sure my smile wasn't wavering. "Look, Inspector…"

Someone had answered a phone. Now they called across the room, "John, someone called Masson for you."

My heart dropped like a stone.

The inspector picked up his receiver, pushed a button, and leaned back in his chair.

"Mr. Masson? What can I do for you, sir?" The way he spoke, I knew this Masson had clout to spare. Rebus's face hardened as he listened. "What?" He began writing on his notepad. For the moment, I'd been forgotten. "A pet? When was this?" He listened some more, scribbling furiously. "Why didn't you come to us straight away? What make of car?"

His writing was appalling, but I read the words "Volvo" and "car park."

"And there was no note? Where's your wife now? Can I speak to her, please, sir?"

He put his hand over the mouthpiece. "Be with you in a minute."

I nodded, feeling like my head might actually fall off. Mrs. Masson was coming to the phone! Her husband was bringing her! So she hadn't been in the van. She was nothing to do with it. What had he said about a pet and a note…? My hand went to my jacket pocket. The envelope was still there.

"Mrs. Masson?" Rebus said now. "How are you? Yes, must be terrible. They were supposed to leave a note? Have you seen these men?" He listened, started scribbling again. "You've only spoken to one man? But he spoke in the plural? Well, it might be important, Mrs. Masson. When was this?" He began writing again. I could feel sweat trickling down my back. "No, it's serious, all right, I just wish you'd come to us right at the start. I'd like to come out there and see you." He listened again, scribbled—by now the top sheet of the pad looked like a blackboard at the end of a school day. When he put the receiver down he did so slowly, still writing. Then he got up abruptly and went to talk with someone at the far end of the room.

I slipped my hand into my pocket and felt the envelope. It hadn't been stuck down. I felt inside. Sure enough, there was a sheet of paper there. I eased it out, my face blank, unfolded it on my knee, and read the pencilled capitals.

£2,000 TO GET THE BITCH BACK. GET MONEY READY, WE'LL CALL.

The squeal I'd heard had been human, but it had been the roadie's voice. He'd just been bitten by Mrs. Masson's pet dog: *You won't do that again, you bitch!* Maybe he'd muzzled her, tied her up, knocked her cold. Maybe he'd done worse. If there's one thing I abhor more than the cruelty we inflict on each other, it's cruelty inflicted on animals.

Especially dogs.

It was as clear as day now. Mrs. Masson had been instructed to leave her car in the car park, and to return sometime later, when she'd find a ransom note on the passenger seat. Only I'd chanced by and lifted the bloody note. So now she didn't know what was expected of her and was going up the wall. And her husband, driven by this, had at last called the police—perhaps against her wishes. All she wanted was her dog back. Meantime, I had the note *and* a description of the dognappers. I had more than any of them.

And I was stuck here.

Rebus came back and tore the sheet from his pad, folded it into his pocket. By now the other note was safe in my pocket. He looked at me for a long time, as if trying to place me. I went dewy-eyed again.

"I've got your licence plate, your name, and your address," he said quietly. "I've got everything I need—for the moment. I'll want to talk to you again tomorrow. Be here at ten-thirty, understood?"

Two choices: stick with innocent bewilderment, or nod. I nodded. Not that I'd be here tomorrow morning: I'd be packed and gone by midnight.

He gave me another long stare. "Your car's outside, get the keys from the desk." He moved away, but paused and turned. "See you tomorrow, Mr. Croft." He made it sound like a threat.

It didn't bother me, I knew I was off and running. That was the only sensible course, I kept telling myself. And I believed it, too.

I sat in my car, hands trembling as they ran over the steering wheel. I didn't know whether to laugh or cry. In the end, I think I did both simultaneously. I leaned down and felt beneath the passenger seat. The envelope was still there. Everyone deserves a lucky break, I thought, starting the engine.

I'd go back to the B&B, pack my things, and never come back.

Wouldn't that be a callous ending?

But as I drove, I thought of the two men and wondered what kind of dog Mrs. Masson owned: something small and snapping, or a big hearty beast fit for walks across the golf course? I hoped for the latter, for something like the blind man's Labrador. I heard the squeal again. It could have been a dog squealing. And the thump I'd heard: Had the roadie smashed its head? My hands tightened on the steering wheel and, first pub I saw, I pulled over and went looking for another phone book.

This time I had a whisky—a good-sized one. Well, they weren't going to stop me twice in the same night, were they? And I needed the courage. I looked up Masson's address and took down his telephone number. I couldn't call from the bar: too noisy. But there was a box fifty yards along the road, and I used that. A man answered, Masson himself, I presumed.

"Inspector Rebus, please."

I heard the man say, "Someone for you," as he handed the phone over.

"Hello?"

"Just listen. You're looking for two men." I gave my descriptions, eyes squeezed shut as I tried to make them as accurate and telling as I could. Then I described the van and the BMW. "And they want two grand. They'll probably be phoning later."

Rebus had listened to this in silence. Now he spoke.

"Mr. Croft, is that you?"

This time my heart sank like something altogether more massive than a mere stone. A block of city granite, maybe.

"Was it your car Mr. Masson saw?" Rebus went on.

I licked dry lips. "Yes," I said.

"Are you mixed up in this?"

"Only as a…well, I saw the van. I thought I heard something. I was worried, so I went back tonight."

"You found the note?" He sounded amused.

"Yes."

"Why didn't you come forward?" He caught himself. "No, stupid question. Thanks for your call."

"Do you still want me at the station tomorrow?"

"Were you planning on coming?"

"It doesn't really fit with my schedule."

"Get out of the city, Mr. Croft. Don't ever come back."

"Inspector, one question—what breed is she?"

There was a pause while the detective checked. "Persian Blue," he said at last.

"What?"

"Persian Blue."

"But that's a cat."

"Sorry?"

"A cat."

"That's right."

"I *hate* cats!"

I slammed the phone down, went back to the B&B, and packed my suitcase in a blind fury. I had paid till noon Sunday, so there was no problem. I just left my key behind, got back into the car, and drove. I was heading down Dalkeith Road, making for the city bypass, when I saw the van. I blinked, shook my head, but it was definitely the van. I knew not only from the black roof, the missing wing-mirror, but because it was being shadowed by a black BMW. They were going around a roundabout as I approached it. I watched them turn off, then followed. Cameron Toll Shopping Precinct. They were driving into the car park, the only vehicles around at that time of night. I switched off my lights and hung back, watching as they came to a stop. The roadie got out of the van, and was joined by Mr. Smooth, who checked his watch. There was a wall-mounted telephone close by. The roadie opened the back of the van and got in. After checking his watch again, rocking on the balls of his feet, Mr. Smooth got in too, closing the doors after him. I kept my lights off and lifted my foot from the brake, rolling down the slight incline towards them, keeping going until my front bumper touched their rear. My car's a big old Merc, same axle height as a transit. They felt the impact and tried opening the doors, only they were jammed shut by my radiator grille. I got out and jumped up onto my bonnet, my face close to the inch-wide gap in the transit's rear doors.

"A female cat isn't called a bitch!" I screamed at them.

I might have screamed it more than once, actually, before getting down and going to the telephone.

The Advent Reunion

by Andrew Klavan

1. Ghost Hunter

I've wanted to tell this story for a long time. It began when I was a young man, during my junior year at Harvard.

To come, as I had come, from a crumbling house on a sandy lane in a dying town just west of nowhere to the aged brick and history, high culture and customs of one of the most prestigious universities in the country was a daunting journey for so inexperienced a boy. I spent my first year holed up in my room, buried in my books, working on my writing. Only after a very unpleasant summer break at home did I return to school determined to make friends.

I soon fell in with an aspiring composer named Jonathan Wilson and, through Jonathan, I found myself part of a little clique of brilliant artsy types—brilliant in our own minds, anyway. Among this group was a girl named Amanda Zane. She was blond and willowy and had a dreamy, wistful quality about her. She wrote songs and played guitar and sang. Her voice was high and clear and sweet, with a sad, yearning tone that just grabbed me by the heart. I was crazy about her pretty much on sight and, for some reason, she seemed to like me as well. We became a couple within the clique. It was the first truly happy time in my life.

No wonder that, as the Christmas break approached, I began to dread the thought of going home again. And when Jonathan came up with an alternative, I was delighted. His parents had decided to spend the holidays in Hawaii. Their house in rural upstate New York was going to be empty. Jonathan invited our little gang to spend Christmas there with him. Five of us accepted the invitation, David, Lucy, Rosemary, Amanda, and I.

It was, it turned out, a perfect setting for Christmas. The house was enormous, stone and stately. It sat in a little valley with hills of forest on every side, everything white with snow as far as the eye could see. When we first arrived, we tried to behave with our usual pseudo-sophisticated pseudo-detachment but the spirit of the season very quickly overwhelmed us. Within an hour of tumbling through the front door, we were laughing and shouting like the excited children we were. We found decorations in the attic and spread them all about the house. We found sleds in the garage and raced each other down the slopes. We cut down a large pine tree at the edge of the forest, tied it up with stout ropes, and dragged it home over the snow. We hung ornaments on it and sang carols around the piano and basically had as much good, clean fun as it's legal to have.

We were having so much fun, in fact, that I didn't notice—none of us noticed—that Amanda had begun acting very strange. Shy and distracted at the best of times, she'd grown almost silent in our boisterous midst. More and more often, she withdrew from our festivities without excuse and went wandering on her own for hours.

Finally, one afternoon, when the others were planning a shopping excursion to the nearby mall, she asked me if I would remain behind. When we were alone together, she broke the news to me: She was pregnant.

She had actually managed to convince herself I might be happy to hear about the child. But how could I be? I had no money. I had worked like a slave, year after year, to win my place at school. I had ambitions—big ambitions—to become a writer, a novelist—not exactly a very secure profession, not something you can count on, not in the beginning, at least. I was in no position to take on the support of a wife and child.

I didn't have to tell her any of this. Amanda took one look at the expression on my face and saw it all. The next moment, she was in hysterical tears, raging at me, completely irrational. I had never seen her like that before. She screamed that I was selfish. I was thoughtless. I was this and that and the other. And when I tried to reason with her, when I suggested there might be another, better time for us to have a child together, she lost control completely, took it in the worst way, practically accused me of being some kind of homicidal maniac.

Thankfully, the worst of it was over by the time Jonathan and the others returned from their outing. When they burst through the door, shouting and laughing, I was in the living room, sitting alone in an armchair by the fireplace, staring into the flames, torn between panic and despair.

"Where's Amanda?" they all cried out at once. "We're going to play games! We're going to make cookies! We're going to play Ghost Hunter!"

I hesitated—but I finally managed to smile and tell them Amanda had gone to bed early with a headache. I didn't see the point of spoiling their good mood with the truth.

It was already evening, already dark. We all went into the kitchen and made popcorn and cookies, swilling wine and beer as we did. I forced myself to join in the fun with a show of enthusiasm. After an hour or so, we began our game of Ghost Hunter.

Ghost Hunter, for those who've never played it, is basically just hide-and-seek in the dark. One person is designated the Ghost Hunter, then you turn off all the lights and everyone else scatters and hides. The Hunter moves through the house with a flashlight and if he leaves the room in which you're hiding without finding you, you're allowed to jump out and scare him. Each person who comes out of hiding then joins the hunt for the others.

I didn't want to sit out and ruin the game, but with everything that was weighing on my mind, I didn't know how long I could keep up the pretense of high spirits. I came up with what I thought was a brilliant idea. I hid down in the basement behind the boiler. It was, I felt sure, literally the last place anyone would look.

It was pitch dark down there, absolutely black. I could bring my hand within inches of my eyes and still not see it. I sat on the floor just behind the boiler, staring, blind, feeling sorry for myself. More than half an hour went by. All the while, I could hear the screams and giggles of my friends upstairs.

Finally, I heard the basement door open. A flashlight beam shone on the cellar stairs. Jonathan was the Ghost Hunter. He'd already collected all the others. I could hear them murmuring to each other.

"He must be here. Where else could he be?"

Laughing nervously, they came thumping down the stairs behind the flashlight beam. When they reached the bottom, Jonathan swept the light across the pitch darkness. It went over me once, then, a second later, snapped back to pick out my face.

"There you are! I see you!" they shouted together.

Someone—Rosemary, I think—said, "I'll get the lights."

The basement lights came on. And the next thing I knew, Rosemary let out a high, ragged, terrible scream. I lifted my eyes, following her horrified gaze. Then I started screaming too.

There, just above my head, Amanda's corpse dangled in the air, one end of a rope tied around a heating pipe in the ceiling, the other end pulled tight around her neck.

She had been there, right above me, the whole time I was sitting in the dark.

2. She Haunts Us

The aftermath of Amanda's death was ugly, especially for me. The coroner had no trouble deciding she'd committed suicide and he also had no trouble figuring out why. I was forced to tell the police the whole story: the pregnancy and our awful argument. This got back to Jonathan and the others, of course. I won't say they blamed me or anything, but they didn't exactly forgive me, either. After that, we'd see each other around campus from time to time, and we were always pleasant enough with each other, but their underlying coldness toward me was unmistakable. To my great sorrow, the days of our true friendship were over.

When I graduated, I moved to New York City. I didn't see any of them again for a long time.

Seven years went by, in fact. Some hungry times, a lot of hard work, then I started to make some progress. My first couple of books came out. I scored some movie sales. I hit some bestseller lists. Things began to go well.

But all the while, I was aware that, in some way, what happened with Amanda continued to cast a shadow over my life. I had never been close with my family, but now I cut off communications with them altogether. I had girlfriends from time to time, but I never established another long-term relationship. Most of the people I called friends were really just casual acquaintances. Somehow, after Amanda, there was always a part of myself that I kept in reserve, that I was never quite willing to share with anyone else.

One day, in early December, I came home from a party to find a message on my answering machine. The message was from Jonathan Wilson. He said he was in New York and he wanted to meet with me. You would think I'd be surprised to hear from him, but the truth was, I'd been expecting that call—expecting it for as long as I could remember.

The next evening, Jonathan and I met at my local tavern, McGlade's. It was a cold, drizzly day. I stepped into the bar and stood brushing the damp off my overcoat as I looked around for him. At first, I didn't see him. That is, I must have passed over him without recognizing him. Then I did. He was seated at a table in back by the brick fireplace. He was staring into a glass of red wine. He was a shocking sight. Only seven years had passed since I'd last seen him, but he seemed to have aged decades. He was thin and sallow and drawn.

I sat down with him. Ordered a drink. Before the waitress even returned with the glass, Jonathan had begun to tell me his story. Things had gone badly for him since school, he said. He'd been ill off and on. He'd abandoned his composing. Gone from job to job until he finally ended up at his father's investment firm, where he was doing only moderately well. The same was true of the others, he told me, the other three who'd been at his parents' house with us that Christmas. Rosemary had struggled with drugs and alcohol. David had been through an ugly divorce that left him depressed and nearly broke. Lucy had gone through a series of abusive relationships, including one that ended with her in the hospital with a couple of broken ribs.

"It's about her somehow," Jonathan told me. "It's about Amanda. We all feel it. She haunts us. She won't let us move on." Then, after a pause, he said, "I read about you in the papers all the time. You seem to be doing well."

It felt like an accusation. I was the one most closely connected to Amanda's death, after all. If anyone was responsible for it, obviously it was me. And I had my problems, as I said, but basically he was right: I was doing well. And I said so.

Jonathan stared into his wine a long, silent moment. Then he looked up rather sharply and said, "We have to go back. We've all agreed. We're going to meet up at the house in a week. We're going to spend Christmas there again."

"What's that supposed to accomplish?" I asked him.

"I don't know. None of us knows. We just have to do it. Will you come?"

I said I would think about it. And I did think about it, all that night. And I thought: That time of my life, even that Christmas at the Wilson house before the tragedy—those were the happiest days I'd ever known. For all the success I'd had, nothing else had ever come close. I thought: Maybe they're right. Maybe if we could go back, if we could capture some of that spirit, lay our guilt about Amanda's death to rest…maybe we could be happy again.

I called Jonathan in the morning and told him I would drive up to the house next weekend.

3. A Voice in the Storm

I left the city on a gray Saturday morning and headed upstate. When I was about fifty miles north of Manhattan, it began to snow. Pretty soon, the grass by the side of the highway was dusted with white.

I pressed on. The snow kept getting heavier and heavier. The traveling wasn't all that bad as long as I was on the thruway, but once I got past Albany, once I got off the main roads and into the back country, the conditions deteriorated fast. Soon, the snow was falling so thickly I could barely see—and when I could see, leaning forward to peer through the windshield, all I could make out were the vague hulking shapes of the surrounding forest. The roads here had not been ploughed. They wound perilously through narrower and narrower passages between higher and higher drifts. I probably should have pulled over someplace, tried to find a motel and waited out the storm. But the idea of this reunion had captured my imagination. I didn't want to get there late. I didn't want to miss anything.

I turned on the radio, hoping to hear the weather—news—any sound of civilization. Nothing came out of the speakers except a steady hiss of static. I hit the search button. The digital readout spun from number to number without stopping. A murmur of voices rose and faded. A whisper of music died beneath the unbroken windlike sough.

Then, after another moment or two, the tuner seemed to catch hold of something. For several seconds, I could hear—soft beneath the interference—the wistful sound of an acoustic guitar. It was playing a sad, lilting melody I had never heard before. A woman's high, clear, sweet, and mournful voice was singing.

"I wait for you," she sang. "I wait for you."

I turned from the windshield and stared at the radio. That voice…It was far away, riddled with static…but I recognized it…

Just then, the car went into a skid. I faced forward—but too late. I had lost control and was sliding, blind, through the whiteness.

Before I could get my bearings, the car dropped off the edge of the road and buried its front end in the deep drifts beneath the winter trees. I tried to rock it out, but the tires just whined uselessly. I couldn't get any traction. The car was stuck.

I sat back in my seat breathing hard as the full dimensions of the situation became clear to me. It was cold, very cold. I hadn't seen a building or a turnoff for miles. I had only about a quarter tank of gas. Maybe two hours of daylight left at most. If I stayed in the car, the engine would probably die right about the same time the light did. There was a real possibility I could freeze to death out here.

I decided to try to find help or shelter before nightfall. I stepped out of the car—and dropped into snow up to my knees. I stared around me into the blinding white. I saw nothing but the dim shadows of pine trees standing like sentinels watching me. I shouted for help. My voice was lost in the wind. Clutching my overcoat closed against the cold, I pushed forward until the snow grew more shallow and I could feel the road under my shoes. I followed the pavement as best I could up a small hill.

Just as I got to the top, something wonderful happened. A gust of wind pushed the snow aside like a curtain. The view cleared. There, nestled in an empty valley not a quarter of a mile away, stood the old Wilson mansion, the very place I was looking for.

I didn't go back to the car for my luggage. I was afraid of getting lost. I stumbled down the hill until the road wound around to the Wilsons' long driveway. Then I shoved my way through the driveway's big drifts until I was at the front door. I pounded with the old iron knocker. No one came. Finally, shivering, I tried the knob. Luckily, the door opened. I spilled inside.

I shouted. No answer. It was clear the place was empty. I tried the lights. Nothing. The phones were out, too. There wasn't much time before sunset. I had to find some supplies. Some matches; flashlights. Logs so I could start a fire.

Yet, I hesitated. I stood in the front room at the window, staring out at the falling snow. I watched the light grow dimmer and dimmer. Alone in that house with the night coming, all I could think about was that moment in the car just before I hit the final skid. That familiar voice lilting through the static on the radio. That song:

"I wait for you. I wait for you."

4. Reunion

The day grew darker and darker at the windows. I made preparations to get through the night. I stacked some logs in the fireplace with old magazines for kindling. I rattled through every drawer I could find, searching for matches. Luckily, just as the last light was dying away, I opened a hall closet and found a flashlight on the top shelf. I followed the beam to the kitchen. But I stopped on the threshold.

I could see by the flashlight that the door leading from the kitchen down into the basement stood open, the cellar stairs disappearing into the blackness below. The open door unnerved me somehow. Alone in the dark house, my mind returned to that moment seven years ago when I saw Amanda's corpse dangling above me.

I stepped decisively to the basement door and swung it shut.

I took a second to calm myself. Then I searched the kitchen. I looked in the small pantry. Went through some more drawers. Finally, the flashlight beam picked out a box of wooden matches on a small shelf over the stove. I was reaching up to take hold of the box when my hand froze in midair.

I heard something. A guitar was playing. Slowly, I turned around, brought the flashlight around. The basement door was standing open again. A voice wafted up to me from below, singing softly, sadly.

"I wait for you. I wait for you."

I moved quickly back to the door, intending to shut it again. But just as I reached the top of the stairs, the singing stopped. The lightless basement fell silent. I stood there, staring down into the darkness. I felt a sour, burning fear rise in me as I realized I couldn't just close the door, I couldn't just walk away. I couldn't spend the night in this house wondering what was down there, not knowing.

I had to look. I started down the stairs, holding tight to the flashlight. The basement dark seemed to crawl up my sides and close around me. I reached the bottom. Immediately, I guided the beam to the place where I'd seen Amanda hanging. There was nothing there.

No. Wait. There was. The light picked out the shape of a rope. My hand trembled as I raised the beam to see that one end was tied around the heating pipe. My breath caught as I lowered the beam.

The bottom of the rope was tied in a noose. But the noose hung empty.

I lowered the flashlight and saw Amanda come walking toward me out of the darkness.

She was just as I'd seen her last. Her body was horribly bloated, her face disfigured, the eyes bulging, the skin bluish-green. In terror, I stumbled backwards. And the flashlight slipped out of my hands. It fell to the floor and went out. The blackness was complete.

I gave a strangled cry. I knew she was still coming toward me, but I couldn't see her. I couldn't see anything. With my hands out in front of me, I stumbled in what I hoped was the direction of the stairs. I found them. I grabbed the banister. Started up. But in the darkness, I tripped. I went down on one knee.

Cold fingers wrapped themselves around my ankle.

I cried out and yanked myself free. I charged upward blindly, tripping, stumbling, but finally plunging through the doorway into the kitchen. I slammed the basement door behind me and looked desperately this way and that, lost in the darkness. I had to get back to the stove. To the matches on the shelf. I started moving—and, as I did, I heard her again. Through the basement door. Singing softly.

"I wait for you. I wait for you."

Her voice was growing louder as she slowly climbed the stairs.

I staggered across the kitchen. Bumped into the stove. Reached up, feeling for the box of matches. There it was. I grabbed it. I fumbled for a match, concentrating so hard that I barely noticed that the singing had stopped, that the darkness had grown silent again. I brought out a match. I struck it against the side of the box.

The flame flared and she was standing right in front of me, reaching for me with those dead hands.

I screamed and dropped the matches. Hurled myself headlong away from her. By sheer good luck, I bumped into the edge of the pantry doorway. I rolled off into the pantry itself and shut the door fast. My hand still clutching the knob, I braced my shoulder against the door. The knob turned in my hand. I could feel her trying to push the door inward.

I held it shut.

5. I Wait For You

All night long, I heard her at the pantry door. Sometimes she rattled the knob, trying to get in. Sometimes she knocked softly or called my name in a laughing, teasing voice, trying to coax me out. I tried bracing my back against the door, covering my ears with my hands, but I still heard her. I hugged my knees to myself, trembling. It was enough to drive me mad.

I knew what she wanted. Revenge. She'd been waiting for it for seven years. She would never forgive me for what I'd done. Not just getting her pregnant. Refusing to marry her, refusing to sacrifice my future, my whole life, to take care of her and a child. Not just for shouting at her so that she stormed off, crying.

I think she would've forgiven me for all that if I hadn't killed her.

But what else could I do? She never would have gotten an abortion. She would've had the child and used it against me. Forced me to come up with child support. Ruined any chance I had to be free, to be a success. I mean, deep down, Amanda was a very vindictive person. Well, that was obvious, wasn't it? Look how long she'd waited to get back at me, nursing her bitterness all the while.

So anyway, I'd taken a rope—one of those stout ropes we'd used to haul the Christmas tree home from the woods. I went upstairs to her room. I pretended I wanted to make up with her so that she ran to me, put her arms around me. Then I slipped the rope around her neck and pulled it tight.

It took a long time. A long time. I don't like to think about it. Finally, she slumped, unconscious. I carried her down to the basement and strung her up on the heating pipe. That was kind of awful too because she woke up for a while and struggled, hanging up there, before it was finally over for good.

It really was a brilliant idea to hide downstairs in the basement during the game. It gave me a chance to collect myself—and to act surprised and scream in horror when they found her. And no one would believe I would just sit down there like that in the dark for so long, knowing she was with me all the while.

Amanda had never forgiven me for any of it. She'd waited for me all this time.

All night long, she knocked and called outside the pantry door, trying to draw me out. But finally, I saw the first sunlight slip in under the door. I heard her voice grow softer and softer until it vanished.

I climbed unsteadily to my feet. I opened the door. Peeked out. She was gone.

I rushed out of the house. The snow had stopped. The sun was shining. I was delighted to see that the road and the driveway had been ploughed and sanded overnight. It was easy to get back to my car, easy in the daylight to push it free from the drift where it was stuck and get it back onto the road.

As I was driving away from the Wilson house, a Volvo came past me in the other direction. It was Jonathan. I don't think he saw me. He didn't stop.

When I reached the top of the hill, I looked back. I saw the Volvo go down the driveway to the house. A moment later, two more cars reached the drive from the opposite direction and joined the first. Jonathan got out and then David and Lucy and Rosemary. They all came together, hugging and kissing and shaking hands.

I left them to their reunion. Let them live in the past, not me. I wasn't going to waste my one and only life wallowing in remorse about Amanda.

Although I must admit, as the years go on, as I move toward the end of middle age, I find myself wondering about that sometimes. Whether this is, in fact, my one and only life, I mean. Death wasn't the end for Amanda, after all. Recently, more and more often, I hear her in the night, in the dark, in the distance, singing in that wistful voice:

"I wait for you. I wait for you."

I believe she does.

Dear Emily Etiquette

by Barb Goffman

Dear Emily Etiquette,

I recently received an invitation to my cousin's wedding. It was addressed to me plus a guest, which I thought was lovely, especially since my cousin and I aren't close anymore and not everyone can afford to offer plus-ones. However, I was completely taken aback by an asterisk (!) on the invitation that said "Black tie. Dates required. Sorry, we can't accommodate singles at our wedding."

I've seen demands for black-tie attire before, but a date? Seriously?

Not that I can't get one, but on behalf of singletons everywhere, I'm so steamed about this, I'm tempted to bring a blow-up doll as my plus-one just to piss off the happy couple, which I know is not the right attitude for a wedding guest. Thoughts?

Sincerely,

Plus-One My Ass

My dear Plus-One,

While I like your style, you are quite right. Aiming to annoy the bride and groom by bringing a blow-up doll as your date would not be proper. You'd likely infuriate the bride and distress her mother, although other people might be amused.

That said, I must note that the date requirement itself is a breach of etiquette. Hosts are supposed to make their guests feel comfortable, and I can't think of anything more uncomfortable than having to find someone to drag along to a wedding just so you can share in the joyous occasion. Has the time truly come that the singles table at a wedding is no more? A place where the lovelorn and dateless can mingle amongst themselves and perhaps find true love over chicken or fish? Emily Etiquette certainly doesn't think so.

So I suggest, my dear Plus-One, that you decline this gracious invitation. I'm sure you and your inflatable friend can find something better to do that evening. Perhaps involving your back massager.

Sincerely,

Emily Etiquette

* * *

Dear Emily Etiquette,

Thanks for responding to my letter regarding the asterisked wedding invitation. I took your advice, RSVP'd no, and planned a fun evening instead with a back massager and DVD of *Fifty Shades of Grey.*

But it seems it's not to be. I got an angry call from the bride, demanding to know what I had going on in my life that could possibly be more important than her wedding. Her highness insisted I attend, calling me selfish for wanting to ruin her day. How would it look, she screeched, if her cousin didn't come?

Long story short, I felt guilty because we were good friends when we were kids—before she became incredibly selfish and materialistic—so I gave in and said I'd go. (And yes, I'll have to bring a date.) But I've found myself so aggravated that I just went online and nearly posted an embarrassing picture of my dear cousin from a sleepover when we were teenagers—can you say bed head, retainer, and a face full of zits?—with the comment, "So happy for Cuz! Who knew she'd grow up to be a beautiful bride?" Knowing that I should be better than this is all that kept me from hitting *post.*

Any suggestions for how to get through the wedding reception? How

early is too early to leave?
Sincerely,
I Need Stiches
From Biting My Tongue

My dear I Need Stitches,

Your cousin appears to be the model for an obnoxious term that is so popular these days, *bridezilla*. It's not a word I like to use, but I also believe in calling 'em like I see 'em. Weddings are supposed to be celebrations of love and commitment. But all too often these days, they are turned into productions, with the bride as the star. Emily Etiquette gives all such shows two thumbs down.

Moreover, while it's true some people might notice if a cousin of the bride doesn't attend the festivities, attendance is certainly never mandatory, and guilting anyone into attending one's wedding is far from mannerly. A wedding should be a joyous occasion, and why a bride would want anyone at her wedding who doesn't want to be there is beyond me.

I applaud you for holding your tongue on social media. I hope that since you've agreed to attend the wedding, you'll go with an open heart and mind. Make conversation with your date and tablemates and enjoy some dancing. Before you know it, the cake will be served and you and your date can bow out. I bet that DVD of yours might provide some interesting ideas to tie up the remainder of the night.

Sincerely,
Emily Etiquette

* * *

Dear Emily Etiquette,

It's me again, the cousin of the no-singles-allowed bridezilla. I'm sorry to keep imposing on your time, but I need help (etiquette and psychological). Today my aunt called, insisting I throw my cousin a bridal shower. And not just any shower: a kitchen shower, because a plain old generic shower apparently isn't good enough. Auntie claims it would look bad for Cuz if no family member threw her a shower, and since Cuz doesn't have any sisters, I *have to* do it.

I might feel more inclined if no one else was throwing her a shower, but the bride's two best friends are hosting a lingerie shower and a honeymoon shower. The groom's sister is throwing a Great Gatsby shower. (When did this become a thing? Guests wear twenties attire, and the only permitted gift is alcohol so the happy couple will have enough hooch to survive should Prohibition somehow be reinstated.) You'd think three showers would be enough, but no. One of my cousin's coworkers is throwing a shoe-themed shower in which people are "highly encouraged" to buy designer shoes that Cuz has registered for. And her college bestie is throwing a New York City getaway shower, which Cuz will evidently need in order to get away from the stress of being honored at all these other parties.

Anyway, I've been *instructed* to host the kitchen shower, not that Cuz needs it. She's been living on her own since she graduated from college three years ago, and between her and her fiancé, they already have more than enough appliances, plates, and wineglasses to fill the beautiful new house they've purchased. I understand that showers are designed to help newlyweds start their married lives on the right foot. But my cousin's feet are already walking just fine—straight from the Louboutin boutique.

I'm not good at saying no (obviously), but would it be wrong of me to scale back the madness by asking the attendees to each bring a favorite recipe that we can compile into a book for the bride and groom, instead of buying more stuff for their cabinets? And maybe each person could bring a sample of their dish for everyone to try, and we could share funny cooking stories. I have a charming one about Cuz and me back when we were kids, when we each snuck pieces of cake at Thanksgiving and ended up with icing all over our faces and hair, the result of laughing too much while watching the movie *Airplane!*. The bride was a fun and nice person back then.

Sincerely,
Nostalgic for Nicer Days

My dear Nostalgic,

I too long for nicer days, when people threw showers out of the goodness of their hearts, not to satisfy the demands of a greedy bride, or in this case, her mother. Insisting someone throw a shower is the height of impropriety. I guess there is some solace in knowing that the bride's mother isn't throwing a shower herself, keeping up the pretense that she's not using the upcoming wedding as a gift grab.

Alas, you and I know better. That is why I think your version of a kitchen shower is a wonderful idea. It centers on the spirit of a shower—giving the bride and groom things they truly need for their kitchen and lives,in this case, recipes, memories, and laughter. It also tweaks your aunt right where she lives, and if some icing were to accidentally get smeared into your aunt's hair during the shower, well, those things do happen.

Sincerely,

Emily Etiquette

* * *

Dear Emily Etiquette,

I threw the kitchen shower this afternoon for my cousin. It did not go well.

Since the bride had other showers planned, and since my rental town-house is not that large, I invited only about fifteen people: the bride, her mom and bridesmaids, my mom, the groom's sister, and several aging relatives on our side of the family—women who might not appreciate a lingerie shower but who would enjoy sharing their recipes and know-how. I expected maybe a dozen people would attend.

My aunt wasn't happy with my guest list, so without asking, she invited nearly fifty extra people. I only learned about it when women I hadn't invited started RSVPing yes! And my aunt was dissatisfied with my bring-a-meal-and-recipe plan. She told everyone their gift should include an appliance needed to make the recipe. (I understand she described my original plan to people outside the family as "quaint," yet she asked my mother if I recently had been "hit upside the head with a crowbar.")

The result: Nearly sixty women crowded into my small kitchen and living room for the shower. If the fire marshal had come, we'd all be in jail right now. People were squeezing on top of each other, setting the food they brought and the plates they filled everywhere, including on the narrow mantel above my fireplace. Yep, you know how that played out. There'll be no security deposit returned to me when I move out. New carpeting is expensive.

On top of that, there wasn't any room for people to work on the recipe book—not that they wanted to. When I began handing out paper, glue, and fun stickers, the bride stared at me like I'd grown a second head. "You're not still actually planning on doing that *craft project,* are you?" my aunt asked. "What is this? Summer camp?" And if you're wondering why my mom didn't stand up for me, she has the same problem with confrontation that I do—but worse.

Anyway, then the bride decided it was time to open the presents, telling me it was my job to keep track of who gave what. I would have been happy to do that anyway, but it's never nice to be treated like the help, especially in your own home. And you can imagine how things went from bad to worse when Cuz and Auntie realized my only gift was the uncompleted recipe book. I'm inclined to finish it now, filling it with full-fat recipes of Cuz's favorite foods. Maybe she'd gain ten pounds and be unable to fit into her wedding dress.

Sincerely,

Daring to Dream

My dear Daring to Dream,

I applaud your intent to still make the book. I even like your high-cal recipe idea. Normally I wouldn't approve of passive-aggressive tactics. It's always best to stand up for yourself directly to the source of your grief. However, in extreme circumstances like this, all bets are off.

Accordingly, since the recipe book is, as your aunt so nicely put it, a *craft project,* I suggest you go all out and add some glitter to it—multicolored glitter on every page. Lots and lots of glitter that will land on your cousin's clothes, face, and hair. Glitter that will float throughout her kitchen, settling onto every surface and into cracks and crevices, making the room sparkle for years to come. And every time she notices the glitter, your dear cousin will remember how joyous you made this special time in her life. Really, what more could you want than that?

Sincerely,

Emily Etiquette

* * *

Dear Emily Etiquette,

What more could I want? Sanity. A little sanity would be nice.

I had to buy Cuz a wedding gift. I figured between the six showers and the two hundred plus wedding guests who RSVP'd yes, she'd be overwhelmed with stuff. So I decided to do something different. Cuz met her fiancé at a sports bar they both frequent, so I splurged and bought them a bunch of tickets to see their favorite team.

You'd think she'd have been delighted when the tickets were delivered in the mail. Alas not. If I understand correctly, my cousin complained to my aunt who complained to my mother who complained to me that dear Cuz only went to that "dumpy bar" to land a man, and now that she had one, she had no intention of wasting any more of her time watching *sports*. And since Cuz hated my gift, it was "only right" that I get her something else. "Please don't make trouble," my mom told me. "Just buy her something off the registry."

As if that's not bad enough, the happy couple still intends to keep the tickets! The groom and his best friend will use them, allowing the bride to have "me time" while they're at the games—as if she didn't fill every day with me time. Can you believe it?

Sincerely,

No Good Deed Goes Unpunished

P.S. For my mom's sake, I bought some china off Cuz's registry. I may have accidentally dropped the box onto the cement parking lot on the way back to the car. A few times. But don't worry. I'm going to make up for it by covering the box with glitter before I wrap it, so there will be much joy when Cuz opens it.

My dear No Good Deed,

Unfortunately, after all these years in this business, I can believe your story. I thought your tickets gift was extremely thoughtful, and it's a shame this bride can't appreciate it. I don't know where people ever got the idea that they have a right to dictate what presents they receive, nor that any response other than "thank you" is appropriate. (I'm assuming you haven't received a thank-you note. If one actually comes, please don't let me know; I don't want to drop dead from shock.)

As to the china you purchased, I would not worry even if the plates have chipped. This insufferable bride will surely insist that the store exchange them for her, and I expect they will oblige, if only to make her leave as quickly as possible.

Sincerely,

Emily Etiquette

P.S. The glitter was a nice touch indeed!

* * *

Dear Emily Etiquette,

My bridezilla cousin had her bachelorette party last night. I was thrilled to not be invited. I was less thrilled to get a call this morning from a friend who was at one of the clubs the ladies went to and heard the bride talking sh—sorry, saying rude things about me, including my "small, tacky house," the "lame" shower I threw for her, and the "mannish" (mannish?) wedding gift I sent. She's apparently embarrassed to be related to me because I'm a "sad, old-maid cow." In case I haven't mentioned it, I'm only twenty-six (a year older than dear sweet Cuz) and in no rush to find Mister Right.

I get that my cousin was plastered when she said these things, but that doesn't make it right, especially since I'm sure these are her true feelings. What happened to the cousin I played with as a child, the one who giggled with me during sleepovers, long after we were supposed to be dreaming? The one who schemed with me to distract our parents so we could steal extra desserts? She seems to be long gone now, so I'm done being nice to the woman she's become. I'm done with decorum. I'm done with holding my tongue. And I'm done with being afraid of confrontation. Cuz's wedding is next weekend, and it's going to be a night that won't be forgotten in these parts for a long, long time.

Thank you, Emily Etiquette, for all your support these past few months. I'll let you know how it goes.

Sincerely,

Finally Looking Forward

To This Wedding

My dear Finally Looking Forward,

I'm not sure what you have planned for the festivities, but I urge you to reconsider. However horrible your cousin has been, it's in your best interest to hold your head high. The wedding will be over soon. The memory of your cousin's rude behavior will fade in time, but the loss of your dignity could last forever.

That said, if my words don't persuade you, I do hope the videographer will record whatever you have planned. I'm not that adept with technology, but I understand tapes can get released publicly—by accident, of course. And these instances can be for the best. Sometimes drastic measures are necessary to make a dramatic bride understand the lines she's crossed. And, after all our correspondence, I would like a front-row seat when that happens.

I'm waiting eagerly for your next letter.

Sincerely,

Emily Etiquette

* * *

Dear Emily Etiquette,

I'm sorry this letter hasn't arrived quickly. Sending out mail from here isn't that easy.

You're eager to hear about the wedding, I know, so here goes. The ceremony was lovely. The groom stood at the front, smiling and dapper. The bridesmaids seemed cheery despite wearing lime-green dresses with puffy sleeves and bows that made them resemble Little Bo Peep. (Shocking that the bride made them look bad, right?) I myself looked pretty good in a long dress covered by a large pale-pink wrap. Then the music swelled, the guests stood, and my cousin, with a smug smile, began walking down the aisle, her beautiful bouquet of flowers held up proudly.

I think God was sending a message of approval, because the sneezing started right as Cuz was passing me. One sneeze, then another and another. She must not have wanted this problem to impede her procession down the aisle, because Cuz kept walking even as she sneezed. Her head bopped up and down with each step, like a dime-store hooker going down on a john. Sorry for the language, but I know you wanted video, and since I don't have access to that, I figured I should paint the picture for you.

It was handy that I know Cuz is allergic to certain perfumes. Being the bigger person, I stopped into the bridal suite shortly before the ceremony to wish my cousin well. While there, I picked up her bouquet from the counter to breathe in its beautiful fragrance—and spritzed perfume on the flowers from a tiny bottle I'd clutched in my palm. By the time Cuz began her vows, her nose was red and runny and she sounded totally congested. When the pastor pronounced them married, Cuz's new husband looked like he wished he'd said "I don't." Talk about for better or worse.

Then it was off to the country club for the reception. I'd asked my date to meet me there after the party started—I'd text him when I was ready for him—because I wanted to save his grand entrance for when it would have the most impact.

In the meanwhile, I headed inside with my other date: a four-foot-tall blow-up doll that resembled Otto the automatic pilot in that old *Airplane!* movie that Cuz and I had loved as kids. I'd considered bringing an X-rated doll, but my plan required I annoy the bride without going so far out of bounds that she'd ask me to leave, so Otto had to do. He and I hustled inside. People stared, as anticipated.

We made our way to our table—near the kitchen, natch—but at least the room's setup was picturesque. Each table sported a white linen tablecloth with lime-green linen napkins and a lit candle in the center. I plopped Otto on his seat just as the newlyweds entered the room to applause. When that died down, the salad course was served, and I introduced Otto to everyone at our table. Reactions ranged from confusion to horror to big smiles from a couple who recognized him. I knew I'd chosen the perfect date, because the party hadn't been going on more than ten minutes before the bride and her mother—a twofer!—stormed over, apparently having spotted my guy from across the room.

"What do you think you're doing with…that thing?" my aunt demanded as she and Bridezilla stood over me.

I smiled demurely. "Is there a problem, Auntie? The invitation said I needed a date. It didn't say he couldn't be plastic."

"She's ruining my wedding, Mother," Cuz shrieked.

"Don't make a scene," Auntie told her.

"But she's ruining my wedding," Cuz pouted in a lower voice.

Lord, she hadn't seen anything yet. I had quite the show planned. Pushing back my chair, I stood and grinned as I flipped my pink wrap off my shoulders, revealing my snug, low-cut satin sheath dress. The bride wasn't the only one wearing white, and I wore it better.

"I don't understand the problem," I said. "You said you couldn't accommodate singles. So I brought a date to fill the chair. He's even wearing a suit. You remember Otto, don't you, Cuz?"

A tiny part of me hoped Cuz's eyes would twinkle even for a moment, that she'd recognize Otto and remember how much fun we had as kids when she wasn't so uptight. I hoped my old friend was still in there somewhere. If she were, I might have called off the rest of my plans. But her eyes were an icy blue, as cold as her heart had become.

She pointed, first at me, then the doll, then back at me. Then she stamped her foot. "You can't wear that white dress here. I'm the only one who gets to wear white. And you can't have that"—she pointed at Otto—"here. You just can't."

Talk about discrimination. Just because Otto was plastic. Tsk tsk. As Auntie gave me a dirty look, I sighed loudly. "Well, all right. If you want me to get a real-life date, I guess I can do that. Let me make a call." I turned to my tablemates, picked up the doll, and waved his hand. "Say bye to my date, everybody. I'll be back soon with another one."

"Make sure this one's breathing," Cuz hissed as I walked away.

Okay, Cuz. You asked for it. I texted Johnny, my alternate date. He met me by my car as I stuffed Otto back in the trunk.

"Va va va voom!" Johnny whistled. "Let me get a look at you." I twirled for him. I don't usually wear such tight outfits, but when circumstances require…And I must say, Johnny cleaned up well. With his brown hair and goatee both trimmed, he reminded me of a young Matt Dillon. He even wore a tux. I think the chance to annoy my cousin was all he'd needed to agree to accompany me—that and the promise of an open bar. You see, Cuz and Johnny dated right after college, and Cuz told everyone who'd listen that Johnny was "the one" until he dumped her in a spectacularly public fashion because she was "a bossy bitch." I'd felt sorry for her then. But not now.

To my disappointment, nobody noticed us as we walked inside. We ate our dinner peacefully. (I had the chicken; he had the fish.) Meanwhile Cuz and her hubby started going around to every table with their money bag, putting people on the spot for cash gifts on top of whatever other gift they'd already brought or sent. I know. You're dying. But not me. This was something I'd anticipated. I'd seen this tackiness at another wedding maybe a decade ago and recalled Cuz calling it "genius." I pulled Johnny away to the bar and encouraged him to partake—all part of my little plan—and I waited, at one point actually rubbing my hands together in anticipation.

Johnny was all liquored up when the first dance began. Would you believe the song Cuz chose was…wait for it…"Linger" by the Cranberries. Apparently after all these years, Cuz still doesn't pay attention to the lyrics of a song. So here she was, dancing with her brand-new husband to a song about being unable to get over an old love, and here I was leaning against the bar, right next to Johnny.

That's when I sent out a tweet letting folks know how delighted I was to be at Cuz's wedding. It ended with, "Who would've imagined she'd grow up to be such a beautiful bride?" But instead of attaching a picture of Cuz in her wedding dress, I accidentally—I assure you—attached that old photo I previously mentioned. You remember? Bed head. Retainer. Zits. Even before "Linger" ended, the retweets began.

As soon as we could, Johnny and I took to the dance floor, and I made sure he twirled me past the happy couple a few times. I feared Cuz hadn't spotted him, though, because I hadn't heard any screaming. So when the next song came on, Johnny and I cut in on them. Cuz looked apoplectic as Johnny grabbed her waist, and I decided to kick things up a notch more by planting a big wet kiss on my new cousin-in-law to welcome him to the family. I might have welcomed him with a little tongue.

That's when the screaming started. Cuz wrenched me away from her hubby, and just when it seemed like we were about to rumble, the groom jumped in between us and danced my cousin away—but not before winking at me first.

There was a little more dancing. Then came the toasts. Cuz probably didn't want me to make one, but when the opportunity presented itself, I zoomed to the microphone.

"Hi," I said. "For those of you who don't know me, I'm the bride's cousin. I'm thrilled to be here today to share in the happiness of the loving couple. And that wedding gown? So lovely. I mean, not everyone can rock a white dress like I can"—some people laughed—"but my cousin looks pretty good in hers, especially considering the happy news that…well, I'm sure you all can see that the seams are straining and she's become a little puffy around the middle. And in her face. But—"

"Shut up, you stupid cow!" Cuz stormed toward me. "I am not pregnant."

Please note that she's the one who started name-calling. Not me.

"Are you sure?" I said into the mic, tilting my head, looking questioningly at her stomach. "Because *I'm* sure your mom must be thrilled. I mean, after you tried lesbianism in college, we all wondered if there'd ever be any children." Not that Cuz had actually done that. And I wouldn't have cared if she had—actually, I'd have been impressed—but I knew my saying so would mortify her.

"What?" she screamed. And as mouths dropped open around the room, Cuz tried to yank the mike from me. The champagne in my glass flew through the air, drenching her face. I know I shouldn't have laughed. But I did. I roared.

That's when she came after me. Her hands were around my throat when her hubby and Johnny both tried to pull her off, grabbing her by the torso and lifting her horizontally. Then somehow they each had one leg, like a wishbone, and Cuz's dress swung up high enough to show off the garter (and way too much else).

"Let go of me," Cuz screamed, kicking backward with both of her legs, and hitting each of them in the nuts. She always was pretty dexterous. They both dropped her at the same time, and Cuz hit the floor like the worst mike drop ever. Meanwhile Johnny moaned, stumbling backward into a table, knocking over some glasses, and causing folks to jump from their chairs.

"Johnny," Cuz cried and ran to him. Yep, she didn't check on her brand-new husband. She went to care for my date. Maybe Cuz had listened to those "Linger" lyrics after all.

Anyway, that didn't sit well with Hubby, who ran at Johnny and took a swing. Johnny was drunk by this point, but he still had some fight in him. Good thing, because before you knew it, the groomsmen and bridesmaids had joined the melee. Folks were shrieking. Tables were being overturned. Plates and glasses shattered. Someone slammed into the cart that the wedding cake sat on, and its top tier flew, landing in dear Auntie's hair. Prayer works! People were brawling, others were screaming, and the elderly relatives were inching away for their lives.

Meanwhile, with all eyes off me, I hurried over to the bridal table and snatched the money bag. Last I saw as I made my way to the exit, candles on several of the tables had toppled over, the linen tablecloths had caught fire, and Cuz, Johnny, and her brand-new hubby were in a three-way slap fight.

The end result: Everyone made it out alive, but the country club sustained major damage. I'm sorry I didn't get video for you, but I understand the riot—that's what they're calling it, the Bo Peep Wedding Riot—made all the papers and went viral on every social-media platform, so hopefully you've already seen the pictures of Cuz, Auntie, and a few others sopping wet and covered in fire-extinguisher foam. The whole wedding party was arrested, and they're all now awaiting trial on charges ranging from assault to destruction of property to rioting. (Johnny too. I'll have to make it up to him.) And I'm sitting on a beach in a foreign country, sipping a mai tai. Overall, I think things worked out pretty well. Sure, no one in my family's going to talk to me anymore, but I don't think that's a big loss.

Thanks for all the good advice, Emily Etiquette. I owe you one. And if you're ever in my new neck of the woods, please call on me. You have an open invitation to dinner at my house. No date required.

Sincerely,

Single and Loving It

A Complicated History

by Daniel C. Bartlett

I had no idea people like Domingo existed until he showed up at my apartment and invited himself in to stay. Domingo wasn't someone you refused. And back then, as an eighteen-year-old kid who'd been kicked out of college and then my parents' house, I wasn't good at telling anyone no. We both worked at Sal's Grocery, a meat market where he trained me to grind, mix, and stuff sausage into tubes. That's where we met and how he knew where I lived. After we'd worked together three days that's when he knocked on my door knowing full well I'd let him stay. I was an easy target, and he was good at getting his way.

He had a gorgeous girlfriend, Melanie. She was the kind of gorgeous that made my insides ache just to look at her. He was in love with her. He didn't trust other guys around her, and he moved in and took over my life trying to hide away with her, to keep her to himself.

Two cops were waiting in the parking lot after my second day's shift with Domingo. This was before he moved himself in with me. We were walking out together and one of the cops called Domingo's name. "Later, man," Domingo said to me. He walked past the cops like they weren't there. The cops exchanged smiles with one another and turned to me.

"Michael Larue?" one of them said.

"Yeah," I said.

"New on the job, huh?" The other cop leaned against their car, silent but watching me over the top of his sunglasses. "Just wanted to have a little chat with you."

"Okay," I said. I felt myself shiver even in the warm afternoon sun.

"You know him?" A nod over his shoulder, in Domingo's direction.

I shrugged. "He's training me."

The cop nodded. He folded his arms over his chest. "What can you tell me about him?"

"I don't know anything about him." The cop waited, so I added, "His name's Domingo. He's pretty good at stuffing sausage." Across the parking lot, Domingo got in his car and drove away, keeping a steady gaze over half-open black-tinted windows. A gaze not on the cops but on me. So far all I knew was that Domingo was fast at stuffing sausage and that he didn't waste time talking. He got several calls or texts on his cell, answered with quick responses, then got back to work. I didn't say that to the cops. From my experience, the best strategy for dealing with anyone—cops, parents, university officials, any authority, really—was to answer questions without committing to anything specific.

"That all you know?"

I shrugged, meaning *I guess so*.

"Keep it that way. We'll be talking with you."

The first time I was confronted by cops was when I shot and killed my brother. I was fourteen. Derek was sixteen. We were hunting squirrels in the woods not far from home.

"What happened here?" I remember the sheriff asking.

I couldn't seem to recall where I was. I blinked at the .22 rifle the cops had tagged and placed in a plastic bag. I thought it was my rifle, but I didn't remember ever touching the trigger.

"Michael."

Then I remembered a clap. The gun had been lying across my lap. I was sitting on a fallen tree. Did I lose my balance? Yes. I started to fall off and jerked to catch myself. The rifle was on safety. I never even touched the trigger. I remembered the clap and thinking, *Now someone's really stupid firing a gun with us out here.* My brother slumped over as though leaning to tie his shoe. The most ordinary gesture in the world. If death was that easy, it didn't bode well for life.

It was ruled accidental. The cops absolved me legally, which meant nothing in any way that matters.

Back then I thought I was in love with Charla. She'd tried and failed to move on from me so many times it was ridiculous. How many times in high school did I stand by while she made plans with another guy? It was okay with me if I was just her fallback plan—at least I was in the picture.

When I came home after being expelled from the university, the first thing I did was call Charla. She agreed to let me come pick her up at her parents' house, where she still lived. It was right around the corner from my parents' house. My new apartment, which my parents had found for me while I was on my way back from college, was only a few blocks the other direction. My parents had also gotten me the job at Sal's, because they knew the manager there. That's the way it was. They managed my life but kept their distance.

When I pulled up at Charla's house, she got in the passenger seat of my car and pulled down the sun visor. She looked in the mirror to touch up her makeup. "I don't know why the hell you came back here," she said. "Give me a ride to Sherry's house."

"I thought we'd have dinner," I said. "That's why I called."

"That's not why you called. You always call. You can't *not* call."

This was true. For the two months I was away at college, I called her every night. More often than not, she didn't answer and I left a message saying that I loved her and that I was sorry.

"I don't know if you're punishing yourself or punishing me," she said.

"I don't know either," I said. "I think we're punishing each other."

I drove her to her friend Sherry's house, where a party was raging across the front porch and the lawn. I stopped the car in the street and Charla got out. A guy with a beer in each hand swaggered over, gave Charla one of the beers, and wrapped his arm around her waist. They did a dance step to the booming music and stumbled off together. Charla had left the passenger door wide open when she got out. I leaned across the seats but couldn't reach it, so I had to get out and walk around the car to close the door. My heart was thumping. I didn't know if it was the music or the realization that I was pathetic and didn't have it in me to do a thing about it.

Driving away, I ruled out the music.

When there was a knock on my apartment door on the evening of the third day I'd worked at Sal's, I hoped it might be Charla. I knew it wouldn't be, but there's a fine line between optimism and stupidity. I opened the door half expecting to find my mom standing there with a plate of cold leftovers, my dad assuring me in his resigned way that we'd survive this too. Although my parents never verbally blamed me for my brother's death, how could they not harbor some resentment? Their stopping by was as much a long shot as it would be to find Charla at my door, but there wasn't anyone else who'd know where to find me. Or who'd want to.

"Hey, man," Domingo said. "This your place, huh?" He walked past me and looked around. He picked up a framed picture of Charla and me, studied it, put it down. It was a prom picture from our junior year in high school. Our senior year she'd gone with another guy.

"My mom threw me out," Domingo said. He was nineteen, maybe twenty. He seemed much older.

"Oh," I said. Domingo sat on the futon. I felt the need to add something. "I been there, thrown out."

Domingo nodded. He looked at me over the rims of his glasses. "Sit down, man. Make me nervous standing over me like that. I need a place to stay awhile." It was as easy as that. He took over.

My place was a one-bedroom apartment with cheap wood-panel walls and thin carpet as hard as concrete. The futon in the living room was held together with duct tape. In the bedroom I had a single mattress lying on the floor. In the kitchen refrigerator I had a bottle of mustard, a half loaf of bread, and a partial package of oily lunchmeat. My clothes and what few personal things I had were piled in three cardboard boxes along the bedroom wall. It looked like I barely existed.

"What you got to drink?" Domingo asked.

Nothing was what I had, so within a couple minutes we were headed to the car to get some beer at the store.

"We'll take yours. Hand me your keys," he said. I gave him the keys and we got in. "What's your story, man?" Domingo asked once we were moving. "Why you by yourself in that shit-hole apartment?"

I hardly knew Domingo, but I couldn't help telling him the truth. I told him I was there because I'd been expelled from college for a stupid prank I'd let myself get talked into by some frat guys who figured out I'd do anything for acceptance. I'd wanted to impress them. College was a new start away from the ghosts of home. In the end, the frat guys got away clean, and I got sent home, where my parents pointed me toward a job and a place of my own so I'd work on understanding what I'd done to myself. Domingo took in everything with a slow nod, occasionally said, "Yeah, man, I hear you," and he didn't seem to care that I was a loser.

There was also a dangerous ferocity that emanated from him.

"Who's that chick in the picture?" He meant Charla in the prom picture. I told him that she and I had a complicated history and that she wasn't all that into me but didn't mind calling when she wanted something.

"You let her run all over you. You let those guys at college screw you over. Your parents throw you out. Why you let people push you around?"

I didn't mention that he'd just told me his mother kicked him out. Or that he'd just pushed his way into my apartment and my car. "I don't know," I said. "That's just how it is. Life pushes you around."

Domingo gave me a look that suggested I was full of it.

"You can't control everything, is all I'm saying. Even when you think you're in control, you're not," I said.

"Don't think so?"

"No. See...you can't control that jerk behind us."

Some guy in a jacked-up pickup truck had pulled up right on our rear bumper. Any closer and he'd be riding in my backseat. "That pisses me off, man," Domingo said. He slammed on the brakes and cut the wheel so the car skidded to a stop at an angle across both lanes of the street. The pickup behind us screeched to a stop.

Domingo was out of the car and at the other driver's window before either car completely stopped. He pulled at the door handle but it was locked, so he slammed his elbow into the window. It shattered as he jumped up and followed with a kick. The driver sprawled across his seat, trying to get away but fighting his seatbelt to do so. Domingo reached in through jagged glass and hit the man with a solid punch to the head.

"Stay off my ass," Domingo said. Then he strolled over and got back in my car. "I'd say I took control of that situation, wouldn't you?"

He looked at me until I nodded in agreement.

Domingo assigned the bedroom to me, and he spread out in the living area. This was now his apartment. I was simply an occupant who paid the rent. I wasn't his friend, exactly. I wasn't his partner in anything. And I wasn't part of any gang. But I knew enough to follow his lead or stay out of his way.

Dangerous-looking guys in baggy jeans and sleeveless shirts started coming and going from the apartment to see Domingo. Usually he'd step outside with them. I caught on pretty quickly that Domingo was dealing. I just didn't know what he was dealing. I didn't want to know. The first time I walked out of my bedroom to find Domingo peeling bills off a huge roll of cash and returning the roll to his pocket, I did an about-face and went back into the bedroom without comment. From then on, I was more careful about walking in on Domingo when he had visitors.

Unless the visitor was Melanie. It terrified and thrilled me when she came over, which got to be about every night. She'd bring homework from her classes at the community college. She wanted to be a nurse. I wanted to absorb her presence. Domingo, Melanie, and I would hang around watching TV. He always seemed to find a slow, seemingly endless game of baseball. With baseball, he could come and go to make deals and not really miss much. My dad loved the game. Derek had been an All-Star in high school. All my life I'd watched Dad and Derek throwing the ball back and forth in the yard, talking stats and technique. I hated baseball. Domingo usually bet on the games, though, so we watched, and he cussed the players, and he made phone calls to bookies, and he stepped outside to make drug deals with guys who knocked at the door. All the while, Melanie studied, keeping one hand free to caress and reassure Domingo of her devotion to him.

I felt my stomach in my throat when a knock would come at the door and some guy would slouch in, give Domingo a nod, and the two of them would go out to Domingo's car. That left Melanie and me alone. She seemed to wait for those moments too. As soon as the door closed, she'd turn and ask me to help her study. She always waited for Domingo to leave before talking to me. When all of us were together, she directed her attention on him even if she was saying something to all of us. But when he left, she'd hand over her books and have me quiz her. Usually we sat on the floor, leaning against the futon. She'd stretch out her legs, and I'd go fuzzy in the head trying to contain myself.

"You're sweet," she said each time she handed me her books.

I nodded. Sweet was not what you wanted to be with women like Melanie who went for guys like Domingo. We'd study for a few minutes until Domingo came back in. Then she'd close the books and turn all her attention to him again. She never said anything about him forcing himself on me, but I sensed an apology in the sympathetic smiles she shot me every so often. Or maybe she just felt sorry for me in general.

One night after Domingo stepped outside, Melanie handed me a book filled with pictures of tattoos. "I'm trying to pick one. Which do you like?"

I flipped through, elated because she'd deemed me fit to ask for an opinion. I pointed at an image of a green tree frog, the kind I thought most women would find cute.

When the door opened and Domingo came back in, Melanie beamed a smile at him. "Hey, babe. Which one you like?" And she was up taking the book from me and handing it to him and directing him to sit and nestling herself against him. He held her close to him, stroked his hand along her head. He watched her like he couldn't stop taking her in.

I slipped away to my bedroom.

My phone buzzed in the middle of the night maybe two weeks after Domingo had moved in. It was Charla. "Can you come get me?" This was the first I'd heard from Charla in that time. She'd been ignoring my daily calls and messages. I crept out of my own room, past Domingo and Melanie murmuring to each other under the covers on the futon in my living area.

Charla was waiting for me in front of her parents' house. She got in the car and gestured for me to drive. "Craig got a job in Houston," she said as we pulled away. "He leaves next week. He wants me to go with him."

"Craig's the guy from the party?" I said.

She nodded yes and wiped at tears budding in her eyes. "I don't think my parents will let me go."

"Okay," I said. We both understood that what I meant was, *Why are you calling me about this?* And we both understood that she called me for the same reason I kept calling her. Neither of us could *not* call.

I drove slowly to the end of the street. We sat at the stop sign. I didn't have a clue where to go. I didn't know what to tell her about Craig or her parents. There wasn't much left for us to say to each other.

"We were fighting over you that day," I said. She knew what I meant. The day I shot Derek.

Charla, Derek, and I had grown up together. Derek and I developed teenage infatuations with Charla, who started to return his feelings. Probably because he was older and athletic. After his death, she and I developed a mutual dependency. Over time, I needed her more, and as much as she wanted to pull away and go on with her own life, she couldn't manage to do it. Our codependency made her vacillate between resentment and guilt while it simply made me more dysfunctional.

"Jesus, Mike," she said. "Do we have to go through this again? You didn't do it on purpose."

"That doesn't change anything," I said.

"Just take me home."

I put the car in reverse and backed down the street until I stopped in front of her parents' house. "It's kind of funny. We go up the street and back down the street. Back and forth. That's us. In all these years we haven't gotten anywhere."

"I don't think it's funny at all," Charla said. "We might as well not have even done it." She turned away and started getting out of the car.

"Charla," I said.

She paused, listening without turning toward me.

"If you really want to go with him," I said, "you're old enough to do what you want."

She got out and shut the door. We both knew it wasn't that easy, if it was possible at all, to do what you wanted.

Domingo and I were stuffing sausage one afternoon when one of the stockers, Chad, came into the back room with a bottle of window cleaner. He'd been wiping down the store's front windows when he was called to carry out an old woman's groceries.

"Some old lady just tipped me a quarter," Chad said. He flipped the quarter into the air and caught it. Chad was usually trying to impress Domingo. "You believe that? A quarter."

Domingo tied off the end of a roll of sausage. He glanced at Chad and back down. "People are crazy, man."

"Yeah." Chad was encouraged by Domingo's more or less agreement. He stood there wide-eyed, obviously hoping to spur more praise. Then he smirked and sprayed a couple squirts of the glass cleaner into the sausage I was mixing. "Hope they enjoy our new secret ingredient." He danced about, pleased with himself and expecting Domingo to be pleased too.

Domingo looked at the sausage where Chad had sprayed it. He looked at Chad. Then he looked down at the tube of sausage he'd just stuffed. He coiled it and stacked it on the tray with the other coils. When he was satisfied that it was right, he walked around the stuffing table toward Chad, who had stopped dancing. "That's not cool, man," Domingo said.

Chad withered.

Domingo went on. "Ain't no reason to do that. You expect people to eat this?" He picked up a clump of the ground meat in his fingertips. "How about you eat it."

Chad glanced at me. I didn't want any part of this, but I couldn't look away or move.

"I'm waiting," Domingo said.

Chad tested a laugh but Domingo was dead serious. Chad took the red shreds of raw meat from Domingo's fingers and put them in his mouth.

"Chew it up good. Don't just swallow it whole."

Tears brimmed in Chad's eyes. He chewed until Domingo nodded.

"Got anything to say now?" Domingo asked.

Chad swallowed. "Sorry," he said.

So Domingo not only made Chad eat raw sausage with window cleaner in it, but he made him eat it and apologize for it.

Of course I was terrified of Domingo, but I was also mystified by him. His self-certainty. His strange code. It wouldn't be right to call it a code of honor. A code of expectation, maybe. He expected certain things from people, and he generally got what he expected.

Domingo woke me up early on a Sunday morning by tugging lightly at my covers. "I'm heavy, man. I got to go to church. Come on. Go with me."

The words didn't make sense. I pulled the sheets across my shoulder and rolled over.

"Hey," Domingo said. "Get up. Come on."

"I don't want to." I carefully slurred my voice with grogginess, although by then I was wide awake and felt my blood rushing. I lay still, my back to Domingo.

The last time I'd been in a church was my brother's funeral. I didn't need to go to church to have it shoved down my throat that my own life wasn't in my hands. This was the first time I'd challenged Domingo's demands, though. I could sense him deliberating.

"I'm not going to say it again," he said.

"Come on," I said. "Please. You don't underst—"

I was yanked by my ankles out of the bed. I slammed flat on the floor, my breath knocked loose. The sheets fluttered and drifted down on top of me.

"Don't ever tell me I don't understand," Domingo said. "You're coming. I ain't asking."

I cleaned up a bloody nose and tenderly got dressed with a sore, possibly cracked, rib. Then I went with him to church, where we knelt, crossed ourselves, took Communion, and sought forgiveness. Afterwards, I felt no better, though Domingo swaggered out light and unburdened.

I knew I had to get free of him. Things would only get uglier. But there was no way I could kindly ask him to leave. It had also gotten to where I depended on Domingo. I was afraid to go to my apartment unless he was there. The thugs who came looking for him were suspicious of me but were too afraid of crossing Domingo to bother with me. When I was there alone one afternoon some guy had pushed his way inside the apartment, asking me where his shit was. He paced the living area, his eyes darting around. After a minute, he came to his senses and got nervous. "Forget it, huh? Forget it, okay?" he pleaded with me. "Don't tell him about this, okay?" The guy hugged me as he left, and I felt the hard bulge of a handgun in his waistband.

Since that episode, when we left work and Domingo went to "make my rounds," as he put it, I'd piddle around a while before going to the apartment. I'd drive out by the college, maybe hoping to see Melanie walking between classes. I didn't know if she'd talk to me in public, or what Domingo might think of us meeting without him there. I knew it was best not to find out. I drove by there anyway, almost every day after work.

Some days I drove past my parents' house, slowing to a near stop until my nerves got the best of me and I hit the gas. As much as I wanted to stop and go inside, I couldn't make myself do it. Most days I drove past Charla's house too, both hopeful and afraid she'd be there and see me. The best thing that could happen would be for us to never see each other again, never speak again, never even think of one another. But shared misery is a strong bond.

Obviously someone did see me driving by Charla's one of those afternoons. My phone rang just moments after I passed by her house.

"What's your problem?" a guy's voice said when I answered.

"Who is this?" I asked, although I knew right off that it was Charla's boyfriend.

"You know she cries every time you call," he said. "She stares at the phone and sobs."

I kept driving toward my apartment, held the phone to my ear, and said nothing.

"Here's what's going to happen," he went on. He was menacing, but deeper down I heard something else. He was menacing not because he was a jerk but because he cared about Charla. To him, I was the bad guy. We're all someone else's bad guy. "You'll leave her alone."

I couldn't agree more, I thought. I said nothing. I hung up as I pulled into the parking lot of my apartment, where the two cops were waiting for me. They watched me drive up and met me as I got out of my car.

"You don't listen so well, do you?" said the one who'd done all the talking before. They got right up on me. One, the *good cop*, leaned casually against my car with his arms crossed over his chest. The other one, the guy playing *bad cop,* I guess, stood back, poised and ready for something to go down. "We know he's been staying here, son."

I looked past them to see if Domingo was here yet.

"Thing is, Mike, you don't know what you're dealing with." This came from the bad cop. "You think it's cool playing want-to-be gangster? I got news. This guy's no want-to-be."

"See, we don't think you want to be involved in any of this," said the first one.

They were right. I didn't want to be involved. In anything at all.

"You keep up like this and one thing's for sure. Things won't end well."

"What do you expect me to do?" I asked. "I don't understand what's expected of me."

The truth was, they probably didn't know what they expected of me either. They were fishing for answers too, and, like Domingo, they were willing to use me to get what they wanted.

"Just watch yourself," the one cop said. "And be ready to answer questions when we ask them."

They fixed hard stares on me, then got back in their car and left. Domingo pulled into the lot as the cops pulled out. They followed him with their stares. He followed them with his. Then both cops and Domingo looked to me. As they turned away he pulled up but didn't get out of his car. He eyed me over his partially open dark window.

"Come on. I want you to go somewhere with me," he said.

"Isn't Melanie coming over?" I asked.

"Naw, man. Let's go."

He'd never invited me into his car. This wasn't an invitation, though. I got in. The car was immaculate. A little green tree air freshener hung from the mirror. We drove awhile in silence, deeper into the part of town where most of the buildings were boarded up, broken up, and coated in graffiti.

"What'd they want this time?" Domingo asked.

"They asked if I wanted to go down with you."

"What did you say?"

"Nothing."

After a moment, he nodded. "That was the right answer."

We drove past an old school, closed and left to rot years ago, surrounded by rusted metal fences with barbed wire coiled at the top. Across from the school were little houses with peeling paint, chipped asbestos siding, sagging roofs. It was dusk and just starting to get dark. Domingo slowed to a crawl as we passed one house. The doors and windows were open to let in air. Light from inside fell in distorted patches onto the dirt yard and broken sidewalk. Someone was moving around inside.

"That's my mom's place," Domingo said. "You'll come Friday night for Melanie's birthday party. My mom loves Melanie. It's me she's got problems with."

This was the first I'd heard of a birthday party. It was the first he'd revealed of his family too, except when he initially moved in and told me his mom had kicked him out. Apparently it was a ridiculous ritual we shared, creeping by the homes of loved ones.

"Show you something," Domingo said. He dug into his pocket and pulled out a ring with a diamond so brilliant it gave off its own light in the dark car. "What you think?"

"Are you…is that an engagement ring? You're going to ask her to marry you?"

"I want her to know we're serious. That we got a commitment to each other," he said.

I understood that it wasn't so much a commitment to each other he wanted to nail down. He needed to confirm Melanie's commitment to him.

"Think she'll say yes?" he asked.

Normally, any guy in this situation would be obligated to needle his friend and express doubt about the woman's willingness or sanity. With Domingo, I wouldn't dare express even the slightest doubt about Melanie's commitment. Before I could say anything, though, headlights swept up behind us. Domingo cussed, slipped the ring into his pocket, and drove on around a corner.

The car behind us turned the corner. Domingo slowed down and the other car did too. When Domingo turned another corner, the car followed. Finally, Domingo stopped in the middle of the street and watched in the mirror. The other car idled back there. "I'm getting tired of this, man. They always testing me." Domingo got out and walked toward the other car. He held his arms out wide in a show of open challenge. When he got halfway there, the car reversed, turned around, and cruised off the other way. Domingo yelled, "I know you. I know where to find you."

He got back in the car, slammed his door, and floored the gas pedal in one fluid motion. After we cleared the screech and smoke of burning rubber, he said, "It's always something I got to deal with. If it ain't this, it's college dudes hitting on Melanie. If it ain't that, it's my mom bitching at me. The cops coming around."

By the time we'd stopped careening around corners in the dark streets where the city didn't bother replacing burned-out lights, Domingo had driven us to a place that didn't have a name, just a neon sign in the shape of a naked woman. "Let's go in here a minute. Take a load off."

Before I could catch myself, I said, "What about Melanie?"

"What about her?"

I shrugged, not wanting to challenge him.

"Look, man. I don't want to take out my frustrations on Melanie. You telling me you ain't got urges?"

"No, I mean, yeah. I have urges."

"Damn right you do. We all do. We got bad shit inside us, man. You don't let it out somehow…" He shook his head. "I don't want to always look at Melanie as a piece of ass. I just showed you I want to have something more with her. So I got to get this need out of my system. You know what I'm saying?"

"Yeah," I said. I wasn't sure I liked it or agreed with it, although I wouldn't say so to him.

He saw it on me, though. "You're a smart guy," Domingo said. "But you're naive. You been sheltered."

"No," I said. Anger flashed across his face. I went on quickly. "Not sheltered. Stunted. Emotionally stunted."

Domingo said nothing. Then he grinned. He clapped his hand down on my shoulder, squeezed like we were the closest of friends. "I like that. Yeah. Emotionally stunted."

But who isn't? We're all stunted, at the mercy of much greater forces. Domingo's trick was manipulating those forces to his advantage. For a couple of hours in that club he peeled cash from his roll and threw it at the waitresses and strippers, buying both of us drinks and lap dances. I didn't think of Charla or Derek or much of anything at all.

The next evening, Domingo, Melanie, and I sat over a dinner that Melanie cooked in the tiny apartment kitchen. I helped her clean up while he sat on the futon. He watched us and ignored the baseball game on TV even though I knew he had a bet on it. Domingo usually couldn't keep Melanie close enough to satisfy him, but I sensed something more needy, more dangerous, in his demeanor. I also noticed that he kept slipping his hand into his pocket, then bringing it out empty. Was he waiting for the right moment? Or was he having doubts?

"Come here, girl," he said eventually.

Melanie put down a dish and went over to sit on his lap. I turned away and finished cleaning up while they nuzzled. After a moment, a knock came at the door. Domingo muttered a curse. He stared at the door. The knock came again. "All right, goddamnit," he yelled. Then to Melanie, "Be right back." He left her sitting on the futon and slipped outside.

"Everything okay?" I whispered when the door closed behind him.

"He's just…stressed," she said. "He's having problems with some guys. And his mom, she doesn't like how he lives. She's on him all the time."

She gestured for me to come closer. I went and settled on the floor in front of her.

"You know that he…." I didn't know how to say it. Or if I should.

She nodded. "I know he's involved in stuff he shouldn't be."

"So why, you know?"

"Why stay with him?"

"Yeah."

"I don't think I have a choice."

"Do you love him?" I asked.

She was staring at her schoolbooks stacked on the floor near me. "He looks out for me like no one else ever has. But he's always afraid I'll go off with some other guy. It makes him mean."

"He loves you. He's afraid of losing you." Because that's what love is. The constant fear of loss. I'd figured out why Domingo imposed himself on me. It wasn't that he trusted me. It was that he knew right off I wasn't a threat.

"Hey, check it out." Melanie suddenly extended her leg across my lap. "Feel it," she said.

She had a tattoo of a tree frog clinging to her ankle. It was the image I'd pointed out in her book. I reached to touch the tattoo, then hesitated. What line were we crossing? My hand trembled. I felt the heat and weight of her leg on mine. This felt innocent and intimate at the same time.

"It's okay," she said.

I touched her skin, tracing the lines of the ink. She smiled.

Behind me, the door rattled and swung open. Melanie yanked her leg away, nearly pulling me flat onto my face. I jerked myself upright. Domingo stood over us. He'd come in pissed off, either about being pulled away from Melanie when he was trying to nail down a commitment or about a deal gone wrong outside. Standing there, he sensed the anxiety in the room, and looked from me to Melanie and back again.

"I tell you what pisses me off," he said. "You turn your back for a second, someone's going to screw you over." He pulled out a handgun and took out the clip and blew as if to clean it. He put the clip back in and put the gun down on the table. He stood there looking at it. Then he looked at Melanie. Then at me sitting on the floor. "Don't like guns?"

I shook my head.

"Worst invention in the world, man. If I could go back in time, I'd get rid of these things. I'd kill the guy who invented them."

"So why do you carry one?" Melanie said.

Domingo answered as if I'd asked, though. "That's just it, ain't it? I got to. Because they exist. Because everybody else has one."

We sat there. Domingo seemed lost in thought, but he had that jittery physicality as if he were about to do something ugly. He couldn't seem to reconcile his thoughts. He knew something was going on, but he also *knew* I was harmless, a pushover.

"Michael was telling me he's thinking about taking some classes next semester," Melanie said, obviously attempting to steer us in a safer direction.

For a moment Domingo said nothing. He looked at Melanie with that blank expression. Then he looked at me. "Yeah?" he said.

My voice was lost. I nodded.

"So what's keeping you?"

"Money," I managed to say.

"Money, that's all that's keeping you from college." He pulled the roll of cash from his pocket and peeled off several hundred-dollar bills. "That get you started?"

I nodded.

"Tell me when you have to pay again. I better see a report card or something too. All A's."

Another knock came at the door. Domingo's shoulders slumped. "Can't get a single minute," he said. Then he put the gun back inside his waistline and went to answer the door.

I didn't sleep well that night. Twice I started dialing Charla's number but hung up in the midst of dialing. I lay awake. I heard when Melanie left the apartment. I heard Domingo shuffle around, then settle down for the night. Apparently he never came out with the ring. I stared at the outlines of the boxes I hadn't touched since moving in. Finally I got up, got dressed, and crept out to the car.

I drove awhile absent-mindedly, staying in the neighborhood. There was nowhere to go. Eventually I found myself parked in front of my parents' house. I got out and went to the side door. I still had a key, so I let myself in. The kitchen was dark and quiet, just the hum of the refrigerator. On the door of the freezer side was a dry-erase board where Mom and Dad kept a weekly schedule for meals. They planned each meal of each day at least one week ahead so they wouldn't find themselves at a loss for what to do.

I went on into the living room where my dad lay asleep in the recliner. The TV flashed before him. His face went light then dark then light. His chest rose and fell. His mouth was open. His dinner plate sat on the coffee table before him. From the day I shot Derek to the day I left for college, we'd eaten hunched over our plates in the living room, staring at the TV so we wouldn't have to face one another or live with our thoughts. I wished he would wake up and talk to me. We could talk about baseball.

Down the hall was my parents' bedroom. Mom was in bed asleep on her side, a book open but facedown in Dad's spot. The lamp was on for Dad to find his way. They'd survived the years—as Dad said when things got tough, "We'll survive"—but it seemed they'd gotten so old, so run-down. I knew that I'd started this downward spiral. If only I knew how to turn it around.

Upstairs, Derek's room was to the left and across from it was my room.

I didn't have to go up there to know that his was exactly as he'd left it the day we went squirrel hunting and he didn't come back. There would be clothes hanging in the closet. The bed would be made. There would be baseball posters on the wall. Trophies along the shelves. There would be the appearance of life.

Meanwhile, my room was cleaned out, leaving nothing more than indentations in the carpet where my computer desk and my bedframe used to sit.

On my way in to work the next day, I drove past Charla's house. If she were going off to Houston with what's-his-face—I couldn't remember his name—they'd have to leave any day now. As I slowed in front of her house, two figures walking out paused to look at me. Charla and her guy. We all made eye contact, and I panicked and hit the gas. I took off down the street and around the corner.

I wasn't but a few blocks away when he raced up behind me in his truck, blowing his horn and flashing his lights. I kept going. He pulled beside me, yelling, pointing. Charla sat in the passenger seat refusing to look at me. He swerved in front of me and slammed on the brakes. I veered into the gutter at the edge of the street to keep from colliding with him, and I came to a stop there.

He was at my door when I looked up. He hit the door with his fist and gestured for me to get out. I felt a hot fear in my head and chest, but I knew there was no avoiding this. I got out. He backed up just enough for me to open the door. He was a bit taller than I was but wasn't bigger in any muscular way. Still, he had the hard look of someone who did physical, outside work.

"Damn, dude," he said. His face was red and his hands were balled into fists. He kept stepping back and forth, up on me, and away just a bit. "You got to stay away from her. Why can't you get that?"

I nodded, unsure if my voice would work. I expected him to hit me any second. I wasn't sure what I'd do then. Would I fight back? Would I roll into a ball and let him pound me? I found myself wondering what Domingo would do. No, I knew what he'd do. What I wondered was why I couldn't do it.

Charla sat in the truck, not looking at us. I could see that she was crying.

"The next time," her guy said, "I won't keep my cool. One of us will get his ass kicked. You can guess which one that's going to be."

I nodded, whether in agreement or simply acknowledgement I didn't know.

At work, Domingo was edgy. He ignored his cell phone. When Chad came into the back room, Domingo watched him. Chad kept his head down, loaded a cart full of boxes to stock the shelves, and left without a word. Domingo turned off the radio that usually buzzed staticky music in the background. I was already wound tight, so Domingo's tension didn't help. After an hour or so, I had to say something just to keep from losing it myself. "Melanie's birthday party's this evening, right, six o'clock?"

He finished tying off and rolling up a tube of sausage. Then he scraped the mix of blood, water, and scraps on the stuffing table into a large trash barrel. He didn't look up at me.

"She's pulling away," he said. "I feel it, man."

"What?" I said. "I don't think she's—"

He slammed a fist into the stuffing table. "Don't screw with me." His face flushed with a sudden rage. He took a breath as if collecting himself and walked away into the meat cooler, closing himself inside.

I finished cleaning up and waited for him to come out. When he did, he was no longer angry. He was something worse, a cold calm like predators must have when they kill not out of anger but out of nature.

"I got to do it tonight," he said. "I'll get there early and surprise her with the ring when she walks in. Down on my knee and all that shit." He seemed to be talking himself through it while also asking for my opinion on the scenario.

"Yeah," I said. "Sure."

"You need to take care of your business too," Domingo said. "You need to get right with your parents. And with that girl of yours."

"You right with your mom?" I asked.

He studied me. I knew he was thinking about how I'd gotten testier recently. I knew he was torn about this. He didn't tolerate being challenged. But he also knew he'd helped bring this out in me. "I call my mom every damn day. I tell her I love her. I tell her I'm going to straighten up," he said.

I knew this was true. It was too vulnerable an admission not to be. We needed a change of subject to save face. I asked him, "Why do you work here? I mean, I don't think you need the money."

"Got to keep up appearances," he said. "Besides, maybe I really will straighten up one day. Then I'll have to live like a real person."

My phone rang as I was leaving work. At the same time, Domingo was saying, "Going to make the rounds. Catch you at the party."

I wasn't sure I had it in me to go to the party, but I nodded at him and answered my phone without looking to see who was calling. "Can you meet me?" the voice asked. It took me a moment to realize that it wasn't Charla. It was Melanie. I couldn't make my voice work as I watched Domingo drive away. "Please," she said.

"Okay," I managed.

Half an hour later I found her in a study carrel behind rows of books in the college library. A pretty unlikely spot for Domingo to find us. She gave me a relieved but worried smile, and I felt a tingle of fear.

"I guess this place is kind of pitiful compared to when you were off at the university," she said, gesturing for me to sit in a chair beside her.

I sat. "Wouldn't know. I wasn't there long enough to see the inside of the library."

"Most students never do anyway, I guess," she said. "But I like coming here. It reminds me how much there is to see and know. So much besides what I live every day."

While we talked, I watched other guys notice her. They'd size me up in a glance, then slow down to take her in as they rounded the corner of the shelves. Every one of them obviously waited for her to notice them. I saw how gracefully she tuned them out.

"I think there are a lot of guys who wouldn't come here if it weren't for you," I said.

She smiled. It was genuine and flattered. "You're sweet." Her phone rang. She looked at it but didn't answer. "Guess who," she said. Her smile faded. "I told you before how Domingo's mom doesn't like how he lives. That's not all of it. He nearly beat his brother to death. And he gets in fights with his cousins all the time. We lived with them before he moved back home with his mom. Then she threw him out."

I wanted to tell her about Derek, about the tremendous difference between *nearly* killing your brother and really doing it. I didn't, though, because if I did then that shared knowledge would always shape us. Instead, I said, "That's when he showed up at my door."

She nodded. "I do love him. You asked me that before. It's just, sometimes he scares me. A lot lately. He's losing his grip or something." Her phone buzzed that she had a message. "He'll be freaking out. Wanting to know where I am."

"He thinks you're pulling away."

She closed her eyes. Wiped her hair away from her face. Opened her eyes and looked at me with a tired expression. "What would you do?"

"What do you want to do?" I asked.

Her phone buzzed again. She gave me a hopeless smile. "Does it matter? I better go. I'm going to be late. See you at the party?"

I nodded, only then making up my mind to go.

But she didn't move, and I found myself reaching out to place my hand on hers. My heart thumped. All I could hear was my own breathing. We didn't look at each other. We looked at the floor, across the library, at the books. We sat there for a long time. Terrified as I was, I found it peaceful. I understood why Melanie said she liked going there. All those books. If there was that much worth writing about, there had to be something worthwhile in the world.

From where I parked down the street from Domingo's mom's house I could hear the music thumping and smell the burgers grilling in the yard. I took my time getting out of the car and walking to the house. After Melanie and I had left the library—separately, I let her leave first then followed a few minutes later—I drove slowly and took a roundabout way to get to the party. I didn't want us to arrive at the same time. I felt out of place walking up to the yard under scrutiny from the five or six sleeveless-shirted tattooed guys standing around the grill drinking beer. One of them was probably the brother Domingo had almost killed in a fight.

As I stepped inside the front door of the house, I felt the atmosphere of argument and the blur of sudden action as Domingo lunged to grab Melanie. It was like everything had been going on forever, yet like it had been waiting for me to enter. Just when I did was when he jumped. Domingo pressed her against the wall. His hand gripped her jaw, fingertips digging hard into her face. She cried out, tried to push him away. The music played on. People pretended not to notice. There were maybe eight people in this room and others milling around in other rooms.

"Where you been?" he screamed. "Tell me!"

Melanie thrashed. Her frantic eyes found me. Somehow I'd crossed the room. Had I run? I couldn't recall. But there I was, right up on Domingo and Melanie. I put my hand on Domingo's wrist. I felt his brutal strength. "Come on, man, let her go," I said.

"Who you been with?" Domingo screamed, ignoring me. "Who?"

Melanie made a gagging sound.

Terrified, I pulled on his arm. Melanie flailed. He rared back with his free arm. I grabbed it before he could strike. I felt a sharp blow in the gut. His elbow. A woman—it had to be his mom—bolted around the corner, yelling at him and pounding on him with the flats of her fists. He pushed her away. I grabbed at him again. His mom came forward again. Domingo was wailing, crying fierce tears. He let go of Melanie's jaw and watched her slide to the floor. He slung his mom off of him again with a swipe of his arm.

"What is wrong with this world?" he said. "This isn't how it's supposed to go."

He looked at me. He was asking me. What could I say? *This is exactly how it goes*. That was the only answer I had. I said nothing.

"All right," he said. "All right. To hell with all y'all. I'll show you how it goes."

He pushed through me, knocking me down. He stopped at the door, turned around to us, and reached beneath his shirt into his pants. For a second I saw a blurred hint of his handgun, but then he was holding the ring between his thumb and one finger. He flicked it toward Melanie. Then he turned away and bolted out into the yard. He punched one of the guys outside. Kicked over the grill. Red coals and burgers scattered across the yard. He tore off in his car, leaving behind a trail of smoke and chaos.

The two cops collected Domingo's things from my apartment. They asked me to describe what happened at the party. Then they made me repeat it. They asked what time it was that I last saw him. I told them I didn't know, I guessed somewhere around seven or seven-thirty. They asked if he came back to the apartment at any time in the night. I told them no. The last I saw him was when he stormed away from the party. His mom and several people had gathered around Melanie, collapsed in a sobbing heap on the floor. Sick and terrified, I'd staggered out unnoticed and gone back to the apartment. The cops nodded, made a few notes. They already knew all the answers.

It was six in the morning. A few hours earlier, Domingo had been arrested for a spree of drive-by shootings. He shot several rounds into the buildings at the college. He shot at cars parked on the street. He shot at the houses of his rivals. The cops had a list of known associates and enemies. They showed me page after page of guys who looked a lot like the ones who came and went from the apartment.

"Who was he after?" the cops asked me. I didn't know. Truth was, I doubt Domingo knew. There wasn't any obvious villain. That was his problem. It was his mom. It was Melanie. It was Chad. It was his cousins, his brother, rival drug dealers, buyers. It was himself. It was me. Take your pick. It was me she was with, and that was the straw that broke him. He'd been wrong. Anyone could be a threat, even me.

He shot five rounds into a house where an off-duty fireman was sleeping. Hearing the shots, the man ran into a bedroom where his two young daughters were in bed. He shielded them with his body and took two rounds in his back. He died on the spot. The cops told me a former resident of that house was on their list of Domingo's known enemies. Domingo had gotten out of his car and stood out front firing as if he were hoping to be shot at in return. The fireman and his family had lived there less than a week.

Domingo had the gun on him when they found him sitting on the front porch of his mom's house, arms folded across his knees, head down. He didn't even look up when they approached him. He stood, then knelt, then sprawled facedown and let them take him in. The cops told me all of that while watching for my response. They wanted to see the lesson sink in. "Just thought you should know what you've been involved in," they said.

I nodded. I said nothing. I wanted to tell them that I wasn't involved in it, but that wasn't true. I was right in the middle of it. Try as you might to avoid the worst of life, you are always right in the middle of it.

The cops eventually left. For a long time I sat and tried not to think. I felt hollow. The apartment was quiet. Domingo wouldn't be back. I was free of him. He was awful and dangerous and I despised what he did, and yet the apartment suddenly felt very empty.

Melanie wouldn't be back either. Somehow I knew that.

I loaded up the boxes I'd lived out of and carried them to the car. I left the broken-down futon and the mattress. I left the picture of Charla and me. I closed the door and got in the car and left that pathetic apartment.

I went looking for Charla. I hoped her guy would be with her. They weren't at her parents' house. I kept driving around and finally found them at the house where I'd taken Charla to that party on the very first evening I'd gotten back home. They were sitting on the front porch. They each had a sweating bottle of beer. It was early afternoon. He laughed at something she said, and she laughed with him. She leaned into him, laid her head on his shoulder. I saw them as I screeched to a stop in front of the house. I jumped out of the car, leaving the door wide open, the engine running. I crossed the yard and came up on them so fast they seemed stunned.

"Michael," Charla said.

"Dude, what did I tell—" he started.

I lashed out and kicked him. Right through the beer bottle and square into his stomach. He fell backward gasping. Charla didn't even scream. She scuttled away, mouth wide open. She needed this. Now she could hate me. She could blame me without guilt and she could be done with me.

I walked away without a word and got in my car and drove home.

I let myself in the front door. My parents weren't home, the house still and quiet.

I carried a couple of my boxes upstairs to Derek's room. I dumped my stuff out onto the floor and set the now-empty boxes in the center of the room. For four years this room had remained like this. Like it was waiting for him to come back.

I took down the posters. I pulled clothes from the closet. I collected the trophies lined on shelves. I put everything in the boxes. Then I started ripping from the bed the sheets that still held his smell.

Behind me was the open door to my old, empty bedroom.

My parents would be stunned and heartbroken when they got home, but I didn't know how else to tell them they'd cleared out the wrong son.

I enrolled at the community college the next semester using the money Domingo gave me to get started. In the mornings I took classes, in the afternoons I went to work, and in the evenings after work I hung around the library. I often wandered along the aisles looking for books that grabbed my attention. The computers might have been more efficient at finding specific titles or subjects, but I didn't know what I was looking for so I liked the random chance of coming across an interesting old book that probably hadn't been opened in years.

One evening I'd settled down with a few titles when I noticed Melanie on the other side of the room. She'd come in accompanied by several guys.

For a while they sat at a table talking. It wasn't until she got up to leave that she noticed me sitting in the same spot where she and I had hidden away the night of Domingo's breakdown. She froze for a second, then finished gathering her things. I stayed where I was.

When she looked up again, we nodded slightly toward each other and she went along her way and I turned back to my books. We did each other the favor of letting go.

Summertime & The Livin's Easy in Saratoga

by Tom Tolnay

Though madcap betting and extravagant feting have been going on for over a century in Saratoga Springs, my fiancée and I stumbled across the "Spa City" only a few years ago, and we've been making the pilgrimage every summer since: That's the season in which favorites and long shots kick up clumps of turf, when casino games gobble up players' cash faster than they can blink, and pleasure-seekers of all persuasions lose themselves in epicurean delights, hot-oil massages, and photo finishes. Bottom line is that everyone in Saratoga is looking to get a leg up on the competition, including me and my lovely business partner. The only difference is that we collect our payoffs not at the betting windows and slot machines but among the hedonists who stagger around dazed by the uproar of race day, barely able to stuff their wallets and purses away for safekeeping.

Lucky Lucy and Danny Boy (sorry, we never divulge our last names) enjoy monetary withdrawals of this nature in New York as well, among the throngs at the Thanksgiving Day Parade, and on "Black Friday," when Bergdorf Goodman and Saks Fifth Avenue attract bevies of bargain hunters. We've also profited at Macy's on Christmas Eve, when shoppers are too loaded down with packages to pay attention to the whereabouts of their cash and credit cards, and on New Year's Eve, when a million revelers are jammed hip-to-hip in Times Square, staring bleary-eyed at the glittering globe shimmying down the pole. Occasionally we'll do the Mummers Parade in Philadelphia and St. Paddy's Day in Boston. Once the major holidays have died away, however, there's a conspicuous drop-off in our commerce, at least until the Mets and Yankees start playing home games in April. But when all the receipts for the year are tallied (I keep reliable records, having been employed in the accounting field), and these figures are weighed against the amount of time and money spent on each venture, the best setting and season to pick up ready cash is Saratoga from July through Labor Day.

If you've got it in your head picking pockets is a mean-spirited way to earn a living—well, more or less a living—I'd suggest you check out the history of this profession. No less an authority than Charlie Dickens recognized that picking pockets helped equalize the playing field a smidgen between rich and poor: That's why he got Fagin to teach the Artful Dodger, the treacherous Bill Sykes, and even the blameless Oliver Twist the art of using sticky fingers in London's merchant quarters. Same goes for me and Lucy: We are constantly teaching each other tricks of the trade, and in our own little way we're helping to support a more equitable distribution of capital. Not that you need to be concerned about "creeping socialism"—we never share our pickings with those less fortunate than ourselves.

The business of thievery has changed a good deal since Dickens' time. These days virtual crooks are raking in big-time fortunes—the *Daily News* claims a quarter-billion dollars is pilfered electronically every year. The good news for workers in our corner of the industry is that, since the media is focused so intensely on Internet theft, walking off with someone's wallet on terra firma stirs up a lot less hullabaloo. And with the judicial system's attention aimed into cyberspace, too, penalties for getting caught with your hand in someone's pocket are more humane than at the turn of the nineteenth century, when a "hands-on" artist could get a serious pain in the neck courtesy of the hangman just for pinching a handkerchief.

Since our daily needs and future goals are modest, Lucy and I don't begrudge the high returns collected by our brothers and sisters of the Internet. All we want is to keep up with our bills and put away enough to splurge on a Caribbean honeymoon one of these days. Only problem with this dream is that there usually isn't a lot left over after laying out for rent, utilities, and travel expenses. It's mostly our harboring an aversion to working eight hours a day that keeps us at it.

When we met, Lucy'd been employed for several years in the restaurant game as a waitress, cashier, and hostess, and detested every minute of her sentence. I'd worked for an insurance broker, a real estate agent, and an accountant, and resented every day I had to report for duty—a mutual mind-set that immediately attracted us to each other the night I wandered into Luigi's hoping to smother my workaday grievances with a plate of pasta and a liter of vino.

It was Lucy who shuffled over to my table in a tiny black skirt and tossed a menu at me.

"What'll it be?" she spat.

"One thing I don't want is alphabet soup!" I said. "I'm sick and tired of staring at the damn alphabet on my office computer."

Her eyes sparkled with complicity. "And I'm sick and tired of reciting the specials of the day!"

"No problem—I already know what I want."

"Spaghetti and meatballs?"

"I'd rather have a dish of you."

Instead of getting in a huff over my proposal, she sprang this come-home-with-me smile, and the rest, as they say, is history.

I hung out in Rudyard's Tavern on the corner until she finished her shift and she actually showed up for our impromptu date. By the time we'd knocked off half a dozen vodka tonics and tossed around ideas for leaving our jobs behind, half seriously, and totally tipsily, Lucy suggested we go into business together as purse- and pocket-snatchers.

"Let those other sorry souls do our dirty work, Danny Boy!" she giggled.

"Can't think of one good reason why we should *evvvvver* go back to our jobs!"

Talking about slipping our fingers into the pants and dresses of strangers seemed to arouse us, especially the part about walking off with their scratch. Following a couple more get-togethers—highlighted by an unforgettable overnight in her studio apartment—over eggs and toast in her kitchenette, we began prepping a trial rip-off. Unlike many plans made in the muddle of a hangover, this one came to us smooth and fast. We picked a date when the Lakers would be in town to play the Knicks at Madison Square Garden—guaranteeing us a highly preoccupied crowd—and our scenario went off as easily as stealing a lollipop from a two-year-old: On game night, mingling with swarms of revved-up ticket holders, we targeted a white-haired gent in a suit jacket. While Lucy was chatting and batting her eyelashes at him, I moved up behind him, stumbled into him accidentally-on-purpose, and my partner and I walked off with three hundred fifty-seven bucks! Pure profit!

"That was sooooo easy!" Lucy chirped.

"That's because you're my lucky charm," I said.

Lucy and I have been living off the land, or, rather, off the toil or good fortune of our fellow citizens, ever since, and we have a great time planning and acting out our little capers.

Like any business, though, we have our good days and our bad days. At Siro's restaurant in Saratoga Lucy pinched a silk purse off a double-wide dowager before hiding in a restroom stall and tucking more than five hundred bucks into her pantyhose. But on the other side of the coin, we've come away empty-handed after hours of club-hopping in New York's SoHo. That's why we appreciate Saratoga so much: For two solid months everybody's dripping with cash, which fits in perfectly with our business model, since paper money has always been our preferred method of payment.

This year, however, we almost didn't go. Every business has its downside, meaning my fiancée and I have experienced a couple of alarming close calls. Two of the worst came earlier this year: In January, outside Giants Stadium, I spotted this dude's wallet hanging half out of the pocket of his team jacket, so I sauntered up to him and asked if he had tickets to sell. When he dismissed me with a wave of his hand—even though I was wearing a Giants jacket, too—and turned away to look for someone, I flipped my fingertips under the bulging pocket and his wallet plopped onto the pavement. As I was bending over to scoop it up, his tailgate pals, who'd just torn loose from the mega-crowds, saw what I was up to and rushed me like a defensive line trying to sack the quarterback. Lacking hospitalization coverage, I had to leave the wallet behind, bobbing and weaving through the rabble as elusively as an all-pro running back. In those far-flung parking lots surrounding the stadium I climbed into the bed of a pickup truck and lay down until the gang of would-be tacklers finally gave up on me, but it was hours before I stopped looking over my shoulder.

Lucy has had her scary moments, too, like this June when she slipped a Lord & Taylor credit card out of someone's purse, figuring she had enough time to do severe damage to the card before its owner would notice it was missing. But she hadn't taken into account how quickly a victim with a cell phone could report a theft. When the cashier swiped the card, the expression on her face as she read the screen tipped Lucy off that they were on to her. Though Lucy has a gift for talking her way out of a scrape, this time she realized there was no way she was going to be able to explain things away. She barely made it out of the store, hustling down the avenue before store security could lasso her up.

At home that night she announced, "I'm finished with this way of living."

"You don't mean that," I said. "Think of what it was like working nine till five."

"Well, it's better than prison, isn't it?"

"Come on, Luce, our luck will come back, and don't forget, the horses'll be running next month in Saratoga!"

The mere mention of Saratoga melted some of the discouragement from her bright emerald eyes. But I knew it wasn't only because Saratoga's such a great place to do business. Broadway, which cuts through the heart of the old city, is lined with one-of-a-kind shops—from European cafes like Mrs. London's to Victorian-style clothing boutiques and handcrafted jewelry arcades, and there are buckets of fresh flowers on display everywhere. Even the newer buildings have been forced to conform to the brick-and-mortar charm of downtown, where the age of romance is alive and kicking in settings like the Adelphi Hotel, which is where we prefer to bed down. Its leafy lobby is decorated with slow-and-soft comfort in mind, including high-backed, plush armchairs outfitted with embroidered pillows. Within walking distance is Congress Park, where we like to stroll before dinner, sipping from spring-water fountains, eyeing the tuxedoes and cocktail dresses strutting into Canfield Mansion for a high-society party, and sometimes we've even climbed onto a painted plaster horse in the park's carousel. Plenty hungry by this time, we explore nearby side streets to choose one of Saratoga's wonderful restaurants, which feature world-class cuisines to satisfy the most persnickety of taste buds. All this and two racetracks—one for harness, one for thoroughbreds! What more could a couple in love ask for in life?

At Saratoga Race Course, rows of benches are set up at track level so bettors can cool their bunions before elbowing their way to the chain-link fence to watch jockeys whip their ponies to the finish line. I had convinced Lucy to give Saratoga another shot, and as if to show our luck had returned, we were able to latch on to a pair of front-row seats, where we pretended to be studying our race sheets: Actually we were scanning the crowds for a mark to add some bucks to our nuptials account. Lucy had started to relax, getting into the spirit of the thing, when out of nowhere a guy with a camera came up to us and started squeezing off rapid-fire pix. With a self-congratulatory grin the photographer—about fifty years old, with eyes as round as telescope lenses—informed us he was taking pictures of "good-looking couples at the races" for *The Saratogian*. Though we are a handsome couple, if I do say so, I immediately stood up to advise him against taking such a liberty, but he hopped into the mass of humanity before I could finish reading him his rights. Now, the last thing Lucinda X and Daniel Y needed was to have our photo appear in the local newspaper, making us easy to identify if we should have a close call at the track. I had no choice but to take off after him, and Lucy galloped after me like a thoroughbred out of the gate.

Pushing through the bettors gathered ten-deep along the fences was no picnic, and several of them jabbed elbows into our ribs in response to our aggressive maneuvers. By the time we managed to wriggle our way out of that mob scene, the photo-journalist had disappeared like a hundred-to-one shot. Onto the midway under the stands we stomped like a couple of gamblers on a losing streak, searching the crowds that were milling around the betting windows. Mr. Paparazzi was nowhere to be seen.

Stymied and agitated, I voiced a gloomy reality: "Looks like we're going to have to clear out of Saratoga."

"We just got here," Lucy complained. "I was just starting to enjoy it."

"If any of those pictures get printed, we could end up behind bars."

Lucy moaned: "Looks like our luck has finally run out on us for good."

"Not necessarily," I said, trying to boost her morale. "Even if a photo gets printed this year, I doubt anyone's going to remember us next year. Especially if we dress differently and wear sunglasses."

For me, that would've been no problem—all I'd have to do is switch from my blue blazer to my tan sport jacket, wear loafers instead of sneakers, and possibly tug a baseball cap over my coarse blond hair, which has always been resistant to combing anyway. But it would've been a major setback for Lucy, fashion-wise: She was dressed in this lilac cotton pullover that hung down far enough to tickle those pretty ankles of hers, and she'd completed her outfit by tying a lilac ribbon around a brimmed straw hat. So cute! You'd think she just stepped out of Saratoga's Gideon Putnam Hotel in the 1890s, long-lost times when men wore top hats and women dressed in full-length gowns just to stroll down the Avenue of the Pines. I would really have hated to ask Lucy to abandon her charming get-up, but in this business you sometimes have to make sacrifices.

Both of us maddened and moody—our faces stiff with disappointment, as we were thumping down the ramp to join the mass of winners and losers storming into and out of the track, my business partner extended a smooth bare arm toward the front gates: "Look, Danny Boy!"

Sharp-eyed Lucy had pinpointed the photographer with the quick trigger finger. Suddenly we were skipping down the ramp, our faces softening into smiles at the possibility that our good luck might have returned. Through the clusters of race fanatics we pushed until we found ourselves maybe forty feet behind him. Just before he reached the exit gates he pulled up near a food concession stand. Looping the strap of his camera case onto his shoulder, he got into a line of people waiting to place an order.

Lucy and I stopped short and hid our faces behind our racing sheets, but then we swiveled our heads and looked straight into each other's eyes: We understand each other so well, we didn't even have to discuss what our next move would be. "See if you can find a kid who'd like to make a few bucks," I said, "while I keep an eye on the camera creep."

Eyelashes flickering with agreement, she took off into the crowds, and that's when it occurred to me that the biggest reason for our success is my partner's resourcefulness, which includes a brilliant sense of timing, a touch as light as the brush of a butterfly's wings, and a flair for the theatrical—her hands sailing in all directions as she engages a prospect in conversation: My beloved could talk any man, woman, child, or chimpanzee into doing anything she wants. Keeping my face turned away from the concession stand as I waited, I soon caught sight of Lucy striding toward me, and sure enough, she had a kid in tow. By this time the photographer had reached the counter at the stand and was placing his order.

"This nice young feller," Lucy said, smiling her sweet sixteen at him, "would like to earn twenty dollars by helping us play a joke on our friend."

"Perfect!" said I, tapping him lightly on the shoulder to make sure he was real. The kid, who looked about thirteen years old, was already taller than me and had a head of hair that looked like a rung-out mop hanging over his eyes and ears. It was a wonder he could see or hear anything.

"What do I gotta do?"

After I explained the plot to him, he proved he was no dummy: "When do I get my twenty bucks?"

I slipped a twenty out of my wallet, making sure he got a good look at Andrew Jackson's portrait, then tucked it halfway into the vest pocket of my jacket. "Once you've played the joke on him, your money will be waiting right here for you."

The kid glanced at the twenty, then at Lucy, who was still smiling candy kisses at him, and said, "Okay!"

The moment I'd pointed out the victim, the kid started shuffling in the direction of the camera creep, who had just scooped his hot dog and cup of lemonade off the counter, and was backing off to give himself a little elbow room to enjoy his lunch.

The kid moseyed up to the concession stand, grabbed the mustard container, and made his way to the cameraman. "How'd you like some mustard on your hot dog, mister?" he shouted, and began squeezing the plastic container, squirting bright yellow goo all over the cameraman's red face and striped polo shirt. The kid was laughing crazily, as if it was the funniest thing he'd ever seen in his life. Mr. Paparazzi got so angry he took a swipe at the kid, grazing the side of the youngster's head with his hot-dog hand, causing the camera strap to slide off his shoulder onto the pavement. Startled by this reaction, the kid dashed off into the crowds. Lucy and I had timed our approach perfectly. From behind I gave the photographer a shove while she scooped the camera off the ground, and the two of us hurtled out the gates and down the midway. I lost sight of the kid, but I did spot the camera creep—he was running pretty hard after us.

Down Webster Street we scooted, but the cameraman was still making a race of it, closing the gap and drawing close enough that we could hear him grunting like he was heading down the home stretch. Around and between sharpies and harpies we dodged, shoving them out of our way as Mr. Paparazzi shouted, "Stop those two!"

While no one tried to stop us—they just stared at us bewilderedly—his shouts and our dash to freedom were attracting way too much attention. But it wasn't long before our pursuer started to fade, and by zigzagging like steeplechase horses through a bumper-to-bumper parking lot, we finally lost sight of him. Even after we'd stopped running, we kept walking briskly, trying to increase the distance between him and us.

Lucy and I finally came to a cluster of trees a few blocks beyond the roar of the race course, alongside the tall fences that surround rows of stables on the outer perimeters of the track's acreage. In unison, we sank down on a plot of grass, still huffing and puffing, the sun through the leaves making our sweaty faces shine. Once our breathing had calmed down, and we'd made sure the photographer hadn't picked up our trail, Lucy said: "What about the kid's twenty bucks?"

"Looks like we're twenty bucks richer than we figured."

"That's mean."

"Hey, at least we taught him something useful."

"What're you talking about?"

"Sometimes you win, sometimes you lose."

Mumbling something I didn't quite hear—probably something unkind—Lucy took out her handkerchief and started wiping the mustard off the camera case. When she was finished she said, "Now what?"

"Seems to me we have even stronger reasons to quit Saratoga."

Without saying so out loud we both understood the camera caper wasn't finished. While no one at the track would be likely to remember us as the couple that had caused so much trouble the previous summer, the photographer would never forget us: He'd be coming out to the track every day during the next racing season, and the next, equipped with a new camera but with those same telescopic eyes on the lookout for me and Lucy. Getting up to our feet with a kind of philosophical weariness, I looped the camera strap over my shoulder while Lucy brushed off her lilac dress. Taking hold of each other's hand, we moved up to the edge of the road. After several minutes under a pinching hot sun, we managed to wave down a cab. In total silence we rode to the train station, both of us mourning the loss of Saratoga.

In New York, with the downturn in the economy having gotten worse, Lucy and I were forced to become more diversified in our business affairs. These days a transaction can turn out to be as unimaginative as a supermarket shopping cart in which a pocketbook has been left unattended, or the lifting of a jacket off a coat hook in a beauty salon—just in case its owner has been foolish enough to leave valuables in a pocket. I'm equally ashamed to admit we have found ourselves extracting earrings, necklaces, and bracelets out of showcases in Bloomingdale's. Technically this is shoplifting, of course, though it could be said we were picking the pockets of the store's owners. But the word "shoplifting" has always sounded vulgar to our ears, for that class of employment doesn't demand nearly as much expertise as plucking booty directly off a walking-talking human being. Not only that, we didn't have the connections required to turn the stuff we lifted into cash.

Without the easy money of Saratoga to feather our love nest, and with New Yorkers having less in their pockets to extract, it was becoming clear that Lucy and I might be forced to return to the nine-to-five grind, assuming we could find jobs in this lousy economy. But before fully accepting such a distasteful alternative, we made up our minds to withdraw all the money we had saved in our special account and buy a set of wedding bands—so Lucy could lose the zircon engagement ring that's turning her finger green.

We've decided that the day after we exchange vows, we'll board a flight out of LaGuardia to settle down on one of those lush islands in the Bahamas. Checking in at a fabulous oceanfront resort, we'll swim in turquoise waters off golden beaches by day, and by night drift among the extravagant gentlemen and fancy ladies at the casino. After all, as a newly wedded couple with eyes only for each other, we'll have no interest whatsoever in the money belts and cash girdles strapped beneath their stylish jackets and dresses.

Hedge Hog

by Hilary Davidson

Harris Bulger was no gentleman. I knew that long before I got into bed with him. Truth be told, there was actually very little time from when we first shook hands till we slipped between the sheets together. Afterwards, he slapped my bottom and told me that I was better than an escort. Instead of smacking him back, I smiled, and we started seeing each other once or twice a week, always at his Upper East Side apartment. What Harris lacked in charm, his home made up for with its towering ceilings, open-air terrace, and breathtaking view of New York.

Three months after our first rendezvous, Harris's manners hadn't improved. We were in bed again, but when Harris was done, he grunted and pushed me aside. I tumbled to the edge of the bed, sliding along the Egyptian cotton sheets while Harris sat up, lit a cigarette, and started to lay out another line of cocaine.

"You should get going before Meredith comes home," he said.

Meredith was his wife, a tall, blond trophy who, I'd heard, liked to brag about how she used to work on Wall Street, almost ten years after she'd been making coffee for the traders at Lehman Brothers.

"I was planning to stay and play with you awhile longer, darling." I ran my fingers through the thick, matted fur on his back, while he vacuumed up the coke. "I don't get to see you often enough."

Harris turned toward me, making the extra flesh that padded his body and pooled in his belly wobble. "Having you here is a lot more fun, Lacey."

"I could arrange to be here full-time, you know."

"That would be great," he answered, but his tone was noncommittal. I'd heard all of his complaints about Meredith: her temper, her vanity, her bouts of bulimia, her appetite for drugs, her taunting Harris about his growing bulk, and her lack of interest in him. Why he didn't kick her bony ass out to the street was beyond me. It wasn't as if they had kids together. Undoubtedly, Harris's success as a hedge-fund manager was as attractive to her as it was to me, but Meredith was born into a wealthy family, so she must have had other resources. In any case, I didn't need to understand it. I only needed to work around it.

"Tell me what you want, darling," I cooed. "What do you want most in the world right now?"

He took a long drag. "You know what I could really go for?"

"What?"

"A burger from that Frenchie guy's place." He flicked ash on the bed and I shuddered at the thought of beautiful sheets with cigarette holes. Harris wouldn't care. He'd replace them with Frette linens from Gracious Home that cost about as much as a month's rent at my drab little shoebox in Flatbush.

"Frenchie guy? You mean Daniel Boulud?" I asked. "You want the Burger Royale? The one with shaved black truffles?"

"Yeah." Harris's jowls relaxed into a smile and his small, piggy eyes got a faraway look. "Get them to deliver a couple, will you?"

"Oh, I'm not going to have one."

"They're for me." Harris squinted and his lower lip quivered. "What, are you going to start taunting me about my weight like Meredith does? It's genetic, you know." He dropped his cigarette into a glass on the night table and looked at the face of the gold watch sitting beside it. With a lumbering effort, he propelled himself off the bed. "Gotta shower." He didn't turn around, so I was spared the full-frontal view. "See you, Lacey."

"'Bye, darling," I called, aiming for a wistful note, as if I were going to miss him. What I really wanted to do was to wash myself with Lysol. But once I heard the water in the shower go on, that sensation faded. I was alone in the most beautiful apartment I'd ever seen. Slipping out of bed, I put on my push-up bra and stockings and pulled my dress on. My shoes were by the front door, because Harris said my stiletto heels might damage the beautiful parquet floors. Meredith was very protective of the floors, apparently.

I stood for a moment, listening to the water. Then, before I lost my nerve, I grabbed the red thong that matched my bra and marched into Meredith's dressing room. The space was gigantic, with mirrored walls, Art Deco furniture, and a leopard-print carpet. One wall was a shrine to shoes, with Manolo Blahnik, Jimmy Choo, and Christian Louboutin all sharing space on the shelves. The urge to try them on nagged at me, but Meredith's huge size-eleven feet were three sizes bigger than mine. Focus, I told myself. Then I tucked the thong into the edge of the chaise longue, where the back met the seat. No way was Meredith going to miss that.

I turned to her dressing table. Meredith was a neat freak who kept her hairpins lined up in a row. She was smart enough to lock up her jewelry, but she left other treasures lying around. There was a jar of Clé de Peau's precious La Crème moisturizer sitting there, with a delicate silver spatula balanced atop it. The implement actually came with the cream, but since that cost $475 an ounce, it was a relative pittance. I wondered if Meredith collected the little spatulas when she was done with each jar. It seemed like the kind of thing she would do. On impulse, I swiped the cream and spatula and dropped it into my bag. Would she notice that? I'd swiped her bottle of Baccarat's Les Larmes Sacrées de Thebes perfume on my last visit to the apartment. I didn't even like the fragrance, but I craved the pyramid-shaped crystal bottle. That was before I discovered it cost $1,700 for a quarter-ounce. I wondered what she thought was happening to her stuff.

There was a little slip of paper under the jar. I squinted at it.

Tramp, it said. *Perfect for Hedge Hog.*

For some reason, my lips quivered. Was that bleached-blond bag of anorexic bones calling me a tramp? Hedge Hog was her nasty nickname for her husband. When Harris had first told me about it, I'd almost laughed.

That would have been a bad move, because the name almost brought Harris to tears. Still, it was wittier than I'd have given Meredith credit for. But there was nothing funny about being called a tramp.

The note was creepy, as if Meredith were speaking directly to me, something she'd never done when I'd seen her in person. She'd visited Harris's office a couple of times, sweeping in without even a hello as I sat there at the reception desk.

For a moment, I felt an urge to flee the apartment. I backed out of the dressing room and closed the double French doors with a soft click. The shower was still running. Harris had plenty of real estate to wash, after all. No one was chasing me out, but I felt out of place. That sensation lasted until I walked into the living room. Harris's apartment was on the twelfth floor of a Fifth Avenue building overlooking Central Park and was barely a block away from the Guggenheim. Some decorator had mixed French antiques with Southeast Asian icons throughout, and the results were serenely beautiful. I wasn't sure how I'd change it when I finally moved in, though I knew I'd have to. A woman had to mark her territory.

Boulud Bistro was on speed dial on the kitchen phone. Harris's craving for a $150 burger was not a new thing. No matter how much money he raked in, he still had the tastes of an adolescent boy. After I phoned the order in, I pulled a crystal tumbler from a cabinet, marked it with a red lip print, and set it on the counter. There was no way that Meredith was going to miss the evidence of my latest visit to Harris's apartment. If she wanted to keep any dignity at all, she'd have to leave.

As I strolled out the door, I stopped for one last, lingering gaze. In my head, I was already living there. It was going to be wonderful, even if it was with Harris.

Afterwards I walked down Fifth Avenue, along the edge of Central Park. My fantasy of living on the Upper East Side continued to play in my head. It was easy to picture myself jogging through the park in the morning, then having a massage or doing yoga. I'd have lunch at those fancy restaurants favored by the ladies of the neighborhood, places where they brought you a special footstool to hold your handbag. In the afternoon, I'd probably have a board meeting at an art museum. I wouldn't be just another socialite taking up a seat at the table; I could help a museum, say, the Metropolitan Museum of Art, with its acquisitions. I'd been a fine-art major at Butler University, after all.

In fact, when I'd first come to New York, a starry-eyed grad, I'd worked in a series of quirky little galleries in Chelsea. Deep down, I'd always suspected that was where I'd meet my future husband. But the only men who walked in the door were either gay, taken, or bill collectors who were there to repossess the office furniture. After struggling for six years through that, I'd bailed and gone to work for an office-temp agency. That had improved the odds of meeting straight men…that, and the fact that my standards had sunk. I'd given up hope of finding a wealthy, handsome soul mate. I was thirty-two and not getting any younger, so I'd scratched every requirement off my list but one: money.

The fact that I was even seeing Harris showed how far my standards had dropped. Harris wasn't any girl's dream, of that much I was sure. He was of average height but above-average build. Most of the hair on his head had already waved bye-bye, at thirty-eight, though the carpet on his chest, back, arms, and legs grew thick and furry. He had sweaty palms, bad breath, and an overbite that should have been corrected years ago.

Still, he knew how to make money. So he had a certain charm. I had to give him that.

Harris ignored me when we were at work. I was on a contract, filling in for a receptionist who'd gotten knocked up by a married trader. That was one smart cookie, I thought. Still, the thought of carrying Harris's spawn made bile surge up my throat. I waited for a couple of days, then shimmied into his office after the market closed for the day and closed the door behind me.

"I've missed you, darling," I cooed.

"Busy," Harris barked back, his eyes not leaving his computer screens. He had three monitors that told him what was going on in markets around the world. The room reeked of cigarette smoke. Of course, it was illegal to smoke in the office, but the higher-ups didn't care what the hedge-fund managers did so long as they produced big returns. If you looked closely, there were traces of white powder on his desk.

"Do you want me to come over tonight?"

"No."

If I'd cared about him, my feelings would have been hurt. *You stupid jerk*, I thought. *I'd like to shove you out the window.* I was tempted to call him Hedge Hog, but worried that would cross a line. "That's too bad," I said instead. "Want me to come over tomorrow?"

"No."

It was frustrating that he wouldn't even look at me. "Is your wife in town?"

"Uh-huh."

"Does she have any trips planned soon?"

"She's ditching me next week to watch polo in Barbados." The hurt in his voice was clear. Poor Harris felt like he was being abandoned. This was my way in.

"How could she want to leave you?" I sat in Harris's lap, not an easy thing to do given how much stomach surged over it. "She doesn't appreciate what a good thing she's got."

We went at it for a little while. When we finished, he was sweaty and panting. I got up and made sure I looked decent. The last thing I wanted was for anyone else at the office to know about us. If there was a better prospect in these waters, I wanted to catch him and toss this one back.

"That was fun, Lacey," Harris said, lighting a cigarette. "I'll tell you when she's gone so you can come over. We can have some more fun together."

The *fun* was one-sided, but I kept that to myself. "That sounds wonderful, darling. I can't wait."

A smarter, less conceited man would have heard the sarcasm in my voice. But Harris just sat there, happy as the proverbial pig in mud.

"Hey, Lacey," he said on my way out.

"What is it, darling?"

"Order me up some pizza, will you? Bacon, peppers, extra cheese, caviar."

I smiled and closed the door.

The next time I went to Harris's apartment, I was prepared. I brought perfume so that I could mark my territory, feminine hygiene products that were a different brand from what Meredith used, and a book of love poetry that I was going to leave under her bedside table. I had doubts about that last one. She'd been living with Harris long enough to know he wasn't the love-poetry type. Still, the message would be loud and clear. *You're losing this battle*, it proclaimed.

My ace was inside a pink box that came from a Lower East Side shop that most people wore sunglasses to go inside. It was an adult toy called the Flower Power, and it promised hours of solo pleasure. That was going inside Meredith's bedside table. I was still mulling over writing a note to go with it. *You must be lonely*, I wanted to say, wondering if that was enough of a taunt.

And then I found her note. It was on a plain yellow Post-it note on her dresser, under a jar of Valmont skin cream that cost roughly the same as my monthly rent. *Hands off Hedge Hog*, it said. *None of this belongs to you.*

Was this woman nuts? Did she think that writing little notes to me was going to scare me away? There was something creepy about it, true, but it spoke volumes about her, the fact that she knew I was in her home, and that her only defense against me was through Post-its. She must be feeling threatened. She knew that I was there. She didn't know my name, or any details about me, but she'd gotten the message. I was winning. Poor Meredith.

The only thing was, I wasn't entirely sure I wanted the prize that was within my grasp. True, I loved trying on Meredith's designer clothes, but I wanted my own. I stole her lotions and potions; Meredith's dressing table was like a candy store for women who'd had to give up edible treats to stay thin.

"You'd better not be getting vain like *her*," Harris huffed one morning when he caught me staring into the dressing table's mirror. I'd been examining the fine lines that had etched themselves into the delicate skin under my eyes. If they'd been obvious enough for Harris to see, he'd replace me in the time it took to get more black-truffle burgers delivered.

That was the thing about Harris: His life was all about what he wanted. While I stayed with him that week, I discovered how brutish he really was. It wasn't that he was cruel; he just didn't think that anyone else had needs. He'd order food for himself and forget about me. In bed, he acted like I was his slave. But I pretended to enjoy every moment, and that made him very happy. One night, after he pushed me off him and rolled over to snort down another line of cocaine, I asked him if he'd ever had this much fun with Meredith.

"No," he answered. "Never."

"Really?" I was intrigued. "What's she like in bed?"

"We don't do much anymore. I have more fun with other girls."

Other girls? Was there one besides me? Tension shot down my back, straightening my spine. "Oh, you have other girls?" I said, in a teasing voice. "Why don't you ask them over so we can party together?"

"I'm not seeing anyone else right now. Just you, Lacey." It was probably as close to a declaration of affection as I'd ever get from him.

"But there have been other girls, before me?"

"Sure." Harris lit a cigarette and lay back.

"What happened to them?"

"Sometimes I get tired of them. Sometimes they meet someone else. And sometimes…" His eyes looked hazy, as if he were working on a puzzle. "Things just don't work out."

Who wouldn't want to take your calls? I thought. "Have you ever thought about breaking up with Meredith?"

"Sure."

"But you haven't done it."

"I did once."

"Really? What happened?"

"There was this other girl who I…well, I fell for her, and Meredith…well, Meredith was being Meredith." He dragged on his cigarette. If only it could have made him more articulate. "But it didn't work out. The other girl…changed."

"Changed how?"

Harris stared at the ceiling. I repeated my question, but he wouldn't look at me. "It just didn't work out," he said finally.

"So Meredith moved back in?"

"Yeah. She makes my life…well, not easy, but it's…familiar, I guess. Even though I kind of hate living with her." He took a long drag. "Sometimes I think she likes it that I sleep with other women, so I don't bother her. My own wife doesn't want me." His eyes were watery.

"You mean she doesn't work at pleasing you?" I leaned over and kissed him.

"She's not like you, Lacey. You work really hard at making me happy." He was staring at me intently. "If she moved out would you move in?"

"Are you asking me to?" In spite of everything, I was still eager. I wanted to live in that apartment.

"Yes." His voice was quiet, almost shy. "I don't like to be alone. If she moves out, you'd have to move in immediately."

"I think that could be arranged."

"It would be fun, having you here all the time." He crushed his cigarette. "You wouldn't travel all the time and leave me here, would you?"

"Never," I promised, tempted to cross my fingers.

"I bet we'd have a lot of fun together," he said.

"Oh, we would."

"I'll think about it," he said.

I wanted to slap him. The way he sounded made it seem entirely his decision, not mine. His job at the hedge fund and his money had made him incredibly arrogant. Still, that money was what I wanted.

"I'll make you happier than she ever has," I said, going on to argue my point without words.

When I left Harris's apartment after that extended visit, I was pleased with myself. But as I stepped outside, into the sunshine, it hit me that he hadn't so much as given me cab fare back to Flatbush.

It hit me then what a sweet deal Meredith had.

There I was, standing on the street with my overnight bag, crammed full of little luxuries I'd pilfered from Meredith's dressing table. Perfume, skin-perfecting serums and creams, luxe makeup, and a pair of silver earrings that she must have deemed not important enough to lock up. I'd picked up her leavings and kept her husband occupied while she was off in a tropical paradise.

She didn't want Harris, but she wasn't going to divorce him, either. The fact that he was sleeping with me actually enabled him to stay with her.

That realization hurt. I wandered, dazed, to the subway entrance on Lexington, but I couldn't make myself walk down the stairs. It wasn't that I was afraid of the subway, but I dreaded the moment when I would have to return to my crappy apartment in Flatbush. The thought of turning all three locks and stepping inside a room that stank of mold and mu shu pork was more than I could bear just then. Instead I wandered south, found myself in front of a church, and was drawn inside.

It had been years since I'd stepped into a church, much less a confessional. I wasn't ready to go that far now, but I reflexively dipped my hand into the font, then slipped into a pew. There were a few other people sitting in the church, and they stared ahead, almost as if the priest were performing Mass. I opened my bag and extracted the Post-it note: *Hands off Hedge Hog. None of this belongs to you.*

How many times had Meredith written notes like that to the different women Harris had cheated with? I was just the latest in a long line, and suddenly, it didn't seem worth it. It wasn't as if I loved Harris. I adored his apartment and craved his lifestyle. But I didn't even like him, and I shuddered to think of the life ahead of me, with Harris pawing at me and then shoving me aside. I was doing wrong, and it wasn't even getting me anywhere.

Stop now, I told myself. *Move on*. There are plenty of other rich guys out there. I decided then and there that I wasn't crawling after Harris anymore. And I was going to run the other way if he came after me. There had to be someone better.

My resolution lasted almost three months. That was long enough for me to have the satisfaction of blowing Harris off the next several times he tried to get me to sleep with him.

"But why not?" he asked me, once he realized I was serious. "We have a good time together, Lacey. I thought you cared about me."

"You're married, and I'm not interested in a married man."

The wounded expression on his jowly face was priceless. Better yet, I met Nigel, another hedge-fund manager, but one who was a handsome triathlete with a sexy South African accent. For a month, I thought I'd died and gone to heaven, until I actually almost died. Nigel had flown me—on a private plane—to Bermuda for a weekend.

"What I love about you, Lacey, is that you don't have any inhibitions. You don't, do you?" he asked.

"None at all," I'd answered. His hands caressed my neck, and then he started to throttle me. I tried to scream, but no sound came out of my mouth but a choked gurgle. His green eyes were wide with excitement, and the more I panicked, the more they gleamed. Then I blacked out. When I woke up, Nigel was sipping champagne and smoking a Cuban cigar. I was on the floor.

"That was lovely, Lacey," he said. "You do bruise up terribly, though."

There were marks on my throat where he'd gripped me, a necklace of black and blue. After that, Harris started looking pretty good again. Especially since he was pursuing me. There were flowers and plaintive phone calls. He bought me a bracelet from Tiffany & Co., and when that didn't work, a necklace from Harry Winston. He couldn't understand what had happened, but he'd do anything to get me back, he said.

"Then get rid of Meredith," I told him.

He did, and I moved into his apartment the next day. It was even more gorgeous than I remembered. Meredith hadn't smashed any glass or done any damage. Instead, she'd packed up her jewelry and some clothing and personal items and left. Harris didn't know where she'd gone. Her clothing was still on hangers and most of her shoes were there, but the luxurious toiletries and makeup were gone.

But there was a note on her dressing table: *Hedge Hog is all yours. Enjoy it while it lasts.*

It amazed me that she hadn't put up more of a fight. She'd vanished with barely a whimper. Was that note her attempt to mock me, or make me feel insecure or guilty? It was a failure. I crumpled it up and threw it out.

It was true that living with Harris wasn't going to be any picnic. While I was in the apartment, I still didn't have any money, and Harris wouldn't give me any.

"If you need something, tell me and I'll buy it for you," he said.

I'd already made a list of things I wanted to get. The top of my list was an appointment with a Park Avenue dermatologist known for her amazing ability to suspend her patients' aging process.

"Are you kidding me?" Harris asked. "Meredith wasted so much of my money on crap like that. No way."

The only thing he seemed to think of as a reasonable purchase was lingerie. He ordered a selection of it for me. On the same day that my French maid's costume arrived, so did a box for Meredith. It was from a department store, and it was filled with her monthly supply of beauty products. It seemed heaven-sent. There was a collection of small bottles from Sisley-Paris, filled with their famous elixir, and RéVive's precious serum—$600 an ounce!—that promised to turn over dead skin cells at a rate eight times faster than normal skin. My heart skipped a beat. I ran with it to the bathroom, washed my face, and put on some serum. It immediately stung my skin, which seemed a sure sign that it was working. I gently tapped on some eye cream, and it made my fingers sizzle as well as my face. *That's some powerful stuff*, I thought. But it was only when I misted my face with what was supposed to be a skin-softening balm that I felt scorching pain. It was as if someone had seared off the top layer of my skin. I screamed and splashed water on my face, but when I looked in the mirror, my skin was completely red, and my eyes were puffed up like a bullfrog's.

"Acid burns don't heal normally," the doctor told me in the hospital. That was much later, after they'd sedated and restrained me because of the pain.

They put me on an IV that gave me the means to push the pain away, but it lurked by me, trying to get closer. What I wanted was a mirror, but they wouldn't let me near one.

"Plastic surgery will help," the doctor added. "But it will take several operations. Insurance won't cover most of it. Do you have anyone who can help you financially?"

"My boyfriend," I said. The words came out garbled, because the thin skin of my lips had been burned away.

"All right. We'll talk with him when he comes in," the doctor said.

Harris came in once, while I was sleeping, I was told by a nurse. I waited for him to come back, then asked a nurse to call him, then tried calling him myself. The bandages on my hands made it hard to do. Or maybe that was the pain medication. Either way, I couldn't reach him.

Then the note arrived.

> *Dear Lacey, I'm so sorry that things didn't work out between us. I wish you all the best.*

It wasn't signed, but it didn't need to be. I recognized Meredith's handwriting.

Jenny's Necklace

by O.A. Tynan

The last time I saw Jenny, she was lying unconscious in the sandy hollow at the foot of Danagher's Head. Its looming shadow concealed us from the eye of the summer sun. Her cheek lay against a sea-smooth stone, her blue dress flared from her waist like the gown of a fairy princess, a fleck of green seaweed was caught in her wavy brown hair. Her white high heels, her Sunday best, were nowhere to be seen. Her necklace, too, was gone. It was quiet in the hollow; even the seagulls wheeling overhead were silent. The only sound was the tide whispering in under the barrier of rocks and then a sudden hoarse shout as someone found us.

That was long ago, in the summer of 1961. I was nine years old at the time and still remember the horrible hushed atmosphere about the house after I was dragged, kicking and screaming, my dress soaked from the tide, away from Jenny. The window blinds were drawn halfway down, a sign a death had occurred. Jenny had only fainted, so perhaps it was the uncle who suffered from a weak heart. "Mark my words," my mother often said. "One minute alive and breathing, the next dropped down dead at our feet. That is how it will be."

The dead person was the uncle who suffered from a weak heart and who had dropped down dead at someone's feet, and I was supposed to mourn

155

him, but I could think only of Jenny. My mother warned me to stay out of the way in my room, but I stole out and flitted about, a skinny pigtailed ghost keeping watch for Jenny's return. Any minute I expected to catch sight of her coming in the back door, hear the clang of the iron kettle as Philomena, my mother's cook-housekeeper, a moody woman given to violent likes and dislikes but devoted to Jenny, offered her a cup of tea.

The comings and goings continued on through the afternoon. I recognized Sergeant Monaghan's voice several times. He had a habit of coughing to clear his throat and then sounding hoarser than ever. Towards evening the doorbell stopped ringing, but Jenny still hadn't returned. I was in the hall near the coat stand and burrowed just in time into the scratchy folds of a tweed greatcoat as my parents emerged from the sitting room. I stood statue-still and they stopped a few paces from my hiding place, unaware I could hear everything they said.

"My summer has been ruined," my mother was saying. "Utterly ruined."

"My dear, it is most unfortunate." My father tried to console her in his courteous, elderly way and I imagined him patting her arm. "Perhaps," he added tentatively, "we might consider putting the house up for sale?"

"Good gracious, don't be absurd!"

I knew my mother when her voice sharpened like that. She said an unhappy fatality had occurred, tragic and shocking, yes, but they had more than exonerated their responsibilities in the matter by offering to shoulder the funeral expenses. Perhaps they might go abroad for the last week of August, fortunately imminent, saying the trip had been planned all along, but selling was *absolutely* out of the question. Summer holiday houses were becoming the fashion, and this particular stretch of Ireland's southwest coast was very much sought after. "Where," she asked my father, "would we ever find another summer house of the same distinction and in such a dominant position overlooking the town? Nowhere!" she answered for him.

In a more satisfied tone, she went on to say it might be wiser to remain at the seaside until the week was out, their departure from Kilcurtan mustn't seem hasty. They could fly out from Shannon to somewhere on the Continent; Rome, or maybe Paris, several of her friends had already travelled to both places more than once. Or perhaps Vienna; the Austrian capital was becoming fashionable. As for me, it would be better to send me back home to Roscrea first thing in the morning; she would inform the caretaker's wife of my arrival. But there was no real cause for concern; it was sufficient never to mention Jenny's name in my presence again. "The child," she said to my father, "will soon forget she ever had a governess named Jenny. And so will you."

My father sighed, and I heard the faint brassy pop of a shirt-collar stud coming loose. "Stop that!" my mother snapped, and I imagined her pressing a wrist to her forehead as she told him to fetch her cigarets and a small glass of gin because she had a migraine coming on.

I never saw Jenny again and I was supposed to forget her, but how could I? When, in the winter before she disappeared, my mother led her up to the gloomy Roscrea schoolroom, I couldn't believe that someone like Jenny was to be my new governess. Except for the darned woollen gloves and shabby clothes, Jenny looked nothing like my previous governesses, and I thought it was some kind of trick. Jenny's cheeks bloomed with fairy softness. From under an old navy beret her hair descended in gleaming brown waves almost to her shoulders. I was probably glowering with mistrust, but Jenny smiled and held out her hand to me, and the bloom on her cheeks didn't fade and her smile didn't wither.

I hesitated, then started to inch away from the scratched schoolroom table and hurtled into Jenny's arms. I hugged her so tightly I'm sure I almost choked her, but when at last I released my grip, Jenny's brown eyes were still smiling and her scent of violets remained on my cheek. My mother glared at me for my bad manners, but said nothing as she left the schoolroom. Now it was up to Jenny to do something about my comportment and scholastic education.

From the first day, Jenny allowed me into her tiny bedroom, forbidden territory with my other governesses, and I could have watched for hours while she brushed her wavy brown hair. At night, Jenny went to bed without applying steel hair clips and a hairnet as my mother did, and woke the following morning with the same gleaming waves, which meant they were natural.

My mother was tall, fair-haired, and fair-skinned and much admired for her sophistication and the elegant way she held a cigaret. My father was plump and silver-haired and, because of his courteous manner, considered the perfect gentleman. I was an only child and didn't resemble either parent in appearance or manner. My starved looks and thistly black pigtails were a trial to my mother and to me, although I pretended I didn't care. But I knew how similar misfortunes came about. Sometimes mischievous fairies exchanged newborn babies in their cradles, and that was what had happened to me.

But it didn't matter to Jenny how I looked, and she never pulled my pigtails. Her scent of violets, I discovered, came from a gold-capped flacon which she kept, together with her makeup and treasured keepsakes, in an old cardboard chocolate box with Christmas robins and snowy holly sprigs on the lid. Jenny never minded when I took the box onto my lap to examine each precious item: a rayon handkerchief printed with orange tulips, two lipstick stubs, a Pope John XXIII medal, a cracked pancake compact, a postcard signed by three orphanage nuns who'd taken a pilgrimage to Lourdes, and the gold-capped perfume flacon on which was written *Nuits à Paris* in violet lettering. Jenny and I pronounced it *Newts a Pond* and how we giggled over that. Jenny hadn't known *nuit* meant night in French, which confirmed she wasn't a very good governess, but that didn't matter one jot to me as long as my mother didn't find out. Instead of poring over schoolbooks, we played Beggar-my-neighbour, Noughts & Crosses, or daubed the pages of old copybooks with the colours from a tin paint box Jenny bought me one day as a present. The instant I heard my mother's footsteps climbing the narrow wooden stairs up to the schoolroom, I would grab a schoolbook and start calling Jenny "Miss."

"The Lord save us from all harm!" Jenny would gasp as soon as my mother had finished her sweeping inspection of the schoolroom and had left. "Sure, hasn't she eyes in her head that would frighten the wits out of you."

It was true that there were times my mother stared so intensely the whites of her eyes seemed wild and bloodshot. As the sound of her footsteps receded down the stairs, Jenny, still affrighted, would mumble a Hail Mary, sketch the Sign of the Cross—a hasty circuit of her forehead, breast, and left and right shoulder as though she wished to set a miniature windmill going—and then look relieved as though absolved from some guilty act or sin. I could never imagine what someone as gentle and devout as Jenny could do wrong; she always said her morning and night prayers, paid attention at Mass, and went to Confession once a week. I was the wicked one who sooner or later would end up breaking all the Ten Commandments.

Jenny was an orphan brought up by the Good Shepherd nuns, and had nowhere to go during the summer months, so my mother invited her to spend the holidays with us at Kilcurtan. The agreement was that, on half-pay, Jenny would keep me occupied and "help a little around the house."

Afterwards, I discovered what that innocuous little phrase meant. It meant that Jenny had to get up at six every morning to sweep and clean and do the laundry, which included starching and ironing my father's collars and shirts and my mother's linen dresses. While my parents breakfasted, Jenny cleaned the bedrooms and made the beds, after which it was time to take charge of me and make sure I stayed out of everyone's way. Everyone's way included Philomena, the cook-housekeeper, who complained that I had a look in my eye that could turn milk sour.

But I didn't care about my elegant mother, about my gentlemanly father, about half-mad Philomena, or even about Jenny when I discovered how overworked she was. I was filled with delight. The seaside had always seemed a dull place to me, but with Jenny everything was different. It was the most wonderful summer of my whole life—a summer that ended when Jenny disappeared. Jenny had never been to the seaside before, and together we made many exciting discoveries. We would skip down to the little town feeling the sun on our faces. We would take the shallow steps down onto the beach, where we paddled and splashed and built sandcastles that never lasted. We would stroll along the promenade, then take the winding path up to the top of Danagher's Head, where we would gather pink and white sea flowers to make caterpillars that blew away with the wind.

Quite often, we would find that Sergeant Monaghan had followed us up to Danagher's, and he would cough and clear his throat and try to talk to Jenny, or sometimes just stare at her. I would snigger behind my hands without quite knowing why, and Jenny would stop picking flowers and tuck her flapping skirt between her knees. Once, when my father anticipated his postprandial constitutional to the summit, Sergeant Monaghan happened to be there, staring. My father raised his Panama hat, bowed courteously to Jenny and to me, then paused, tapped the ferrule of his silver-knobbed cane on a rock, and said "Good day," to the sergeant in a stern way. I watched as Sergeant Monaghan's face became swollen and red. "Sure what would I be doing up here on a windy day like this," he muttered hoarsely, "unless 'tis to warn ye keep away from the edge."

Not long after that, Jenny said she didn't want to make flower caterpillars anymore, so instead we found a spot on the barrier of rocks at the foot of Danagher's Head. There, we would sit on a slab of pewter rock to gaze at the shifting jewel colours of the sea and laugh if sea spray caught us unawares. Sometimes, we would search among the rock pools for shells and unusual sea creatures, or play hide-and-seek using the gaps and hollows in the rocks as hiding places. When Jenny won, she would pounce and then cuddle me in case I'd taken fright.

As the days went by and my mother had no complaints to make, Jenny and I became bolder. We broke my mother's rules and wandered through the little town like day-trippers, munching on chocolate bars or licking penny ice creams. We bought periwinkles wrapped in newspaper from noisy vendors and learned to extract with a pin the whorled mollusks that tasted so tart our tongues curled. We crossed the threshold of the moth-eaten cinema where musty smells clung to our clothes as we gazed at true love conquering all in flickering Technicolor.

And one Saturday afternoon, following the source of strange, chaotic music coming from a field behind Danagher's Head, we plunged into the dizzying excitement of the carnival.

It was shortly before my bedtime on the evening of that same Saturday, in Jenny's poky bedroom beside the pantry, that I first set eyes on Jenny's necklace. Jenny was brushing her hair in front of the sea-rusted mirror propped on the warped dresser, and I kept bouncing up and down on Jenny's rickety bed and breaking into hectic bursts of laughter, still excited from our afternoon at the carnival.

"Hush!" Jenny set her brush down and sketched the Sign of the Cross—the windmill dab on her forehead, breast, left and right shoulder. "Your mother might hear you."

"And what if she does!" I shouted.

"Hush now and I'll show you something."

Jenny opened the top drawer of the dresser where she kept her cardboard treasure box, and I jumped to the floor and held my breath as she removed the lid and held up something pearly and white for me to see.

"Oh, Jenny," I said. "It's like something a princess might wear."

Jenny smiled and with her free hand, stroked my cheek. Then she turned back to the rusted mirror, lifted her brown waves from her nape, and clipped on the pearly necklace. The bloom on Jenny's cheeks never faded, but that day, wearing the necklace, she glowed with an enchanted radiance I had never seen before. She smiled and again came the sketchy windmill gesture, but with her left hand because with her right she was touching the necklace. I remembered that Father Clooney often warned against making the Sign of the Cross with the wrong hand, because it brought bad luck. He said it must always be the right because the left hand belonged to Beelzebub himself. But I didn't say that to Jenny. Instead, I pulled at her skirt and asked if she could give me the necklace.

"I can't give it to you, honeybunch," she said. She often called me "honeybunch," which I liked; the nickname came from the Hollywood film-star magazine she had found one day on the beach. "I just can't."

"But why can't you give it to me, Jenny? Why?"

"Oh, honeybunch, I can't. I just can't."

Jenny seemed truly distraught that she had to refuse me and tried to console me with a stub of crimson lipstick instead. She made a game of painting my lips with it and adding some pancake to my cheeks, but the result was disappointing because my skin had turned a grubby brown from the sun and my pigtails seemed spikier than ever. I wasn't ungrateful for the lipstick, but couldn't help thinking that if Jenny had given me the necklace instead, my ugliness would slough from me like the skin of a lizard and I would look beautiful too.

"At least tell me *why* you can't give it to me," I kept saying. Poor Jenny, how I pestered her. I can still hear that petulant childish whine, and in the end, I wore her down, because she told me.

"It's a present from my boyfriend," she said softly. "I can't give it to anyone—not even to you."

"Sergeant Monaghan!" I said.

Jenny shuddered. "That fella!"

So Jenny had a boyfriend who wasn't Sergeant Monaghan, and I was glad at least for that because I didn't like him either. But I couldn't speak. I felt betrayed, excluded, unloved by the one person I believed truly loved me.

But Jenny understood me. "Don't be upset," she said, kissing the top of my head. "That doesn't mean I'd ever leave you. Sure, I'd never leave my little honeybunch. Never."

She dabbed a spot of perfume behind her ears and dabbed a little behind mine too. Her gentleness and the scent of violets warmed me a little. "You never told me you had a boyfriend," I said sullenly. "How long has he been your boyfriend?"

"I met him this afternoon at the carnival."

"But I didn't see you with anyone!"

"It was while you were on the swings," she said apologetically. "He came up to me and asked me my name. He gave me the necklace and asked me to be his girl. He said he'd seen me in the town several times before, so it wasn't as if we were strangers."

Much of Jenny's meagre salary was spent on Holy Masses for her mother, whom she had never known, but she had set aside a little pile of silver sixpences and shillings for cinema matinees, chocolate bars, and ice creams. At the carnival, Jenny had paid for several rides for me on "the swings," a merry-go-round with seats suspended on chains that spun faster and faster and wider and wider so that it felt like flying above the earth. While I had been spinning through the air, Jenny had been below, a blur, talking with her boyfriend. And I hadn't noticed.

"You were going to keep your boyfriend a secret from me, weren't you?" I said.

She hesitated. "If the mistress ever found out…"

"Jenny! You don't think I'd tell my mother on you."

"Sure, don't I know you wouldn't. It's not that at all."

"What is it, then?"

Jenny's smooth forehead wrinkled in a small, worried frown. "The Lord save us, I don't know who to be more frightened of, your Ma or me boyfriend! He said I was to swear never to tell a soul about the pair of us."

There were times Jenny lapsed into her country brogue and we usually giggled together over that. But not now.

"Jimmy's after havin' a little trouble with the police," Jenny went on, "but it wasn't his fault at all, he explained all that to me, they had it in for him. But if the mistress ever found out about him, she'd march the pair of us down to the police station and then sure wouldn't he kill me stone dead!"

"Is he tall, dark, and handsome?"

"Is he *handsome?*" Jenny's eyes sparkled. "Sure, isn't he just like a Hollywood fillum star!"

I was eaten up with jealousy, but also thrilled that Jenny was being courted by someone who looked exactly like a film star and what was more, someone innocently in trouble with the police.

"So you're going to meet him tonight," I said, having understood the significance of the perfume and that she was changing into her Sunday best, her blue flared dress and white high heels.

Jenny nodded happily. "We're going to meet on top of Danagher's Head. He said he'd something very important to ask me, so I mustn't be late."

I looked up at Jenny. She was again touching the necklace.

"Can I try it on?" I asked.

"Of course you can."

Jenny went to the trouble of removing the necklace and clasping it around my neck. Even standing on my toes, it was difficult to see the effect properly in the rusted mirror, and I gave the necklace back to her reluctantly.

"I know what I'll do," she said, smiling. "I'll leave it to you in my will."

"Does that mean that one day the necklace will be mine?"

"All yours, honeybunch. Cross my heart and hope to die," she said, making the well-known gesture of sworn promises, as binding as any oath on the Bible.

Jenny raised her brown waves and clipped the necklace on again. Then she took my hand and led me off to bed. I was close to tears. I couldn't have Jenny's necklace and Jenny dying was something I couldn't bear to think about. But that same evening, Jenny had blessed herself with her left hand and less than sixteen hours later, she was lying unconscious in the sandy hollow at the foot of Danagher's Head.

The morning after Jenny disappeared, I was sent back to Roscrea by train. Just before dawn, I had tiptoed to Jenny's poky room for a last time, wary of Philomena, who slept near the kitchen too and was a light sleeper.

But Jenny still hadn't returned. Instead, I found her rickety bed stripped, the mattress rolled up, the dresser drawers emptied, Jenny's few garments removed from their wire hangers which hung askew on the back of the door. The little room was bare of her presence but for the chocolate-box lid, a snowy corner of which I spotted protruding from under the dresser. I searched the little room again, but the rest of the box and its precious contents had vanished into thin air.

My parents left for the Continent and I remained in Roscrea. When my parents returned, my mother engaged a new governess who looked nothing like Jenny. I never stopped thinking about Jenny. I dreamed of her almost every night. Sometimes the dreams were nightmares. Jenny's hair would be damp and straggled by the tide, her mouth silently agape, her nylon stockings torn, her toes bleeding, her white high heels gone, her necklace gone. There were times I smelled violets, as though Jenny stood behind me, but when I turned, she would not be there. I considered running away from home and taking the train to Kilcurtan to look for Jenny, but my mother would inevitably find out and send me to a reform school where they kept you forever if your wickedness knew no bounds.

Children are strange; they form strange ideas. When I think of myself as a child all those years ago, I see another person acting with an illogical childish logic. We are joined only by our sad memories of Jenny and the unsolved mystery of her disappearance.

That last evening, the evening I first saw Jenny's necklace, we met my father in the corridor as Jenny led me off to bed. He bowed and complimented her, as he always did, on the way she starched and ironed his collars and shirts, and helped him find the shirt-collar studs he was constantly losing. He held her hand and patted it sadly, and I remember thinking it was because someone else had given her the necklace. As an afterthought, my father wished me pleasant dreams. Before Jenny came, I rarely saw my father, although when we happened to meet, he always had a kind word for me and when, ten years later, he died from pneumonia, he wished me to have his Panama hat.

"I'll stay with you for a little while," Jenny said as she arranged the bedcovers about me. "I'll stay with you till you get to sleep."

Jenny, sweet gentle Jenny, had realized I was still upset she couldn't give me the necklace, and didn't have the heart to rush away to meet her boyfriend until she was sure I had fallen asleep. But how cruel children can be. I can't bear to remember how cruel I was. That evening sleep eluded me. I was wakeful and fretful and clung to Jenny's hand as though I might die without her. When she tried to slip her hand away from mine, I gripped her fingers tighter. I heard the clock in the sitting room chime midnight, twelve slow notes. Jenny removed her blue dress to avoid crushing it, but not the necklace, and lay beside me. That was how Jenny passed the night—lying beside a fractious nine-year-old child who refused to sleep.

The following morning was warm and sunny. After ten-o'clock Mass, Jenny suggested we might take a stroll along the promenade in the direction of Danagher's Head. She looked thoughtful and subdued. Because it was Sunday, she was wearing her Sunday best. And her new pearly necklace. She was fingering it every now and then and pausing to look anxiously over her shoulder. Perhaps she was thinking of her boyfriend and of how angry he would be because of the missed date. The "something very important" was surely a proposal of marriage. He would have gone down on bended knee, opened a small velvet box to reveal a sparkling engagement ring, and asked Jenny to do him the honour of becoming his wife.

I glanced at Jenny. Her cheeks were pale. I thought that if she sat on a rock with her legs folded under her, wearing the pearly necklace and singing a mournful song, she could be mistaken for a mermaid. She had the faraway look mermaids usually wore when they were sad or lovelorn.

When we came close to Danagher's Head, Jenny wanted to take the path up to the summit, but I wanted to go down onto the beach instead and from there, climb onto the barrier of rocks at the foot of the cliff. A purple sea urchin we had captured a few days before had died, and I wanted to look for another among the rock pools. Jenny agreed halfheartedly, but by the time we had tramped over the sand and clambered onto the barrier, I had developed a sulk and told her I didn't want the sea urchin anymore, that I wanted to climb to the top of Danagher's instead.

"Oh, you mustn't do that," Jenny said, looking up at the summit. "It's very steep. If you want to get to the top we must take the path." Jenny hadn't removed her white high heels or nylons for clambering onto the rocks, and I wondered if it was because she still hoped to meet her boyfriend.

"I don't *want* to go all the way back," I said. It wouldn't have taken us long, but I wasn't going to be crossed. "Besides, it's not all that high and I'm sure lots of people have climbed up from here before."

"They might have," Jenny retorted. "But you're not to. It's very steep and you might slip and fall down onto the rocks. You could even get yourself killed."

"But I *want* to!" I said.

"You're not to go climbing up there now," Jenny said even more crossly. It was all so unlike her. Then her brown eyes seemed to soften as she added sadly, "What would I do if anything ever happened to my little honeybunch?"

She was touching her necklace again. At the foot of Danagher's it was more secluded, because swimming from the barrier was dangerous. Jenny hadn't stopped looking over her shoulder, perhaps both hopeful and fearful that her boyfriend had followed her and might suddenly appear from nowhere.

There's no doubt that Jenny was unlike herself that day. I was already more than halfway up the craggy face of the cliff when I heard her cry out from below. She called out I was to stay where I was, that she was coming for me. I continued to climb. I felt no fear, I wouldn't fall, nothing could happen to me. I felt secure as a spider that can go anywhere it likes, my stick-thin arms and legs moving steadily. I heard Jenny's voice getting closer and closer; she kept repeating I mustn't move until she reached me, I mustn't move.

"Please don't move, please don't move," she kept saying. I looked down. She was a little below me, her beautiful face upturned, her lips moving all the time, coaxing, urging, soothing. I was glad she seemed to have forgotten her boyfriend, that now all her concern seemed only for me.

It's hard to describe what happened next. Each time I remember a different version of those dreadful moments. I can still feel the pitted rock under my fingers, then the sudden hurting dazzle of the sun as I neared the summit. It seemed to me as Jenny reached my side and stretched out her hand to me, that her expression changed. But had it really? Had Jenny's brown eyes seemed strange and unfamiliar because I was blinded by the sudden dazzle? And had the silent shadow that loomed over us been just a passing cloud? Or someone standing among the pink and white sea flowers, leaning over and staring down with ill intent as we clung to the rock face looking blindly up?

I often wonder about the silent shadow that had startled Jenny. The devil, I used to think, because the evening before she disappeared she had blessed herself with her left hand, Beelzebub's hand. I worried too that I had put an evil spell on her because I had coveted the necklace, but as the years went by and Jenny still didn't return, I evolved more rational theories.

Perhaps the shadow had been my father, concerned for Jenny's safety and looking forward to an eternal search for shirt-collar studs. Or Jenny's criminal boyfriend, angry for the lost night of love. Or Sergeant Monaghan, who hoped to keep Jenny all to himself. Or my mother, who had seized the moment to harm Jenny, afraid her circle of friends might start gossiping about her husband's infatuation with a girl young enough to be his granddaughter. I even considered moody Philomena struck by a sudden rage, although she rarely left the house and, unlike my mother, I had never known her to walk as far as Danagher's Head.

My father fell ill when I was eighteen and before he died he gave me his Panama hat. "It is my favourite hat," he said, "and I should like you to have it." As he spoke, I wondered if he was thinking of Jenny and the number of times he had raised that same hat to her.

My mother's health deteriorated when I was in my forties and I left my job with a pictorial artists' supply firm to look after her. My mother and I never spoke very much. Once, I asked her if she knew what had happened to Jenny, but she pretended not to remember the name and drifted off into a doze. It seemed a mercy to keep my mother supplied with gin and vodka; the clear, innocent-looking liquid went a long way towards easing whatever pain it was that had always tormented her. For what troubled her worn body she had other therapies that worked less effectively.

When she died, I sold the house in Roscrea and settled in Kilcurtan to be near the place where I had last seen Jenny. Sporadic pilgrimages when I could get someone to stay with my mother were never enough.

What is time? Time is that which has turned an unsightly child, girl, woman into an ageless crone, hard and sinewy as a whip. Winter and summer, I set myself up with my easel on the barrier of rocks at the foot of Danagher's Head, overlooking the hollow where I had last seen Jenny.

I probably never will know who loomed over us the day Jenny disappeared.

Perhaps it was only a passing cloud. Perhaps, had I kept looking upwards, the dazzle might have lessened and I would have seen if someone had really been there. In any case, Jenny, who must have kicked off her white high heels to climb after me, was beside me by then and as she reached out her hand—I am certain it was to help me down to safety, not because she was angry with me for the missed date with her boyfriend—but when I reached out my hand it was to grab for her necklace. Jenny's outstretched hand flew to her throat as the string snapped and the pearls flew like magic dewdrops around in the air and she uttered a small cry, like a seagull lost at sea. Then she floated like a bird away from the cliff, down, down, down into the sandy hollow below.

I have never learned to paint. My pictures are just coloured copybook daubs, but the easel is my rationale to come here to this place where I last saw Jenny. I set aside palette and paintbrush, remove my father's Panama hat, place a stone on the shredded brim so the breeze won't carry it away. I look up at the craggy face of the cliff and start to climb. I feel as steady and fearless as I was on the day Jenny disappeared, all those years ago. I have searched for Jenny in her poky room, in the carnival field, in the cinema, until it was knocked down, in the town, for Sergeant Monaghan's secret cellar. I have searched for Jenny among the pink and white sea flowers, on the curving beach, among the rocks where we used to play hide-and-seek, in the sandy hollow where I had seen her last. Perhaps I will find her here, close to the summit of Danagher's Head, still wearing her pearly necklace, still clinging with one hand to the pitted rock, her other hand outstretched towards me, caught in the evermore, seconds before she fell.

Tradition

by Ed Gorman

At least the caller had the good grace to wait until Amy and I had finished making love. What with a kid and both of us working, the old days of spontaneous and frequent lovemaking were long gone. Now we made appointments, and tonight we'd penciled in a frolic in our bedroom. I can't say it was a frolic as such, but it was one of those times when lust and tenderness reminded me of how much I loved my wife of nine years and how nice it was afterward to lie with her sleeping on my chest.

We'd been a little late getting started because she'd gotten a call from Paula Crane, a fellow high-school teacher. She'd wanted to know all about the English teacher who joined the faculty recently. Since Amy also taught English, Paula assumed that she'd have lots of gossip about the man. Several of the female teachers had been at the house a few weeks back and all they'd talked about was this Bruce Peters. Apparently the women couldn't stop flirting with the handsome bachelor. As Amy hung up, she'd laughed and said, "Sorry, honey. If I didn't know better I'd swear Paula wasn't married. She talks like she's still single."

The clock radio said 11:24 as I reached to pick up the receiver. I had to roll to my right to reach it. I tried to do this without waking Amy up but my acrobatic skills failed. Her blond head snapped up and she looked at me with the fuzzy confused gaze of a child. "What's wrong, honey?"

"The phone."

"Oh." Then, brushing hair from her face, alert now: "Oh, God."

I suppose that is a phrase common to many women married to law-enforcement officers when their phone rings late at night. A mixture of irritation and vague fear.

She sat up and began running a slender hand across her face.

By now I could see Caller ID. My father.

"Just got a call that David Neely is dead."

"Dead? How?"

"All I know is that he's lying on the river road straight down from the cliff behind his A-frame. Dink Hopkins was out on his motorcycle and found him about five minutes ago. Didn't call the shop. Phoned me at home."

"I'll meet you there in about ten minutes."

"Tell Amy I'm sorry about the late call."

Amy was up and hurrying out the bedroom door to check on our daughter. Even though Cindy is six, she still checks on her three or four times a night, the way she did when she was smaller.

I grabbed socks, my L. L. Bean Bison Chukkas, black sweater, jeans, and the plastic loop that carries my official ID, dressing quickly in the Halloween shadows from the naked tree limbs on this cold October night. The last two items were my fedora—and I'm well aware of the vanity involved with wearing it—and the .38 I holster on my belt.

Amy was back in a rush, sliding her arms around me, holding me tight, letting me smell the good clean scent of her hair and recently showered skin. "Did somebody die?"

"David Neely. Dink Hopkins found him on the river road a few minutes ago. That's all I know."

She leaned back. "Oh, God. I wonder if he was murdered—I wonder if it was one of his married women." Then: "Oh, listen to me." Her hands dropped from my sides. In the wan streetlight she looked like a sensual college girl. "Can you be any more of a bitch, Amy? I shouldn't have said that. The poor man's dead. It's just that he was—"

"An asshole."

"Yes. An asshole. He ruined my best friend's marriage."

"Well, Donna had a little something to do with it, too. He didn't exactly force her into that affair." I leaned in and kissed her. "I need to get going. I'll call you on your cell in a while so it won't wake Cindy."

"Love you."

"Love you, too."

Alveron, population 4,680, is in Northern Illinois, fifty-three miles from Lake Michigan. At this time of night everything except a few taverns and convenience stores is closed and the houses, which tend to be small except for a handful of McMansions on the eastern edge of town, are hunkered down in dreams and darkness. There was no reason to use a siren. My father, the county sheriff, would already have dispatched an ambulance as well as the county medical examiner, a capable middle-aged black doctor who had yet to find complete acceptance in the mostly white community. I liked him. Our previous M.E. had been something of a showboat. Our new man had come here to get his kids out of the city. We had the lowest murder rate in the state. Our badge of honor.

I couldn't drive these streets without being at the mercy of memories good and bad. Being the son of the sheriff in a small town means you'll have lots of friends, whether you want them or not. You enjoy something like celebrity. My folks are good and decent people. My father believes that physical force is always the last resort and he has fired more than a few men over the years who have taken their problems out on their prisoners. Last year he hired a young woman as his newest deputy. She and Dr. Thomas face about the same amount of resistance. A black doctor? A female officer? What the hell is going on here? That's Chicago foolishness and not at all for Alveron.

I was the detective in the five-man sheriff's department, meaning that I had gone through the police academy in Chicago and taken four night-school courses in criminology. At that, I was lucky to be anything in the way of law enforcement. I had been the law-breaking son of the town cop. Drugs, reckless driving, more than a few fights, and ten nights spent in one of my father's cells over a two-year period. Amy had been my salvation. We'd been high-school lovers until she could no longer deal with my drinking. Four years after graduation, when my father had a serious cancer scare, he made me promise that I would give up drinking. Even though I promised, it shouldn't have worked. Liquor trumps loyalty. But between giving my word and meeting Amy again after she'd worked in Chicago for a few years, I've managed to stay dry since the day I told the old man I would.

The river was on my right. Pale full moon riding the far piney bend in the river; the silver-limned water cold and forbidding; and several cars lined behind the blue-flashing box of ambulance.

I could see my father talking to one of the paramedics. Like most of us males who bear the name Winters, Con (for Conor) Winters is a tall man who gives the impression, and a true impression it is, of rangy prairie-boy power. He has the red hair, now going to gray, and thoughtful, somewhat melancholy face of our tribe. His pride is that he is not a hayseed lawman. He is, like his own father who preceded him as county sheriff, a reader and a thinker and a man who weighs his words.

The limestone cliff loomed in the lights. I parked and started walking toward the ambulance. Behind me I could hear cars pulling up, parking. The vampires. No matter how late at night, no matter what the weather conditions, they come out. To stare at death. Maybe they think it will buy them some extra time of their own. Voodoo.

The paramedic saw me before my father did. "Here's Cam now," he said, watching me approach.

The night was cold enough for breath to run silver. Mike Sullivan was the paramedic's name. We played softball on the same team in the hot months.

My father said, "Neely's on the gurney over there."

If we'd been alone I would have pointed out that procedure was to leave the body for the detective and the medical examiner before moving it. But I didn't want to criticize my father in front of Sullivan.

"Looks like he won't be bed-hopping much anymore," Sullivan said.

"Not anymore he won't." My father had disliked Neely from the first day the man had moved here six years ago. I remembered sitting in Millie's

Cafe and my father saying, "He'll be trouble, you wait and see." Neely had been here all of two days then. His feelings had never changed. Even the mention of Neely had always brought a harshness into my father's blue gaze.

"Head caved on the left side from the fall," Sullivan said. His lean face brightened into a smirk. "I'm sure even Dr. Thomas'll be able to figure this one out." Sullivan was one of those who found it hard it believe that a black man could be a competent doctor.

"You think you and your crew will ever give him a break, Mike?" It came out harsh, the way I intended.

"You think you two could hold off the bullshit till we figure out what happened here?" my father said.

The children had been chastised.

I walked over to the gurney and pulled back the sheet. In the beam of my flashlight the left side of Neely's head was a stew of blood and bone and brain. His carefully kept dark beard gleamed with soaked red highlights. Neely had been a commercial artist working from the A-frame he rented. But his real work had been in posing as a serious painter. He lectured at the local library frequently, spending most of his time talking about Van Gogh and hinting that his own work, which even I could see wasn't very good, might someday be compared to the man he called "his mentor." If he hadn't been a swaggerer and a pretty-boy none of the married women he'd slept with would have paid any attention to him.

Sullivan came over and stood next to me. "I piss you off?"

"Yeah."

"I'm sorry I shot my mouth off."

"Dr. Thomas is a good man. I'm sick of you and everybody else in this town cutting him down."

"I'll watch it." He nodded to the body. "You can see bone sticking out of that arm."

"Yeah."

"Your dad found three of his imported beer bottles near the cliff. He must have been drunk off his ass. He drank all the time anyway. I saw him half in the bag plenty of times in the afternoon. I was surprised he could service so many women when he was like that." Neely had indeed had a problem with alcohol. Two DUIs and a pair of drunk-and-disorderlies.

Sullivan smiled. "I have a few too many and my little man goes right to sleep."

My father stood beside us now. "Dr. Thomas just pulled up, Sullivan. You heard what Cam here said."

"I hear you, Sheriff. I already apologized to Cam."

"You want to get to work, Cam? I'm assuming this is an accident, but I won't settle on that until you tell me that that's what it is."

In the academy I learned all about such modern crime scene techniques and tools as blood spatter and flight interpretation, electrostatic dust print lifters, portable lasers, and alternate light sources. The problem our little shop has is that these are way too expensive for our budget. On a homicide, we have to get the state boys and girls involved.

One other thing I learned in the academy is that most detectives approach crime scenes pretty much in their own way. They develop their own approach over the years. The two rules are to gather evidence scrupulously and to document everything to help the county attorney make the case when the time comes.

Josh Cummings, our night deputy, arrived at the scene after helping the highway patrol with a two-car accident on the asphalt strip north of the town limits. Teenagers drag racing. Bad pileup, nobody killed. I tried to sound as angry about it as Josh did, but since I'd done a lot of drag racing in my teenage years I suspect my words sounded hollow.

We spent an hour inside the A-frame. At one point, Josh came out grinning. He held a super-size box of super-size condoms. "No wonder the ladies liked him." That was the highlight of our search. No evidence of any foul play. Three dozen or more bad paintings lay against the wall of Neely's large office. No sign of any of the advertisements or brochures he produced. He apparently wanted to keep them secret even from himself.

When we got back outside, my father was working the backyard with a flashlight big as a trapped sun. He had his pipe going, too. The cancer scare had had to do with throat cancer. My mother and I had badgered him into quitting for a few months, but he started smoking again down at the shop and gradually eased back into it at home. My mother told me that she lights a special votive candle once a week for him. But she'd quit arguing with him about it. My father reasoned, quite unreasonably, that all the bike riding he did kept him healthy. A bright, ordinarily realistic man kidding himself into an early grave.

Josh and I used our smaller flashlights to join in the search. The brown autumn grass gleamed with frost. I walked toward the pine trees that formed a windbreak on the far side of the A-frame, the scent of them sweet on the cold night. A narrow trail ran down the center of them. Long before the A-frame had been built, kids my age had ridden their bikes up here much against their parents' will. The cliff, of course, dangerous to play near. And, in fact, since both my grandfather's time as sheriff, there had been three deaths of children who'd fallen from it, smashed on the road below. I'd walked right on the edge of it many times; one time, on a dare, blindfolded.

When the light found something red flashing in the grass I stopped and bent down to see what it was. A large reflector used on the rear fender of a bicycle. With a jagged crack down the middle.

"You find something?" Josh said as he walked toward me.

"Nah," I said, slipping the reflector into my pocket. "I dropped my keys and was just picking them up. You find anything?"

"Just a few beer cans. He sure liked his booze."

We drifted back to the A-frame, where my father stood talking to Dr. Thomas. The doctor is a quiet, slender man who, at forty-five, is starting to lose his hair. His clothes of choice run to button-down long-sleeved shirts, dark neckties, and dark slacks. He carries both a beeper and a BlackBerry. In addition to being the county M.E. he also oversees our little clinic, which he's improved considerably with the meager funds the county has been able to give him.

"Evening, Stephen."

"Evening, Cam."

"I was just telling your father that I should have something for him around breakfast time."

"That makes for a long night. What's the rush?"

My father put his hand on Stephen's shoulder and said, "Cam doesn't understand how us old-timers like to get things done right away."

I smiled at Stephen. "Dad's sixty-three, in case you didn't know."

"Oh, that's all right. My kids think I'm an old-timer, too. I'm used to it. And I don't mind pulling an all-nighter. Have to earn my keep." He nodded to the

A-frame. "Well, he didn't die the way I thought he would."

"Oh?" my father said.

"He's been a patient of mine for the last year. The alcohol was starting to do serious damage to his liver. I suggested him trying AA or even going to a rehab center somewhere. He wouldn't hear of it." He zipped up his blue windbreaker and said, "I'd better get going. Night, everybody."

We said goodnight and watched him walk to his gray Saab.

"Good man," my father said. Then: "I guess that's about it for tonight. Thanks, Cam. Sorry I had to drag you out of bed." He pointed to Josh. "You may as well start making your rounds for the night."

"Right," Josh said. "See you two later."

As we were walking back to our cars, my father said, "You all right?"

"Tired, I guess."

"You never could kid me, Cam. You seem tense. Everything all right at home?"

"Why wouldn't everything be all right at home?"

He stopped and looked at me. Studied me, actually. "You're wound pretty tight, Cam. I just asked a question. A harmless one. And you climbed on my ass. Now I'm asking you, is everything all right at home?"

He was wrong. I'd kidded him all my life and gotten away with it. I kidded him now. "You're right, Dad. We just had a little argument tonight about that outboard motor I want to buy. You know how Amy is about staying on a budget." There'd been no argument, of course. But in the chill and shadow and weariness of the moment it sounded true.

"I knew it," my father said. "I knew something was wrong. And I'm the same way Amy is about budgets. About staying on them. You've always been like your mother. Budgets are just something you write down and then throw away. I'd give that new outboard some more thought before you buy it. The one you've got now is fine."

"Good idea, Dad."

Then we said good night and got into our cars.

In the morning I drove over to the county seat. I had to testify in a trial in which a drunken driver I'd arrested had caused considerable damage to a house he'd rammed his car into. When I got back to the shop just before lunchtime I stopped where my father's bike was padlocked to a steel pole. He rode the ten-speed back and forth to work. I saw what I was afraid I would find.

Millie's was crowded. Tuesday lunches are meat loaf and mashed potatoes. They're as good as the Wednesday spaghetti lunches are bad. There should be a federal investigation into what Millie can do to spaghetti.

My father was in the last booth with his newspaper. It was town etiquette that you did not bother the high sheriff when he was reading his newspaper. Sons were the exception to this rule.

"How'd it go in court?"

"No problem. Open and shut."

He yawned. "Late nights remind me that my retirement's coming up in another year or so."

"I'll believe it when I see it."

"Oh, you'll be seeing it all right. Even if I didn't want to turn in my badge, your mother would force me to. She watches those damned travel channels on cable all the time. She thinks we should spend the rest of our lives being tourists."

"Here you are, Cam."

Millie had gotten her hair tinted red again. The color clashed with her pink waitress uniform. Her dentures gleamed in one of her soft smiles.

"Now tomorrow, young man, I want you to tell me how good my spaghetti is."

I'd been coming in here since I was fourteen. I would always be "young man." "As long as I don't have to swear it on a Bible."

"I think you should arrest this boy of yours, Sheriff."

We laughed as we always laughed. It was a ritual, the dialogue, the smiles, the laughs.

I cleaned half my plate before I said anything. "I saw the autopsy on your desk."

"Accidental death, just the way we figured."

"Drunk and walked too close to the edge."

"Forty-five-foot drop. That'd kill anybody. Plus, he landed on his head."

"Still."

He had his coffee cup halfway to his mouth when I said it. He looked at me straight and hard. And set his cup back down. "Still? Still what, Cam?"

"It's possible—just possible—that somebody gave him a little help falling off that cliff."

"You read the autopsy report."

"Nothing wrong with the autopsy. But an autopsy doesn't give us any sense of whether he fell off or was pushed off."

The blue of the eyes was that special simmering color of my teens and twenties, the eyes that assessed me with anger and disappointment. "I'm halfway through finishing up my report. I'm listing it as an accidental death. Nobody who knew him would have any doubts about that." He made a show of smiling. "Except my son the detective."

I took it from my shirt pocket and laid it in the center of the formica-covered table.

"What's that?"

"Bike reflector."

"I can see that. But what's it supposed to tell me?" But the voice was tighter now and the gaze nervous.

"Nothing special about the reflector. Round, red. One of those that ignites in the dark when light strikes it. There's just one thing wrong with it. Notice the crack down the center."

"I've got eyes, Cam."

"Same as your bike reflector. Cracked in shipping. You took it because it was the last one they had."

He sat back in the booth. "All right. And this is amounting to what?"

"It's amounting to nothing, Dad. I found it near the pine trees at Neely's last night. Right about where the trail was. All I'm wondering is why you didn't tell me you were up there recently."

"I ride my bike all over this town. Up on Indian Cliff included. Not that it's any of your particular damn business. I lost that reflector several days ago—though I don't know why the hell I owe you an explanation about it."

"Look at the condition of it, Dad. That reflector hadn't been there very long. The adhesive on the back still works if you press it against something hard enough. It rained yesterday morning and there was frost last night. The adhesive would have been ruined by either one of those if it had been there for more than a few hours....And you had the body on the gurney before I could look at it."

He was out of the booth before I could say anything else. Out of the booth and out of Millie's front door.

Halloween came and went with the usual damage to a few gravestones and dirty words spray-painted on the high school. In a town this size, it was easy to find the culprits and put them to work undoing their damage. Cindy insisted on wearing her Halloween Cinderella costume every night before bedtime. We had a light snow one night but it melted by noon. And the few downtown stores that had survived the outlet malls a few miles to the west started putting up Christmas decorations. Or Xmas decorations, as a few of them insisted on calling them.

I never mentioned the bicycle reflector again to my father. I'd even begun to wonder if he'd been telling the truth after all. Maybe the reflector really had been in the grass for several days. The first few days after our talk at Millie's had been strained, but one night he and my mother were sitting at our dinner table talking to a delighted Cindy. She much preferred them to

Amy and me. They never gave her orders or scolded her. And they gave her a king's ransom in gifts. Finally, Cindy, as she often did, climbed up on my father's lap and gave him a kiss. Seeing them together I realized how much I loved him and how I needed to let it go with Neely. I wasn't sure what had happened. And now I didn't want to be sure. I wanted to will it all out of existence.

After the meal we were father and son again. With icy rain coming down every other day, we were busy with traffic accidents large and small. And it was because of one of the accidents that I found the photographs.

I was alone in the office, working late, on the computer. Even with a Mac, reporting on traffic accidents is tedious work. My father was bowling that night and I told him I'd file his work, too. I was grabbing his reports when I realized that I needed a requisition form for more supplies. The town council takes its work too seriously. We always joked that one day they'd make us requisition permission to take a piss. The requisition forms were in my father's middle drawer. There was a pile of them. I skimmed three off and was about to close the drawer when I saw the edge of a photograph sticking out from under the stack I'd dislodged.

Who can resist looking at a photograph? I tugged it free and held it up. A minute later I'd pulled four more photographs from under the requisition forms. I took them back to my desk and sat down and stared at them for a long time. They were the kind of thing a private detective takes for a client worried that his or her mate is cheating. They'd been taken with the digital camera my mother had bought my father for his last birthday.

I spent five minutes with them. Given that they showed David Neely and two different women from town entering one of those old-fashioned garden motels, they didn't need to be pornographic to tell their story. In some ways they were worse than pornographic. The prurient mind, and I certainly have one, could paint any picture it wanted to.

The clock stood at nine. My father would still be bowling.

I had two beers while I sat in the cafe section of the bowling alley. I'd never taken to the game. I had too much cool-kid arrogance left over from my youth to ever wear one of those shirts, for one thing. And for another, there was something suffocating about watching adults take it all so seriously, a certain desperation, I guess. Amy always said that I was a snob and in many ways I suppose she was right.

My father came up a couple of times but I didn't mention the photographs. I wanted to be alone with him. The second time he stopped by I caught a look of concern in the blue eyes. He stared at me a bit too long but didn't say anything.

Outside in the parking lot, after all the interminable beery good nights among the two teams, my father started toward his car but I grabbed his arm. "I need to talk to you, Dad."

"Everything all right at home?"

"Fine."

He seemed confused. He had his pipe going. "Then it couldn't have waited till later?"

"I found the photographs, Dad. I was looking for a requisition form in your desk and I came across them."

"I don't know what the hell you're talking about."

"Sure you do."

He not only knew what I was talking about, he gaped nervously around to make sure that we were the only ones in this section of the parking lot.

"Maybe it's not what you think."

"Then again, maybe it is."

He nodded to his car. "Get in. I don't want to talk out here."

He started the engine and turned on the heater. We sat next to each other but didn't talk for some time. His pipe smelled good. The wind was strong enough to rock the car. The lane shut off its lights. There was a prairie loneliness to the way it looked now, a pastel green icon alone on the fields.

"You followed him and then you killed him."

He angled himself so that he could face me. His yellow bowling shirt was gaudy inside his open brown suede jacket. "I'm going to tell you something and after I'm done you can decide what to do about it."

"I'm listening." Then: "I don't enjoy this, Dad. I'm pretty sure you killed him. Murdered him. This isn't easy for me."

"I know it's not, Cam. But at least listen to me."

I listened.

"When your grandfather was sheriff he had three murders in the first few years after he took office. One of them was a tavern fight and two of them were husbands killing wives for being unfaithful. The women had both slept with the same man, a car salesman named Blount. Your grandfather didn't like that at all. Here were two women dead and two men in prison—one of them eventually got executed—and two entire families destroyed. And here was Blount still strutting around town looking for more women to land on. And he seemed to prefer married women, I suppose because there couldn't be any permanent attachments. Well, one day your grandfather saw this Blount coming on to the wife of your grandfather's best friend. The marriage was having some problems so he was afraid the woman might be vulnerable. He told me that after that day he wondered what life would be like here without Blount causing so much pain. But he didn't do anything about it until a woman who worked at the courthouse got into a shouting match with her husband over at Millie's. The story was that Blount had been sniffing around the lady and the husband was jealous. A couple of days later, Blount drowned. It was all accidental, of course."

"Grandfather killed him."

"Then another tomcat showed up a few years down the line. He was even worse than Blount. He was a rock musician. Nobody famous, mostly played little jobs up and down the lake here. But he flaunted it. He wanted people to know he was a lady-killer. Your grandfather watched him ruin the lives of three different families and then he just couldn't put up with it anymore. This Boehner kid electrocuted himself with his guitar equipment one night."

"Grandfather again."

"There was a woman once, too. Came back here when her Chicago sugar daddy dumped her because she'd had the gall to turn thirty-five. Sarah McBain was her name. Damned good-looking woman. And she cut a wide swath. Caused three divorces the first year she was here. Died in a tragic fire."

"And now you're carrying on the tradition. That was what Neely was all about."

"You have any idea how much pain that man caused the people in this town? You ever see the faces of the little kids when their folks are going through a divorce? And here was some drunken so-called artist not giving a damn about any of it. I was pretty damned patient. I even warned him. I was careful not to make it a threat—not anything he could sue the town for—but he got the message and all he did was laugh at me. Said I was just jealous. I would've been mad but I figured that was just par for the course with somebody like him."

"You committed first-degree murder."

He looked straight at me. "Yes, I did. And I don't regret it."

"You've just confessed a capital crime to me, Dad."

"Who the hell do you think you're talking to, Cam? I was sheriff while you were still riding a tricycle. I know damned good and well that I just confessed to a capital crime. But I'm not going to turn myself in for it. I'm going to leave that up to you."

He angled back so that he faced the steering wheel. "Now I need my sleep, Cam. I'm not as young as you, in case you hadn't noticed. I'll see you in the morning."

He put the car in gear and waited for me to get out. He didn't have to wait long.

"Hey, you didn't eat any of that macho-man breakfast I fixed you."

Soy bacon. Egg Beaters and wheat toast with soy margarine. I guessed that was what passed for breakfast macho these days when I was trying to keep weight off and avoid a heart attack before fifty.

"It's good, Dad," Cindy said. She pointed her fork at her empty plate. "I ate every bite."

The smile and the blue, blue family eyes made me reach across the table and take her small hand. "I'll do my best."

"Unfortunately, Cindy, you've got to get ready," Amy said. "The bus'll be here in less than ten minutes. Scoot now. I'll help you with your backpack."

Leaving me alone with a breakfast I had to force myself to eat.

Cindy always went out the front door. She ducked into the kitchen, gave me a tiny wet kiss on the cheek, and then charged through the house, Amy right behind her.

I managed to eat one piece of bacon and half the toast by the time Amy reappeared.

"If I had time I'd find out what's bothering you, honey. But that's always a long, involved process so I'll have to wait until tonight. I counted you getting up three times in the middle of the night and you were sitting down here staring into space when I came down for breakfast. I worry about you. But you know that."

This kiss was on my mouth. And it lingered. But as I was kissing her I had a thought that made me hate myself. Neely had certainly gotten around with married women....Amy had her nights out. I'd always taken her word that she was out with her female friends, usually shopping at the outlet malls and then getting a pizza afterward.

I brought her to me. Kissed her tenderly, ashamed of what I'd been thinking. Then, like Cindy, she was gone.

All the way to the shop I prepared myself for an awkward morning. I wondered if I'd even be able to look at my father. He murdered a man. And basically he was daring me to turn him in.

This morning was his turn to put in a court appearance, so he didn't come through the front door until after eleven o'clock. I was at my desk on the phone, enduring my monthly call from an auxiliary deputy who had a library full of ideas on how to turn our sheriff's department into the same kind of brave and fearless crime-fighting he saw on cop shows every night.

My father remained in the doorway, watching me as I watched him. After I hung up, he said, "Mason want us to start carrying grenades?"

"Ground-to-air missiles."

"Sounds good to me."

He came in and poured himself some coffee and went over and sat down at his desk. His in front of mine. He swiveled his chair around. "It wasn't easy to tell you what I did last night."

"It wasn't easy for me to hear it."

We didn't have to worry about being overheard. Daytime we had two officers in the field—three when I had the time—and so we were left alone frequently. The dispatcher and the jail cells were in a small adjoining building.

Long, lean fingers drew his pipe from his suit-jacket pocket. "You ever think Amy might step out on you?"

The terrible thought I'd had at the breakfast table came back to me. "That's a hell of a thing to ask."

"Think of what would happen to little Cindy if you and Amy split up. If she'd stepped out."

"Well, she hasn't stepped out and she won't step out. Any more than I'd ever step out on her. We're not programmed that way."

"That's what your grandfather used to think. And I used to think it, too. But there's always somebody who comes to this town—usually a man but sometimes a woman—and they destroy people. I'm not naive. They don't force people to sleep with them. Unfortunately, the people want it. Want excitement, want something strange and new. But if that person hadn't come to town, hadn't offered them the opportunity—"

"You murdered a man."

"I'd murder him again. He was going to cause at least two families to come apart. Good people, by and large. Friends of mine. People who belong in a town like this, where they don't have Neelys prowling around like some rabid animal."

"You murdered a man."

He stuck the pipe in his mouth. "Then turn me in, Cam. Pick up that phone and turn me in."

He swiveled back to his desk and went to work.

I enjoyed a hearty meal at the Quick-Pick's microwave. Nothing more refreshing than standing in a convenience store that smells of disinfectant and gulping down a hamburger of questionable origin. But I didn't want to face my father at Millie's.

The manilla folder was on my desk when I got back. I sat down at my desk and opened it up. Inside were copies of three divorce notices from the local weekly. I knew two of the families very well. I'd gone to high school with the man and woman from one divorce and with the woman from the second divorce. The third couple were younger than me.

My father came in just as I was closing the folder. "They missed you at Millie's."

"And the point of this is?" I said, jabbing my finger at the folder.

"The point of it is that when you count up all the children involved, the number comes to nine. One of the fathers is now a useless drunk. One of the women is living on food stamps and can't get much medical care for her kids. And one of the kids who was a very bright student has now turned into a monster who may get kicked out of ninth grade. And Neely was involved in all of it."

"And you murdered him."

"And I murdered him because this is my town and I care about the people here, and because I owe it to them to help them through life as well as I can. And given all the things you did when you were younger—and given the way the town forgave you—I'd say you owe it to them, too. And another thing—" The blue eyes blazed; the voice was furious. "You're so damned smug about this. Like I said last night, you're lucky Amy's never been unfaithful. I half wished I could have told you that she was one of Neely's conquests. She wasn't, but I know damned well how you would have reacted. So don't be so quick about judging me. Now give me that folder back and get it over with."

I was so caught up in his rage that I wasn't quite sure what he meant.

He cleared it up by reaching over to my phone and picking up the receiver. "You know the number of the county attorney. Tell him what I told you. Tell him that he knows where he can find me and that I won't be any trouble at all."

He shoved the receiver at me and then went to his desk and sat down, facing the door.

I don't how long I sat there with it in my hand. Long enough for the dial tone to change into a beeping sound. I wasn't even aware of hanging it up or going to the back near the four empty cells. In the bathroom I washed my face and stared into the mirror. He'd murdered a man. And my grandfather had murdered even more. And now he wanted me to carry on the tradition if I started to see the same pattern happening again.

He was gone when I came up front. I spent the afternoon working on several things, enjoying the luxury of temporary amnesia. He came back later. The temperature had dropped to the low thirties, so his gaunt cheeks were red and the green woolen scarf he wore looked almost festive.

He stood at my desk once again. "You need to turn me in, Cam. For your own sake. I had no right to drag you into this thing, and I don't have any right to ask you to act the way your grandfather and I did. Just give me a little advance notice before you make the call. I'll need to prepare your mother." Then came the real surprise. He leaned over and put his hand on my shoulder and said: "I love you, son. You've turned into a hell of a good man. A lot better man than I've ever been."

My father never played on my sympathies. He was straightforward. Nobody had ever called him a coward, and he wasn't being a coward now.

"I told your mother I'd pick up a pot roast for her over at Shop-Rite. I should be home in half an hour if you want to talk to me." He nodded goodbye and left.

Given all that had happened I'd almost forgotten about picking up Amy at school.

Alveron High came into existence ten years ago when three different small high schools consolidated into one. Better for the budget and for attracting more qualified teachers and expanding the curriculum. Amy had been there six years. She'd spent Cindy's first year at home, but given my salary she had to go back to teaching.

The building was two stories and red brick. The windows were on fire with the dying sun. I pulled up out front. Twisted brown leaves scraped across the grounds, collecting around the silver flagpole. The students were long gone. Teachers began drifting out in twos and threes, talking and laughing. Not that I paid much attention. I was thinking about my father and the copies of the divorce proceedings he'd shown me. And what he'd said about me being so smug. I hadn't suffered any of it, but now as I thought about it, I remembered some of the domestic disturbances I'd covered. The rage and the pain. There is no equivalent to a domestic, seeing people at their rawest. The children are the heartbreakers, crouched in the corner, sobbing and pleading with their parents, or so stunned and afraid that they are frozen in the moment, scalded in their misery, lucky even to have a heartbeat. And the Neelys of the world—some of them married, some not—are often at the center of it all.

And what my father had done was try to relieve some of his people of some of their pain. I saw that now even though I still could not forget that in protecting his town—and I had no doubt he thought that was exactly what he was doing—he'd had to take a life.

And then Amy was coming out of the front door. Sight of her comforted me. I wanted to be home, sitting with Amy and Cindy on the couch. Being goofy the way we got so much of the time. A good dinner finished and a lazy night of watching some good TV shows.

Then he came out right behind her. He put a hand on her shoulder to slow her down. He was laughing and she was smiling. I had no doubt who I was seeing. The new English teacher. The one even Amy's married friend had a crush on.

He was tall and tanned, with dark curly hair. In his white shirt and blue V-neck sweater and chinos he had a young preppy look about him. He was very handsome.

Amy stopped and he came up to her and slipped a piece of paper from one of his books and handed it to her. It was the way she stood hugging her books and staring up at him. A familiar sight from our own high-school days. Except instead of him, it had been me.

Then she said something and started walking toward my car.

I thought of my father and how he said I'd been spared the pain that had ripped apart so many other families.

I was going to have to keep a very close eye on Mr. Bruce Peters. And not only for myself, but for all the good true people of our little town.

Cleopatran Cocktails

by William Burton McCormick

I stare at my reflection in the jewelry case's glass. I'm not a young woman anymore. Lines in the forehead and under the eyes. A bit jowly at the cheeks. A middle-aged face, if I'm honest. Well past time to do something with life.

> *Bob Beamon's leap lasted twenty-three years before being broken.*
> *Roger Maris's sixty-one home runs made it thirty-seven years.*
> *Dan Marino's passing yardage a mere twenty-seven.*

I could never break an athletic record. I'm terrible at sports, as much as I love them.

Beneath the case's glass, on a lavender silk pillow, lies the Tabatskaya Necklace: a string of pearls conservatively valued at thirty million dollars. The third most expensive in the world.

So, here we go.

I glance over at this room's lone guard. Ronnie's away from his station, at the museum window, as he always is on school days at this hour, waving down to his wife and son in the convertible. Her name is Joyce, the boy Jonathan. Ronnie introduced me last week.

A before-school tradition. Very sweet.

And it gives me an extra thirty feet.

I pull the hammer from my purse, smash the glass, seize the necklace.

Alarms go off. People scatter. They don't know I'm unarmed.

Ronnie sees me. Shock in his face. The exhibition security is designed to keep thieves contained, each exit accounted for. Automatic iron doors descend over the windows and stairwell.

But I don't wish to leave.

I run towards a washroom. Not the ladies', but the handicap and baby-changing facilities. A sole-occupancy bathroom. No stall. No surprises.

Ronnie is closing fast.

The race is on.

The Statue of Liberty, at 225 tons, is literally the biggest gift in history.
A record that's lasted 131 years.
No dice.
I can't lift fifty pounds, can't afford even an Amazon gift card.

The Thuggee strangler Behram killed 931, the last in 1840.
A murder mark still standing 177 years later.
I could never harm someone.

That Russian woman, Mrs. Vassilyeva, who bore 69 kids.
Twins, triplets, quintuplets at every birth.
The final set born in 1765. 252 years.
That much time in labor?
Forget it. I would rather harm someone.

World records all.
None even a millennium old.

Ronnie won't pull the gun, it's there for defense, intimidation. He'll try and tackle me. But I've made the washroom. One small toilet. No interior walls, no stalls. One bolt to keep out the rest of the world.

I latch it. Hear Ronnie pound on the door.

He doesn't carry any keys. He'll call the office on the ground floor.

Probably five minutes to find the janitor. Three more to bring them up in the security elevator.

I lower the diaper-changing platform, withdraw the Styrofoam cups, rubber mortar, and plastic safety scissors from my purse. I remove the two heavy packets of vinegar from my ill-fitting C-cup bra. Clip the packet ends with scissors. Pour the liquid into the Styrofoam cups.

Cutting the necklace string, I slip the pearls onto the changing platform. Crush them to dust with the mortar.

The Gewandhaus Orchestra of Leipzig, Germany, formed in 1743.
The longest-running musical group in history at 274 years.
And you thought the Stones were old.

Swedish newspaper Post-och lnrikes Tidningar *established 1645.*
Still published.
I can't write a word in another language.

The Nishiyama Onsen Keiunkan company of Japan, founded in 705. 1312 years.
A family-owned hotel for fifty-two generations.
Thirteen centuries of operation is impressive....
Millions upon millions of man-hours.

I'll eclipse them all today.

As Ronnie beats on the door, and alarms blare outside, I brush the pearl dust into the cups, let it dissolve inside the vinegar. My stomach knots and I feel a little dizzy as the priceless powder disappears within the murky liquid. Somehow, I forgot a spoon. I stir with my finger.

Then I drink the first cup.

And the second.

And third.

Most would gag at this much vinegar, but I've practiced months for this. . . . The vinegar is acidic, the pearl remnants a natural balancing antacid.

No mistakes. I've waited millennia.

The door latch turns. Ronnie has obtained a key.

Only one more cup to drink.

One morning in 41 B.C., to impress her lover Marc Antony with her wealth,
Cleopatra VII of Egypt dissolved a single great pearl earring in vinegar.
By historian Pliny's account, the pearl was worth ten million sesterces.
Estimated value today?
Fifteen million, five hundred thousand dollars.
Antony and Cleopatra shared the drink. An aphrodisiac.
The most expensive breakfast in history.
A record that lasted 2,057 years.
Until now.

Ronnie throws open the door. Gun in his hand. A custodian and another guard at his side. They see the cups, the empty packets, the bare necklace string. Their eyes fix on the mortar. Confusion covers their faces.

I down the last cup.

Thirty million dollars for breakfast. None will ever think of little Janet Millsap as a listless, unemployed divorcee from Panama City, Florida, again. One whose life will pass unnoticed by history.

Now, friends, look upon the woman who surpassed Cleopatra, Queen of the Nile. As none has in two thousand years.

Today, forever, a record-breaker!

I lick the last of the pearl solution from my lips. Cleo was right. It is an aphrodisiac. Where is my Antony?

Somehow, I doubt poor Ronnie here is in the mood. . . .

Best Served Cold

by Alice Hatcher

Revenge is a dish best served cold, Kate has observed on two occasions. Both times, we were drinking beer, though I might be remembering things incorrectly. I might have been the only one drinking beer two days ago, when Kate visited me in Arizona for the first time, to see how "her old friend turned out in the end." For the past hour, I've been trying to fix the details of Kate's visit in my mind. What I drank. The filigree of Kate's silver jewelry. The texture of her shirt. Silken and soft. The color of the sky at nightfall. Kate's questions about a car accident that happened thirty years ago, in Illinois—a place I had almost pushed from my mind. Everything keeps slipping in and out of focus, though.

Maybe I'm developing a cold, but something came over me this evening. I didn't even bother to reheat the leftovers from Kate's visit. I just sat down at the kitchen counter and ate dinner straight out of jars and off serving dishes, even though eating this way usually inspires a certain loneliness. At some point, I overturned a jar of mango salsa, and I didn't bother to clean it up. The mess. I just stared out the window above the sink, watching twilight fade above the mountains and shadows engulf the garden. The erratic movements of a bat flitting above the pool. Drinking cheap beer from an old coffee mug. Talking to my reflection.

I don't always drink alone, but I haven't been myself since Kate left. I've been alternating between grief and regret, and relief that Kate is gone.

I'd feel guilty admitting my relief if it weren't for Kate's circumstances. I couldn't stand to see her in such pain, between her physical constraints and enduring sense of unfairness. Weakened by illness and burdened with hatred. Whatever she said about seeking inner peace, she seemed so angry. About her own suffering. Her mother's pain. Her father's cruelty. About Julie, the woman who nearly killed us, and the car wreck that upended our lives. Two days ago, when Kate talked about revenge, it seemed like nothing had changed since she was seventeen. As though she was still waiting for justice, unable to recognize its moment has passed.

The first time Kate said revenge is a dish best served cold, we were high-school seniors drinking beer on a bluff above the Illinois River. The night before, Kate's dad had packed his bags and moved out, leaving Kate's mom with little more than a crushing mortgage and the keys to a beat-up Granada. I didn't know this when I showed up at Kate's with a six-pack of beer. I just knew Kate had sounded distracted when she called and asked me to come over, saying she needed to get out of her house.

When I pulled into her driveway, Kate was sitting on the sagging couch on her porch. The shades in every window were drawn, even though Kate's mom had always kept them raised to hide their stains. Kate's mom didn't come out to greet me. I had never once made an appearance at Kate's house without Mrs. Ettleson asking about my parents or plans for college. She always asked if I was going to Harvard. It was probably the only college she knew by name.

Kate was a wreck when she climbed into my car. It wasn't her appearance that worried me. She always wore thrift-store clothes and looked like she hadn't slept in days. It was the way she sat with her head inclined toward the house, as if listening for a disturbance while she described her father's resolve packing his bags. Her mother screaming about another woman. The brush of a hand that became a shove, and then a punch. Her mother leaving for the liquor store with a bruise forming on her jaw. Breaking every mirror in the house and passing out on the couch. Backing out of the driveway, I kept wondering how Mrs. Ettleson looked. To be honest, I was morbidly curious.

Minutes later, I parked on a dirt pull-off near the trestle spanning the river. We followed a trail through tall grass to a short outcropping of rock where we could smoke and drink with little chance of being seen by adults, or, as I hate to admit, by my other friends. People like Julie. I had known Kate since first grade, but we went to different high schools, probably for the best. She couldn't have afforded the tuition at my private school, and she would have been shunned there for her secondhand clothes. The ledge was a narrow strip of common ground connecting our diverging worlds, one of the few places we could escape everyone's expectations, even our own, of what we might become.

It was early September, and mosquitos were still swarming above the reeds edging the river. Shifting clouds cast indistinct shadows, as if uncertain of the day's mood.

"She cut her hand up pretty bad punching the bathroom mirror," Kate said, after smoking a cigaret down to its filter.

I felt sick. Mrs. Ettleson had always called me her second daughter and offered me dinner whenever I came over. Even though Mr. Ettleson humiliated her with comments about the doctor's kid slumming on the wrong side of the tracks and eating shitty cooking just to see how the other half lived.

"You could have called me."

"I would've called an ambulance if she wasn't okay. And she was covered in blood."

I twisted a beer tab between my fingers, suddenly ashamed to be driving a new Prelude with leather seats. For questioning Kate's judgment. "We should go back to your house. Your mom won't care if we drink."

"She'll end up drinking with us, and she's had enough." Kate loosened a stone from a crack and threw it into the river. "My mom always thought my dad was lying about overtime so he could get high after work. He was, but he wasn't getting high alone."

"Can she take him to divorce court?"

"She can't afford a lawyer. And she's too messed up."

I felt guilty for suggesting we drink at Kate's house. I had taken advantage of Mrs. Ettleson's drinking more than a few times. Had beers at her kitchen table. Told friends at my school how I got messed up with Mrs. Ettleson, sometimes in the morning, because she needed company. Because she was a lonely alcoholic.

"He beat her after he told her he was leaving her," Kate said. "I should have knifed him."

I watched the river's snaking movements over submerged rocks and grew uneasy. I'd long sensed an undercurrent of violence in Kate, and I'd dismissed it for years. By the time I was seventeen, though, I was thinking about law school. Anxious about situations that might jeopardize my future.

Kate lit another cigaret. "I was thinking about this movie where this guy gets diagnosed with some heart condition. He's only got months to live, so he tracks down the guy who murdered his wife and got off on some technicality. To kill him. He's got nothing to lose."

"You have a lot to lose. And your dad isn't worth it." I trailed my fingertips over a set of initials carved in the rock. "Someday, he'll regret everything."

"That's what I mean. Someday. In this movie, the husband shows up at this guy's house twenty years later. The guy doesn't even recognize him."

"What happens to the husband?"

"He's not even a suspect. At the end, he's drinking on this hotel patio, talking to some guy who's been ripped off in a business deal. He says, 'Revenge is a dish best served cold.' If you act on emotion, you get careless. He tells the guy to be patient."

"Maybe that's the point. Things will get better."

I fell silent. There was a leaden quality to everything, between the heat and suffocating humidity. The slant of sunlight through gauzy clouds.

"I should get back," Kate said when the sun began to set. "I've left her alone too long."

Kate's house was dark when we pulled into the driveway. I didn't ask to go inside. The truth is, I didn't want to see Mrs. Ettleson. I wouldn't have known what to say, and Mrs. Ettleson's humiliation would have been too awful to witness. That evening, I went to a party with Julie. I felt a little guilty, but then Kate had always been able to handle herself. She wasn't prone to dangerous bouts of depression. She wasn't like Julie.

For an hour, I've been staring at the spilled salsa on the counter and thinking about that afternoon on the bluff, when Kate talked about revenge. Two days ago, on my patio, Kate again spoke of murder. As if it were a normal subject of conversation with a friend who happens to be a lawyer. With each moment, Kate's visit seems more like a slowly unfolding dream formed from the murk of suppressed memory.

The dream began last week, when Kate called. I hadn't spoken to her in almost a year. She spoke my name before I uttered a word. Stated it. Angela, she said, compressing the vowels and giving anything soft in my name a cutting edge. Before I could ask about her health, she said she was about to drive across the country and hoped to pass through Scottsdale on her way to California.

"I finally scattered my mother's ashes," she said. "It made me think of you. That I've been meaning to visit."

Chronic pain makes it difficult for Kate to travel, and I was touched. I spent the morning of her arrival polishing granite countertops, brushing off leather cushions, and rearranging satin throw pillows. If I'd thought at all about Kate's dingy apartment, I might have been more sensitive. Less ostentatious. I wouldn't have bought decorative soaps to fill the crystal dishes in every bathroom or filled every vase in the house with gladiolas. I wouldn't have pulled my nicest stem glasses from the buffet. I wouldn't have bought such a wide array of cold cuts, or such expensive Chardonnay. I wouldn't have bought gourmet mango salsa. I did think to buy Kate's favorite beer—something watery that always reminded me of formaldehyde. I felt embarrassed dragging the case from the convenience-store cooler and had to remind myself I was buying what Kate always drinks. What she would want. At home, I settled into the couch with a glass of wine and tried to read through a legal brief, returning over and over to the same sentences and realizing, after I drained the glass, that I hadn't made it through a single page.

Nothing Kate said on the phone prepared me for her appearance. I recoiled slightly when I opened my front door. Except for the shadows beneath her eyes, Kate was deathly pale. She seemed lost in clothes unlike anything I'd ever seen her wear. She had always worn baggy skirts to disguise her limp. Now she was wearing flared slacks and a silk shirt with a Chinese collar—things I might wear on a casual day at work—a softly patterned headscarf, and a lapis ring, and leaning on a polished black cane that might have suited a woman of a different social class.

Kate made a sweeping gesture down her shirt. "It's a special occasion. Seeing you, finally. In your own digs."

"You look nice." I wrapped my arms around her, only to stiffen when I felt the pronounced edges of her shoulder blades.

"You can say it," she said. "The clothes are nice. I look like shit."

As she drew back from my embrace, I saw the black Lexus parked on my driveway. "That's a step up from your last car."

"Don't get too excited. It's a rental."

"With some miles on it," I said, noting the splattered mud on its lower panels.

"I took a few back roads. Made some stops. But here I am."

Kate limped into my living room, and I saw myself, as I have so often, through her eyes, according to her shifting expressions and pointed comments. She examined the clothing catalogues on my coffee table. The Navajo rugs mounted on my walls. The iron candleholders on the adobe hearth. The full-length mirror framed in pressed Mexican tin.

"I'm punishing myself," I said. As Kate knew, I had always loathed my own reflection.

"I doubt that." Kate wandered into my dining room, considered the framed photographs on my credenza, and touched the portrait of my parents. "How are they?"

"My dad's still obsessed with his boat. My mom's still a hypochondriac."

"Still? That can't possibly be." Kate pointed at my colleagues toasting each other with margaritas. "And who are they?"

"Happy hour," I explained. "We'd just won a case for the firm's biggest client."

"I hope I'm not being nosy. I'm just curious about how my friend made out in the end."

In the kitchen, Kate paused beside my table, a slab of polished mesquite covered in woven placemats, cloth napkins, and an empty fruit bowl. The table was set, I realized, as if a large family might sit down at any moment. Mercifully, Kate didn't comment. She had turned her attention to a glass display cabinet. Balancing on her cane, she pulled a chipped coffee cup from an upper shelf.

She looked at me with wonder. "I can't believe you still have this."

"I remember the day your mom gave that to me. Right before I left for college. She told me I'd be drinking a lot of coffee over at college. Remember how she used to say 'over at college.'"

"She was happy for you." Kate studied the mug's chipped handle. "And proud."

Thinking about Mrs. Ettleson, I felt more like Kate's sister than a friend who had been drifting for years. "Let me get you something to eat. You need something decent after being on the road. We can sit on the patio."

Pulling trays of food from the refrigerator—steamed green beans, peeled shrimp, mixed olives, rolled prosciutto, and soft cheeses—I realized I had prepared an obscene amount for two people. My colleagues would have thought nothing of the extravagance, but Kate was staring silently at the trays. With a twinge, I remembered how we'd avoided my house when we were growing up, and met at dive bars once we were old enough to drink. Avoided situations that made Kate feel out of place. Or ashamed.

"I'm so happy to see you," I said. "Down here, I feel so distant. From home. It's hard to stay in touch." I drew a bottle of Chardonnay from the refrigerator and gestured at the cardboard case on the bottom shelf. "I picked up some of your favorite beer."

Kate glanced at the bottle. "I'll have wine, actually."

I don't know why, but I laughed. "I didn't think you drank wine."

"I'm acquiring the taste," she said, looking at the mug cradled in her hands and running her fingers along its rim, as if the stains on its surface contained traces of her mother.

When Kate and I stepped onto the patio, the sky looked exactly like I describe it to friends in Illinois. Cloudless. Vast and unchanging. It's easy to feel disoriented beneath the desert sky. To feel as though time has evaporated. Become meaningless. The sky allowed Kate and me to ease into conversation divorced, at first, from our past. Kate spent fifteen minutes studying the pads of Indian figs. The blue stripes of giant agaves. The blood-red fruit of a prickly pear. The spiny canes of an ocotillo in bloom.

"These plants are so primal," she remarked.

"They seemed strange to me when I moved here. Primeval. Everything has to be covered in spines or be toxic to survive."

Kate paused before a wooden bench surrounded by potted sage, and a small Buddha on a stone pedestal. "You're not getting religious?"

"I meditate." I took a sip of wine. "It helps me deal with stress. Sitting quietly and letting my mind go blank."

"I've never been able to do that," Kate said, turning from my meditation bench. "Clear my mind."

When we sat down in a shaded corner of the patio, Kate considered the chairs crowding the pool's mosaic deck. Again, I realized I might give the impression of someone with a large family; I saw my longing through Kate's eyes.

"I could get used to it." Kate dabbed the perspiration on her neck with a linen napkin.

I noted a mesquite seedpod floating in the pool and settled into the slowness of the afternoon. "The heat?"

"All of it." Kate convulsed, smothered a cough, and spent a long moment gasping. "I should get it over with," she said, once she caught her breath. "You probably already guessed."

"I haven't guessed anything," I said. Crazily, I hadn't.

"It runs in the family. Or smoking runs in the family. I have cancer."

I lifted my hand to my mouth, conscious of something cliche in the gesture. I forced my hand to my lap and started grasping for information, as I often do, to impose coherence on a world coming apart.

"What kind?"

"Ovarian. It's spread pretty much everywhere except my lungs. It's the only reason I'm still standing." She reached into her purse and tossed a pack of cigarets onto the table. "And smoking."

I stared at the cigarets, and Kate, in disbelief. "How long have you known?"

"Nine months. I wanted to tell you in person."

"Are you doing chemo?"

"I stopped two months ago. With the other meds, my body couldn't handle it."

"How are you managing?"

"Credit cards. I applied for a bunch when I started feeling sick. Before my diagnosis. When I could still get them." Kate flecked a bead of moisture from her glass. "I just tear up the statements when they come."

I pressed my fingertips to my temples. "You can't keep this up."

"My mom was sick when she lapsed on her mortgage. No one cut her any slack. I don't care if I die owing a few banks a million dollars."

"I wasn't judging. I just wanted to know how you're doing. Emotionally."

Kate's face grew slack. "I just need time. I don't know if I have enough time to take care of certain things." She pulled her scarf from her head and dropped it into her lap. "Or energy."

I looked at the scars covering Kate's scalp, and the patchy hair above her ears.

"Between seizure drugs and chemo, the hair's gone. But I finally got a leg that doesn't hurt. Just in time to walk to the funeral home." Kate rolled up her slacks to reveal the prosthetic affixed to her thigh with a padded brace.

I should have risen from my chair and hugged Kate, but I was feeling unsteady. For the next half-hour, I drank to numb myself to a conversation about cremations. Operations. Illness. Kate was so matter-of-fact, but I barely held myself together. When we finished the Chardonnay, I retrieved a second bottle and placed several beers in an ice cooler beside the table.

"I'll stick with wine." Kate drew a cigaret from her pack and I twisted in my chair, looking for a flowerpot. "I'll ash in the empty bottle," Kate said. "This will make me dizzy, but I can't resist. Seeing you."

Kate struck a match, and I had a sympathetic sensation of my throat muscles tensing and a warm chemical tide flooding my skull. I remembered all the times Kate and I had sat on the bluff, sharing cigarets, and without thinking, I reached across the table.

"I thought you quit." Kate blew a stream of smoke over her shoulder.

I drew my hand from the cigarets. "I was just tempted. Thinking about the times we hung out by the river."

"I was just thinking about that too. That conversation we had when my dad left." Kate took another drag off her cigaret. "The funny thing is, I'm on my way to see him."

"I didn't know you were in touch."

"I wasn't. But we ran into each other on the street three years ago. Right before he moved to California with his wife. Her. Guess she inherited some money."

"Why would you want to see him?"

"When I ran into him, he said we should get together sometime. Just talking shit. But I decided to take him up on it. Called him three weeks ago and told him I'd be passing through. He seemed surprised."

"Does he know you're sick?"

"I've been sick for years, and he's known the whole time."

"I meant—"

"Yeah, I told him."

"Why put yourself through this?"

"I need to know if he's sorry for what he did," Kate said. "And he's my dad. Some people change. Take a hard look in the mirror."

The air was completely still, and I had no sense of time passing until Kate spoke again.

"Around the time I called my dad, I thought I'd look up a few other people from our past and see how they ended up. It was probably a bad idea. The crazy thing is, she's in California too."

I knew she was talking about Julie. The woman who crawled from a car wreck unscathed. Who lifted her face to a tower of cloud and saw God. A woman Kate met only once. On the last day Kate and I were both healthy, and whole.

It was spring break. My senior year in college. Strange as it is to say, it was a beautiful day, with billowing white clouds massing in a bright blue sky. A sky perfectly suited to my mood. After years of maintaining a perfect GPA, I had just gotten accepted to the University of Michigan's Law School, and I wanted to enjoy a few weeks of indeterminacy after so much focused effort. Kate was busy working at the grocery store that week, so I spent almost every night drinking with Julie. Doing lines of coke. Even so, Julie seemed relatively stable. So I didn't worry about introducing her to Kate on Kate's only day off. I was tired, anyway, of worrying about what people might think of Kate. I was tired of worrying about Kate.

Julie picked us up in front of the theater downtown, in her dad's Mercedes. Kate was uncomfortable, I knew. She'd heard stories about all-night parties in sprawling houses. She'd seen Julie's class pictures. Now she was seeing, first-hand, Julie's highlighted blond hair and all the money reflected in its shining strands. Whatever her anxieties, Kate was polite, even formal, although she was wearing jeans with bleach stains and a repurposed dog collar for a bracelet.

"Nice to meet you," Kate said, crawling into the backseat. "I've heard all about you."

"I've been hearing about you for years," Julie said. "It's weird we've never met. Angela's probably ashamed of me. She probably told you I'm a complete mess. A cokehead."

So many times, I had said these things about Julie, though never to Kate, and I resented the tension edging into the afternoon.

Kate twisted the ring on her index finger. "She told me you were a lot of fun."

Julie reached over the gearshift and patted my knee. "You're the only friend I can trust." She glanced over her shoulder. "Well, you should meet the girls in my sorority. Even Angela can't put up with them when she visits. And she'll hang out with just about anyone."

I held my breath until Julie pulled away from the curb.

Kate leaned forward. "Where are we going?"

Julie barely slowed at a stop sign. "What about that place you guys used to hang out? The place you told me about, Angela. By the train tracks. I want to see it. I've got some vodka in the glove compartment."

"It's probably muddy," Kate said. "It rained last week."

I twisted around to see Kate digging her nails into the leather seat and shaking her head. "Kate's right," I said. "It's going to be muddy."

"Then we can go to Kate's house," Julie said. "Have a few beers. In the kitchen."

"Let's just hit the bluff quickly and then go somewhere else," I said.

I faced the road ahead and trailed my hand out the window as strip malls gave way to cornfields and patchy forest. Near the bluff, Julie skidded onto the pull-off near the trestle. A cloud of dust settled on the windshield.

"See, it's not muddy." Julie opened the glove compartment and drew a bottle from beneath a small plastic bag. "You guys need to chill."

I led the way to the river, because Kate wouldn't. Julie trailed behind, humming an unrecognizable tune. Making disjointed observations about pillars of white cloud and the colors of butterflies. About the afternoon's perfection. On the ledge, Kate sat down and lowered her head between her arms. Julie stepped up to the precipice, took a swig of vodka, and handed the bottle to me.

"All yours," she said. "I'm quitting. Right now."

I sat down beside Kate. "You'll be asking for it in one minute."

"I don't want to get drunk," Julie said. "Ever again."

"When did you decide this?"

"Just now. I don't want to ruin what I'm feeling."

Kate lifted her head. "What are you feeling?"

"Like everything's perfect." Julie said. "Like there has to be a God."

Kate laced her fingers together in front of her shins.

"I hope I'm not offending you," Julie continued. "It's not like I don't usually believe in God. I just mean it feels like God's right here. Like God's one of those clouds."

Kate looked in Julie's direction. I knew she was studying Julie's French manicure. The cut of Julie's designer jeans. She snapped a twig between her fingers. "It doesn't matter to me what other people believe."

I took a swig of vodka and extended the bottle to Kate. She looked at the bottle as if it were dirty. I grew annoyed, even though Kate was being gracious and even tried to engage Julie in conversation again.

"What's Santa Barbara like?"

Julie turned from the precipice. "The guys were pretty hot."

I threw a pebble at Julie's feet. "What's with the past tense? Go through all of them?"

"Almost. But you already know that."

Kate picked at a scab on her elbow. "What do you do there? I mean, study?"

"Not much. I'm not interested in anything. Even sex. I never feel anything." Julie took a step toward Kate. "That probably sounds cold. To you. You seem really nice."

Kate drew her shoulders forward. "You just met me."

"I can tell. And Angela told me you're really sweet. But she never told me you had such curly red hair. You should get highlights."

"I don't have time," Kate said.

"That's the problem. Even this week's almost gone." Julie pivoted to look at me. "And now you're about to leave me."

"The internship isn't going to take up the whole summer."

"But then you'll start law school. What am I going to do?"

"You've been doing fine without me for a long time."

"I can get you both jobs at the grocery store," Kate said.

Julie didn't seem to notice the edge in Kate's voice. She had grown fixated on the train trestle. Without a word, she started back up the trail and turned into the tall grass lining the path.

"Where the hell's she going?"

"I have no idea," I said. "Maybe she's taking a piss."

"She's messed up. And it's got nothing to do with drinking."

I went silent and, I suppose, tacitly agreed. It was as close as I came, that day or any other, to admitting anything.

"There she is." Kate nodded at the trestle.

I looked up and saw Julie moving along the tracks, leaping from one railroad tie to the next. Halfway across the trestle, she stepped onto a rail, wavered, and looked down at the river. I stood up and lifted my hand to shield my eyes from the sun.

"If she falls, she'll hit the rocks," Kate said. "Does she do this kind of thing a lot?"

I didn't answer Kate. At least a train wouldn't be coming anytime soon, I told myself, as Julie stepped onto a railroad tie and started back toward the end of the trestle. When I turned around, Kate was standing at the base of the trail.

"We should go," she said.

"I'm sorry. I thought you guys would—"

"She can drop me off at my house. See another tourist attraction."

"It was amazing up there," Julie said, when she appeared. I gestured toward the trail, and Julie clambered up the hill, humming sporadically and pausing at points to look at clouds.

I'll never be sure what my real reasons were for taking the backseat. Maybe I thought it would be easier for Kate to direct Julie from the front seat. Maybe I was acting on instinct. The fear I felt watching Julie slide her keys into the ignition.

"Kate needs to go home." I slid the vodka bottle beneath the passenger seat and rested my head against the window, regretting the afternoon and thinking I didn't care if Kate spent the rest of her life wearing dog-collar bracelets and faded shirts. When Kate named the road to her house, I closed my eyes.

"You missed the turnoff," Kate said a moment later. "Did you hear me?"

I opened my eyes and looked out the window. Julie had turned onto a narrow road winding through a stretch of woods. The trees lining the road seemed too blurred, and too close.

"You should turn around," Kate said.

I heard fear in Kate's voice and tensed as the trees on one side of the road gave way to a fallow field. Near a sharp curve, I thought to say something and then saw the speedometer. Saw Julie straining to depress the accelerator. I gripped the back of the passenger seat. The last thing I remember before the car rolled was Kate's hair brushing my knuckles.

I woke up facedown on a bed of leaves. I was just lucid enough to move my fingers and toes to test for paralysis, and to run my tongue across my teeth. I must have been in shock when I sat up, because I spent a long time staring at the tear in my jeans and the dark stain spreading between my thighs before I saw the car, an accordion of crushed metal lodged against the trunk of an old tree. Its doors were hanging open, and Kate was still in the passenger seat, pressed against the dashboard. Just before I passed out, I saw Julie sitting cross-legged on rutted ground. She was cradling her wrist in her hand and smiling at the sky.

I often think of Julie's smile on that afternoon. A mindless, ecstatic smile. A smile that's hardly changed over the years, though it's a little tighter at the corners now. A nipped and tucked smile adjusted by incremental doses of prescription pills. That's what I was thinking two days ago, on the patio, when Kate interrupted my thoughts, as if she had read my mind.

"I guess she married a doctor," Kate said. "A bone doctor. She walked out of a car wreck and into the sunset. It's a sick joke."

I startled at the sound of Kate's voice. "I didn't know she married an orthopedic." The statement, the lie, seemed harmless enough. I knew Julie had married a cardiac surgeon. "She's probably had her difficulties, like everyone else."

"Not like everyone else."

"At my high-school reunion, I heard she went through detox a couple times. Therapy. She's had her problems."

"She's gotten over them pretty well," Kate said. "You can find tons of pictures of her online. Vacations in the Caribbean. At ski resorts." Kate stroked her ring. "She has three kids."

I emptied my glass and drew a can of beer from the cooler. For years, Julie has been sending me holiday cards with family photos. Images of smiling children on tropical beaches. Julie always wears her hair pulled back in a thick ponytail. A tank top to show off her toned arms. She wasn't at my high-school reunion, I knew, because she was in Cabo. "We'll never know what she went through after the accident. She's probably suffered in her own way."

"I wouldn't know. You were the one who knew her. You were close friends."

"We hung out. But I was too young to realize how disturbed she was."

"But she was one of the few high-school friends you kept in touch with," Kate said.

"For a while, but I never really knew her. Not like I know you."

Kate set her glass on the table. "I didn't know her at all. But I think about her every day."

I might have said that I thought about Julie every day too, but I suddenly felt out of sorts and excused myself to go to the bathroom. When I stood up, I realized how much of the afternoon had passed. The sky was suffused with a sanguine glow, and shadows were unfolding across the yard. There are, in fact, times when the sky here changes, usually in the fleeting hour before nightfall. When stark forms and certainties dissolve.

In the bathroom, I ran my hands under cool water and took several deep breaths, only to find myself drawn to the mirror. Against my better judgment, I pushed aside my bangs and traced the trail of knotted tissue along my hairline. To indulge my self-loathing. Then I unzipped my slacks. Touched my abdomen and traced ridges of scar tissue until my hands started shaking. Kate had been right. Julie stepped from the wreckage and walked into the sunset. Onto a California beach with a good-looking husband. I know. I was a witness at her wedding.

I leaned over the sink and told myself, as I often do, that Julie's success is superficial. Julie has had as many relapses and breakdowns as she's had heartbreaking affairs. But then I thought about Julie's smile and started to wonder what, if anything, she's ever lost. A few weeks to rehabilitation at upscale spas. Idle hours on leather couches, talking to psychiatrists with thick prescription pads. But she never lost that smile. A smile opening into an endless abyss.

She had that smile on her face three days after the accident, when she walked into my hospital room with a temporary cast on her wrist. She didn't seem to care that her hospital gown was slipping from her shoulder. It's strange, now, to think of how calm I was seeing her, but then I was sedated, and too unfocused to take her in all at once.

"I overheard some nurses talking." Julie placed her hands on my bed's guardrail. "Saying you were right down the hall."

My facial muscles felt slack, and I struggled to speak. "You almost killed us. Kate's in a coma. They amputated one of her legs. Why did you do that?"

"I heard God's voice out on the train tracks. He wanted us to come home."

I felt a dead weight on my chest. "You've never talked about God before."

"When I was standing above the river, I knew God wanted us all to be with him. That it was time."

"But we're still alive, Julie."

"Sometimes God changes his mind. When we were in the field, he told me he wanted us all to be happy. In this life." She leaned over the guardrail to touch my hand, and I formed a loose fist to prevent her from wrapping her fingers through mine.

"God never wanted you to kill anyone."

"It's not what you think. It was beautiful. The doctors want to make me see a psychiatrist. But I know what I heard."

"I'm really tired, Julie."

I rolled onto my side to face the wall and felt goose bumps along my spine, on the exposed skin between the folds of my hospital gown. When I heard Julie leave, I touched the gauze covering my forehead. Slipped my hand beneath my gown and examined the bandages covering my abdomen. Reached between my legs. Felt rubber tubing and the tug of a catheter. Then I faced the ceiling and imagined Kate with needles buried in her arms and electrodes taped to her head. Metal screws in her femur and bandages around her truncated thigh. I cried until I was exhausted and slipped into morphine dreams.

"You can't let this destroy you," my mother said one week later. Two days after a doctor explained the nature of my injuries. "You can still graduate on time. And someday you can adopt children. You and Julie need to put this behind you. The accident."

I closed my eyes and said nothing. I now see that, in my silence, I was choosing survival. I had known about the turbulence in Julie's mind. I had known about the cocaine in her glove compartment. I knew of her delusions—delusions that became collective once my parents and Julie's began covering up the cracks in Julie's fragile façade. To save Julie. To save me. My embryonic career.

Five weeks later, Kate was still unconscious. Julie's parents had convinced a psychiatrist to give their daughter a diagnosis of mild depression. My parents had talked a college dean into letting me make up missed exams, and the head of a D.C. law firm into deferring my internship for one month. They paid someone at City Hall to expunge every reference to alcohol and cocaine from the accident report. I had been named in the report and had plans, after all, to attend law school. Kate's father never visited Kate in the hospital. Neither did my parents. Mrs. Ettleson visited me every day.

People in law school always talked about having too much to memorize. I had too much to forget and filled my mind with fine print to crowd out painful memories. After law school, I could have worked for a top law firm in Chicago, but I ran away to Arizona. In such an alien environment, I thought, I might forget the past. But I kept in touch with Julie. Visited her in California. Around Julie, I never felt guilty about the advantages I had. The privileges I have. The person I've become. Maybe in trying to forgive Julie, I was trying to forgive myself. But I never forgot anything. Or forgave anything.

When I pulled away from the bathroom mirror, I felt the emptiness of the house more acutely than ever. I felt a hatred for Julie that I had never allowed myself. I felt closer to Kate than I had in years. If I had been able to muster any courage, I would have gone out to the patio and confessed my own part in what happened after the accident. Instead, I told myself what I have been telling myself for decades: It wasn't my fault; I wasn't the one driving the car.

When I stepped onto the patio, Kate was standing at the edge of the pool, smoking a cigaret. I flipped a switch to light a paper lantern above the table.

"I wasn't ashing in your pool." Kate limped back to the table and sat down.

"Why would I think you were?" I reached for the pack of cigarets. "I was going to ask if I could have one."

"I shouldn't be tempting you, but I figured you quit."

"I have one now and then. When I'm dealing with a big case." I slid a cigaret from the pack and opened a beer. "You don't need to feel guilty."

"I don't. You're an adult. You can make up your own mind." Kate watched me take my first drag. "Just like old times."

"When I was in the bathroom, I was wondering how things might have turned out if we hadn't gotten into the car that day."

"Now that I don't have much time, I don't sit around wondering what might have been," Kate said. "I'm just trying to understand what happened. So I can make peace with the past."

I opened my mouth, as if to speak, but remained silent.

"One time, you told me she came to your hospital room," Kate said. "You said she was hearing voices out on the tracks."

"I was drugged up. It's all a blur."

"She never approached me. To see how I was. Maybe I was too much of a mess to look at. My leg kept bleeding through the bandages. My head was full of stitches."

"She probably felt terrible—"

"She never apologized. Not even in a letter. Or an e-mail." Kate dropped her cigaret into the wine bottle. "She could have gotten my address from you."

I gripped my beer to steady my hand. "She was probably ashamed. And we were young."

"We're adults, now," Kate said. "It's never too late to admit something.

It's what mature people do. An apology might have made everything less painful. It would, even now."

I took a drag off my cigaret, if only to avert my gaze from Kate.

"She's not the only one," Kate continued. "My own dad never visited me in the hospital. Probably didn't want to get tangled up in our lives after cutting loose. I spent years waiting for him to apologize for that. He'll say something or he won't when I see him."

I took a sip of beer and felt a chill. "You didn't have the dad you deserved."

Kate pressed the stem of her wineglass between her thumb and finger. "Remember when we were sitting by the river and I told you about that movie? About the guy that says revenge is a dish best served cold?"

My cigaret had almost burned down to the filter and I pinched its smoldering tip, only to realize how drunk I'd become. My fingertips were nearly numb, and I almost knocked over the empty wine bottle when I tried to drop the butt down its neck. "You were so angry."

"I'm not angry like I used to be. Still, I think about it, sometimes. Revenge."

"Your dad isn't worth it."

"It's funny. You said the same thing back then. My memory is hopeless because of chemo, but I remember that. You said I had too much to lose." Kate tugged at a fold of fabric caught in the lattice of her titanium leg. "Even before I got cancer, I didn't have much to lose. I'd already lost my leg. My hair. Mom and I lost the house."

I rested my hand on my abdomen. "You have friends, Kate. We're like sisters."

"My mom did think of you like a daughter. It's too bad you never saw her when you were in town for your reunion." Kate looked at the shadows massing in my meditation garden.

"I meant to get in touch." I paused. "You e-mailed, but I didn't realize she was that sick."

"I said she was on oxygen. In too much pain to do a crossword."

"I think I was worried I would tire her out."

"She would have rallied for you. Even at the end, she was always asking about you."

I gazed out across the pool, remembering how I'd spent the weekend of my reunion drinking gin and tonics at a country club. I never got in touch with Mrs. Ettleson because I couldn't bear the thought of sitting in her tiny apartment, drinking fortified wine from a dirty glass. Trying to ignore the musty smell of stained carpeting and carry the weight of awkward conversation.

"Maybe it's just as well you didn't see her. She got bitter at the end." Kate rested her fingers on the base of her glass. "She didn't hate anyone. Not even my dad. But she hated them. Your friend Julie. And her family."

"Of course she would have blamed the person who was driving during the accident."

Kate seemed confused by my remark. "My mom could have forgiven her. And her family. If it had been just an accident."

"What do you mean 'just an accident'?"

"My mom got talking to people and heard how crazy Julie was. I guess there had been other incidents. Even that month. Her parents knew about them. Smoothed things over by making donations to the right people. Paid off cops. Then gave her the keys to that car."

I reached for the pack of cigarets. "That's horrible."

"My mom thought so. For a long time, she thought of suing Julie's parents. She needed some way to pay the medical bills. She pulled herself together and even quit drinking for a while. Gambled everything on a lawyer who tried to depose some doctors. To prove Julie's parents knew about her mental illness. And drug use. And still gave her a Mercedes."

"Who knows what the medical records would have shown? Psychiatrists can be creative with diagnoses."

"I suppose. But my mom's lawyer couldn't find anything in the police report either. Nothing about vodka. Blood-alcohol levels. The coke in the glove compartment." Kate tapped the side of her glass with her ring. "Her dad worked downtown. As a judge. I guess you knew that. He must have expunged things from the records. Is expunge the word? Anyway, my mom ended up calling your parents. Figuring they might know something. Hoping you might testify."

"I had no idea. That she called my parents."

"Your parents said you were too fragile. So, my mom told her lawyer not to contact you. She didn't want to make you relive the accident. When you'd just started law school. She loved you like a daughter."

"I could have said something, Kate, but—"

"You didn't know. That my mom wanted to call you." Kate pulled a beer from the cooler and set it in front of me. "I should add Julie to the hit list. I'm headed that way."

"If you started that kind of list, there would be no end—"

"My mom worked herself to death to pay for my physical therapy."

"I know," I said.

"But you can't really know. You didn't see her at the end. You didn't see her much after the, what did you say, the 'accident.'"

"I'll always regret that," I said quietly.

"I'm not trying to make you feel bad. My mom wanted you to focus on school. Do well over in college. At your new job." Kate lit a cigaret and took a long drag. "I still think about Julie every day."

"She can't be happy. Knowing what she does."

"Then maybe she'll apologize. If I run into her in California."

A strange laugh escaped my throat. "Do you really think about her every day?"

Kate tapped ash onto the patio pavers. "I've spent thirty years in constant pain."

"If there's a price, I'm sure she's paid it," I said.

"With a platinum card." Kate massaged her temples with her burning cigaret trembling between her fingers. "She has a nice house. Three healthy kids. Maybe I told you that. Or did you know that already?"

"I heard about them," I whispered. "Her children."

"In crazier moments, I really thought about doing it. But it wouldn't be right to kill the mother of three kids. That would be sick."

I must have been angrier than I'd realized; I felt disappointed. "But it would be justice. You said it yourself. She walked into the sunset. Everyone else paid for her reckless behavior. You. Me. Your mom. I can't even imagine what kind of mother she is."

A sip of beer caught in my throat, and Kate waited for me to stop coughing. "You would have been a great mother," Kate said. "I always imagined you with lots of kids. You can still adopt, you know. It's not too late."

"I'm not in a good place. I never have been." I looked out across the yard and heard my own voice, a stranger's, it seemed, pleading. "There's an argument for killing her. So she never hurts anyone else. Like she hurt us. She's really disturbed."

Kate fingered her ring. "You were right, though. For all we know, she's changed. Didn't you say she got help? Went to therapy and rehab?"

"A few therapy sessions don't change someone like that," I said. "She's no different than people I've seen in court. Paying a few small fines and cutting deals."

"Being a parent can change people. Maybe she's a great mother."

I drained my can of beer. "But she didn't change. She's walked through life without a scratch."

Kate pulled another can from the cooler and set it on the table. "People used to make assumptions about me. Based on my house. My clothes. Maybe we're doing the same thing."

"This is different," I insisted. "I knew her. She's exactly what you would imagine."

"Maybe I need to believe people can change. So I don't go crazy."

"She was old enough to know what she was doing. She never apologized." I pulled the tab from the beer can, thinking about my massive kitchen table, the empty rooms in my house, and the scar tissue inside of me. "Julie's dangerous. You would be doing the world a favor."

"She posts tons of pictures online," Kate remarked. "All sorts of personal stuff. She acts like someone who has no reason to be ashamed."

"Why would she be ashamed? She has no conscience."

Kate studied my face. "You should hear yourself."

"I know people who keep in touch with her. I hear things."

"Do you honestly think she deserves to die?" Kate asked.

"I hate myself because of her," I said, feeling sick from expensive

Chardonnay and cheap beer. "She took everything from me."

Kate lifted her glass. "Then here's to both of us having nothing to lose."

In my drunken state, I smiled at the thought of Kate driving across the country to kill someone. For both of us. "Maybe I'm crazy, but if I thought you were actually going to do it, I wouldn't try to stop you."

"I know you wouldn't," Kate said. "I've known you for thirty years."

For the next hour, we drifted in and out of unfocused conversation. About the people who bought Kate's childhood house. The small theater where we used to see third-run movies for a dollar. The large houses being built along the bluffs. At some point, I excused myself again, this time to sit on the edge of my tub and cry. To get a respite from the past. From Kate.

When I emerged from the bathroom, Kate was in the kitchen, covering trays in sheets of foil. She was leaning on her cane and working with one hand, and her arm was trembling from the effort. When she saw me, she reached for the lid to the salsa jar.

"It's funny, but I knew exactly where you'd keep the tin foil." She screwed the lid onto the salsa jar. "I normally don't like salsa. But I loved this." She gave the jar a shake. "It has the right consistency." Her hand was still trembling, and I thought she might drop the jar.

"I'm not sure you should see your dad. It'll just stir up more pain."

Kate placed her hand on the counter to steady herself. "I could spend what's left of my life trying to find happiness. But I don't have time. Or energy." She screwed a cap onto a pill bottle standing beside her purse. "I just want clarity."

She drew a second pill bottle from her purse and studied its label. I pulled a glass from the cabinet and filled it with water.

"There's so much they don't tell you when you start chemo," Kate said. "I have pills for every lingering side effect." She slipped a capsule into her mouth and lifted the glass to her lips. Water dribbled down her chin, and she wiped her face with a silken sleeve.

I looked out the window and struggled to compose myself. The sun had set. A thin band of purple afterglow remained above the mountains. "Why don't I get your things from the car?"

"I should go back to the motel. The pills for insomnia cause indigestion, and the pills for indigestion cause insomnia. I don't want to keep you up. Shuffling around."

"Look at this place. It's huge. I won't hear a thing."

"It will be easier to stay in a motel," Kate said, gathering her purse. "I should get going before I'm too tired to drive."

"Do you want to come over for breakfast? I have so many leftovers."

"I should get back on the road."

"Will you be passing through on your way back?" My voice cracked, and I grasped, for the first time, that I might never see Kate again.

"Everything's hard to predict. I might just hole up in some beach hotel. Sit on a patio, drinking." She gestured at the corner cabinet. "You should use the mug. Put some whiskey in it. My mom would approve. You could never do any wrong in her book."

"I can't believe you drove all this way," I said, as we walked to her car.

Kate drew a key from her purse. "I've been meaning to do this for a long time."

"Why don't I visit you in Illinois?" I said impulsively. "I'll take time off next month."

"I'll have to see where I am by then," Kate said.

I wrapped my hand around Kate's and felt her bones shifting beneath my fingers. I tried to imagine her as she had once been, with thick red hair, a shy smile, and bargain-bin jewelry on her wrists, but she had changed beyond recognition. "Don't do anything rash."

"I never do." She drew her hand from mine and lowered herself into the Lexus.

"Drive safe," I said.

"Don't worry," Kate said. "I'm completely sober."

When Kate's taillights disappeared, I inhaled the scent of creosote and allowed a sense of relief to wash over me. Inside, though, I felt unnerved by the emptiness of the house. My reflection in the bathroom mirror was so oppressive that I draped a towel over the glass before I undressed, all the while thinking about Kate's parting words. Her assurance of sobriety. I had been the only one drinking, I realized. Numbing myself. Because I couldn't stand the pain. Or myself. After I undressed, I knelt on the tiles and got sick, taking care to retch quietly, even though I was alone. All night, I drifted in and out of troubling dreams, and in waking moments, imagined different conversations with Kate. Different confessions.

Now, two days later, I'm still having imagined conversations with Kate. I spent all day working in the garden without gloves and then scrubbed the kitchen floor on my knees, letting ammonia work its way into the cuts on my swollen hands. Just to feel something. To sweat out the sickness that has been inside me for years. I kept repeating to myself that Julie was the one driving the car. That I would only have hurt Kate by confessing my part in what happened. That it was a mercy to leave certain things unsaid. As if Kate couldn't handle pain.

An hour ago, I decided to eat something substantial after two days of nibbling on crackers. I took out the tray of cold cuts, a bag of chips, and the salsa Kate liked so much. I pulled the coffee mug from the cabinet and filled it with beer that reminds me, more than ever, of formaldehyde. I wanted to feel like I was having one last drink with Kate, and with Mrs. Ettleson.

I've been sitting at the counter since, eating by candlelight and holding whispered conversations with a pane of dark glass. Maybe I am exhausted, but I feel lightheaded and unmoored. My mind keeps slipping between the past and present, flitting between a snaking river and a ridge of desert mountains, and then going blank. But then the desert can induce a certain amnesia. It's the emptiness and infinity of a cloudless sky. The slow bleed of days into one another. A sun too close to Earth. The infernal heat. A fever feeding an infection coursing through my bloodstream. Filling me with fear.

The fact is, I haven't felt quite right since I sat down.

My thoughts are growing fragmented, slipping away in rapid succession. Memories of torn blinds shrouding Mrs. Ettleson's solitary pain. A polluted river uncoiling beneath a trestle. The rattle of a train that never comes. Bits of litter catching on reeds. A figure poised above it all, preparing for a doomed flight. Kate looking at a jar of salsa, the salsa she never even sampled but claimed to love. Turning it over in her hands. Giving it a slight shake. For no reason. For one reason. To watch tasteless white powder dissolving on bits of mango.

This evening, I dipped my spoon into that jar. Over and over. Swallowed the poison Kate started preparing decades ago.

I see Kate sitting on the patio, studying my face with a pained expression. I hear my confused talk. About love. Friendship. Justice. I could have argued for Julie's life. I would have been arguing for my own.

I just stood up, thinking it can't be too late, and nearly collapsed. My phone is somewhere in the house, but there's no time to find it. There is no time left to change. For me. Kate recognized that. She saw to it. She saw to everything. The candle is guttering, and the smell of hidden rot reeking in the drain is growing worse. I never imagined life ending this way. Extremities chilled by air conditioning. Shaking uncontrollably in the middle of the desert. A last sunset muted by a pane of polished glass. Streaks of purple bleeding into red above a mountain. A dark bruise spreading across the sky where God should be. I lower my hand and touch my abdomen, where a baby might have been, and with newborn clarity, I imagine Kate driving to California by herself, for both of us.

The Kim Novak Effect

by Gary Phillips

Here I was, running a sweet little hustle, not really hurting anybody, and yet I find myself strapped spread-eagle, chest down, across a piece of three-quarter-inch plywood plunked across two sawhorses. My pinpoint Oxford Raffaello shirt was in tatters. This gruff cornfed ol' boy in a cowboy hat standing behind me, ready to wail on my bare, bleeding back again with his heavy-buckled belt. The other ruffian leaned on a beam of the unfinished wall of the tract house. This one bopped his head to *The Best of Warren Zevon* playing on his iPod.

"'Roland, the Headless Thompson Gunner,'" Leaning Man mouthed as Hat Boy took another chunk out of me. "Talkin' about the man…" He smiled, absently scratching his threadbare beard. He took another swig of his bottled water.

Hat Boy cocked back again like Roger Clemens goofy on the juice and let another one go. The leather sizzled on my flesh and the edge of the buckle dug another groove.

"Ke-Rist," I screamed into the gag tied around my mouth.

"He looks about primed," Leaning Man said, yawning. He straightened from the skeletal wall, wire conduits snaking through the holes cut into the framing lumber. He removed his earpieces and methodically wrapped them around his iPod. He then placed it carefully on a juncture of wood beams.

"Yeah?" Hat Boy said dubiously. "A few more love taps would make sure." Eager bastard.

"He's got to be conscious when Bishop George gets here," Leaning Man pointed out. "That sonofabitch'll skin our hides if sugar lips here isn't conscious."

"I suppose," his compatriot agreed reluctantly. He wiped at his forehead with his forearm, the Vegas heat particularly stuffy inside the raw plywood shell of the house's second floor. Despite this, Leaning Man wore a bulky nylon windbreaker, shades, and a baseball cap.

We were in what the blueprints indicated was the master bedroom—the homes in development on one of the higher plateaus of Red Rock Canyon. On the other side of the ridge, down in the womb of a valley, was an eighteen-hole golf course I frequented. Beyond that was the tail end of Summerlin, this where my latest operation was bivouacked.

Leaning Man walked over and doused my back with what was left of his water. It wasn't much, but I was mutely thankful. Funny how things work out, I reflected, as we waited for the big boss to arrive. Less than two weeks ago, my golf game was improving, my off-shore bank accounts were fat, and I was in my office doing, with gusto I might add, the wonderfully preserved late-'70s sexpot Jerri Rocklyn. She of the *Ava of the Underground* WWII actioners, wherein each installment included heady doses of sadomasochism.

"Thank you, kind sir," she joked as we finished up. On the lower right cheek of that gorgeous Nautilus firmed butt of hers was the mole made famous in the photo layout the real Jerri Rocklyn had done for *Gallery,* one of the slick skin mags, back in '78. Looking dreamily from that image I gazed out of my office window, which offered a view of Rainbow Boulevard. Life sure was good.

Back in her clothes, Jerri sat on my desk crossing tanned, muscular legs. She lit a blunt and inhaled. Her real name was Helen Hobart. She was thirty-six years old, originally from Redondo Beach, California. But for the escapade we'd just pulled, she'd been modeled to look like Rocklyn, whom she happened to favor.

"Do I really have to go back under?" she asked, blowing fumes and offering me a toke.

I took the joint, sampled it, then answered, "We can't have the mark spotting you at the craps table, now, can we?"

She sighed heavily, getting off the desk with a flourish, those marvelous gel-filled breasts of hers swaying hypnotically. "But I like this look. And so do you." She sucked in more smoke and put the joint on the edge of the desk.

I stepped forward and we kissed while she guided my fingers slowly along her leg. Momentarily lost in lust, I eventually got back on track. "Doc's ready to go, baby. And we've already agreed you can keep the tatas," I murmured as I nibbled her scented neck.

"But," she started, then didn't finish. She knew I couldn't force her to get re-cut. But she also knew it would mean the end of any future lucrative assignments if she insisted on keeping the Jerri Rocklyn look. For like me, Helen was addicted to those pretty little green ones.

"Fine," she said, giving me a last peck and sauntering out of my office after putting the dead blunt in her handbag. I checked my appearance in the mirror of my tiny private bathroom, making sure my hair was just so and my eyes weren't red from the weed. Then I opened the floor safe beneath the rug upon which sat a cylindrical glass case of sports memorabilia I'd pushed aside. I took out the acrylic-encased page from the 7/21/73 program book of the Braves versus the Phillies at Atlanta. I smiled crookedly, like Mel Gibson speaking at a synagogue, and put everything back in its place. Aluminum attaché case in hand, I left.

Not forty minutes later I was sitting across from retired dental-clinic king Eldon Dudley in the Blue Velvet Lounge on Bridger. In fact, there was a Dr. Dudley Discount Dental facility several blocks away on this street. His big smiling face, circa thirty years ago, beaming down on the abscess-plagued and broken-toothed citizenry from the 3-D logo.

"Wonderful," Dudley said, examining the inauthentic certificate of authenticity I'd laid on him. I was especially proud of the hologram work on that bad rascal. That lab in Taiwan knew its stuff. He picked up the encased program page again, savoring the item. On that date in 1973, Hank Aaron hit home run number 700 in his irrefutable quest to equal, and eventually surpass, Babe Ruth's home runs. Say what you want about Barry Bonds, Hank did it without 'roiding up, while also putting up with racist death threats from jealous crackers. Sure I was a con artist, but I could appreciate the real thing when it came along.

Scouring, as I do, antiques stores and estate sales, I'd chanced upon the actual program book from that auspicious day. The rest, faking Aaron's signature and the certificate, then working the network I'd established for high-end sports memorabilia, was simply reeling in the right fish.

"Okay," he said, sipping his cranberry juice. "You've got yourself a deal."

"This," I said, reverently touching the artifact, "is not only a wise investment on your part, but a legacy to leave your children."

He snorted. "My grandkids, maybe. 'Fraid my son and I don't see eye to eye," he lamented.

He was like that, regurgitating those clichéd homilies now and then. I said nothing, merely sat back, tenting my fingers as he wrote a check for fifteen grand. The waitress came by our table.

"Can I get you gentlemen refills?"

"I believe we'll settle up," I said, adding after the right pause, "Noreen, is it?"

Dentist Dudley looked up from his checkbook.

"Yes, it was my grandmother's name." She put on a neon smile and glided away in her skimpy outfit after laying the tab on us. Naturally I picked it up. Dudley stared after her.

"You okay?' I asked.

"Yes, uh-huh," he said, handing me the payment. "Was she our server originally?"

I hunched my shoulders. "Maybe her shift just started." I rose and said my goodbye, reassuring him once again about the timeliness and efficacy of his investment. I strolled out, sure that he was staring at the waitress named Noreen as I passed near her. She was earning her tips laughing politely at the inane *Girls Gone Wild* level of word foreplay of a couple of 'SC frat boys.

I'm sure they were in Vegas to show us hairy-knuckled droolers how to party. I got in my platinum-colored 300, put on the factory air and a Celine Dion CD—what can I tell you, I actually like the way that broad belts out a tune. I drove over to the kitchen of a downtown casino to make a pickup. Then out to see my man.

Dr. Mathias Steiner was the cat you'd cast to play the Nazi doctor if you were of a mind to make another *Ava of the Underground* flick. He was about medium height, stocky, with good-sized shoulders even at his age. Apparently back in the day he wrestled at Düsseldorf U or whatever the institution in Germany he attended was called. He wore a pencil moustache, touched up his gray locks, and his fashionable rimless glasses stood in relief over his steel-blues. His hands were long like a pianist's, and it annoyed me to no end that his golf game was better than mine, even though he had a couple'a decades on me.

"I'll have Shauna call Helen. I'll schedule her for the day after tomorrow," he told me in the hallway of his cut shop after his new receptionist had buzzed me into the back.

"Where'd this one come from?" I said, meaning the new receptionist called Shauna. She was a statuesque hottie I took to be no more than twenty-four or -five. Once upon a time, Helen had been his receptionist.

Steiner took my elbow and guided me toward his open office. He liked nothing better than thinking about, touching, smelling, and pursuing women. He had an invalid wife. While he was a sucker for female flesh, he did right by the wife when it came to care and whatnot, so he wasn't a total ogre.

"Shauna Cheung. She's studying Economics and Nineteenth Century English Lit at UNLV." We were standing just inside his office and he gazed around the room as if worried his wife had planted a bug. "She made her college money with one of those Web sites where you watch her in the morning, rant about her boyfriend, feed the cat, and all that." The tip of his tongue wet the center of his top lip as he grinned. "Of course she did these tasks mostly in short nighties and silken underthings, earning quite a few male and female subscribers."

He tipped back momentarily on his heels as he conjured up those carnal cyber images in his head.

"You hint to her about our sideline?" I asked, conversationally. Her online thing struck me as someone who had a taste for larceny. Or maybe she was just a stone exhibitionist. Either way, she seemed to be a likely candidate.

"Not yet, but yes, she certainly seems prime material. There must be plenty of these bourgeois fools who have fantasies about the Asian goddess or Dragon Lady."

Steiner was a study in contradictions. He justified his arrangement with me as a way to strike back at the nabobs of convention and conformity. Going on about his patients, the vain, jowled men and the sun-aged, vodka-breathing blondes deluded they could defy gravity and time. Yet I also knew he was spiteful that he got the low-rent chin nip or outpatient tummy tuck, with the high-end work those vodka blondes wanted flying out to Beverly Hills to get done.

"Here you go," I said, laying the packet of blow on his desk. That was the item I got from my connection at the casino. Women weren't Doc's only weakness.

He put the dope away, relocking the drawer. Randolph Scott looked down on us from behind him. Steiner was also a movie-cowboy aficionado, and had several such portraits—Glenn Ford, the Duke, Eastwood, and so on—tacked to the walls. All of them were autographed. I'd sold him his Ford. Hey, Western memorabilia brings in a decent buck.

"Noreen make contact?" We were walking back out of his office.

"Yeah," I said. "I still think it was too dead-on to use the name of his dead wife."

"We all want to believe that the second chance can be had," he said wistfully. "The heart forever overrules the intellect, does it not?"

I demurred. Since my research had shown the dentist was into mysticism, it did seem Dudley was more inclined to fall for the bit the more he glommed that this Noreen could be the spirit of his departed. This was the first time we'd done the Kim Novak this nose-on, and I hoped it didn't jinx the con.

Shaking Doc's hand in front of the receptionist, it looked like I was simply some sort of pharmaceutical salesman making his rounds. Which in a way was true. I gave her a nod and she returned that with a brief smile that could be interpreted a couple of different ways. Could be Doc had let on more than he allowed. Yes by golly, she was a candidate.

The slap across my face brought me out of my daydreaming and back into my current unpleasant situation.

"Got your attention now, asshole?" Hat Boy followed his question with a jab from his steel-toed boot into my chest. They'd untied me from the makeshift table and dumped me in a corner. A brief wind rippled the blue plastic covering the cutouts for the windows.

"The bishop will be here soon," Leaning Man said, pocketing the cell he'd been talking on. He crossed his arms and looked down at my pitiful form. "Then we'll get down to it, won't we, sugar lips?"

I feebly managed to give them the finger. Instead of knocking the crap out of me, which I expected, Hat Boy and Leaning Man laughed like they were watching a Chris Rock routine. Hell, why not? They were holding all the cards.

I know I should pace my intake. I am a doctor, for God's sake. Once I was in demand, and know more than some windshield-washing addict what this heavenly narcotic does to you physically and mentally. But the feeling it purveys, that, well, that is almost like sex itself, is it not?

I know too that as I sit here in the tomblike dark of my office, Wagner softly on my stereo, the hum of the thoroughfare beyond a desensitizing lullaby of normalcy, current matters are far from that. And yet a kind of throttle of inertia embraces me as I ingest more powder, my self-image that of the immigrant gangster Pacino played in that movie all those rappers sample. The cocaine gives me spine. The coke will give me the *eier* to reach for the pistol in my middle drawer should I need to.

This I must believe because I know my erstwhile partner in the doppelgänger enterprise is not a heroic man. I dip my head and partake of more of the powder. Mein Gott, it is an amazing substance. I wipe the residue from the rim of my nostrils and lick some left off the back of my index finger. I certainly don't mean to say that he is a coward. You can't be gutless and perpetrate the sort of bold swindles he pulls off. You have to project the veneer that reflects what the person you're taking wants to see, and he certainly has that.

But what am I to him? I, who used to be a surgeon and now create cartoon heart-shaped derrieres for the self-perpetuating, self-absorbed class. I have more coke and I wait. I could go downstairs and get in my Cadillac CTS with the temperature-controlled seats and the surround sound, the vehicle purchased from the profits I made doing my part, but where would I go? I am very comfortable in my newly obtained condo in nearby Summerlin. And really, as I have more coke and analyze it further, I am an asset, am I not?

Here I was, having driven to his office to tell him the important news I'd discovered about Shauna, anxious as I was not to speak on the phone. Cocaine makes one wary. But then spying that large one with the cowboy hat taking him away forcibly. The other one I couldn't see so well at the wheel of their car. Together those Macheaths will squeeze my name along with the other particulars of the operation out of him. What if they aren't giving him the works, and will simply offer him money? Or drugs. The judicious use of psilocybin or scopolamine, that would disorient him or create fright or paranoia and that could get him babbling as well.

Yet when he does give them my name, why would they give me the treatment? It would seem to me their boss would want to keep me in the picture, assuming he wants to keep the effort going. And why wouldn't he? Whoever was in charge of the hoodlums must be a man of means, a gangster of some sort, surely. Unless it was over a personal matter that he was taken away as he was. That might be. And if so, then all my worrying is unfounded, and I should cease my consumption. I will, just after this next line.

"You do have amusing qualities," Shauna Cheung said condescendingly. She set her margarita down on the pub table and fluffed out those raven tresses.

"But why should I kick back anything to you or to Herr Doktor?" She put a finger up. "More than, say, the cost of getting the remodeling done, as you call it, and some sort of finder's fee? Though when you really think about it, why are you necessary at all?"

I pantomimed for two more drinks from the waitress in the faux-moll outfit. The third-floor game room in the Riverhead Casino was called Nitti's. Leaning just so across the pool table, Shauna steadied herself and smacked the cue ball dead-on. She dropped her solid into the awaiting hole. I appreciated a woman who could work the stick. She walked to the short side of the table, eyeing her next shot.

"It's not just setting the job in motion that matters," I said. "But lining up the marks does take a certain specialty." That had come out more harshly than I'd intended. I couldn't let this chick get ahead of me. "But sure, you're right, you don't need me. Only, who's gonna soothe that old croaker sack's nerves when you're off playing slap and tickle with the mark? Riddle me that, Green Hornet."

"It's not hard to find a crooked cutter," she said. "Half of them are sniffing their Xylocain or whiffing their patient's panties…or want to."

The cue ball glanced off the solid seven and it spun on its axis but didn't have much trajectory. She left me with much of nothing on the table but I was cool. I positioned myself confidently. "You figure to branch out with my idea, that it?"

She smiled radiantly. "I'm not saying that, homeboy. I could see where you might be an asset."

"Now you're just jerking me to make me miss." I did anyway. My striped ball bounced off the padded corner.

She lined up her next shot. "No. But I was thinking this hustle could be a two-way thing."

"How you mean?"

"There're plenty of lonely widows, you know. Fact is, statistically, there's more older broads with some savings than older men." She let loose with her cue stick and, banking her shot, knocked in another solid.

"I'm not taking the denture-cream money from some gummy grannies.

That is not what this is," I insisted.

"My bad." She gave me that smile of hers again, well aware that it got to me despite my anger. "The point remains, you're not tapping your market's full potential."

"Maybe that's where you come in," I suggested. "Lining up some of these beefcake boys for the work."

She seemed to consider that while she sunk her last solid. "Who knows? I might take a semester off and show you how to properly expand your operation." She pointed the cue stick at the middle pocket and put the eight ball away in a smooth stroke. "See you, champ."

I stood watching her walk away, allowing as she did a bit of a swing of those wonderful hips in those designer jeans. Yeah, Ms. Cheung was a real go-getter. And if I wasn't careful, she was going to run me like she did this pool game, and put me out of the picture.

"Really, you don't need to keep doing this."

"It's my pleasure to see that look on your face," I said.

She yawned and stretched on the bed. The diamond and white-gold pendant I'd just given her was resplendent against her magnificent bronzed skin. Noreen—and I understood she wasn't that Noreen, the woman I met in those days of want in Tulsa—pulled me closer from where I stood gazing down on her.

"How will I ever thank you," she giggled, reaching for my boxers. Oh these modern women. I was glad I no longer wore the traditional undergarments. Much too much fuss to get out of. She laid back on the bed again, giving me an eyeful of that young and fit body of hers clad only in the frilly panties I'd bought her. What a self-deluding fool I was. How pathetic I must be to this gorgeous girl who could have her way with any of those snarling boys with their bunching pectorals prowling Vegas to satiate hedonistic desires. Yet here I was, a slave to my baseness.

"What's wrong, baby cakes?"

I sat on the edge of the bed and she snuggled close. "I'm not so gone that for one minute I would suppose you have real feelings for me," I began, touching her hair. "Sending orchids and chocolate bunnies to you at that bar and grill like some teenager." I wiped a hand over my face. "Why did you agree to see me?"

"You have to stop doubting yourself, Eldon. I told you. Men my age have grown up playing video games blowing up monsters and making it with digitally animated babes with balloon boobs. Salivating over how they can get a house like they've seen on *MTV Cribs* and a car featured on *Pimp My Ride*."

She kissed my far too rotund belly. "I was and still am flattered a man of your experience would find me of interest."

I grabbed her by the shoulders, tighter than either of us expected. "What if I'm crazy, Noreen? I know full well you aren't her, she died some thirty years ago. There's plenty of Noreens in this world, and no doubt a fair share in Las Vegas. And sure you favor her some, but she never had a body like yours or—"

I stopped myself, ashamed and excited all at once.

"She never did this, did she, Eldon?" She pushed me onto my back and demonstrated a technique, shall we say, I'd never experienced before in sixty-seven somewhat sheltered years. Then she had me reciprocate. Oh my. But I believe that's what the article I read in the *AARP* magazine advocated— to keep your mind active in the Golden Years, you should learn something new every day to keep sharp. Well I was a damn needle that night.

Afterward, as we got dressed for dinner, I asked her, "When you decide to leave me, do it quickly, will you? I've convinced myself I can take it easier like that, as if it were a gut punch, okay?"

"Why do you always talk like that? And why would I leave someone who is so kind to me?" She was combing her hair. As I'd noticed before, she didn't look in the mirror. I suppose I assumed all beautiful women regarded themselves, primed themselves for a night out. But then, what did I know of women such as this second-chance Noreen? She patted my cheek and gave me a look that rolled the tops of my socks.

Of course at dinner, like before, there were those who ogled, wondering just what sort of relationship we had. Her laughing at my shopworn attempts at humor and me grinning like Tom Sawyer must have when he tricked others into painting that fence for him. They were envious, I convinced myself. Here I was, not particularly handsome nor commanding, yet I was the one who'd struck it rich in Las Vegas. The Wheel of Fortune had spun in my favor.

The next day in my office, as I sat and admired my Hank Aaron prize, marveling at how that transaction had brought me such luck, my private line rang.

"Bishop George," I said upon hearing his voice. "How may I help you today?" I listened. He was concerned about my being with Noreen. Her age wasn't the issue. I knew that despite the public image he cultivated for business reasons, he still practiced plural marriage. I knew too that his third wife was seventeen. Mine and Noreen's age difference wasn't the issue. This call was of a more temporal nature.

"Oh, no, she has not made such an inquiry." I listened some more. Bishop Abel George rarely raised his voice, but he was persistent in his manner. "Yes, I understand she's just a cocktail waitress. What? Why would I do that, Bishop George? I've certainly not been very strong in our ward for some time, as you are well aware. But her being a gentile is of no consequence." He talked, then I said, "It's enough that we make each other happy."

I wasn't a child. I knew that answer wouldn't satisfy him. Indeed, I was quite aware of where his probing was going. Oh, I didn't know the exact details, but I knew that he would extract what he evaluated as his due from me. Hadn't he always?

That Mormon creep was scary. Good thing he just saw me as a stupid gold digger. He doesn't know I've done *Guys and Dolls* at the Rio, and was Big Nurse in *One Flew Over the Cuckoo's Nest* in summer stock. I know how to play my part. He couldn't rattle me, even coupled with his two bodyguards looking all fish-eyed at me.

Him asking all polite and slithery with his quiet voice and the way he leans in when he's sitting with his fancy cane and all. Eldon showed some backbone, though, talked up for me, for us, really. That must be kinda new 'cause that bastard gave him a stare, that's for sure. Getting it regularly makes a man strong.

Eldon was so ready for the picking, I knew my plan was going to work.

I straddled him one more time and made all the right sounds. Sorry Eldon, but you're just a means to an end. You and that clown who actually believed I was going to kick back a percentage to him like his other girls had 'cause this was his idea and he'd set the con up. Nothing worse than a bullshitter who started to believe his own BS.

"Are you familiar with the Mormon Cricket?"

If I could talk without spitting blood, I still wouldn't have answered. When the bishop arrived, Hat Boy figured to rack up extra points with his boss, and slugged me when I tried to rise from the corner.

"The Mormon Cricket," he continued, "is not in fact a cricket, but a katydid."

The bishop glanced down at his ostrich-skin boots, then back at my battered face. He sat near me, imperial-like in a folding chair, his large hand gripping his dark wood cane topped with a silver bird of some sort. "They are a large insect, though incapable of flight. They live in and on sagebrush and alfalfa, and I've seen them decimate fields of fragrant Black-eyed Susans and Morningstars. These abominations will even eat their own." He got a misty look in his pale eyes, then refocused on me.

"The first settlement's wheat was saved by gulls eating those damned insects," Bishop George said, glaring down at me like Odin used to mad dog Thor in those worn-out Jack Kirby comics I had. My only inheritance from a long-gone mother. Back when I was in one of the several foster homes I'd supposedly been raised in.

"Do you not see the significance of that? Here you had birds, seagulls, that came from the ocean, from California, to save us in the desert in Utah." He pointed his gull-headed cane at me.

I couldn't muster a response. What did he expect me to do, convert?

"The spirit of Joseph Smith was with us then, as it is now.

"Your Jezebel took money from Eldon Dudley and then disappeared. This was some two hundred thousand in cash reserves he kept tucked away for necessities."

"I don't know what you're talking about." Yeah, that was pretty lame, but I wasn't inclined to give him the satisfaction that I was beaten. Not only had he caught me, but the chick I'd set up as the dentist's Noreen had skipped out on me as well. How sad was that?

Given his exertions at tanning my hide, Hat Boy was wiping his face with a handkerchief. He then gulped down some bottled water Leaning Man had passed to him. Bishop George, a tall sumbitch with a mug like a knot of wood and an Abe Lincoln jaw, smiled. That was gruesome. "You make money by setting up lonely, well-to-do men with women who purport to be their lost loves."

Mostly he was correct. I did background research on the marks like you do in any long con. But I didn't coach the women to be the dead wife or high-school sweetheart, endlessly drilling them with facts and dates. That kind of pretend the chump would see through in no time. The art of my approach was for the woman to remind the sucker of the dead wife or the girlfriend. There were other guys hyped on actresses from their teenaged days. Hell, there was even one mark, a software geekonaire, who had this crush on his junior-high teacher. So I had Steiner remodel Helen just enough to suggest her features and he was hooked. We took him for more than three hundred Gs in stock options he signed over to her to save her supposedly ailing son. This setup included a child actor we hired to wheeze and sweat in a hospital bed. His stage mother desperate to get the kid a credit. People.

See I got the idea for the con watching this Hitchcock flick *Vertigo* on TV one night in a motel room in El Monte, laying low from a grift gone south. In the movie, Jimmy Stewart has it bad for Kim Novak, who reminds him of this other woman he couldn't save because of his fear of heights. Only of course it turns out Jimmy's being played. Kim is both women, the dead bit faked to draw him into a psychological trap of sexual obsession. And thus I created the Kim Novak Effect.

I figured the big dog here must have invested money in Dudley's clinics.

I knew from my due diligence the dentist was a lapsed Mormon. "How'd you get to me if my girl lit out?"

Bishop George was smoking a cigaret in one of those old-fashioned cigaret holders. On him, it wasn't gay, just eerie. "Searching for the woman's trail, I worked backwards." He blew a stream of smoke into the still air. "The bartender at the Blue Velvet told me, for a hundred dollars, you'd gotten her hired there. Said he owed you a favor over some sort of misunderstanding. One I'm sure you engineered so as to have him in your pocket when you needed him." He tapped ash. "That put me on to you and," he spread his arms wide, "here you are."

"So what do you want?"

"I'm your new partner, partner. And you will pay back the money, with interest."

Shit. "That right?"

The bishop stood, poking my leg with the end of his cane. "Yes, that is so. You will continue to do what you do, the research and selection of the woman." He showed his blunt teeth. "I have no insight into the type of devious female you seem to be able to ferret out for this work. But I do have ideas on certain businessmen and politicians that we will go after."

"Wonderful."

"Get him cleaned up," Bishop George said to his muscle. Hat Boy made to snatch me off the floor but stumbled and then went to one knee, heaving.

"The hell," he said, and keeled over like a felled rhino.

Bishop George stared at this and Leaning Man said, "Let's go," to me. There was a gun in his hand.

"What's going on here?" the bishop sputtered, gaping at his goon. He squinted, pushing his homely face toward the hood. He started to laugh. "Very good. Very clever," he said.

We left the bishop in the unfinished room, methodically tapping his cane. Out in the dusk Leaning Man helped me into the late-model Mustang they brought me in, and we rode away from those unfinished two stories in a development where the bishop was one of several investors. At a motel on 93, near the Arizona border, Helen was waiting for us as we entered a room.

She was still hosting her Jerri Rocklyn look. "Guess we've worn out our welcome in Vegas," she cracked, noting my condition.

Leaning Man had already removed the bulky coat and now his shirt, revealing the wrap and sports bra Shauna Cheung wore to hide her breasts. She scrubbed off her fake beard and the glue she'd used on her eyelids to make them temporarily rounder and less of her natural epicanthal fold.

I sat on the edge of the bed. "How'd you two work this?"

"The bishop was asking around about you once he got your name from Burt," Helen said. Burt was the bartender at the Blue Velvet. "This I learned from a girlfriend who works the VIP lounge at Caesars."

I looked at Cheung, who had stripped down to her underwear. I supposed that whatever she gave Hat Boy in the bottled water to knock him out, she'd done to the hood she'd impersonated. She'd worn some padding to give her quite obvious female physique more of a manly shape. Pointing at her I said, "You two already knew each other."

"Yep," Cheung answered. "We figured you and the doc needed watching."

That was horseshit. Neither of them gave a damn about me or that cokehead. They'd been setting me or Steiner up for something, only the bishop's intervention presented another opportunity. Plus, they let me take a beating to make me grateful when they got me out of it. They wanted me for something.

"We better get down the road." Helen was up and moving.

I could have split—or tried to, since I was sure Shauna didn't just wave around that pistol for show. I should have gone on and left these two scheming honeys to work their juju on some other sucker. But I was the dude who came up with this and damned if I was going to turn over my most lucrative swindle to them for nothing.

Turns out Helen had been scamming the Leaning Man, the real one, for a while. He was too young to know about Jerri Rocklyn, but was mesmerized by that rack she sported. That's why she'd tried to beg off getting re-cut. She'd recently learned from him that the bishop had a network of non-Mormon business and elected-official types he hobnobbed with, and not just in Nevada.

Relocated to swell Laguna Beach, California, Steiner modeled me to look just enough like the long-disappeared surfer son of a widow whose Frank Gehry-designed glass-and-stone pad overlooks the Pacific. I clip her toenails, make sure she takes the right meds at the right time, and give her back rubs with lotion that, well, let's just say often leads to other duties, if you follow my meaning. Ugh.

I couldn't run now anyway. My real name and face was on some kind of Homeland Security watch list thanks to the bishop. According to this bent-lawyer acquaintance of mine, this also put getting to my funds in the off-shore accounts iffy—at least for now, until I figured that out.

Hey, I know, the situation's somewhat reversed, but I'm also lining up some of the widow's male friends for the women to do their thing. So as I sat here on the deck of the old girl's house, as she napped from our rub-down session, I sipped a merlot and watched the sky turn orange. On the sound system Celine was singing about the Last Plane Out. And I dreamed of being on one some day, no longer trapped by the Kim Novak Effect.

Three Calendars

by Angelique Fawns

My life is full of mysteries. Mysteries and calendars. A calendar by my bed, one on the fridge, and one on my iPhone.

Opening my eyes, I start every day the same way. Birds chirp outside, light filters through my window, and I whisper to myself, "My name is Betty. I'm a retired racehorse groom. And my sister is missing." I know these things. What I don't know is what day it is. Rolling out of bed, I look at the calendar on my bedside table. Before I go to bed at night the first thing I do is X-out the current day. This way when I wake up and look at the calendar I can see right away that today is Sunday, September 30.

Looking beside me in the bed, I notice that there is an indent on the pillow next to me, but the body that should be lying there is missing. My husband. Where is the guy on a Sunday morning? It's not like he's a churchgoer. It seems I see less and less of him these days.

I pull the sheets up on the bed so it resembles something neat and walk into my kitchen. It's not neat in there. My husband has left a mess. Toast crumbs everywhere, a dirty plate in front of the TV with last night's sports highlights playing on mute, and a sludgy half-filled coffee.

I feel a familiar rise of frustration. Twenty-some-odd years married and the guy can't figure out how to put a cup into the dishwasher? Argh. I carry the offending things to the sink and grab my own mug and start a coffee for myself in the Keurig. My reflection stares back at me from the window,

239

distracting me from the lovely view out there. At fifty-nine, I still look pretty good. My auburn hair curls around my face with only a bit of gray sprinkled at the temples. My cheekbones are still striking, not covered yet by the slow spread of weight that gets most of us in old age. It seems the pounds are finding me from the bottom up. My thighs and hips are heavier, but my chest is still boy-flat. with defined collarbones peeking out from my nightgown.

What was I doing? There is a coffee cup decorated with a horse in my hand that says *I've spent most of my life in the saddle, the rest I've just wasted.* That's right, I was making a cup of Keurig's Krispy Kreme coffee. I love the convenience but hate the guilt. I remember a meme I saw on Facebook of all these little used pods encircling the planet in space. Destroying the earth one caffeine hit at a time. Why can't I forget that horrible picture when I can't seem to remember what I planned today?

Good thing I have another handy calendar for that. Taking my coffee and sipping at it, I wander over to the fridge to look at the photocopied calendar given to me every month by my son with my grandchild's schedule on it. It's Sunday, September 30, and the day is wide open. I don't have to pick up my grandson after school today. That is my biggest responsibility these days. Providing a shuttle service and daycare for five-year-old Jack. Both his parents work and need an hour or two before they can pick him up at the end of the day.

This gives me plenty of time to look for Elvie. When I try and talk to my husband Paul?—Phil?—yes, Phil, about how I'm worried about her, he gets belligerent.

"Betty! Elvie is dead. Please, please let this go," he always says, putting his hands on his blond, balding head in exasperation. Then he walks away and turns on the sports channel or locks himself in his office.

I also know what I heard, and it's not too late. That phone call a couple of weeks ago?—I am sure it was just a couple of weeks—when I heard her plea for help:

"Betty, he's got me trapped. You've got to help me. He's going to kill me this time, I am sure of it. I'm running out of..." Then a gasp, and nothing.

Before I could find out where she was, the connection was lost.

Still, I shouted, "Elvie! Elvie! What has the bastard done to you?! Elviiiiee?"

Nothing but the hum of empty space.

Elvie, at only sixteen, had married the devil. He was charming and handsome and had whisked her right off her feet. Johnny Harvey was the son of the local Uncles of Anarchy biker gang and when he saw beautiful Elvie rollerblading around the neighbourhood, he decided he had to have her. Her luminous skin, long blond hair swinging to her bum, and grey-green eyes. She was stunning, naive, and had no idea about biker-gang culture.

I was the elder sister by three years and knew that the Harvey family was suspected in several robberies in the area, dealt drugs, and might even be implicated in a few murders. I warned her, this guy is bad news. His aspiration was to be a career criminal and join the same biker gang his dad ran. But Elvie was smitten. Johnny was like the birds with broken wings she brought home and the stray cats she tried to convince our mother to let her keep. She was sure he could be saved. So, one day she rode off on the back of his bike and officially became Johnny's girl.

I see a yellow sticky note at the bottom of my calendar. It says, *Look in your day planner. It is in your purse.* Still sipping my coffee, I try to remember where my purse is. Looking around, I can't see it and can't remember where I put it. I feel a swell of panic start to roll up in my chest. It's a familiar feeling. Lately, I need to get more sleep or eat more greens. It's getting harder to remember things, but I don't have Alzheimer's or dementia or any of those other brain diseases. My obnoxious daughter-in-law is constantly telling me that I need to go see a doctor about my memory. How dare she? I am fine. Everyone forgets things now and then. She should go see a doctor about her rudeness problem.

My boss at work had a rudeness problem. He accused me of messing up my best racehorse's medication and suggested I retire. I know I didn't screw up. Colic can happen to a horse at any time. And he recovered. It's not like he died. Of course, it wasn't really a suggestion from my boss, so I ended up retiring earlier than I wanted to.

Looking back at my fridge calendar, I see a little yellow sticky note on the calendar. *Look in your day planner. It is in your purse.* A logical place for a purse is on the shelf beside the coat hanger.

Walking down the hall to front door, I see it is there and take my purse back to the kitchen table. It is a lovely item with soft brown leather and fringe tassels hanging from it. I have good taste. Sitting down, I pull my day planner out and open it up to where the little marker indicates. On Saturday, September 29, I wrote *Checked out Uncles of Anarchy clubhouse. No Elvie. Maybe marijuana fields?*

Wow. I am one old, bold bitch. Did I really go check out the Uncles of Anarchy clubhouse yesterday? Those guys are dangerous. But I must have. I scrunch up my nose and try hard to remember. But nothing comes to me. The day planner/bible says I did go there, and I have learned to trust my own notes. Every day for the month of September shows I checked out all Elvie's past addresses and usual haunts, but had no luck finding her. I can see my search clearly in front of me. Every detail of my sleuthing as I look for Elvie.

The run-down trailer she lived in with Johnny is twenty minutes from us. The nail salon/massage parlour she worked at is in town. Her favorite pool bar, where lots of the bikers' "old ladies" hung out, is there too. No one had seen her.

Elvie moved out soon after she started dating Johnny. When my father found out Johnny and some of his wannabe biker friends were hiding stolen goods in our garage, it was like a nuclear bomb went off. That day is etched in my memory. Dad went ballistic. He shouted and swore and threatened to call the cops. Elvie was crying. I was crying. My mom was crying. But that was it for Dad. He believed in following the law and keeping your nose clean. Johnny had to come get his "stolen shit" out immediately and Elvie had to leave her good-for-nothing criminal boyfriend or get the hell out of his house.

Elvie called Johnny, who showed up with one of those nondescript white vans and loaded up the seventeen TVs he'd stashed in our garage and muttered something about how we better not call the cops or else. My Dad's face went so purple I thought he was going to have a heart attack on the spot. Elvie dashed up to her room to quickly pack a bag and then ran back outside and hopped into the van.

"No! Elvie, this is a terrible mistake! Mom, Dad, you can't let her go! Please stop her! Elvie!" I remember crying and shouting.

But my parents had done nothing. I guess even if they had forced her to stay that day, she would have just run off later. She was crazy smitten with that loser. Johnny had taken Elvie and his TVs off in that white van and I only saw her once after that. My sister had joined the world of criminals. I was my father's daughter and also believed in following the law and keeping my nose clean. I told Elvie if she was going to stay with a guy who lived an illegal, immoral life, I didn't want to see her again until she was ready to leave him.

I think she almost got away. Ten years later she showed up at my home in the early afternoon. Phil and I had been married for a while then and he was still at work. As a racehorse groom, I used to nip home for a nap between the morning feed/exercising chores and racing later that day. If you drew a late race on the card, you could be working till one A.M. bedding your horse back down and putting on bandages and poultices. It was just luck I was home that day.

"Betty, Betty, you've got to help me," she said as she tried to cover up a black eye with her long hair. "He's going to kill me one of these days!" There was no hiding the bloody lip. Her words were slurred because of it. The years had been hard on her. She had lost her luminous glow and looked older than I did.

"God! We've got to call the cops, Elvie. You can live with me! I should get you to the hospital!" I blurted, shouting over my shoulder while I ran to the kitchen to get some ice.

"No! If you call the cops, he will kill the both of us for sure. Oh, Jesus. I can't believe this is my life. I'm not his wife, I'm his personal punching bag. And I don't even want to tell you what he has me doing at that filthy massage parlour," Elvie said, sobbing into the ice and paper towel.

I was trying to convince her to at least let me drive her to the hospital, not being able to process what she had said about the massage parlour quite yet, when there was a banging on my front door.

"Oh God," Elvie said, starting to tremble. "It's him. I've got to go." Her eyes went deadpan and the tears cleared up as she heaved a big sigh.

"No! No, you are not going with him," I said as I stomped to the door. There was a bat sitting there that Phil had placed "just in case a bear comes a-knockin.'" I picked it up and swung the door open.

Johnny was standing there with a bottle of wine and flowers in his hand.

"Get lost! Elvie doesn't want to see you! Bastard!" I said, hoisting the bat over my head.

He ignored me. "Elvie, honey, I love you more than my Harley, more than any other of those girls, you got to come home with me. I'm nothing without you. I promise to be better!"

I swung the bat at his head, but he caught it with the hand not holding gifts for my sister.

"Easy there, or I may have to take you over my knee," he said to me with a dark chuckle.

"Next time I am not going for your head. I am going for your balls!" I said, struggling to get my bat out of his hand. I was going to have to go to the gym or maybe buy a big attack dog. Johnny was not going to come to my house again and get away unscathed. I didn't care what kind of patch he wore on his jacket.

"Betty, stop it, honey. I am going to go home with him," Elvie said, coming out from the kitchen. "Johnny, you had better not touch my sister. But I will come home with you."

"No! We'll call the cops! I'll call Phil! You don't have to go with him!" I said, desperately tugging on her arm as she walked past me out the door. I was also still trying to get my bat back from Johnny's leather-clad arm.

"Promise not to hit me with that bat so I can hug my girl?" Johnny said, looking triumphant. He let go of the bat and put that arm around Elvie's shoulders.

She slumped in resignation, and the both of them walked back to his bike, parked in my driveway. He stowed the flowers and wine in a saddlebag. She avoided my eyes as she climbed onto the back of the black Harley-Davidson. I hated those stupid bikes. I'd seen my sister whisked away from me on that ugly, noisy machine.

That was the last time I ever saw her.

Shaking the memory of her blond hair blowing out behind her as they drove away, I go back to looking at the day planner. "Marijuana fields" is written on today. I remember Elvie showing me where the Uncles of Anarchy grew a bunch of their plants when we were hiking in one of the regional forests. This was before Dad kicked her out of the house and her relationship was still new.

I get up to grab a muffin from the counter and look out my back window. As I nibble on it I try to remember where the cornfield was. The group of plants had been subtly inserted in the middle of an unsuspecting farmer's crop. There was a shed not too far from the pot-growing area that Elvie had giggled about having sex in with Johnny. Those early days when she was madly in love with her bad boy. Maybe he had taken a much older Elvie back there, beaten her up, and stashed her in the shed?

Yes, I'll check the shed today. But how am I going to get there? Not knowing exactly where that farmer's field was in the public forest could mean hours walking. And my old legs aren't as spry as they used to be. A bit of Plantar fasciitis here…a bit of arthritis there.

Taking another bite of my muffin, I gaze out the window at the pastoral beauty. We had been lucky to find a small acreage close to Phil's job as a supervisor at a local quarry and less than an hour from the racetrack. When I retired a couple of years ago, I took Ducky, one of the racing thoroughbred geldings I was grooming from the track, with me. He had blown out his tendon at his last race, and his owner/trainer knew he would never race again. Rather than put him into the retired-racehorse program, I convinced them to let me bring him home. I had a small fenced field behind our house and wouldn't mind something to fuss over to fill my days. I had rubbed four racehorses for my trainer and back then my brain was always full of exercise schedules, feed requirements, and special tack assignments. I was very proud of how I could keep every thoroughbred's different needs straight in my brain. As soon as I stopped working, it was like I lost my edge. I did not start slipping while I was at the track, my boss is wrong about that. I did not get that horse's medication wrong. But my brain did retire right along with me and decided it didn't need to hold information the same way.

What was I planning to do with Ducky again? I go back to look at my day planner and see that I wanted to go look for that farmer's shed near the pot field. Because Elvie is missing and in trouble! Grabbing my keys, purse (making sure I put my day planner back in it), and a warm jacket, I walk out of the back door and hop into my pickup truck. It already has the horse trailer attached to it and I keep my saddle and bridle in it at all times.

Walking out into the field with a lead shank and apple treat, I grab Ducky and walk him to the trailer. Like a good boy he jumps right on and we are off to ride in the regional forest. Wow. I can sure handle a horse trailer well. A small bloom of pride wells up in me. If you do an action enough times, there are some things you never forget!

Every time I had a day off at the racetrack I used to ride my old mare Tulip on the trails. As soon as my husband and I bought our hobby farm, I purchased Tulip from a trail-riding barn and financed this little trailer. Sadly, she died a few years ago from old age, and I had been horseless at home until I retired with Ducky. My feet and hands automatically drive me to the trailhead entrance.

What a gorgeous day for a hack! The sun is shining and the fall air is crisp. I can see some of the leaves in the forest have changed, making a colourful canopy to ride under. Before I get out of the truck, I take a pen from my purse and write on the back of my hand.

FIND THE SHED BY THE POT FIELD. LOOK FOR ELVIE.

Sometimes I get lost in the beauty of the paths and ride for hours with my brain happy and free of thoughts. Now, I need to focus and make sure I finish my mission. Elvie could be in serious trouble. This reminder on my hand will keep me on track. Grabbing my helmet, I strap it on. Safety first, right? Even my old head needs protection.

I throw my saddle on Ducky, slip the bridle over his ears, and he stands with patience as I balance on the wheel well to launch myself onto his back. For an ex-racehorse he is a surprisingly lovely ride. He snorts and shakes his chestnut head and starts to walk eagerly along the dirt path.

When we hit a wider sand stretch I let him move into a controlled gallop and the two of us seem united in our glee. The trees brush by quickly and I can feel his muscles tensing and releasing beneath me. What a rush. This is my favorite thing to do. My love of horses had taken me to my career at the racetrack, but riding is my true passion. I could do this all day. When the path narrows again, I pull Ducky up and lean forward to give him a pat.

FIND THE SHED BY THE POT FIELD. LOOK FOR ELVIE is written in pen on my hand. Right! Enough messing around on the trails, I have to go save my sister. I know this trail will lead to the edge of the forest and the farmer's cornfield.

Everything is quiet and the only thing I can hear is the huffing from Ducky's breath as he picks his way along the narrow path. Soon we come out to the edge and I see that the silage crop has already been harvested. This will make it much easier to get to the shed on the other side of the private property. Tall corn is a bugger to ride through. We walk along the edge of the cedar rail fencing until I find the break in. It was probably made by bikers so they could access their illegal crop hidden in the legal one. Ducky pushes his way through the opening and I urge him into a trot when I see the shed way over on the other edge of the property.

Hopefully, no one is out hunting on the land today. It's getting to that time of year when the deer tags come out. And Ducky is sort of like a tall orange deer. After a few minutes, I come to the shed and hop off my horse. Because there's grass surrounding the dilapidated wood structure, I unhook one rein from his bridle and let him eat while I tie the other to a stirrup.

Walking cautiously up to the shed, I try to hear if anyone is struggling inside.

"Elvie? Are you in there? Elvie? It's Betty," I whisper loudly.

I walk up to the door, which is precariously latched with a bit of rusty wire, and I open it. Peering into the depths, I can't see anything, so I take a careful step inside. The shed is empty. The faint smell of old garbage and the more recent smell of skunk tickles my nose. A few beer bottles and the ends of weed joints sit on the ground, covered by the grime of passing time. Taking a deep breath, I can see Elvie is not here. I don't know whether to be relived or disappointed.

Someone has scratched a message on the wall with a knife in the old wood.

Betty, this is a note from yourself. If you are reading this, you need to know Elvie is dead. You did find her here. A year ago. You were too late. Johnny killed her, but because you called in the cops they convicted him for murder and he is in jail. You don't have to look anymore.

I gasp and fall to my knees in the dirt on the floor. Tears start sliding down my face. It's hard to breathe, but I concentrate and count to ten and try to slow down every intake of oxygen. Elvie is dead. My beautiful sister was killed by that rabid bastard. I hope he rots in jail. I hope he's gang raped in the shower twice a day. I hope…I just can't believe she is gone. Using the back of my sleeve to wipe away my tears, I stumble out of the shed and try to get back on Ducky.

There's nothing to stand on, so it's hard to haul my old bones and big bottom back onto his back, but I manage. Sniffling and in shock, I ride back to the trailer. Elvie is dead? I had already found her? I have a vague memory of her blond hair tinged with red. The rope on her wrists…but most of it is a blur. Ducky jumps right back on the trailer and I drive home. I watch the sun setting as I pull into my driveway. The reds and purples reflect the bleeding in my heart. The memory of blood in Elvie's hair.

Ducky is happy to go back to eating grass in his field and I know he has plenty of water in his trough. I walk into the house, trying not to sob, and see Phil sitting on the couch. He has a bottle of scotch in front of him and a big tumbler full of ice. Most of the bottle of scotch is empty. He is probably a few drinks in. As usual.

"Betty! I saw the trailer and Ducky were gone, so I went ahead and made some dinner. There's a plate in the microwave for you. How was your ride?" Phil said, his speech already slurring and eyes out of focus.

A wave of anger washes over me. No sense in trying to talk to him now about Elvie. If he isn't ignoring me and locked in his office, he's three sheets to the wind. When I retired, he started indulging his fondness for single malt. When I try and have a decent conversation with him, he complains I tell all the same stories over and over again. Don't we all? What else do old folks do? I can't bear to try and talk to him about Elvie when he's drunk. Ignoring him and his plate in the microwave, I have a quick shower and slip into my pajamas.

A deep exhaustion and depression rolls through my body. It's like the air has turned to molasses, and I fight my way through it. I need to go to bed. But first, I have to update my calendars. It is the end of the month. I wander out to the fridge, ignoring Phil, and put September in the garbage. My son has October ready to go with Jack's schedule. The second thing I do is flip my day planner over to October and put it back in my purse. All those empty boxes waiting to be filled. Next I go to the bedside table, take a pen and put a big X through Sunday, September 30, and flip that page to October. Tomorrow is Monday, October 1.

As soon as my head hits the pillow I fall into a deep sleep. I don't even hear Phil come to bed.

My life is full of mysteries. Mysteries and calendars. A calendar by my bed, one on the fridge, and one on my iPhone.

Opening my eyes, I start every day the same way. Birds chirp outside my window, light filters through, and I whisper to myself, "My name is Betty. I used to be a racehorse groom. And my sister is missing."

Shall I Be Murder?

by Mat Coward

As for myself, I belong to that delicious subgenre, the *self-confessed* unreliable narrator. I may be a man who has killed someone, or I may be a man who has not killed someone, depending on whether we believe what I say on the matter. And do we believe? Well, we'll see.

It's all very well doctors recommending a daily walk as a tonic for the health, but the thing is, I'm allergic to dogs.

There was nothing very much wrong with me. I had slightly too much wobble around the middle. My blood pressure was mildly high, and my breathing a little laboured under pressure. The moderate pain in my knees, the doctor assured me, was caused by nothing more serious than underexercised leg muscles, and she could cure that—or rather, I could. A good half-hour's walk, every day, if I kept it up and didn't miss days out, would yield a noticeable and clinically significant improvement in all my symptoms within weeks, and she guaranteed that with a smile, a nod, a look of challenge. Walking is a powerful medicine, she said, and it *will*, not might, make you feel better. She was convincing, and I was convinced.

But I'm allergic to dogs. It is very nearly impossible to keep to the discipline of a daily walk, indefinitely, without that walk having a direct and immediate purpose. It's all about motive, in the end. If you have a dog, of course, the decision is taken out of your hands: Dogs must be walked, and that's that. Without a dog, however…

I decided that I would use my daily half-hour to work out a plot. (Maybe I'm a writer? I'm *not,* but maybe I am.) A brisk fifteen minutes from my front door, on the outskirts of a light-industrial estate, there's a self-storage facility. An office at the end nearest the road, and then, behind a locked gate, two rows of windowless, corrugated-metal units, in various sizes. I believe these things are very common in America, but they're still a relative novelty over here. We have a lower divorce rate, of course, and perhaps, on average, we own fewer unwanted popcorn makers.

A little, secure room of your own, to which only you have the key. You can use it as you wish, provided you don't live in it, keep animals in it, or store within it items which are perishable or flammable. A terrible place to hide a body (the smell), but just perfect for temporarily unwanted furniture, ephemera collections, projects you're unlikely ever to complete but can't part with, and privacy. There is no CCTV at Bet's Boxes, because the owners understand that privacy may be the main reason for hiring a unit.

Without delay, I began my regime of restoration: a fifteen-minute march to Bet's Boxes, an hour spent in relaxed contemplation on a public bench opposite Bet's Boxes, and a fifteen-minute stride home.

When the time came, I rented two units next door to each other. I had very little to store in either of them, other than a foldable lawn chair, a laptop, a stepladder, and an electric drill, but that didn't occasion any comment from the staff in the office, as I'd been confident it wouldn't. Once my first week's rental period was up, I unrented one of the units and kept the other.

I continued with my daily walk, never missing a day no matter what the weather or the demands of other business on my time. It was making me feel better, there was no question about that. I could feel my knees strengthening. And all without a single prescription; marvellous. She knew her business, that doctor.

Now, instead of sitting on the bench, I broke my walk each time by making a brief visit to my lockup. There was a recession on—there always is, nowadays—so this phase took a little while, but eventually a new tenant rented the second unit, the one joined to mine, which I had vacated.

This tenant was of little use to me, other than as a kind of dress rehearsal. He used his unit solely for the purpose of drinking. He'd arrive every afternoon, carrying a briefcase. He'd let himself into his unit and then he'd sit on the floor, on a cushion, and drink about three-quarters of a bottle of Scotch, and then he'd leave.

Over the next few months he was succeeded by a young woman in a business suit who used the unit for sleeping in, on a futon, during her lunch break; an older woman who spent her evenings watching romantic comedies on her tablet; and a prosperous-looking middle-aged man who visited every few days, always round about midnight, for the purpose of crying. None of them of any real value from my point of view.

But I wasn't in a hurry. The whole point of the exercise, remember—you do remember I said so?—was to give a point to my exercise. Nothing more than that. Because, according to me, I'm allergic to dogs; I don't know whether that detail is convincing or not, and I suspect it may be redundant in any case, but I rather like it. I feel it adds character, so we'll keep it in for now.

I only spoke to one of the tenants throughout this time. He happened to arrive one day just as I was leaving. His arms were full of toy robots, most of them still in their original packaging, to go with the dozens already stored inside his self-store. He gave me the shamefaced smile of the incurable collector as he wrestled his key into the lock. "My girlfriend says I should sell them, and put the money into a pension plan," he told me.

"No, no, you're doing the right thing," I reassured him. "After all, people will always need toy robots."

The penultimate neighbour during my tenancy installed, with the grudging and sceptical help of his brother-in-law, a full-sized snooker table. He would spend up to ten hours a day practicing his pots, his safety play, and his break-offs, never getting any better at any of them. I found it quite painful, watching his dream die.

Bet's Boxes occupied a fairly quiet spot, except during the evening rush hour when traffic from the nearby road into London was loud enough to overwhelm all other noise: the clack of snooker balls, the shelving and rearranging of toy robots, the screech or hum of power tools, the dry sobs, and the clanking of bottles. Rush hour for the traffic; rush hour for me.

It was when the snooker man moved out that what I had been waiting for moved in: a pair of adulterers.

At least, I hoped they were adulterers, and not just a couple spicing up their entirely legitimate love life with faux clandestinity.

They did the place up to look like a bedroom; to feel like a bedroom, I suppose. Whether for practical or imaginative reasons, it looked to me like the bedroom of young newlyweds, though this pair—like all adulterers, even young ones—were middle-aged. A cheap kit bed. Basic bedside cabinets painted primary colours. Two bedside lamps. An ersatz rattan chest for the sheets. Two flimsy chairs, to rest their clothes on. Nothing else.

If you want to take advantage of adultery you've got to move fast, because adultery is rarely a game of two halves. It's typically a sprint, not a marathon. I'm going to stop those sport analogies now before I inadvertently use the word balls, but you take my point: I was now, for the first time, in a hurry.

On two separate days—and with two days in between, as even in a hurry I remained cautious—I followed the man and the woman to their separate homes. Having seen what I needed to see, in all three loci, I composed a note, sealed in an envelope addressed to "The Tenants," and taped it to the door of their unit while they were out.

It told them—warned them, you could say, though I aimed for a friendlier, more jocular tone than that suggests—that the walls of the units were surprisingly thin and provided little in the way of baffle. When they engaged in the delights of domestic society, I told them (hoping, probably in vain, that they would know the phrase and appreciate its delicacy), I, as their next-door neighbour, could hear every sound. From (if they would forgive the expression) arrival until departure.

This was not a complaint, I assured them; indeed, I made it clear that the arrangement suited my perverse nature admirably. But I felt it was only gentlemanly to let them know.

They left as soon as they'd read the note. He came back later that day with a van to remove the bedroom furniture. I wonder what happened to it. You'd hope he'd give it to charity, rather than just dump it, wouldn't you? In any case, they never came again.

As soon as they'd gone, I rented their unit. I don't blame you if you've lost track a bit, so let me recap: I originally rented units 70 and 71. Then I surrendered 70, and kept 71. Now, I was once again tenant of 70 *and* 71. But only for the minimum rental period allowed; a week later, I moved out of both units, for the final time.

The spy camera in unit 70 was not on a battery. I needed it to run continuously, for extended periods, so to be on the safe side I had drilled a tiny hole between the two rooms, sufficient for an even tinier electric cable, plugged into the mains in unit 71. That hole—Exhibit A, shall we call it?—is no doubt still there, should anyone, for any reason, wish to check.

During my daily rest between the two halves of my therapeutic walk, in that long period when I was waiting for something blackmailable to occur, I would watch the previous twenty-four hours of tapes at very high speed. For the most part, of course, that was an unbelievably dull task, but on the other hand, it was quite relaxing. Those two things are often the same, don't you find? Which is why I almost never relax.

The day after the couple had fled, and I had access once more to both of the little metal rooms, I removed the camera, the cable, my laptop and my chair, and my other scant possessions, and cleaned each unit thoroughly, so that they retained, to the best of my ability, no visible or microscopic traces of human habitation. That was a long, sweaty job, I have to say; very good exercise, though, I should imagine. On top of which, I now had two new places to march to every day: his house, and her house. I would have loved to have told my doctor. She'd have been so impressed.

The key point about blackmail—and in offering this tip, I mean you no offence; for all we know, you may never have occasion to use it—is setting the price. It's got to be low enough that the target can, and will, pay it. But it's also got to be high enough that they will take you seriously.

You see what I mean? Demand a million pounds from an unemployed bus driver and he will laugh and tell you to do your worst. Ask a millionaire businessman for a hundred pounds and he'll laugh and fling a handful of change in your face, and carry on without breaking his stride.

I chose the woman as my victim, after a week or so of study. The two cars in her drive were considerably more expensive than the one car which spent its night on the kerbside outside her lover's marital home. The house itself was a little grander. And, most importantly of all, I observed from my concealment what appeared to be genuine affection between her and her husband; not so much between the lover and his wife. Can pay and *will* pay, remember; both conditions must be satisfied.

Ten thousand pounds, I decided. No, I know—not a fortune, hardly even a decent hourly wage, considering all the time and work I'd put into my plot, but then we must keep in mind that the *plot* was never the point. The point was the exercise. The payoff, you could say, was there only to give verisimilitude. And it is, you'd have to admit, a serious-sounding amount. Even allowing for inflation, the phrase "Ten thousand pounds or I send your husband the tapes" still makes a satisfying noise in a startled adulteress's ear.

She took six days to get the money together without her husband's knowledge. I didn't mind at all; every day of those six I stood outside her house as she arrived home from work, allowing her to see me, giving her a little wave as her car turned into the drive. So that was six more days during which I had an object for my exercise. My knees were as strong now—I really do think they were—as they had been when I was twenty years younger.

All very satisfactory. Ah…but here, I'm afraid, I made what a more honest storyteller might confess as a mistake.

I'd hate anyone to think I got greedy. I'd hate it from all sorts of points of view. I'd hate it because it is so dull and pedestrian and inevitable and seedy. I'd hate it because it isn't true. And I'd hate it because it would mean you hadn't been listening.

The reason I decided to blackmail the woman's lover, as well as the woman herself, had nothing to do with outcome and everything to do with process. If I was greedy for anything, it wasn't money—it was purpose. More days of meaningful walking.

If he said no, I would simply walk away. Walking away counts as walking, after all. I had my ten thousand pounds, and I had no interest in breaking up anyone's marriage. Another crucial thing to remember about blackmail is never to go through with your threat: There is nothing in it for you, and it removes all constraints on your subject's behaviour.

In any case, I no longer had the tapes. They were potential evidence against me, should my target decide to go to the police, and as such had been destroyed as soon as I had printed out a few choice screen grabs. They, in turn, would be burned as soon as I'd shown them to the woman's lover.

Something can always go wrong, though. Essentially, it comes down to this: Even the most rational blackmailer, using the best thought-out plot imaginable, cannot control other people's impetuousness. What I should have done is found a park where there were ducks fifteen minutes away from my house, and taken bread there every day to feed the ducks with. Fifteen minutes there, bit of a sit-down, fifteen minutes back. That would have been much more sensible, instead of going for a double on the blackmail.

"Do your worst," he said, and those were his exact words. He was going to tell his wife about the affair himself, he said, and then he was going straight round to tell his lover's husband, and then I could go to hell.

I shrugged. I could hardly disagree with his analysis of the situation, could I? I'd had my walk, so I walked away. What must have happened next—though of course I have no way of knowing for sure, since I wasn't there—is that the lover must have gone, as promised, to speak to the husband, and somehow that conversation must have developed into a violent confrontation, during which the husband was fatally hit over the head with a rock from the rockery of a nearby garden. It's unfortunate that all this happened in the blind spot between two CCTV cameras, but that's hardly my fault.

When the police came round to see me, I made them a pot of tea, and we drank it together in a civilized fashion while they tried to convince themselves that they'd finally got me. I trust that the detective constable's contemporaneous notes will confirm that it was a good cup of tea, served with an excellent cake from the posh new bakery on the high street.

From the start, I offered to make a full and formal statement, but the detective inspector said she preferred just to chat, for now, and I was happy to do that too. For now. She's a charming woman, so much more intelligent than her predecessor, or indeed his predecessor.

Her version of the husband's death was very different to mine. I didn't tell her mine at that time, because I was saving that, but I was happy to hear hers. I killed the husband. That's the gist of it.

I'd had a long-running feud with the dead man, the cuckold, which gave me motive for killing him. I pointed out that I'd never met the unfortunate man in my life, I'd never had any dealing with him, and that if they believed otherwise they should try and prove it. Which they couldn't, evidently, because if they could, they would have done so long before.

The reason I killed him now, apparently, was because of "deteriorating long-term market conditions" which had forced me to seek drastic solutions. Extraordinary to hear such language from the lips of a police officer! I can remember when the average D.I. could scarcely manage to read the words on the oath card in court without stumbling. So different now: A police detective today is as likely as not to have a degree in Banking Science; I can remember when people joined the police because they'd *failed* their exams.

In any case, market conditions? "Do I look poor to you, my dears?" I asked them. "That cake shop charges an arm and a leg."

There came a point when I decided to move the plot on. It was time for my walk, and I really could not afford to miss my walk. So I gave them the name and address of the widow's lover. "It is my belief that this man committed the murder," I explained. "I can't tell you how I know, not at this point. Let's just say it came to me in a dream. I will perhaps be able to tell you more when I make my formal statement in the presence of my solicitor."

The D.I. recovered very quickly, and I was very impressed. She said that she would check out this lead I had given her before "putting me to the trouble" of a formal interview. So kind, I said. We nodded at each other and shook hands. Thank you for the cake, she said. It was lovely.

The day after her husband's awful passing, the widow went into a charity shop on the high street, a few doors down from the cake shop, and bought every item of female clothing in her size that they had on the hangers. Everything. She explained to the assistant that yesterday her husband had accused her—quite erroneously—of having an affair, and had burned her entire wardrobe on a bonfire in their garden. The neighbours had seen it, and closed their windows against the smoke.

A curiously feminine form of revenge, I thought, when I heard about it. But that was probably just my old-fashioned prejudices, and probably not significant.

Both of the supposed lovers denied having an affair, the D.I. told me when we next met. They had never once set eyes on each other. He had never in his life stood upon the piece of pavement near her house, where her husband met his tragic death, and she, for her part, had never heard of the self-storage facility.

Hardly an unexpected response, I suggested. He doesn't want to be a suspect in a murder investigation, and she is sticking by him. She might as well, now that her husband's dead.

"Possibly," said the D.I., "although our preferred possibility is that there never was any affair, there never was any blackmail. You planned this as a murder from the start."

The purpose of this statement—I make no bones about it—is to provide an alternative narrative to that put forward by the police: one in which I am merely a blackmailer, not a killer.

Every piece of evidence with which the police might try to buttress their theory of the husband's death is, I am confident, covered by my tale of the self-storage, the hidden camera, the weak knees.

I appear on CCTV, in the days immediately before the murder, lurking around the dead man's street. Certainly I do: I was blackmailing his wife.

The D.I. and her team claim that I am a successful career criminal, that they have been after me for years; but they are unable to produce any court-worthy evidence to that effect, and have to admit that I have never been convicted of any criminal offence. The same, incidentally, applies to the man I am supposed to have killed—my criminal rival. I would suggest that the Crown Prosecution Service will be unimpressed by this as the basis of a motive.

If I wasn't blackmailing the wife, I should like to know, how did I end up in possession of her ten thousand pounds? I have voluntarily handed that money in to the police, and I don't doubt that their forensic service will be able to link it to her, one way or another, through fingerprints or hair samples or banking transactions. The D.I., rather weakly (if you'll forgive me saying so), suggested that I stole it, though so far no one has offered even a hint of an explanation of when or how.

There is no trace of the widow at the self-storage unit, according to forensics. Well, I should imagine not: As I have already said, I cleaned it thoroughly to remove traces of me. In doing so I have clearly removed traces of her too. I'll bet there's no trace of her lover either, and yet it is undisputed that he did rent that unit, during the period which I have specified. I say he rented it for the purpose of adultery; the man himself, apparently, says he used it to store personal possessions during a temporary estrangement from his wife which saw him briefly barred from the marital home. Neither claim can be verified now.

I am in fact allergic to dogs and I have quite a history of visits to the doctor, conversations with the pharmacist, and prescriptions to prove it. A relatively recent history, perhaps, but a history even so.

That is why I disposed of the clothing I was wearing on the day of the murder. Not, as the police wish to believe, because the clothes were bloodstained, but because during my walk home on that occasion I was subjected to unsolicited affection from a large, hairy dog which covered me from head to foot in its dander before I was able to escape its friendly embrace.

The dead man's widow is adamant that she was not having an affair, and therefore I was not blackmailing her. Her reasons for this insistence are obscure and of no interest to me, except insofar as they make a prosecution of me for blackmail seem a rather remote possibility. By my account, I blackmailed one person and attempted to blackmail another—but since neither of them is willing to give victim statements to that effect, I think the police realise that this is a dead end.

As things stand, neither the police's story, nor my story, can be wholly substantiated. I would be insulting my audience's intelligence if I pretended that this was accidental: I am, by my own admission, an unreliable narrator. Or at least, I claim to be.

The police in this country do not decide whom to prosecute. That is the job of the Crown Prosecution Service, and that body, under its own guidelines as posted on its website, must proceed only where there is a "realistic prospect of conviction." The purpose of this unreliable confession is to confuse, to obfuscate, to undermine. To render such a prospect unrealistic.

It is time for bluntness—without, I do hope, giving offence. I don't trust the police. The D.I. is a very pleasant young woman, and her colleagues have been unfailingly civil in all their dealings with me, but it is not in my nature to trust any police. I do not trust them to get their murder investigation right, and would far rather put my trust in the austerity-crippled budget and bureaucratic self-protectiveness of the CPS.

To be on the safe side, I must stress that this voluntary statement to the police should not be seen as an admission that anything it contains is actually true. (I think I could survive a charge of wasting police time, if it comes to that.) My narrative unreliability, I must formally reiterate for the record, applies to that which incriminates me as well as that which exonerates. No doubt there are laws against lying in statements to the police, but if the CPS were to prosecute me for lying in this statement they would be admitting that parts of it are untrue—and wasn't that rather my point all along?

My lawyer warns me that I'm being too clever for my own good; she flatters me—I consider all this to be little more than an opusculum.

And that, I think, is about it. Have I missed anything? Any gaps in the plot? Any little bits of characterisation that don't quite ring sweet? We managed to weave the dog allergy into the weft, didn't we, so I'm glad that's not been left dangling. You might be wondering what I use as a destination for my walks now and I suppose I could tell you, but actually I'd rather keep that to myself, because you never know where these things might lead.

We don't need to waste any time on this last-minute theory of the detective inspector's, in my opinion. The one that made her eyes suddenly pop open, and her mouth dilate, and her heartbeat skitter; the one that caused her to interrupt my statement halfway through—much to the horror of my solicitor, whose belief in the sanctity of procedure was quite shaken.

"She *did* give you the ten thousand pounds," said the D.I., and I've only settled for "said" because I couldn't decide between "breathed" and "blurted."

According to this new version—exploding from the D.I.'s subconscious, it seems to me, as a consequence of desperation rather than inspiration—I didn't kill the husband, and the lover didn't kill the husband: The wife killed the husband. Afraid to leave him and afraid to stay with him—afraid for her life, that is—she resolved to rid herself of the violent criminal to whom she was welded, and she recruited me to supply her with a plot and various other assistances. She perhaps approached me because I am her lover, or perhaps because I was her husband's rival, with almost as much wish as she had to see him dead. Or both; perhaps we started as partners and ended up in a bed in a self-storage unit in the afternoon. I can't say; it's not my story. The ten thou is either payment for professional services in bullying-husband removal, or else a theatrical prop to prop up the blackmail story. Or (once again) both.

As my solicitor rightly and deftly pointed out, there are an awful lot of "fill in details later" moments in the D.I.'s latest outline, and I don't think we'll be hearing much more about it. Any forensic evidence of the widow's guilt presumably went up with the clothes on that bonfire. There's no CCTV.

There are no witnesses; the D.I. herself has insisted all along that the alleged lover was nowhere in the vicinity. There are motives here and connections there, but each one fits two other stories just as neatly as it fits this one and I can't see the Crown Prosecutor being keen to choose between them.

In any case, I've had enough of talking. The rest is up to the D.I. The CPS. The fates or the forensics. I am allergic to dogs. I walk for my health. I am unreliable. That's all you're getting.

Motormouth

by S.J. Rozan

Hey, long time! How you been, okay? What's going on? Yeah, me either, same old same old. You gonna be on that much longer? Two more miles, that's cool, I'll wait. What are you doing, ten? See, you're the patient type, I can tell. Just do it, whatever it takes. Not me. I get bored, know what I mean? My mind keeps racing, this thing, that thing. No, I stretched already, I'll wait. Around this gym, you gotta keep your eye out, or some guy'll jump right in on your machine. Half the time, a woman's waiting, they don't even see you. Especially if you're the type like me. I just zone when I'm working out. Probably doesn't happen so much to you. You, like, stay alert, see what's going on. And you got attitude, probably you can stare them down, even you being small. You got attitude, you don't take nothing, I can tell. You go, girl! Me, I figure, whatever. I just get into it, know what I mean? Put on the headphones, crank up the music. Man! That's the best, know what I mean? Not that I get, like, oblivious or whatever. That's the right word, right, oblivious? What I mean is, I still know, like, where I am, what's going on. Pisses me off when people say I don't. Like this cop, two nights ago? I was here, I do arms and back on Tuesdays. Don't you usually come Tuesdays? Thought so, but didn't see you. Anyway, so when I'm done I drive down to the 7-Eleven. I'm still pumped, so I've got the headphones on, I'm cool. I'm picking up a few things, beers, whatever, and these three little guys come charging in, ski masks and everything, they're robbing the place! I'm, like, what is this, a midget robbery? And then I see they're not guys. They're women! Women! Don't that kick ass? Girls rule! I'm all, like, wow! Then I'm, like, girl, you need to be scared, what the hell's the matter with you? Women, men, they got guns, they could blow your head off either way. So I'm thinking that, and Blammo! One of them shoots the clerk. Blood flying everywhere, he, like, explodes! I guess I never saw anybody shoot anybody before, I'm frozen to the spot. Maybe you saw it on the news? No? I mean, she really blew this guy away! Well, so I'm frozen there, my mouth is probably open, I look like a dork, and I should be scared but I'm just thinking, this is too cool, a girl gang. Like, where do I sign up? And the coolest thing: the whole time I got Lil' Kim in my earphones, like the holdup has a sound track or something. What've you got, another mile? Cool. No, I'll wait. So anyway, I guess they don't even notice me, they're in and out so fast. They drive away. I stand there some more, then I get unfrozen. Duh, call the cops, girl. So I do. The cop who comes, he gets pissed at me right away for the earphones. Like I was really gonna be able to identify their voices if I wasn't wearing them. What does he think, they stood around talking? Anyway, I told him what I saw. I mean, I'm his only damn witness. He should be grateful. He's hot, too. And I saw a lot. Like I said, I'm not oblivious. They were all kind of small, I told him, and the one who shot the guy, she had this tattoo on her left wrist. Sort of like yours, now I look at it. You're Dominican, right? This is like some Dominican thing, tattoos on the wrist? Hey, cool, so maybe they were Dominican. He'll like that. The cop. We're having a drink later. I told you he was hot. I called him, said I remembered something about the robbery. What? No, of course I didn't, he was just hot. But check it out, now I have something to tell him, about the tattoo being Dominican. Cool. You believe this, he was even pissed I couldn't identify the car they used. Well, hell, it was one of those damn SUV's, a Fourrunner or something, how should I know? Some bumper sticker on the back, dent in the side. That should be enough for him, don't you think? Was it black? he asks. Well, duh, they're all black. There must be ten of them out here in the gym lot right now. You drive one, right? Everybody drives one. Except me, I drive that little yellow Toyota. Well, I mean, it goes. Just keeps going, just like me. You done? Cool. I didn't rush you or anything? I hate that, when people stand around talking, make you feel like you got to rush. Bet it doesn't bother you, though. You don't take bull, just do what you have to do. How far am I going? Hey, I only do two miles. What? Fast as I can. I got to race through it before I notice what I'm doing, otherwise I get sick of it. Then? Well, hell, then I shower and I'm done. Did all my lifting already. Got to go meet that cop. You done too? Don't you usually lift after you run? Oh, you gotta be someplace? Cool. Well, have a good time. The cop? At Stardust, you know, that bar on Market. Yeah, tell me about it, there's never a place to park over there. I guess he doesn't care, he can park anywhere, you don't get a ticket in a cop car. Me? Around the block, over by the church. No one's ever there on a weeknight, that whole block's deserted. I always park there. No, never had trouble yet. Well, time to crank up the Discman. Yeah, thanks, you have a good night too. Will I see you tomorrow? Why, you won't be here? Well, if you will, then I'll see you. What do you mean, you don't think so? Oh, whatever. See you some other time, then. Stay cool. Bye.

Never Enough

by Liza Cody

As every woman of intelligence knows, a certain sort of man offers a relationship when all he wants is sex but doesn't want to look like a sexist chimp. Equal and opposite, a man of experience knows that a certain kind of woman, if she's sober, offers sex when what she wants is a relationship but doesn't want to look predatory.

Everyone knows the game. An ambiguous deal is struck. It's where a battle begins. It is fun—unless the wrong one wins, so I'm told. I wouldn't know: I always win.

I snagged the husband by the usual method before I was thirty, and the annoying kid meant that the husband stayed sober long enough to provide me with a fairly decent house. It could have been better. Maybe nobody knows what they want till what they've got just isn't good enough.

Then, years later, when the marriage was worn as thin as the hall carpet, I landed a man my friends envied me for. An artist. "How romantic," they said.

After a while I said, "I love you," because I wanted to hear him say it to me.

"I love you too," he said. And although the commitment is implied in the words, it didn't sound passionate enough. Men really do take effort.

I wanted him because, at the bar, someone told me he was a painter. I bought him a glass of the wine he was drinking and said, "I hear you're an artist. I adore Lucian Freud."

He turned to introduce me to the woman he was standing next to but I pretended not to hear, and after a moment she walked away almost as if she'd heard me say, "Get lost." Then there was only him and me. And I hadn't done a thing to make it happen.

We didn't talk about Lucian Freud. We talked about me.

"A guy like you can't want to know about an *ordinary* woman," I said. Men never recognise flattery. They experience it as true admiration. But in his rarefied arty gallery world, he said, he didn't often meet down-to-earth people. I was a "breath of fresh air."

After a while, he went on his way because he'd promised someone a lift home. I smiled coolly and said goodbye, but not before he'd told me how to contact him through his website.

The next day I looked at his website with my friend Penelope. She wasn't interested in the paintings but she pored over the photographs of him.

"I don't know, Sheena," she said. "He's a bit old and overweight."

"But he's quite famous," I countered. That shut her up. And I was thinking, old and fat: good. The older and fatter he is, the younger and slimmer I'll look by comparison. One of the biggest kicks I get when I'm out with a guy is when someone mistakes him for my father. A girl has to think about these things when she's facing her…well, a big birthday.

After Penelope left, I studied the website again. There he was, Hal Yaeger, in his studio and at various gallery openings. He'd had a picture bought by Tate Modern, which seemed to be a big deal. But the pictures were confusing. I didn't understand them at all.

I'd seen a TV program about Lucian Freud, and I'd wished someone famous like him had wanted to paint me. Even though he had a cruel eye for age, and saw women as the colour of corpses, he'd *really* looked at them. He'd turned those hawkish eyes on a model and looked and looked. I'm sure a woman felt properly seen when she modelled for him. But as far as I could tell from Hal Yaeger's paintings, he didn't look at women at all.

Timing is important. I'm a professional woman, and I don't like to seem too keen, so it was eight days before I composed a careful e-mail to him. I said, politely, that I'd enjoyed meeting him and asked if he could recommend a book or a blog to help me because I didn't understand modern art at all. I realised, I said, after looking at his website, that I was missing something important.

It didn't take him eight days to reply. So I won that round.

The other guy I was writing to at the time was a client—someone I met when showing him a city-centre flat. He'd come to the point far too quickly, offering me a "quick bonk" after only four exchanges. I wasn't really tempted because, although he was looking at very expensive properties and the commission I'd earn would be substantial, he was too bad-mannered. I am not destined to be "a bit on the side."

"What about Barnaby?" asked Nancy, my other friend, who I don't like much.

"What about Barnaby?" I said. "I've pleaded with him about his drinking. Has there been one occasion he hasn't spoiled by making a scene? We can't go on like this."

"I know, but you *could* get him into rehab or something. Breaking up a family is a really big deal."

Well, she should know. Both her kids are in therapy. I said, "I can't make Barnaby do anything."

"But it sounds as if you're trying to replace him before he's gone," she said. This is why I don't like Nancy—she's an inconvenient thinker as well as being slim and stylish.

"If you'd been married without complaint to a lush for as long as I have, you'd want a little harmless fun too."

Barnaby is a techie, but he should pay more attention to the papers he signs. He was either stoned or lazy when we talked about mortgages. As an estate agent, I knew way more than he did, so he left all the work to me. I'll cash in on that work soon. In eleven months, the deal will let me buy him out for the price we paid years ago, which is a fraction of what it's worth now.

It pays to think ahead. And I have earned every penny.

Hal sent me a list of books about art history. I asked him questions about Joan Miró, Alexander Archipenko, and, of course, his own work. After about a month I felt we'd got to know each other sufficiently to drop in a few personal details, for instance that Barnaby and I were only occupying the same house because of the annoying kid. He responded by telling me he was divorced. I began to sign my e-mails with a kiss. He followed suit.

Then he sent me a catalogue of his latest one-man show. I admired it excessively but couldn't help noticing it was four years old. He said he was working towards a "retrospective."

Meanwhile I had subscribed to an online *Art Today* site and saw from the photos that he had attended a "vernissage" for a weird "sound sculpture" performance that had attracted many luminaries and a lot of unexplained praise.

He should've invited me to that as his plus one, I thought, after I'd asked my phone to define vernissage. I bet the crowd he was with hadn't worked as hard as I had on an exchange of probably fifty e-mails. A vernissage is a private viewing, in case you didn't know—and even if you did, understanding it doesn't make you more intelligent than me. Just pompous.

In one of the photos I noticed the woman he'd been talking to the evening we first met, the evening I count as our anniversary. She was clearly older than me and therefore of no importance.

"You're actually going to meet him?" Penelope said. She was almost as excited as I was but only half as cool.

Nancy sipped her coffee and raised one eyebrow. "Seriously?" she said. "You've only met him the once and already you've bought new underwear?"

Something of the accusatory way she said this reminded me of my mother. I said, "And you stick your fingers down your throat every time you eat cake."

She stared at me with wet eyes, then picked up her bag, snatched her coat off the back of her chair, and walked stiffly out of the cafe.

"Why on earth did you say that?" Penelope asked.

"Because it's the truth," I said.

My mother turned my daddy against me when I was sixteen. She caught me in her bed with a boy in Senior Two. I was wearing the see-through garment I bet she hadn't worn for decades. She was supposed to be at Aunt Suzie's for the whole afternoon, so it was her own fault. On top of that, she couldn't get it through her thick head that I was now more of a woman than she was. She was old dried-up bones in a skin sack. Why did she deserve the big bed and see-through negligee? Why did she think she could control how much lippy I wore or how high my heels were or how late I stayed out? Why was it okay for her to drink vodka and tonic but not me?

What gave her the right to snitch on me to Daddy? I don't know what she told him, but from then on he wasn't *my* daddy anymore, he was *her* husband. There were no more country hikes or trips to the garden centre. He cut me out of his life; all because she told him to.

I'd written, "Wouldn't it be weird if, after all this time, we never saw each other again? x."

He wrote, "I feel as if I've known you forever. x."

At last! I thought. Because this had taken baby steps. I know when not to rush. But now we had exchanged so many virtual kisses he couldn't claim we didn't have a relationship.

I wanted to meet him at a gallery, but he suggested Kew Gardens, which I thought was a bit odd. Plus, it was a long way from where I lived. But we arranged to meet at two-thirty in the car park.

I'd had my roots done, my eyebrows tidied, and my legs waxed. My clothes, however, were casual. I didn't want him to think I'd dressed up for the occasion. I wore tight jeans and a new blouse that showed off my tan and just a hint of the new lacy bra.

I can't remember what he was wearing, but he had that scruffy artistic look that made me want to straighten his shirt for him. I'd arrived a few minutes early and was leaning nonchalantly against my car. The car park was crowded, and he pulled up in front of me, beckoning and leaning over to open the passenger door.

That was my plan: I didn't want him to see the interior of my family car with its debris from a sloppy drinking husband and an annoying kid.

As soon as I got in, he turned to me, saying, "I'm glad you suggested this. Good to see you." And before I could protest that I'd worked quite hard to make it *his* suggestion he kissed me lightly on the lips. He pulled away, but only a little. It could've been simply a Hello kiss. What a cautious bunny, I thought. I didn't withdraw even an inch although I raised my eyebrows in a way that could have been interpreted as surprise. A delicate moment. But then he leaned in and the next kiss was, without a shadow of a doubt, a sexual invitation.

All right! Game on! It was the payoff for months of pussyfooting around. I prolonged the kiss.

Then some bastard behind us hooted and Hal had to find a parking space of his own. I leaned my head back, breathing deeply as if emotionally stunned. Or overcome by desire, if he preferred to see it that way.

He switched his engine off and said with a roguish smile, "My place or yours?"

It could've been a joke, but at that moment jokes didn't serve me at all.

I said, "If this is to go any further it has to be secret. I still have a husband in residence."

"Agreed," he said promptly. "I need secrecy too."

"Why?" I said, surprised. "I thought you were divorced."

"I've been divorced for going on fifteen years. I told you. But there *is* someone."

This was news I didn't like. "Who?" I wanted to sound curious but not chagrined.

"No names," he said. "But it's an important relationship. I love her. I'm committed to her."

We were holding hands when he said this. He was stroking my smoothly moisturised knuckles with his warm dry thumb.

"Then why…?" I let the question hang.

"Because." He turned my hand over, lowered his head, and kissed the inside of my wrist. No one had ever done that before and I shivered. That's how they do things in Art Land. I imagined describing this to Penelope and Nancy. They'll cream themselves, I thought.

Then he went on, "It's not what you think. It hasn't been…well, I'm not going to talk about it…I'm sure you understand. She's my age. Women change."

She isn't putting out, I realised happily. He isn't getting any. I was glad I'd gone on HRT early. I was not *ever* going to lose the juice if I could help it.

"Is this a problem?" he asked.

I turned and kissed the spot where his jaw, neck, and ear met. I felt *him* shiver.

If he loves this other woman, I mused, it's a watery sort of love and she won't last long. It would be my new project. Beating out another woman is part of the buzz.

"Then what?" Penelope asked, breathless.

"If it's a secret, why are you telling *us?*" Nancy asked. She'd been snarky since the last time at the cafe. But here she was. She's got no willpower.

"Obviously it's a secret from Barnaby," I said. "I'm going to Hal's place tomorrow afternoon."

"Wow! You've scored an artist!" Penelope said almost as if I'd written a script for her. She's a kindergarten teacher and impressed by anything adventurous.

"So, you're hooking up with a bloke you scarcely know who is in love with someone else?" Nancy began.

I cut her off. "I'm going to his house," I said. "I'll see how I feel when I'm there. We've been getting to know each other for months."

"Pen pals." Penelope sighed. "It's romantic, Nancy, you've got to admit it's romantic."

"What about the woman he says he loves?" Nancy said. "How romantic will it be for *her*."

"That's his business, not mine."

"I wonder how long *that* will last," Nancy murmured.

"Maybe I shouldn't tell you," I said sweetly. "I saw your daughter at the bus stop while I was driving past the other day. She was smoking a spliff with an older guy. But that's none of my business, is it?"

Barnaby opened a second bottle, topped up my glass, and refilled his own. He was more mellow than plastered. Timing's important, and I wanted to make sure that, whatever happened with Hal, my late spring break to Ibiza with Barnaby was still on. I'd worked hard and was due a holiday.

He said, "I haven't paid yet. You've been so cold with me lately I didn't think you'd want us to go away together."

"You haven't made it easy for me to be warm," I said. "But you know that our best times are in the sun."

He took a deep swallow. His lips were glazed with wine. "I thought maybe you were seeing that boss of yours again. Or someone new."

"Paranoia," I said flatly. "But if you don't arrange Ibiza the way we agreed, I might be tempted."

He stared at me for a moment. But he reached for his phone.

Sometimes it's just too easy.

Hal's house was potentially wonderful, if only he'd look after it. I ran a professional eye over the frontage, noticing a cracked gutter, some flaking putty and exterior paintwork, an original but battered front door with original but blackened brasswork. It was in a short road of Victorian houses of character. Except for Hal's, all of them clearly had pots of money lavished on them.

It was a primo patch. Hal was sitting on a gold mine—but didn't recognise it. I was surprised—an artist who didn't look at his surroundings?

Hmm, I thought, as I tapped the elegant but grimy knocker against the peeling front door: definite potential.

"Not surprising," Nancy said, sipping her espresso in tiny abstemious sips.

"I imagine, being an artist, he's above such bourgeois considerations." That woman just can't help sounding bitchy.

"What's his bedroom like?" Penelope, on the other hand, can't help sounding prurient.

I don't know why I bother with friends, I thought. But I smiled mysteriously.

"You look like the cat that swallowed the goldfish," Nancy said.

Both of them looked jealous.

This is why I bother with friends, I thought.

Alone in my own bed, I sometimes think of the things I wouldn't *ever* tell my friends.

I suppose all relationships can be seen as wars. If so, Hal Yaeger couldn't even fire his own gun. He seemed keen enough when he came to the door— so keen that he hurried me straight to the bedroom.

I was at my finest: sexy but tasteful, willing but not slutty, hot but not demanding. Hal Yaeger, on the other hand, couldn't even find his bullets.

"This has *never* happened to *me* before," I said, sitting up. I was offended. It wasn't the tribute to my desirability I'd expected.

"First-time nerves," he said. "I was overeager. Stay awhile. Things will get better."

But I got up. I said, "My other lovers could never seem to get *enough*." I almost added, None of them has been as old and fat as you are. *I* was doing *you* a favour. But I stopped myself because he was quite famous.

"Not very tactful," he said, laughing it off.

I was in no mood to laugh but I said, "Well, I have to get back to work now. That's the trouble with nooners." It was as dignified an exit as I could muster.

"I don't want to leave it like this," he called as I scurried as fast as I could down to the front door.

That was what I didn't want to think about when I was alone in bed and Barnaby was comatose on the sofa, an empty bottle by his side, while the annoying kid still had his light on, lost in some cyberwar.

Sometimes the failure of everyone around me weighs heavy, and I have to remind myself that it isn't *my* failure; it's theirs.

Then, a couple of days later, Hal wrote, saying, "I miss you. I miss your e-mails. Your friendship's important to me. x."

Sealed with a kiss, I thought, and went downstairs to pour myself a glass of wine. Barnaby was splayed in an armchair watching sports. His eyes were half shut already.

At that moment I realised three things: first, that Barnaby was history; second, that what I really wanted was someone *important* to want *me*; and third, that Hal's e-mail told me that he was still in the game. However, if all he wanted was to recover his self-esteem in bed, it wouldn't be enough. But if I kept him off balance now, I could get way more out of him in the long run.

I'd leave Hal hanging for a few days, to undermine his confidence. Then I would make sure that when I finally relented he'd realise that he'd given me power. I'd start using it by forcing him to tell me who the other woman was. Because, one way or another, she had to go. There wasn't room for both of us.

He'd said, "No names," but after only a couple of weeks' work he told me she was Esti Ezra. She was a sculptor who'd had a certain amount of success when she was younger.

Later, he was adamant that he'd never reveal any intimate details. So listen to this list of betrayals: She was abused as a child; she'd spent some time in the nut house; she'd chosen to have an abortion rather than allow a child to interfere with her work. He would've been the father of the child, but he'd been married at the time. And, best of all, she'd had a difficult menopause—so I'd guessed correctly about that. He said he was always very careful not to hurt her because she was sensitive. Well boo-hoo. There was a load more stuff but I already had enough to work with.

She had an entry in Wikipedia and I looked her up. She was the woman with Hal on that first, fateful evening when we met. Then there was a picture of a supposedly famous statue called *Mother and Child*. The hypocrisy of the cow! I wondered how many of these fancy-pants art lovers knew about the abortion, and what they'd say when they found out.

Of course, I was not openly critical. I never derive pleasure from the failings of others. But I did counsel Hal on the danger of living in the past, of compromising the future for the sake of an outdated commitment.

"I'm having a dinner party for my birthday," Penelope said. "Of course you and Hal are invited."

"Fat chance," Nancy said. "Haven't you noticed, Penny? Sheena's been 'seeing' this guy once a week for nearly a year and we've never even been asked round for tea and toast."

"We" and "us": such loaded words. They applied to Hal and me when we were alone together in his dark Victorian bedroom, in the bed that used to be his parents'. He hadn't bothered to change or redecorate anything in that horrible, old-fashioned gloom. I told him once, "I could snap my fingers and, without any trouble at all, add a million to the value of this house."

"Why would you want to do that?" he asked, lazily stroking my back.

"To help *you*," I said soothingly. But the notion that I was with some old hippie to whom owning property was an embarrassment really bothered me. As usual he treated my assurance with silence. But I was not yet ready to expose the fact that I felt anything for him but unqualified approval and desire.

"And why only once a week?" Nancy persisted. "And what about Little Miss Psycho? Any progress?"

I gave her the friend-killer look that usually shut her up. But this time she went on, "We're only trying to be supportive. Aren't we, Penny?"

Penny said, almost inaudibly, "We're worried about you, Sheena."

I said, "I'm with someone I love and admire who loves me back and, unlike you two, I'm having the best sex of my life. And since you're so worried about me, perhaps I can return your kindness: Penelope, has Richie stopped putting you down in public or spent enough time at work to take you on holiday for a change? And you, Nancy, has Beatrice quit hitting you yet?"

A couple of months later, Barnaby had moved out and I'd cleverly remortgaged my house with enough money left over to give the place a total makeover and buy a better car—both more fitting to my status as the agency's Saleswoman of the Year and the bonus that went with it. Amongst other successes I'd collected the commission from persuading the "quick bonk" buyer to complete on an even more expensive property in Belgravia.

I'm good at my job, so I'm assigned to the most lucrative prospects. The other agents mutter behind my back about why so many favours come my way. But they're just eaten up with jealousy.

I was riding high. On top of professional successes I'd pretty much landed a famous artist who'd repeated that he loved me.

But it wasn't enough. There was still Esti Ezra. Despite all the time and intimacy we'd shared, Hal hadn't told her about me. Once he said he was afraid of "what she might do" if she found out. Another time he told me about a so-called genius poet called Sylvia Plath who was barking barmy and topped herself when she found out her husband was playing away. So my name for Esti became Sylvia and Hal took to calling her that too.

That was good, because it put Hal and me together against the Ezra woman. And I thought, If she's barmy and neurotic enough to kill herself, it won't be any great loss to the world. But it'd be a great relief to Hal and me.

Hal's refusal to meet my friends, even if it was only for a drink in a trendy bar, was irksome. They were taunting me about whether Hal existed at all.

Nancy in particular had taken to calling him the Hal-lucination. And Penelope, who always has to follow someone, occasionally referred to him as the Invisible Man.

"What does he do in the evenings?" Nancy asked. "How come you and he don't go to the cinema or theatre? And what about all those arty parties?"

"He does his best work at night," I said.

But the criticism stung. Hal refused to go anywhere with me, although I would have loved to meet some of his friends and contacts.

"Are you ashamed of me?" I asked as we lay skin-to-skin in the saggy old bed.

"Is that what you think?" He turned to face me.
"Well, you never take me out anywhere." I was surprised that the little shake in my voice was almost genuine. "I feel like I'm your dirty secret."

"That's not it at all," he said. "It's just that when we meet, the only thing I want is to take you to bed." He rolled over on top of me, which ended that conversation.

Another time I said, "Barnaby knows about you. He's moved out. Wouldn't you feel better if you put Sylvia P straight too?"

This made him sit up in bed, silent for a beat too long. Then he began, "I told you at the beginning that I loved and was committed to someone else. I get it—you want more. You deserve more. But I'm on a promise—hard as it seems for both of us." He reached out and took my hand. "So if this isn't enough for you, maybe you should look for what you really want elsewhere."

It was not what I was expecting, and I felt a sudden chill. I'd put too much hard work into this relationship to lose Hal or the prospect of his house now. It would mean that Esti had won, and I will never be defeated by another woman. Never.

So I set the chill to one side, took my hand back, and stuck out my chin. I simply got out of bed, dressed, and went home. I was demonstrating wounded self-respect.

I did not refer to this disagreement in our next e-mail exchange. But I did mention casually, when telling him about the troubles of one of my colleagues, that a woman would be grateful for information that affected her life choices. Would he take the hint?

He did: Almost immediately, Hal invited me to his studio. He'd never before let me see what he called "work in progress." It wasn't that I was particularly interested in the work, but I hadn't liked being kept out of an area so important to him. This was a big deal.

Unbelievably, Hal's studio was at the bottom of his garden. I say unbelievably because I simply hadn't realised that the wall at the end of his tangled, weedy lawn was not an ivy-choked community wall. It was a two-storey, stone-built studio. I'd always imagined that he had a converted warehouse or garage somewhere. But all he had to do was walk about thirty steps down a half-hidden gravel path to a door concealed by an ancient cherry tree.

Renovated and remodelled, I thought, it could be a perfect granny flat, and I added another million to the value of the property. Looking back towards the gate at the side of the main house, I revised this valuation upwards. The so-called studio might be converted into a small dwelling sold separately.

Doing the sums in my head, I strayed a couple of steps off the gravel and almost tripped over what looked like a naked giant lying in the weeds. It was too smooth to be a man with his arms over his head like someone afraid of gunfire, but that was my first reaction, until I saw it was just a lump of metal.

There was another lump with bindweed crawling all over it that might have been someone leaning against the fence. It was the sort of crap I would always advise a seller to get rid of before a viewing. I was going to comment, but then Hal took a key from a nook between a branch and the trunk of the cherry tree and opened his studio door. I followed him into what looked like a builder's workshop. He turned on the lights.

There was wood stacked higgledy-piggledy, rolls of fabric, shelves of paint pots, at least two industrial air-brushes and electrical equipment to run them, rollers, brushes, stacks of masking and gaffer tape. There was scaffolding, a small tower, and step-ladders. Canvases, slashed and stabbed with garish colours, leaned at all angles against the walls. There was a desk sagging under the weight of three computers, piles of books, magazines, catalogues, beer cans, and possibly half a dozen dirty coffee mugs. There was paper everywhere—some written on, some drawn on, some with other coloured paper stuck to it. Postcards and posters were tacked to walls.

I was confused. The light was painfully bright, so every inch and corner of the chaos was sharp. There was hardly any place to stand. I didn't know what to look at or what to say.

Hal laughed suddenly. "Satisfied?" he asked. Then he opened the door and switched off the painful lighting. I followed him back into his jungle of a garden that looked almost orderly compared with the disorder of the studio. I was too shocked to say a word.

"Fancy a drink?" he said unexpectedly. He unlocked the gate at the side of the house. This was the first time he'd ever suggested we go out together in public. It was a second victory.

We walked to a small pub where, disappointingly, no one seemed to know him, and found a table in a dark corner. He went to the bar and brought back beer for himself and a vodka and tonic for me. The barman didn't recognise him either.

I held his hand across the table and asked, "What's above your studio? There's a second floor, isn't there?"

"No one's allowed up there," he said in a spooky voice. "That's where I keep the mutilated corpses of women."

We laughed. "Seriously?" I persisted.

"Seriously," he said, still laughing. "I can't even remember where the door to the stairs is. It used to be a storeroom. As you might have guessed, I've lived at the same address almost all my life."

"You never thought of moving?" I said. What was it like, I wondered, to be someone who didn't always want something better?

"Nothing's ever enough for you, is it?" His tone was patient but I felt the chill.

I laughed lightly and said, "If you were born with everything you could possibly need or want, I suppose it would be hard to understand someone who wants more." I said this sweetly, without an ounce of blame in my voice. But I almost hated him at that moment.

He said, "I wasn't criticising you."

"Good," I said. "Now tell me about the lumps of metal in your garden."

I said, "It's all crap."

"The contemporary-art establishment doesn't think so," Nancy said. "A couple of her pieces were chosen for the Venice Biennale."

"Who died and made you an expert on Esti Ezra?" I said.

"Please don't quarrel, you two," Penelope pleaded. "Sheena, you're in a world we don't understand. Of course we're interested. You're so lucky."

"It's not a matter of luck," I snapped. *Lucky?* It isn't luck; it's what I worked for, what I'm owed.

"I'm sorry you feel threatened," Nancy said, "but you know Hal has a history with the woman. Of course she'd give him some of her work."

"I'm not threatened by shapeless lumps of metal," I said. "Hal has let weeds grow all over them and he's let weeds grow all over the so-called relationship. Esti doesn't *have* a history; she *is* history."

"Then what's your problem? Is it because you're still only seeing him once a week?"

"If it's any of your business, we go to the pub as well."

"Does that mean he's fed up with you in the bed department and has to have a drink instead?"

"Why don't you worry about your own relationship instead of poking your nose in mine? I've seen your 'partner' out with other women."

"At least I've *got* a partner," Nancy said, getting up to go. "At least I'm not a bit on the side." And she stalked out before I could get in with the last word.

"She's jealous of me," I said.

"She's one of your oldest friends," Penelope said.

I went on, "I've got something Esti Ezra, a.k.a. Sylvia P, doesn't have. I've got a boyfriend. She can't claim Hal's her boyfriend. He's mine in every way that counts."

"So why does she bother you?"

I drained my coffee cup. "What bothers me is Hal's integrity. Of course I understand an unstable elderly woman like SP would want to cling to something long after it's bitten the dust. She doesn't want to die alone. But Hal should give her the chance to make a new life for herself, even at her age."

"How old is she?"

"Years older than me. The point is that I'd respect Hal more if he told the poor old girl the truth about us. That's what every woman wants—*honesty*."

"Is it?" Penelope asked. "Why don't *you* tell her then?"

"Because she's *Hal's* problem so it's *his* job."

"Does he know that?"

"He knows how I feel." Was Penelope getting at me? But she gazed back with that stupid, innocent look that explains why her husband treats her like a moron in public.

I'd learned early that Hal is not confrontational. When I push, he doesn't push back. He goes silent, which can be quite useful. But it does mean that we dance all around a subject like Sylvia P without coming to the point. When I want information I can work with all I get are insubstantial generalities.

I parked well away from the nearest streetlight. I flattened the driver's seat and, using a hand mirror, I watched Hal's house. Some of Nancy's bitchiness had stuck: Why *did* we only meet in the afternoon? What do you do at night, you shifty bastard? Because while he always told me he worked at night, all the photos of him on that *Art Today* site had been taken after dark. That's when he enjoyed the social life he wouldn't share with me. What else did he enjoy without me?

Over an hour later I saw a woman carrying a bunch of flowers and a bulging carrier bag approach his house. She did not go to the front door like I always did. She went straight to the side gate and let herself in. No lights came on in the house.

I waited half an hour. She didn't return.

I phoned Hal. He didn't pick up.

I waited some more. He still didn't pick up. And she did not appear.

By now it was past my bedtime. I had three viewings in the morning. I went home.

Hal told me he worked nights, not going to bed till three or four in the morning. So I never rang him till lunchtime. When I visited him on a Tuesday it was always after my lunch and his breakfast. I remember thinking that if we ever married or lived together I'd have to train him to keep normal hours.

I rang him from my office and he picked up on the fourth ring. I could hear him yawn.

"Hi, sweetie." It was what I always said.

"Having a good day so far?" It was what he always said.

I'd had a good morning in spite of fatigue. But I didn't tell him this. Instead I said, "Where were you last night?"

He took a beat, and then said, "Excuse me?" like he hadn't heard properly. But at least he'd stopped yawning.

"I called you three times."

"Did you? Why?"

"Why not?"

"You don't usually ring at night."

"Maybe I will from now on." I kept my voice light, almost flirty.

"Okay," he said equably. "But I don't take my phone to the studio when I'm working. What did you want to talk to me about?"

"I was lonely; I just wanted to talk to my boyfriend. Where were you?"

"I told you; I don't take my phone to the studio."

"Well, too late now," I said cheerfully. "I was just feeling low and wishing we saw more of each other. Then I could come round and surprise you with a kiss like a proper girlfriend."

He laughed. "I don't want a proper girlfriend. I want an improper one, and you're perfect."

"Was Esti Ezra improper too?" I asked, keeping the smile in my voice.

That stopped him laughing. When he didn't speak, I said, "I'm just saying that what's done in the dark always comes to the light in the end. If you respect her so much, tell her about me. If *you* don't, someone else will. Wouldn't it be better coming from you?"

"I'll bear that in mind," he said evenly. "So, are you coming round tomorrow as usual?"

"Of course," I said. "Oh sweetie, I can't wait."

"Nor can I," he said.

"Please may I borrow your car tonight? Mine's in the garage having a tire change."

"You had your MOT and a service a month ago," Nancy said. "What's your game this time? I'm not paying your parking fines ever again."

It was only once, years ago. I hate people with long memories.

I drove Penelope's little tin can to Hal's street just as the sun went down and slotted it into a tiny space between two Chelsea tractors. I didn't want anyone spotting me in an ancient Kia Picanto. But it was better than driving my own car. I'd got away with it the night before and didn't want to push my luck.

I waited, lying almost flat, mirror in hand. This is not the kind of behaviour I expect from myself, but sometimes a girl owes it to her self-respect to find out what's going on. I could ask directly. But what's the point when the only source of information has already lied to me?

I suppose, to do him credit, Hal avoided *direct* lies by evading questions. Or by changing direction, as he did when I said I wanted to be a proper girlfriend and he congratulated me on being improper. It *sounded* responsive and hot, but it wasn't.

I should've recognised the technique months ago, because it's one I use. But maybe I'd been too busy positioning myself as a necessary fixture in his life.

At about nine-thirty a black cab pulled up outside the house. Hal came out through the front door, bounded down the steps, and was driven away. He's a big man—bounding doesn't suit him. His shirttails were billowing, his hair was a rook's nest, and he only had one arm in a sleeve of his jacket. Typical Hal—he was late for something and a mess. Worse, he hadn't told me he was going out.

It struck me that he wasn't actually my type at all. I thought it was because he was an artist and bohemian in his ways. But his lack of respect for his property, I now saw, extended to me.

I exited the Kia cautiously, crossed the road, and went to the side gate. It was locked. Last night's visitor had her own key. But luckily I'd noticed a key hanging from a nail when Hal took me to the pub. It wasn't visible from outside, but all I had to do was push my hand through the bars and reach round till I found it.

I locked the gate behind me and went across the garden to the cherry tree where the next key was hidden.

I was *not* breaking in. I was Hal's girlfriend. Girlfriends have rights.

I opened the studio door and switched on the horrible lights. The first thing I noticed was a door on the wall to the right. Previously there had been two very big canvases leaning there, hiding it. Sly, Hal; behaviour unworthy of a boyfriend. Clearly I had just cause. This was not intrusion; it was self-protection.

Stairs led upwards. I found, to my great surprise, that at the top was a small bed-sitting room. I was shocked, both because it was there and because it was beautifully decorated and maintained.

The colours were yellow, green, and terra cotta. I would've advised something more neutral myself, but I had to admit that, for a small space, everything looked fresh and pretty. It was quite unlike the dark heaviness of the main house, where the curtains were never opened.

There was a divan, a small sofa, an armchair, a desk, lots of clever shelving, a tiny bathroom, and a kitchenette. It was a cunning use of space—no sense of overcrowding or claustrophobia.

I checked the kitchen area. There was water in the kettle; milk, pita bread, hummus, cheese, olives, and yogurt in the fridge. The shower room was impeccably clean.

I pulled the cover off the divan and found sheets, clean but not freshly laundered. Under the pillow was a brushed cotton nightshirt that would never have fit Hal.

I stood in the middle of the room, on the colourful Indian rug, shaking. *Secrets*, I thought, *lies, lies, lies*. The only comfort I could take was that the bed was much too small for Hal to sleep in with someone else.

Someone else.

I went to the desk and looked first at the pin board behind it. There were three sets of four drawings almost like cartoon strips. Each sequence started with a drawing of a pregnant woman seen from different angles, front, back, and side. These slowly morphed into the fourth. The first drawings actually looked like the woman, whereas the last hardly even seemed female. They made me feel really uncomfortable. The drawings were the wrong way round. The other way, from shapeless to realistic, would make a lot more sense.

I turned my attention to the desktop. There was a sketchbook, jars of pencils, and an iPad. I turned it on and while I waited I opened the sketchbook. On the first page were four drawings of Hal. He was propped up in bed, reading. He had no clothes on. The second, third, and fourth drawings turned him into a blob any child could've scribbled.

These drawings were done by bloody Esti! And because they were the only drawings in the book, they'd been done recently. So, very recently, she'd seen him without any clothes.

She'd captured, almost photographically, the tilt of his head and the slouch of his body when he was concentrating. She hadn't left out any of the flab, the bits of him I didn't like because they made it difficult in bed. I always shut my eyes. Because I wanted him to see *me*. But *I* didn't want to see *him*.

Whenever Hal mentioned his weight in that humorous, self-critical way of his, I always told him it didn't matter to me. That's what a girlfriend's meant to do. What gave *Esti* the right to be truthful about what she saw?

I was so angry my hands and feet went icy. I got up and went to the kettle. Then I changed my mind and rummaged around till I found a bottle of rum. I don't drink rum because it's crude but I poured myself a slug anyway.

I am not the kind of woman who would fool around with someone else's possessions. But I didn't feel as if I was trespassing. *I* was the girlfriend. She wasn't. Hal was mine. Not hers. His stuff was mine. *She* was the thief. *She* was the impediment to my relationship with Hal.

Taking what was rightfully mine, I folded a slice of cheese into pita bread and ate it without a plate, scattering crumbs and sitting in the comfortable armchair.

If I turned on the gas burners, everything would go up in flames, including those inept drawings and the humiliating evidence that Hal had taken his kit off in front of someone else.

Of course I was too responsible a woman to do anything so destructive to valuable property. Gradually the food and rum settled me.

I went back to the iPad and brought up her e-mail account. She was too stupid to have password protection—an open invitation.

The first thing I saw was from Hal. It said, "Dearest—I'm off to the Hayward. I know you can't stand Damian, but it pays to keep in with the effing in-crowd. And now I'm late. I won't see you tomorrow coz I'm cooking at the shelter. Till Wednesday then." The letter ended with five red hearts. It had been sent over an hour ago and hadn't been opened till I clicked on it. The bitch hadn't seen it.

Tomorrow was *my* day. Well, my afternoon. Cooking at the shelter? Was that how the slippery bastard disguised his passionate nooners with me?

Suddenly my phone buzzed. It made me jump. I too had an e-mail from Hal. He said, "Sweetie, in case you tried to ring me I'm at a gallery where phones are supposed to be switched off. I've thought about what you said yesterday. You're right, of course. So I've begun. But I have to go carefully. Sylvia is already very upset at the thought of me even thinking about another woman. So please don't push me. It won't make things happen any faster and I know neither of us wants this to end in tragedy." He signed off with three kisses.

Had he *really* begun to tell Esti Sylvia Plath Ezra about us? A spasm of pure triumph surged through me, although I didn't like my three kisses compared with her five red hearts.

I scrolled back to previous e-mails. One from her began, "Hal-low— how're you doing, honey? I've talked to Rupert at the Serpentine. He's keen. All will be well. You prob don't need advice but mightn't it be time to reconnect with your therapist? Even though you say you're ok, something's wrong. I hate seeing you like this. All my loving." This was followed by five red hearts.

I can't begin to say how disturbing this was. Was something wrong with *Hal?* But he was the Hal I'd been making happy for nearly two years. *She* was deluded. I took another swallow of rum. Whatever ESPEzra wanted to pretend, Hal was mine. She should not even be writing to my boyfriend without my permission. But he was not behaving well. He should be punished.

I copied her e-mail address into my phone and began, "Hal has been lying to you, as he has to me. I know he feels a historical obligation to you. But the statute of limitations ran out on that years ago. Surely you understand that he needed to move on to someone who treats him like a man. And surely he owes you the truth so that you can rebuild your life elsewhere. Every woman needs to know the truth." I pressed Send before I even had time to check the spelling.

Just as I did this, I began to hear noises from downstairs. Someone was opening the studio door and coming upstairs.

A woman said, "Hal?" from halfway up.

I remained seated at the desk in front of the iPad. I straightened my back and lifted my chin. I felt no embarrassment whatsoever. It was as if I'd summoned her the moment I pressed Send.

"Who the hell are you?" She stood frozen, one sleeve of a velvet patchwork coat on, one sleeve off.

"I'm Sheena," I said with quiet dignity. "Hal must have told you about me." I was going to keep this confrontation civilised. But I was startled by Esti's appearance: Although age had scrawled some white into her hair, her skin was clear and her cheekbones were pronounced. Old women are supposed to be fat; she wasn't. Large dark eyes regarded me with an expression I could only call bewildered.

"Do sit down," I said, politely waving my hand towards the chair.

She didn't move, but I watched her taking in the pulled-down bed, the untidiness of the kitchenette, and the rumpled cushion in the chair.

She said, "Okay, Sheena, what the fuck are you doing here, and what is Hal supposed to have told me?"

I said, "We'll have a more productive conversation if you address me politely. Now, please sit down. Clearly there's a lot for you to catch up on."

Slowly, she hung the coat on a hook by the door. She was wearing worn bluejeans and a long-sleeved T-shirt. I knew she was in her sixties. There's something totally naff about older women who don't act their age.

"Hal said he told you about me," I began.

"Oh, wait," she said. "Are you the estate agent who's been advising him about property prices?"

"I'm an estate agent," I said stiffly. "And yes, I've told Hal he's sitting on a gold mine. But you're missing the point. We've had a relationship for nearly two years."

She just stared at me, covering her mouth with her hand. It was a working hand untouched by moisturiser. I checked my own hands. Perfect. Not even a hangnail.

"I'm sorry you're shocked," I said. "I thought Hal had told you the truth. These men! They're so cowardly, aren't they? It always falls on us women to do the dirty work."

I watched tears drip slowly from the wide dark eyes and slide between the work-worn fingers. It was solace to my heart. I was nearly as satisfied as the time I'd made my mother cry.

At last she said huskily, "What sort of relationship?"

I said, "If you aren't able to satisfy him, you can't blame him for finding someone who not only can but wants to."

"Is that what he told you?"

"I know about your difficult menopause. Hal's told me all about you."

Again shocked tears dripped unchecked down her face. But she said, "Then he'll have told you that the difficulty was as much his as mine."

Well, that would explain our disastrous first meeting. But I said, "He's never had any 'difficulty' with *me*."

"If he's told you everything," she said, "he's told you that he always uses Viagra now."

What a bitch! What a malicious, spiteful cow!

I said, "And of course *you* know that he doesn't cook at a homeless shelter. He spends Tuesdays in bed with me."

I got up. "Well," I concluded, "I've given you the information you need to restart your life. Is there anything else I can do for you?"

She was still standing. Now she looked me straight in the eye. "You can put the studio key on the desk and get out."

It was not what I planned. She should have run away crying, leaving me in possession. So I waited.

And then she said, "What gives you the right to trash the thirty years I've spent working, loving, and playing with Hal?"

"Hal gave me the right," I said.

"I don't think you understand him at all." She held her hand out.

For one awful moment I thought she was expecting me to shake it. Then suddenly I was afraid she'd slap me. I found myself handing her the studio key and leaving.

I remember sitting in Penelope's nasty little car. I was jubilant that I'd wrecked Sylvia Plath's life forever. I'd made her cry. But that pleasure was ruined by the memory of how I'd put the key into her hand. Why had I given her the key as if she had a right to it? Worse, I left because she told me to. I'd been afraid the boo-hooing old bitch would slap me.

I was so furious I thought I'd burst into flames of rage.

Penelope rang me before eight the next morning to ask where I'd parked her car.

"It's at my garage," I said.

Then I rang the garage and told the service manager that I was looking after my friend's car and I was worried about it. He told me to bring it over.

After that I drove my own car to Penelope's house and gave her my keys.

I said, "Last night a drunk driver almost ran into me head on. I swerved in time but I hit a dog."

"Oh my God," Penelope said. "Are you all right? You look awful."

"I whacked my head on the steering wheel and I lost a little time."

"Did the police come? Have you seen a doctor?"

"It didn't seem that serious. When I opened my eyes there was no drunk and no dog. I felt a bit woozy and when I looked at the front of the car there was a dent and something was rubbing against the off-side wheel. So I took it to my garage. The manager says they can sort it out today. So I'm lending you my Audi."

"For goodness' sake, Sheena," she said, drawing me into her kitchen. "I'll make tea for us."

I didn't want to drink her weak milky tea. But I sat down and used my phone to call a cab while she bustled round like the nursery-school teacher she was. She has no ambition: she'll stay in the same job and the same house and be insulted by the same husband till she dies.

In the cab I looked at Hal's last e-mail and realised I hadn't replied. "Sweetie," he'd begun, as he always did. *I was his sweetie.* Me. He couldn't deny it. Whatever Esti claimed, I had written proof.

I typed, "I should have replied last night but I've been having car trouble. I'm so glad you've begun to tell Sylvia P about us. It will be hard but you're doing the right thing. See you later." I ended with six red hearts. But after looking at them I decided they were vulgar—almost like scarlet buttocks. I deleted and replaced them with my usual dignified kisses.

Then I phoned work and said I had a migraine.

All I had to do was pretend nothing had happened.

I'd had hours to think about which of us, Esti or I, had more right to dominate Hal.

During that long night I reviewed my relationship with him and now, this morning, it seemed clear that he had always forced me to make the first moves. That defined him as passive. It meant that he didn't want to take responsibility for his actions. He had given dominion to me.

He wanted us to be together. But he didn't want to hurt Sylvia's feelings or reveal that he was cheating on her. Left to him, telling her would have taken painful *years*.

Therefore he would much rather *I* did the dirty work. So I'd told the truth quickly and cleanly. No one could blame *him* for hurting Esti. I had done him a favour.

The service manager rang at midday. He said, "We've beaten out the damaged panel and retouched the scraped paintwork. We'll need to replace the off-side front tire and rebalance the others." He gave me a price which I agreed to.

Then he said, "One curious thing—while the car was over the inspection pit, my bloke noticed blood in the wheel arch. We hosed it off, but I thought I'd better ask how serious the 'bump' was. Were the cops involved? Coz if they were, maybe we shouldn't have done the work."

"Thanks for asking," I said. "The reason my friend's so upset is because, in trying to avoid a head-on collision, she swerved and hit a dog. Apparently the owner told her that the old bitch had taken to wandering off if anyone left the gate open. He said he'd been considering having her put down anyway. But my friend was devastated."

We left it at that.

I was putting the last layer of mascara onto my lashes when Hal rang. He said, "Something dreadful's happened. We can't meet today."

"Why not?" I was disappointed. I get so few treats in a busy week.

He said, "Esti died last night. I don't know how but…"

"Oh my God," I said, sounding like Penelope when I told her about the dead dog. "I'll come straight over."

"No!" he said, far more forcefully than he usually spoke. "I won't be here. Her family and friends are meeting at her studio—a sort of wake."

"Give me the address. You're going to need support."

"*No!*" he said sharply. "This is a gathering of those of us who knew her best and loved her most. You never met her."

I let my voice wobble a little. "But I know and love *you*," I said. "I'd like to look after you. When will you be back?"

"Sorry to sound harsh," he said immediately. I could still make him apologise. "But," he went on, "I can only deal with this one thing right now. I can't see you."

"Okay, okay," I said, offended. "I'll call you later unless I hear from you first."

"Thank you," he said, although he didn't seem to be listening to me.

I was furious. Hal had no right to reject my generous offer. I removed all the makeup from my face, took off the sexy clothes, and, wearing my gardening anorak and a surgical mask, I left the house.

As I climbed the stairs to the bed-sitting room I thought, Look what you made me do, Esti Sylvia Plath Ezra, by hanging on to a man who no longer belonged to you. You threaten suicide if poor Hal even mentions another woman? You try to pin him in the past? Well, lady, that doesn't work for *me*.

The little room was exactly as I'd left it: the bed pulled apart, the kitchenette untidy, crumbs around the chair, and the iPad still on standby. I looked at the e-mails and saw that there were several new messages, including one from me which began, "Hal has been lying.…" It had not been read. I put it in Spam and deleted the whole file.

There were several after mine which had not been read either. I left them alone. Then I remade the divan, tidied the kitchenette, and swept up the crumbs. Esti had never deserved this pretty little room where she drew her horrible scribbles.

That reminded me. I went to the desk, opened the sketchbook, and tore out the drawings of Hal. She had no right to his body. I crumpled the pages and put them in my bag. They could go out with the rubbish.

I took the Kia back to Penelope. I'd even paid to have it valeted, so it was in better condition than when I borrowed it. I brought her a bottle of wine as well. To say thanks.

She said, "You shouldn't have. I loved driving the Audi."

No sooner had she opened the bottle than Nancy turned up. That woman has a nose for a free drink.

Penelope poured three glasses of wine. But then she asked if I was on pain medicine for my head. I said I thought a little wine would do more good than paracetamol.

"And it's better at overcoming disappointment," Nancy said.

"What do you mean?"

"She's had to miss her Tuesday nooner." Nancy gave me a knowing glance.

"I don't want to talk about it," I said, coughing after too big a gulp of wine.

"It's all over the *Art Today* site." She turned to Penelope. "Her big rival, Esti Ezra, died last night. So I don't suppose Hal was available for nooky this afternoon. Anyway, look at her—she'd never have gone to North Kensington looking like that. Sheena, do you need another splash of Chianti?"

"What happened?" Penelope said, shocked.

"Number one, that poor old woman was *not* my rival, Nancy. And I'll thank you not to repeat such garbage. Two, Hal didn't tell me what happened. And I say again, I *really* don't want to talk about it."

My phone rang. It was the annoying kid telling me I'd failed to leave a meal for him to microwave for his supper. I said, "Go to your father's," and hung up.

Penelope said, "Oh Nancy, do stop laughing. Can't you see she's upset?"

Nancy said, "Not half as upset as she'll be when she sees what everyone's saying about Esti Ezra: like what a cutting-edge sculptor and draughtswoman she was. And how the value of her work is already going through the roof. And what a tragedy it is, because she was such a terrific friend and teacher—a role model for young women. She was a living saint, Sheena, who died way too early."

Penelope said, "How sad. What will this mean for you and Hal?"

"I don't know," I said, drearily. For the first time it occurred to me that Esti Sylvia Crap Ezra might become more of a problem for me dead than alive.

Just then, another phone rang from my bag. I rummaged and found an iPhone. I switched it off.

"Got a new phone?" Nancy asked.

"I always carry a work phone on a Tuesday." I snapped my bag shut. "You never know when a really big deal might go crucial."

My friends were intrusive, unsupportive, and critical. They had absolutely no idea what I'd been going through. I left soon after that, outraged.

When I got home I texted Hal: "Sweetie, what's happening? I want to be with you at this difficult time. It's very hard to be left out. xxx"

He didn't reply till later, when I was eating lunch. He wrote: "I don't know what to tell you. Apparently there's a police investigation. We're all in bits."

No Sweetie. No kisses.

I wrote: "I don't understand. What's to investigate? Who is We? xxx"

When he didn't reply for over an hour I wrote: "Perhaps you are still posing as the faithful friend and lover. Do the people at the studio think you've been looking after her all this time? How would they react if they knew you'd been spending the last two years with me?"

He'd hurt my feelings. His should hurt too.

He replied almost at once: "Sweetie, it's not personal. I'm exhausted and very distressed. You know what Esti meant to me. xxx"

I was pleased that he'd taken some of my words as a threat and backed down. What Esti meant to him was hypocrisy.

I let him stew for an hour. Then I wrote, "Sweetie, I was afraid she'd done something awful to herself. xxx"

"What on earth are you talking about?" he replied.

Had he forgotten he'd portrayed the poor unstable old thing as Sylvia Plath?

I opened a new bottle and relaxed. I wrote: "Sweetie, you said you'd started to tell SP about Us and that she was upset. I know you were concerned about what she might do. I was afraid you might be blaming yourself. xxx"

I fancied a couple of slices of toasted cheese with my wine. So I fixed some and refilled my glass. I watched an afternoon film on TV while I waited for Hal's reply. I'd given him something to think about, so I wasn't expecting a quick answer.

When it came he wrote: "Sweetie, I'm confused. One of my colleagues found an e-mail supposedly from you to Esti on her computer. You would never have done anything so destructive as to tell her *yourself* what you wanted *me* to tell her. But the message *was* sent from your phone. Fortunately she hadn't opened it. Please explain. Also, please would you not call her SP. You know I never liked that and, especially now, it misrepresents and disrespects her. xxx"

I never swear, but I said, "Damn and blast," out loud. How was I to know that as well as her phone and her iPad Esti had a third device?

I could see that Hal felt criticised by my e-mail so, without confronting me directly, he was turning the unstated accusation back on me. What a weasel! I switched the TV off and wrote: "OMG, Hal! I didn't even have Esti's address. But I do see that an e-mail originated on my phone. All I can think of is that my friend Nancy, who has been following EE online for years, got hold of my phone. She was here for supper on Monday night. She is the one who has been pressuring me, for my self-respect, to persuade you to acknowledge me publicly. She even describes me as 'your secret bit on the side.' Which, you must know, distresses me terribly. But it shows how little she understands. Sweetie, Nancy, from now on, is *not* my friend. xxx"

Hal's reply was: "A malicious accident like that is why, when we met, we *both* agreed we should be secret. xxx"

I replied: "Of course you're right. But so much has changed in the past two years! xxx"

It had been an upsetting day, so I awarded myself an extra tipple and an early night. But just as I was getting ready for bed Penelope rang. She had Nancy on speakerphone. She said, "Sheena, are you alone?"

I told her I was going to bed.

"I'll make it quick then," Nancy said. "The head of Music and Arts at the BBC has already commissioned a documentary about Esti. Hal, 'her lifelong partner,' will be contributing and has given permission for the filmmaker to use correspondence and drawings never before seen in public."

Penelope said, "Did you know how important she was in the art world?"

For a moment I was lost for words.

She went on, "Hal and Esti were going to have a joint exhibition at the Serpentine Gallery next year."

"*Art Today* is full of it," Nancy put in. "Everyone says she only agreed to exhibit at the Serpentine if Hal was included."

I found my voice at last. "Hal was using her to boost his career. So what? It's me he wants to be with."

There was a moment's silence. Then Penelope said hesitantly, "I think it's a bit more than that."

"More than a bit," Nancy cut in. "They'd been together nearly thirty years."

"I know that. He was tired of her, her suicide threats and manipulations."

"Did it never occur to you that he was lying about Esti in the same way you lie about Barnaby?"

"I never lie," I said.

"Exaggerate beyond all recognition, then," Nancy said. "Barny may drink too much sometimes. Well, who doesn't? Including you, Sheena. But he isn't a violent alcoholic."

"Unlike your wife, Nancy," I shot back. "Has that fractured cheekbone stopped hurting yet?"

Penelope said, "Calm down. We just wanted to give you a heads up so that you wouldn't be shocked or upset."

"Well, thank you *so* much for your kind thoughts, especially *yours*, Nancy," I said evenly. "I knew all about it. But what Esti had planned for Hal was absolutely redundant when you know what *he* planned for *her*."

"But nobody else knows that," Nancy said. "If it was ever true."

Penelope cut in, saying, "Anyway, her death changes everything."

I ended the call. They, especially Nancy, didn't understand me at all.

I went to my computer and Googled the Serpentine Gallery's calendar for upcoming exhibitions. What I saw there made me as incandescent with rage as I'd been in Penny's car last night.

So I took Esti's iPhone out of my bag and scrolled through her contacts. I did not read the e-mails that passed between her and Hal. I truly didn't want to know what lies they'd been telling each other. I wouldn't sink so low.

I wasn't doing anything wrong, because Hal deserved to be hurt as much as he'd hurt me. So later that night, the head of the Serpentine Gallery, the head of Music and Arts at the BBC, the Head of Acquisitions at Tate Modern, *Art Today*, the Arts correspondents at the *Guardian, Times, Independent,* and

Telegraph received an e-mail from Esti Ezra.

She wrote, "To whom it may concern: Many of you have been my friends for ages. To you I send heartfelt apologies. I have been living a lie. I have falsely given the impression that I have been the long-standing partner of the painter Hal Yaeger. This has not been true for years, but I was too ashamed to admit it publicly. Hal is in love with another.

"I would not be exposing this humiliation now except that I think Hal is going to kill me. He wants to be with his new lover but fears for his reputation if this closely guarded secret is revealed.

"If by the time you open this I am dead, it will mean I was right."

I revised the text several times and checked spelling and punctuation. Then I added Scotland Yard to the list of recipients. Lastly, on Esti's phone I went to Settings and reset the date and time to just twenty minutes before her death.

I pressed Send.

Then I completely destroyed Esti's phone. I would distribute the pieces in several bins on my way to work. It was a job well done.

I climbed into bed. For a moment I lay remembering the tears running between Esti's ugly fingers. With a jolt of pleasure I relived how easily I'd crushed her. That night I slept like a baby.

For the next day or two I scoured the online art sites and all the morning and evening news outlets without finding any mention of Hal's shame or arrest. This surprised me, but there was nothing I could do about it. I didn't hear from Nancy or Penelope either, and that suited me because Penelope was never any help and Nancy was too nosy.

Then, on Friday evening, while I was having a quiet drink and facing a rather empty weekend, someone rang my doorbell. It couldn't have been either of my friends; they know better than to come round without calling first.

The annoying kid ran downstairs to answer it, so I thought maybe he'd broken the rules and was expecting one of his very few mates. Instead, he opened the sitting-room door and showed a man and a woman in.

"It's the cops," he said, for once showing an interest. "What have you done now, Mother?"

"That's not funny," I said. "Go to your room."

"Stay," the woman said.

Have I mentioned how much I dislike bossy women? I stood up. The annoying kid sat down in what used to be Barnaby's armchair, looking expectant.

The woman, who resembled a netball coach, flashed an identity card under my nose and handed me an official-looking sheet of paper. "As you can see, we have a warrant to search this house."

"What for?" The annoying kid's eyes flicked between the two police people and me as if we were in one of his games.

"We have reason to believe that you may be in possession of a stolen item," she said as if she'd learned her lines from TV police dramas.

She was addressing me, but I preferred to talk to the man. He was tall enough and good-looking enough to sharpen my interest. I said, "I really don't know what she's talking about. Do you think I need the protection of legal representation?" I tilted my head and looked appealingly up into his eyes. A little helplessness never hurts when meeting a new man.

"By all means get legal advice," the woman intoned. "Meanwhile I will begin the search."

I was outraged but in a real quandary. The only legal firm I knew worked for the Agency and I didn't want this to become gossip at work.

"If you tell me what you're looking for," I said, "maybe I can save you time and trouble. I have absolutely nothing to hide."

"Okay," the woman said. "If you are in possession of an iPhone belonging to the late Esti Ezra please produce it now. Or, if you have verifiable knowledge of its whereabouts, you'd better tell us."

I only just managed not to gape at her. When I could speak without my voice shaking I said, "What on earth makes you think I'd know anything about that woman's phone?"

The woman smiled frostily. "Maybe my colleague, who is a digital forensic technician, can enlighten you."

The man spoke up at last. "An e-mail was sent to multiple addresses, possibly from the phone in question. Although superficially it appeared to have been sent *before* the owner of the phone was killed in a road accident, it was *received* late the next day. This led us to check if there had been a glitch or interruption to Ms. Ezra's service at the relevant time. No such interruption had occurred. My department can access the server's records and there we discovered that the true time the e-mails were sent was about twenty-two hours *after* her death. Someone had reset the time and date on the device used, probably the iPhone, without erasing the digital footprint retained by the server."

The annoying kid leaped up, his face flushed with excitement. "Why do you think it was my mum?"

"As well as being able to access the correct time and date of sending, we are also able to pinpoint the location of the iPhone at that time."

I only just stopped myself shuddering.

"The iPhone was at this address." The woman's tone was triumphant. I cannot express how much I hated her at that moment.

"Oh, *Mother!*" The annoying kid sounded more disappointed than shocked or sorrowful. "You always think you're smarter than everyone else. You shouldn't have been so quick to dump Dad. He could've helped you. If he wanted to," he added quickly. I hated him as well.

The only one I didn't hate was the digital forensic technician. As I say, he was quite good-looking, slim, and not that much older then me. I needed another win. Maybe a contest between me and a police tech expert could provide it, once I mustered some private tech support of my own.

I'd already had a win of sorts. Although I might have lost Hal, who'd proved he wasn't worth having, I hadn't lost him to Esti Ezra. I had *not* been beaten by an older woman. But it wasn't enough.

Carver (and) [Company]

by Mike McHone

("Five bucks says it'll be a cheater case,") Eddie told her.

"I'm sure it will be. But you don't have any money, so why are you making bets?"

["It's pointless to speculate,"] Gertie said in that judgy tone of hers. ["You can't assume anything in this business, Josephine. You should know that by now."]

"I'm not assuming! Most cases involve cheaters. They're our bread and butter. I think it's an unwritten rule P.I.s have to follow an unfaithful spouse ninety percent of the dang time."

("Bread and butter are all we'll be eating if this one doesn't pay well. Money's tight.")

"I know, I know. That's another unwritten rule. All P.I.s need to be strapped for cash."

"Ms. Carver?"

Jo turned from the window and locked eyes with the brunette standing in the office doorway. Stunning was a fitting word, but far from the complete definition. Jo guessed the woman to be in her late thirties, early forties, but it was difficult to assess with the woman's fair skin seemingly untouched by the lines of age. She was tall, about five-ten, five-eleven in Jo's estimate, and the white blouse and navy slacks hugged her curves in the way most men, and some women, would've wanted. "Mrs. Karn?" Jo asked.

"Yes," she said. "I'm sorry, were you on a Bluetooth?"

"No, ma'am. Why?"

The black mascara narrowed. "I thought I heard... Never mind."

Jo checked her watch. Mickey Mouse showed her it was exactly one minute before noon.

"I know you said over the phone yesterday you wanted to meet at twelve-thirty," Stephanie Karn said, "but I'd hoped we could start early."

"Oh, absolutely!" Jo said. "I happen to be free right now!" And that was the truth. The only reason Jo set the meeting at the time she did was to give herself a few hours to pick up the place, brush the lint roller across herself, and check her hair and makeup in the mirror in the bathroom down the hall. Not that she or the office needed such attention considering both were always orderly, tidy, and professional, but chances were not to be taken that day. It had been two months since her last case, and she needed to make a good first impression.

["And yet she noticed you talking to yourself."]

Hush, she thought, and then told Mrs. Karn, "Come in and make yourself at home!"

The woman entered the office in purposeful strides and lowered herself into the cream-colored chair on the visitor's side of the modest oak desk. The black clutch purse she carried was placed into her lap, and her arms were then fixed upon the rests.

Jo shut the door. "Can I get you anything to drink? I have some bottles of water and a jug of chocolate milk in the mini fridge." She gestured at said mini fridge on the other side of the single-room office.

"I'm fine," Mrs. Karn told her.

"I think I might have one Diet Pepsi left. Or if you want something else, I can run down to the corner store and be back in two shakes! It's no problem at all!"

"No!" she said. "Look, I don't like coming into Detroit for any reason, let alone the reason I'm here to see you. So, if you don't mind, could we please stop fucking around and get down to business?"

("Wow.")

["Wow indeed."]

After a moment's hesitation, Jo proceeded to her desk, undid the buttons of her gray sport coat, and sat down. Nothing sat atop her desk, no computer, pencils, pens, or calendar. She preferred it to be free of things, her thought being this gave her clients a sense of openness and clarity. She leaned forward, pushed a strand of auburn hair back behind her ear, and, in keeping with the theme of the surface, said, "Mrs. Karn, let me be clear. I never eff around."

["Language, young lady!"]

("What language? And she's thirty-four. Not exactly young.")

"How long have you suspected your husband of cheating?"

The steel in the woman's spine held, but a perfectly waxed eyebrow arched itself.

"That's why you're here, isn't it?"

A picket line formed in Jo's head.

["What are you doing?"] Gertie asked. ["Don't be confrontational! You'll drive her away!"]

Eddie agreed. ("Listen to her, Jo! A person doesn't live by bread and butter alone!")

But she did not listen. She believed this woman needed to hear some harsh words. Not for any sadistic reason, but just so she could see that Josephine Millicent Carver was perceptive as all heck, confident in her assessments, and wouldn't take any S-H-I-T from anyone, which meant she was the right person for the job.

She just hoped to H-E-double-hockey-sticks the gamble would pay off.

"I assume you followed him, maybe saw him with a woman you've never seen before? Maybe you caught a few suspicious e-mails or text messages? Or, at the very least, you've been noticing that he's been acting a teensy bit wonky lately?"

Mrs. Karn scanned the stout woman opposite her and then averted her eyes to the carpet. With an exhale, she said, "I did follow him." And added, "He was with someone."

("Told you.")

Pipe down.

"I'm very sorry to hear that," Jo told her. "Really, I am. But to be square with you, I figured that's what it had to be. It's a sad gosh-darned fact that folks like you don't usually visit folks like me unless they get suspicious of the folks they live with."

Mrs. Karn gave a small nod.

"How long have you and the hubby been hitched?"

"Nine months," she answered. "Nine and a half. Not even a year."

"And what led you to believe he might be stepping out on you?"

"Three weeks ago, I called his office to tell him I would be visiting my mother for lunch," she said. "She lives in Monroe and I wanted to let him know I would be out of town for a few hours. I called and couldn't get through, so I tried the main desk. The receptionist said he'd taken a half day. He left the office saying he was sick." She took a breath. "I called his cell but didn't get an answer. When he got home that afternoon I asked where he'd been. He said he had a corporate meeting in Ann Arbor. I told him what the receptionist relayed to me. He said she must've misunderstood what he told her on his way out the door. I didn't press it. There was no reason to. At the time, anyway."

Mrs. Karn opened her purse and brought out a piece of paper folded in quarters. "The following week our bank statement posted. I looked it over, and the day he said he was in Ann Arbor, there were two debits." She handed the paper over to Jo. "One for a gas station, the other for a restaurant. Both were in Dearborn, not Ann Arbor."

Jo unfolded the paper and looked at the debits from the Karn's Lake Erie Bank and Trust account circled in red.

"A few days later, I followed…" She cleared her throat. "I followed him just after he left for work, and…and, uh…"

And the tears came. She tried to choke them back.

Tried.

["Josephine,"] Gertie chided, ["help the poor woman."]

Sorry, sorry!

Jo set the paper to the side. She reached into her desk drawer and pulled out a box of tissues. She plucked two tissues free and handed them to Mrs. Karn. "Thank you," the woman said, dabbing her eyes carefully, taking care not to smear her makeup. "I apologize for earlier. I didn't mean to snap at you."

"No worries. To quote my favorite movie, *'Hakuna matata.'*" She smiled. "But I have to ask, Mrs. Karn, why do you want to hire me? I'm sure as heck-fire not fussing about it, but with all of the ways to track people nowadays, why take the time to pay me a visit?"

She removed the tissue from her face. "That's just it. Time. I don't have any. I've only been at my current job for a month, and I've already taken two personal days over the past week looking into the comings and goings of my husband. I can't take any further time off. But I need to know what's going on. If we rushed into getting married like my mother said we did, if he's not the man I thought he was, if we…If I made a mistake, then I *need* to know. Even if I don't want to know. If that makes any sense."

Jo said, "Before we dig into this a tad bit more, are you sure I can't get you something to drink?"

Mrs. Karn smiled. "Do you have any scotch?"

Jo laughed. "Oh, gosh, no! I don't drink alcohol!"

And judging from Mrs. Karn's expression, Jo may as well have given her reply in pig Latin.

Jo leaned back in her chair and reread each word, each number on the check in her hand.

"Pay to the order of Carver and Company Inc., in the amount of three thousand dollars and zero cents." The memo section was left blank. Mrs. Karn paid her for a full week in advance on the conditions that one, Jo follow Mr. Karn every waking moment for the ensuing seven days, and two, she not cash the check until the week was over so as not to arouse any suspicion from Mr. Karn in case he took a gander at the bank account. Jo was more than willing to agree to the terms and, to her credit, restrained herself from doing a happy dance and giving Mrs. Karn a bear hug.

("That went better than expected,") Eddie mentioned. ("Three thousand bucks!")

Jo smiled.

("And you have to admit, your boy called it. I knew it was a cheater case.")

"If you had a back, I'd tell you to not pat yourself on it. It's not like you're psychic."

("Maybe I am. You don't know.")

"Oh, I'd know." She turned the check over in her hands. "That's for doggone sure."

["Stop with the dilly-dallying and get a move on,"] Gertie said. ["There could be traffic or accidents out on the road. We don't want to run the risk of being late, now, do we?"]

"Oh, cheese and crackers, we're not going to…" She stopped. She didn't argue. It was better not to argue.

Jo grabbed her purse out of the bottom desk drawer and put the check in her wallet. She checked the side pocket of her purse to make sure her digital recorder was inside, and it was. She closed the drawer, locked it, closed her office door, locked that too, walked down the hall, and went outside to her Ford Taurus waiting for her in the very first spot (and safest spot, according to Gertie) next to the Holman Office Plaza. She checked the tires for any signs of wear or air loss, the exhaust pipe for any obstructions, the ground for any sharp objects, and found nothing. She got into her car, fired it up, and headed east on Michigan Avenue, making sure to check her speed limit every so often. Every other car on the road whizzed past her as if they were attempting to time travel. This was how most people drove in Detroit. Not Josephine Carver.

Coming to a red light at the corner of Michigan and Martin Street, she reached into her purse, brought out the voice recorder, pressed the red button, and sat it down in the passenger seat.

"Karn case notes. September eighteen. Day one, summary…Stephanie Leigh Karn suspects her husband, David Edward Karn, of being a Cheatin' Charlie.

"David works as the auditing manager and billing specialist for Supply

Chain Solutions, a shipping and logistics company based out of Dearborn, Michigan. Stephanie is currently the CFO of Kepske Labs, a company that researches fuel efficiency in automobiles. It, too, is out of Dearborn. Previously she was a supervisor at Supply Chain Solutions, and David's former boss. They met at work, took a shine to each other, dated for a short while, and were married the first of December last year. From courtship to current day, their timeline together spans less than sixteen months."

As she recounted the story of the odd debits cropping up in the Karns' bank statement, the light turned green and Jo continued on her way.

"According to Mrs. Karn, as she and her husband were in the middle of having dinner at their home two weeks ago, he received a phone call and stepped away to take it. After he returned, she asked what it was about. He told her simply, 'Work,' and he didn't chew that fat any further. Her suspicions were piqued again."

A Corvette passed her with a blaring horn and the driver's exposed middle finger poking out of the sunroof.

("Ha!")

["Rude!"]

"The next morning, she decided she was going to follow him to work to try and figure out what the heck was going on. Instead of going to work, however, David drove to the Commonwealth Cafe over on Hamilton Row. Mrs. Karn parked out front and from her vantage point she saw him take a seat with a blond woman at a table out on the patio. She snapped a picture of the meeting on her phone."

She made a right off Michigan onto Gulley Avenue.

"After a half-hour, David and the mysterious woman left the cafe, each riding in their own vehicle. They went to a house a few blocks away on Harlow Avenue. Mrs. Karn said she sat outside for a good twenty minutes and restrained herself from kicking in the front door and beating the stuffing out of the B word, which was not her phrasing, by the way. Thankfully, better judgment prevailed, and she left. It was then she decided to look into hiring a P.I."

Jo pulled into a parking lot off Gulley. She picked up the digital voice recorder and held it near her mouth. "Mrs. Karn already e-mailed me the aforementioned photo, along with the addresses of David's workplace, the Harlow Avenue home, and the make and model of Blondie's vehicle. Starting tomorrow, Tuesday, the nineteenth, I will begin following David Karn. To be continued."

She hit stop, placed the recorder back into her purse, and got out. She headed into the Lucky Star Chinese buffet, where she had pepper steak and what was arguably the best hot and sour soup in the area, if not—hyperbole be darned—the universe.

With a three-thousand-dollar check burning a hole in her purse, a bellyful of hot and sour soup, and a new case to keep her occupied, her life couldn't get any better.

But for others, things were about to get complicated.

Truth be told, the days and nights of a private detective are not as glamorous or seedy as the TV shows, movies, novels, or short stories make them out to be. Yes, occasionally there are the cases that have more twists and turns than a pinwheel in a windstorm, and every so often there are the odd characters, the abrasive individuals, good guys that turn out to be bad guys and vice versa. Most times, though, the average job consists primarily of two specific things: sitting on one's duff and trying very hard not to fall asleep.

It was an average Tuesday for her.

She was up, ready, and out the door by seven-fifteen. She parked curbside a few doors down from the Karn residence, a large colonial home with a massive front yard, at seven fifty-one. David Karn's Escalade pulled out of the garage at eight-ten and navigated down the street. Jo followed, keeping two car lengths behind him at all times.

Minutes later, he pulled into the Supply Chain Solutions parking lot. Across the street was a piece of property that used to house an engineering facility for the Ford Motor Company. Jo pulled in there, parked, and snatched her binoculars from her glove box just as Karn stepped out of the Escalade. He was a thin man in every sense of the word. His frame was lanky, his fingers long and slender, and what was left of his hair seemed to cover only the small spaces above his ears and the back of his head in fine brown wisps. He entered the building, and Jo saw the lights of his office click on at exactly eight-thirty.

("We've got a good vantage point here,") Eddie said. ("Talk about good luck.")

"Definitely."

["We can't always rely on luck, Josephine. It happened to work out that his office was located at the front of the building as Mrs. Karn indicated, but when we undertake surveillance for the next case, we should consider the following options…"]

As the impromptu lecture droned on, David logged into his computer and checked his e-mail, then the voicemails on his desk phone, then went back to his computer and checked his bank statement, the *Detroit News* website, and his e-mail again.

And those were the most exciting things that transpired for the first four hours of the day. Over the course of the remaining five, he stepped out to grab a bite to eat at the McDonald's right next to his workplace. He brought a sack and a drink back to his office and ate a Big Mac and fries at his desk, fielded phone calls and e-mails, and spoke with random coworkers who dropped by his office.

Then it was five P.M. Then he went home. And wherever David Karn went, the P.I. was sure to go. She parked in the same spot as she had that morning.

The only thing more impressive than Jo's patience in those situations was the control she had over her bladder. Prior to opening her business, she'd spent six years working homicide for the Michigan State Police, and the six years prior to that as an MP in the U.S. Army. Many a stakeout and many nights spent on guard duty taught her the ways and means to ignore the call of nature, but even the most Zen of bladder masters must eventually submit. There was a Rite Aid a block away from the Karn residence. She went in, asked to use the restroom, and afterward bought a Snickers bar and a can of Mountain Dew to munch on.

["That's what you're eating for dinner?"] Gertie asked. ["Do you *want* diabetes? You remember what happened to your grandfather's foot, don't you?"]

She returned to the Karn house. Just after ten P.M., the lights were cut off. Jo waited another half-hour before heading out and decided to make one quick stop along the way before going home.

During the moments of downtime throughout the day (which, frankly, were most moments throughout the day), she looked up what she could on the blonde's residence. A property-records search for 357 Harlow Avenue turned up goose eggs, and there was zilch by way of info on Zillow or any other realty site. She put a call in to the Wayne County register of deeds office and that venture turned out to be about as lucrative as a gold mine filled with pyrite.

"Register's," was all the female voice on the phone said.

"Hello there!" Jo greeted. "I sure hope you're having a pleasant afternoon!"

The voice offered no reply.

"Anyhoo, I'd like some information on a property located at 357 Harlow Avenue."

"One minute."

It took longer than one minute. In fact, it took fifteen of them before the voice cut through the hold music on the phone and said, "Lemme transfer ya."

Two minutes later, a man's voice said, "Supervisor's office."

Jo said she hoped he was having a pleasant day and told him what she needed.

"Hang on."

And she did, for five more minutes. When he returned…"I'm going to have to transfer you."

And a phone, somewhere deep in that governmental labyrinth of dead ends and no answers, rang three times before a voice-message recording declared that "Larry Bartlett" was "away" from his "desk," but if Jo "would like to leave a message," he'd "call back as soon as possible."

Jo left a message. She didn't receive a call back, as soon as possible or otherwise.

She headed east on Woodward Avenue and made a right onto Harlow. Number 357, a two-story colonial, sat near the end of the street. No lights were on inside or out, nor were there any vehicles in the driveway or parked in front of the home. The neighbors across the street were setting their trash out for pickup the next morning, as were the people next door. Seeing no need to arouse anyone's suspicion by hanging around too long or walking up to the place to peek inside the windows, Jo headed home and was in bed and asleep by twelve-thirty A.M.

Wednesday was a replay of Tuesday, and Thursday was a rerun of Wednesday.

Friday looked as if it was going to fall in line with the previous days, but a few minutes before eleven-thirty, paydirt was struck. As she peered through her binoculars into David's office, she saw the screen of his cell phone flicker to life. He picked it up and entered his passcode. "Twelve-one-nineteen," Jo said in cadence with each key stroke.

["His wedding day,"] Gertie reminded.

A text asked, "U free 2 meet??"

He responded, "Yeah when and where?"

"Noon @ sushi place off Mich Ave?"

"Sounds good. I'll see you then."

A surge of electricity shot through Jo. "Holy cats, this might be it!"

["It may be nothing."]

She started her car. "It might be gosh-darned everything!"

She headed over to O'Sushi Bar and Grill and backed into a space at the rear of the lot where she had a good view of the building and the lot entrance. Twenty minutes later, a newer-model black Lincoln fitting the description that Mrs. Karn gave her pulled in and parked two spaces away from Jo. A squint through the midday sun revealed a woman with short-cropped blond hair and a black leather jacket sitting behind the wheel.

"There's our mystery woman."

The Lincoln must've opened a traffic floodgate somewhere, considering that the lunch crowd started pouring into the lot. Within two minutes most of the spaces were filled, including the space that separated Jo's car from the blonde's Lincoln courtesy of a massive F-350 truck. Within five minutes of that, David Karn's Escalade entered the lot. He parked near the front, got out, and went inside the restaurant. Jo waited for the blonde to cross the lot, but there was no sign of her.

More cars entered. Jo checked Mickey and saw that five minutes had passed. Then ten. Then twenty. Still no sign. "What the heck is going on?"

Jo got out of her car.

["Act casual."]

"For Pete's sake, I know," she whispered.

She sauntered by the Lincoln, acting just like a normal, everyday pedestrian, trying not to be suspicious at all, la-dee-dah, dum-dee-dum, and out of the corner of her eye she saw the blonde still behind the wheel.

In both senses of the phrase.

Jo turned and looked directly at her. The woman's head was leaned back against the seat and tilted slightly to the left. Her eyes were open. So was her mouth.

("Oh boy.")

No wind passed through the parking lot in that moment, but a chill found Jo all the same.

Jo rushed to the car. She reached through the open driver's-side window and checked for a pulse but felt only a smooth neck beneath her fingertips. The pupils centered in the woman's gray eyes sat like tunnels to nowhere.

["Focus, now. Check the body, the sides of the head, and the neck. Wounds? Abrasions? None? Okay, you're going to have to start chest compressions."]

Jo cast a quick glance about. The parking lot was buzzing like a hive a few minutes ago and now it was devoid of signs of life. She opened the car door, unbuckled the seatbelt, and pulled the woman from the car and laid her on a clear space of ground beside her Lincoln. Jo dug her cell phone out of her back pocket and dialed 911.

["You'll have to make sure the compressions are hard and focused."]

"I know, Gertie! Jeez!" Jo stuck her phone between her ear and her shoulder.

"Nine-one-one, what's your emergency?"

She gave the dispatcher her credentials, the location, and the situation. Although she didn't need it, the dispatcher and, yes, Gertie walked her through the CPR. After five minutes, it was clear the woman was gone. The dispatcher asked her to stay on the line until the EMTs arrived. Jo decided to search the woman for ID and unzipped her jacket.

["You may want to ch—"]

("What the…?")

The handle of what looked to be a 9mm tucked inside a shoulder holster jutted out from between the lining of the woman's jacket and her left breast.

Jo forced herself to ignore it for the time being and patted the right-side jacket pocket, felt something, reached in and pulled out a wallet. A passport wallet, to be exact. She opened it and looked for the woman's name but quickly saw she would never find it there. The passport, it turned out, belonged to David Karn.

And he was smiling at Jo from the picture.

("Uh…")

A ringtone chirped from inside the Lincoln.

Jo quickly poked her head inside the car and saw the iPhone sitting in a cupholder in the center console. She grabbed it. A text was sent from David Karn asking where she was. Jo quickly scrolled through their text history, which was short and was mostly comprised of "You there?" or "I'm free to meet Monday," or "Sure," or "Any word yet?"

She soon found the beginning of the text chain, dated three weeks prior.

"I need your help with a problem," Karn told her.

"What problem?" the woman replied.

"About me and my wife. Can you help?"

"Meet me at the house later."

Jo's gaze swung back toward the gun.

("So,") Eddie said, ("I may have been wrong about our case.")

A siren drew close from somewhere in the city.

Saturday morning, just after nine-thirty…

"Are you getting enough sleep?" Dr. Schaumberg asked.

"Oh yes," Jo said.

["Be honest."]

"Well, what I mean is I get darned near my usual six or seven hours. Well, five or six."

["Josephine."]

"Most days." She closed her eyes, took a breath, and opened them again to see a smile shining out from the center of Max Schaumberg's white beard. "A lot of chatter, I take it?" he asked.

Her grin was sheepish. "Yeah."

"From Gertie?"

"Oh yeah."

"Remind me, you named her after your grandmother, correct? The linguistics professor?"

"Yes, my mom's mom, rest her soul. She was the one who told me folks judge you by your language. 'Be clean in all that you do. Vulgar words betray vulgarity in thought and deed.' I guess it was a strange thing to write in a birthday card to a five-year-old, but darn good advice, nonetheless!"

He laughed. "When did she pass?"

"When I was eight. Just before I started hearing the voices regularly."

"And the other voice is named Edison, right?"

"Yep! Eddie for short."

"After Thomas Edison, I take it?"

"Oh no, no. I named him after my grandmother's cat. The voice always reminded me of him. Friendly, but kind of, you know, a bit lazy. And besides, we all know Gertie's the brainy one!"

("Hey!")

"Why don't you go ahead and lie down on your stomach for me," he told her, and she did. He pressed a button on the wall and lowered the examination table about a foot. The doctor's thumbs and fingertips inspected the back of her neck and felt around the base of her skull and the side of her neck. He then placed one of his palms on the upper part of her back. "Relax," he said and pressed down on her spine. A crack that sounded like a celery stalk being broken in half blasted out of her. The pain seared for only a second before a welcome calm drafted through her. She felt his hand move down to the center of her spine. "Relax." Another quick flash of pain, another stream of relief. Down to the base of the spine. Another crack. "Turn over." She did. He moved his hands to the back of her neck, cupped the sides of her face, and gave a quick twist. The snaps and pops echoed in her skull.

After five minutes of this, Dr. Schaumberg pressed the button once more and the exam table rose back to its original position. "You can sit up now," he told her.

She did, and every part of her felt fresh and limber. "Thank you, Doc."

"No thanks necessary," he said.

Dr. Schaumberg was a good man. She'd known him for a little more than three years and started going to him upon the recommendation of Detective Tanya Laxly, a former coworker of hers on the state police force. Jo had wrenched her back after getting into a car accident chasing a van leaving the scene of a bank robbery. Laxly recommended Schaumberg Chiropractic to her. "That man's a miracle worker!"

Jo was sceptical at first, considering that she'd heard that chiropractic techniques were rooted in new-age mumbo jumbo (something that Gertie reminded her of daily), but she gave it a go, figuring that maybe some mumbo and a bit of jumbo would be less painful than the tightness in her spine.

During her initial visit, he'd asked her about having any underlying conditions or mental or physical issues. Without hesitation, Jo told him about the voices. She'd felt comfortable with him and didn't feel embarrassed talking about it like she did with most people. She did, however, make sure to tell him she was declared mentally sound by psychologists when she was a child, and again when she joined the army, and yet again when she joined the police force, nor did she suffer from schizophrenia or any similar disorder. She also pointed out that three percent of all people in the world hear voices, and even Martin Luther King heard them. She then proceeded to trip over herself saying that she "sure as all get-out" wasn't comparing herself to MLK. Dr. Schaumberg told her he understood what she meant.

From there, the two became friendly, and Jo saw their little visits as a form of therapy; a relaxed body helps relax the mind, after all. She was able to share most things with the man, highlights from her personal life and a few of the cases she'd worked on. But that day, when he asked her, "Have anything interesting going on today?" she couldn't tell him what it was. She wanted to, but officially, legally, she could not.

She didn't want to lie either. "Just work," she said.

Eleven A.M. . . .

Jo entered the office building and nodded at the craggy gentleman in the janitor's uniform pushing the dust mop in the hallway. He nodded in return.

She unlocked her door, propped it open, sat down, and put her purse into the bottom desk drawer. As she waited there, her eyes got lost in the swirls in the woodgrain patterns atop her desk.

["Let's focus, shall we? We have to prepare for..."]

She thought of white noise and static, anything at all to drown Gertie's voice. She didn't feel the need to hear it right then.

And Stephanie Karn didn't feel the need to wait in the doorway this time. The woman walked in without introduction and sat down. One leg crossed over the other beneath the skirt of her blue casual dress. "Considering you called and said you wanted to meet ahead of the full week I paid for, I assume you have something for me?"

Jo nodded.

"He was cheating, wasn't he?"

Images of the gun and the dead woman's face flashed in Jo's mind. "No, ma'am," she said, "he wasn't."

"Then who's the woman?"

"Stacey Bettinger."

A sigh came from her. "Telling me her name doesn't explain what my husband was doing with her! Now I want to know what's going on!"

As if on cue, David Karn showed himself in the office doorway, hands shoved deep into the pockets of his jeans. "She was helping me," he told his wife, and said to Jo, "Sorry I'm late. There was traffic on Michigan Avenue."

Gertie, thankfully, kept quiet.

"What are you doing here?" Stephanie asked her husband, but before he could answer, another question was lobbed at him. "Helping you with what?"

"French," he said.

Her nose wrinkled. "What?"

("She doesn't believe him.")

["Defuse the situation."]

"Your husband applied for a passport at the post office in Dearborn," Jo told her. "He asked the employees there if they knew anyone who spoke French. Turns out, Stacey Bettinger, a supervisor at that location, did. They met for a few sessions together, some at a local restaurant, some at her residence."

Mrs. Karn asked her husband, "Why are you learning…"

He pulled two plane tickets from his back pocket and handed them to her.

Stephanie took the tickets and read them. "Paris?"

"Happy anniversary," he said. "It was supposed to be a surprise. But I guess I should've told you."

She handed the tickets back. Her mouth tried forming words.

Tried.

"You always wanted to go," he said, "so I figured our anniversary would be a good time."

"I…I didn't think that…" And that was as far as she got. She slowly rose out of the chair and smoothed the front of her skirt. She turned to her husband and hugged him around the neck. He returned it and smiled at Jo from the other side of his wife's shoulder.

"It was stupid of me not to trust you," Stephanie said.

"It was stupid of me not to tell you."

"No," she said, "don't say that." She breathed deep. "I'm…I'm just glad we're okay."

"Me too."

They kissed.

Jo smiled and informed Mrs. Karn, "I haven't deposited the check, just FYI. If you want, I can tear it up."

Stephanie removed her arms from her husband. "No," she said. "Keep it. You… You deserve it."

("Thank God! I thought that was a stupid part of the plan anyway!")

"Let's get out of here and leave Ms. Carver alone," Stephanie said to her husband.

They turned to go, but before he left, Mr. Karn mouthed a thank-you to Jo.

You're welcome, Jo said in silence.

Alone in the office, her eyes again went to the patterns on her desk.

The man in the janitor's uniform walked in and cast a glance around the place. Jo looked up at him. He leaned the handle of his dust mop against the door frame. "You did good, Carver," he said.

"I sure as heck don't see how," she said. "I got paid for a case that wasn't a case at all."

He shrugged. "Consider it a reward for helping to keep two people safe. Either way, I appreciate it. Agent Bettinger would have too."

By that he meant Special Agent Stacey Bettinger of the FBI, not the post office, shockingly enough.

"Has there been any word from the coroner?" she asked.

"It was a heart attack, like you thought," Special Agent Norman Milewski told her. "She had tons of blockage and didn't even know about it. Sad to go so sudden… She was only forty-nine years old. You believe that?"

The day before, after discovering the texting chain between Bettinger and Karn, Jo sent a text from the woman's phone and told him to come outside and talk. When he did, he saw Bettinger lying on the ground and asked Jo what happened. She told him she suspected it was a massive coronary, considering there were no signs of trauma, or wounds, and Bettinger seemed fine and was able to drive without any signs of impairment just moments prior, which, of course, probably ruled out an aneurysm. Karn asked if she was a doctor. Jo said, "Goodness no, but thanks a million for the compliment!"

"Then who are you?" he asked. And she told him; about herself, about his wife, the case, everything. And the phrase "Oh my God" passed his lips repeatedly, like a mantra.

Once the ambulance arrived and Bettinger was hauled to the coroner's, statements were given to the Dearborn police. The investigator and the husband stayed behind in the parking lot well out of earshot from other people. Jo asked, point-blank, "What's the scoop, Mr. Karn? Is it Wit Protec or are you a CI?"

David stammered. "How…?"

Jo told him that when she saw Agent Bettinger's 9mm and the texts, her first instinct was to assume it was a murder-for-hire case (which, of course, prompted yet another warning from Gertie about assumptions), but when Jo patted down the woman a second time while waiting for Karn to come out of the restaurant, she found Bettinger's federal ID tucked in her back pocket. Things, then, started to take a more discernable shape.

It was doubtful that Karn was working undercover with the feds since he never noticed a P.I. trailing him for three whole days. Also, if he had any sort of training, he wouldn't have been so careless as to sit with his back to a window while at his day job. But with Bettinger being in possession of a passport which contained a very recent photo of Mr. Karn (he was wearing the same exact gray suit, burgundy tie, off-white dress shirt, and black pocket square he had on the day Stephanie Karn snapped a picture of his lunch with Bettinger at the Commonwealth Cafe), it had to be that he was working with the feds in some way to be able to get a document like that expedited so quickly, and that more than likely meant he was either a confidential informant or someone brand new to the Witness Protection Program.

It came out that David Karn's birth name was actually Philip DeMaro, and David Karn/Philip DeMaro was placed in Witness Protection a little under two years prior for turning state's evidence against the Colombo crime family in New York. He'd been the family's "numbers guy" (accountant, in other words) since he was a teenager. After the feds raided a host of strip clubs on the East Coast which were money-laundering fronts for the family, Karn/DeMaro copped a plea in exchange for dropping all charges and receiving a new identity.

The feds made sure he got a new driver's license and social-security card, but a passport slipped everyone's minds. Wanting to head to Paris for his first anniversary, Karn/DeMaro contacted Bettinger to see if there was any way she could help him in not only securing the passport but making sure his likeness and info from his past was removed from the FAA No-Fly List.

After the truth was spilled, Karn/DeMaro called another FBI contact. Enter Norman Milewski, Bettinger's superior.

Milewski asked to meet them both at the FBI safe house. On Harlow Avenue. Jo realized then why it was so darn difficult to track the homeowner documentation of the house, and she could've kicked her own keister for not figuring it out earlier. It also happened to be the place where Bettinger took the passport photo, she was told.

Once there, Milewski stressed to Jo the importance of keeping Karn/De-Maro's identity a secret. Jo understood, and within seconds it was she who proposed the post-office narrative. She also said it might be a good idea to not let on to Mrs. Karn that Stacey Bettinger had passed away, otherwise that could draw a whole slew of questions and queries. Milewski mulled it over and considered it passable enough to cover all angles. Gertie, of course, wanted to take more variables into consideration, but time was of the essence.

Milewski grabbed the dust mop from the door frame. "I'm going to have to get with DeMaro later and tell him to keep his eyes open from here on out," he said. "And to tell him to reimburse me for getting those plane tickets on such short notice."

"Well, that was surely nice of you!"

"I'm only trying to make sure that idiot doesn't get caught," he grumbled. "I wasn't chipping in on a friggin' anniversary gift." He thrust his chin at her. "See ya, Carver."

"Bye!"

He left.

("Guy's got his hands full.")

"Yeah."

["It's a pity we had to lie, even for the greater good. You know I despise that."]

"Yeah, yeah, we know."

["Watch the tone, young lady."]

("Again with 'young lady'? She's thirty-four!")

"Stop mentioning my age, for goodness' sake!"

Milewski returned to the doorway. "What?"

"I'm sorry?" Jo asked.

"I thought you said something to me."

"Oh. No, not you." She laughed.

Milewski stared at the woman for a short eternity before leaving a second time.

Jo's cell phone rang. She opened the desk drawer and brought it out of her purse. "Carver and Company... Oh hello, Mr. Bartlett... You can't locate the docs for 357 Harlow? Oh, that's okay, I don't need them now, but thank you kindly for returning my call!"

Afterword

We live in a world of spoiler alerts and after-reading conversation, and this anthology gives us a wonderful opportunity for such discussion. As mystery fans, we're used to this: We want a chance to solve the mystery on our own but enjoy checking in with other readers afterward. This book, with its deeply personal, profoundly subjective, often conflicted, and sometimes strange voices, gives us a deeper level on which to reflect: Are any of these voices like our own? Which voices did you believe? And do you believe your own?

The last fifteen years have ushered in a renaissance of psychological suspense by way of the "unreliable narrator" in fiction, television, and film. In countless television series and suspense novels, even true-crime documentaries presented in suspenseful narrative form, we constantly question the narrator—to the point of the unpredictability becoming, well, predictable. What we love about this anthology is that it isn't just the twists and turns of the mysteries themselves but the way they're presented, experienced, and solved that draw the reader in—and the delicious quirks in these voices can sometimes help the characters solve their problems and the mystery.

For example, the protagonist in "Three Calendars" deals with a memory disorder, but her particular focus on keeping track of things helps solve a murder, while in "Carver (and) [Company]," a private eye's multiple personalities are what helps her practice succeed.

We can relate to what informs the minds of these characters, as they also inform ours: In "Never Enough," "Hedge Hog," and "A Complicated History," the narrators' desire propels the action forward—for better or for worse—while in "The Belgian," "No Peace for the Wicked," "Jenny's Necklace," and

"Best Served Cold," burning questions about the past dictate what unfolds. A need for survival influences the crime in "What Kind of Criminal?", and a false sense of heroism in "Tradition" and "My Shopping Day."

Isn't it interesting what these characters reveal, and when? Sometimes, it's a dishonest profession of honesty, and other times it's a reveal of something true right off the bat—but not the whole truth ("Summertime and the Livin's Easy in Saratoga"). In "Hey, Dad," the suspense ratchets up and up as the narrator reveals more and more about what seems a celebratory occasion.

First-person storytelling opens a world of possibilities in terms of form and tone too: Some voices break fully through the "fourth wall" and address the reader directly, such as in "Shall I Be Murder?" (answers to a police interview), "The Advent Reunion" (a long-awaited confession), and "Dear Emily Etiquette" (an advice column). In "Motormouth," we see one side of a breathless conversation, and other tellings, such as "Cleopatran Cocktails," are poetic. And in "The Kim Novak Effect," we are dropped intimately into the protagonist's dangerous situation.

Some of our favorite sleuths in mystery fiction are known for their idiosyncrasies, and the way their minds work is what makes them crack detectives; the incredibly methodical is as unique as the incredibly passionate (not to mention the mood-altering substances for which some of the great fictional detectives are known). We discussed the Watson-like, objective narrator in our introduction, but if in some of our favorite mysteries the sleuths—Sherlock Holmes, Nero Wolfe, Hercule Poirot, for example—had narrated their own stories, instead of their sidekicks doing so, they might read more like the stories in this book.

We hope that this book gave you thrills, chills, a laugh or two, and a new way to imagine and experience points of view in fiction and in your own life.

—Jackie Sherbow

Contributor Bios

Doug Allyn

Doug Allyn is one of the leading contemporary writers of short crime and mystery fiction. His first story won the Robert L. Fish Award for best short story by a new American author, and he went on to win two best short story Edgar Allan Poe Awards from the Mystery Writers of America, a Macavity Award for best short story from Mystery Readers International, and a record-breaking eleven Readers Awards from *Ellery Queen's Mystery Magazine*. More than two dozen of his stories have been optioned for feature films or television. He is also the author of eight novels, plus a novel coauthored with James Patterson. His work has been translated into German, French, and Japanese.

Joyce Carol Oates

Called "America's preeminent fiction writer" by *The New Yorker*, Joyce Carol Oates is the author of more than sixty-two novels and forty-seven short-story collections. Although she is primarily a literary writer, her work is not confined to literary fiction: It includes occasional contributions to the crime-fiction and horror genres and even several children's books. The Roger S. Berlind '52 Professor Emerita in the Humanities at Princeton University, she is also the author of numerous volumes of essays and other nonfiction. Her many contributions to American letters have brought her a National Book Award, two O. Henry Awards, the National Humanities Medal, the Jerusalem Prize, and many other honors, including, in the crime-fiction field, multiple International Thriller Awards.

Martin Edwards

The author of more than eighty short stories and both stand-alone and series novels, for which he has received numerous award nominations and the 2018 Dagger in the Library Award, Martin Edwards is also crime fiction's leading critical writer. His books *The Golden Age of Murder* (2016) and *The Life of Crime* (2022) both won the Edgar, Macavity, and H.R.F. Keating awards for best critical/biographical book, with the former also winning an Agatha Award and the latter an Anthony. The British author is a recipient of the U.K.'s most distinguished crime-writing award, the Diamond Dagger for lifetime achievement, and he's the current president of Britain's famed Detection Club.

LaToya Jovena

LaToya Jovena's first professional fiction publication was the story "The Winner," which appeared in *Ellery Queen's Mystery Magazine*'s Department of First Stories in November/December 2020. She has gone on to sell several more stories to both *EQMM* and *Alfred Hitchcock's Mystery Magazine*. Her story "Stingers" was included in 2022's *The Best American Mystery and Suspense*, edited by Jess Walter.

Ian Rankin

Ian Rankin, internationally best-selling author of the Detective Inspector John Rebus series and other critically acclaimed novels, is a recipient of the Chandler-Fulbright Award, the Edgar Allan Poe Award, and four major awards from the British Crime Writers Association: the Golden Dagger for best novel, two best short story Daggers, and the Diamond Dagger for lifetime achievement. His Rebus novels have been translated into thirty-six languages and adapted for two television series. In 2002 the Scottish author was appointed Officer of the Order of the British Empire (OBE) for services to literature and in 2022 he received a knighthood from HM Queen Elizabeth II for services to literature and charity.

Andrew Klavan

Author of more than three dozen novels, including the *Homelanders* series for young adults, Andrew Klavan is a two-time winner of the Edgar Allan Poe Award. Three of his books were made into major motion pictures: *True Crime, Don't Say a Word,* and *Mrs. White* (which he wrote with his brother Laurence Klavan and which was adapted for film as *White of the Eye).* He has also written numerous short stories and screenplays. Among the latter is *A Shock to the System,* starring Michael Caine, from the Simon Brett novel of that title.

Barb Goffman

Short story writer and editor Barb Goffman has been nominated for major crime-fiction awards forty-one times. Her short stories have earned three Agatha Awards, two Macavity Awards, the Anthony and Silver Falchion awards, and the 2020 *Ellery Queen's Mystery Magazine* Readers Award. Her book *Don't Get Mad, Get Even* won the Silver Falchion Award for best single-author mystery short story collection.

Daniel C. Bartlett

A professor of English at Lamar University in Beaumont, Texas, Daniel C. Bartlett has had short stories published in Iron Horse Literary Review, Chiron Review, Crab Creek Review, and other literary journals, as well as in *Mystery* magazine and *Ellery Queen's Mystery Magazine.* His first novel has recently come under representation by a major literary agency.

Tom Tolnay

Tom Tolnay has sold dozens of stories to magazines ranging from *Ellery Queen's Mystery Magazine* and *Alfred Hitchcock's Mystery Magazine* to the *Saturday Evening Post,* the *North Dakota Quarterly,* and *Confrontation.* Awards for his fiction include the Theodore Goodman Short Story Award and first prize in *Literal Latte*'s National Fiction Competition. His story "The Ghost of F. Scott Fitzgerald," winner of the Literal Latte prize, was made into a short film by Sea Lions Productions starring Alexa Davalos and screened at festivals in Toronto, Savannah, and Woodstock. His latest short story collection, *Profane Feasts*, recently won a Literary Titan Book Award.

Hilary Davidson

Hilary Davidson was a journalist before starting to write crime fiction. Her novels include the award-winning Lily Moore series, the best-selling Shadows of New York series, and the stand-alone novels *Blood Always Tells* and *Her Last Breath*. She is also the author of more than fifty short stories. Her fiction has won two Anthony Awards, a Derringer Award, and a host of other accolades. Her novels have been translated into French, German, Hungarian, Polish, and Russian.

O.A. Tynan

O. A. Tynan debuted in *Ellery Queen's Mystery Magazine's* Department of First Stories in 2013, and has sold three additional stories to *EQMM* since then. Born in Limerick, Ireland, she is a longtime resident of Italy, where for many years she worked as editor of an Italian-language golf magazine. She is now a professional translator from Italian to English.

Ed Gorman

Ed Gorman (November 2, 1941 – October 14, 2016) was an American fiction writer, publisher, critic, and anthologist. A cofounder of *Mystery Scene Magazine*, he won a Spur Award for best short story, an Anthony Award for best critical work (for *The Fine Art of Murder*), the International Horror Writers Award, and the Private Eye Writers of America's lifetime achievement award. The *Bloomsbury* Review called him "the poet of dark suspense."

William Burton McCormick

William Burton McCormick is an Edgar, Thriller, Shamus, Derringer, Sliver Falchion and Claymore awards finalist whose fiction regularly appears in *Ellery Queen's Mystery Magazine, Alfred Hitchcock's Mystery*

Magazine, The Saturday Evening Post, Mystery Weekly, and elsewhere. He is the author of the novels *Lenin's Harem, House of Tigers, KGB Banker,* and *A Stranger From the Storm,* and was elected a Hawthornden Writing Fellow in Scotland.

Alice Hatcher

Alice Hatcher is the author of *The Wonder That Was Ours* (Dzanc, 2018), the winner of the 2017 Dzanc Books Prize for Fiction. In 2019, she won the Eric Hoffer New Horizon Award, and in 2023, *Reed Magazine's* John Steinbeck Award for fiction. Her short fiction and essays have appeared in numerous journals, including *Alaska Quarterly Review, Pleiades, Bellevue Literary Review,* and *Fourth Genre.* She teaches at the Tucson branch of the NYC-based creative writing school, The Writers Studio.

Gary Phillips

Gary Phillips is the author of some fifty short stories and more than a dozen novels, including several graphic novels and 1994's *Violent Spring,* which is considered a classic work of crime fiction and was named, in 2020, one of the essential crime novels about Los Angeles. He is also an activist and educator, and an anthologist whose collections include *Orange County Noir* and the award-winning *The Obama Inheritance: Fifteen Stories of Conspiracy Noir.*

Angelique Fawns

Angelique Fawns is a journalist who currently works full-time making television commercials for Global TV in Toronto. She made her fiction debut in the Department of First Stories of *Ellery Queen's Mystery Magazine's* November/December 2019 issue and has continued to write stories in the fields of mystery and speculative fiction. Her work has appeared in *Mystery Tribune, The Mantelpiece Lit, Haunted MTL,* and elsewhere.

Mat Coward

Mat Coward is a British writer of crime fiction, science fiction, humor, and children's fiction. He is also gardening columnist for the *Morning Star* newspaper. His short stories have been nominated twice for the Edgar Allan Poe Award and shortlisted for the British Crime Writers Association's best short story Dagger. His work has been published on four continents, translated into several languages, and broadcast on BBC Radio. In addition to fiction, he's written books about radio comedy and brought out collections of funny press cuttings.

S.J. Rozan

S.J. Rozan, a native New Yorker and a former architect, is the author of eighteen novels and more than seventy-five short stories as well as the editor of three anthologies. She has won the Edgar, Shamus, Anthony, Nero, and Macavity awards for best novel and the Edgar for best short story. She's also won the Japanese Maltese Falcon and the Private Eye Writers of America's lifetime achievement award. *Bronx Noir*, one of the short story anthologies she edited, was chosen NAIBA "Notable Book of the Year."

Liza Cody

Liza Cody is the author of sixteen novels and about three dozen short stories. She is generally credited with creating the first female private eye in British crime fiction. When her work first appeared on the mystery scene in the 1980s it was to immediate recognition with the John Creasey Memorial Prize for best first novel. She has since earned two Edgar nominations, two CWA Dagger nominations, an Anthony Award, and Germany's Marlowe Award.

Mike McHone

Mike McHone is an American novelist, short story writer, poet, and former journalist from Detroit. His short fiction has appeared in *Ellery Queen's Mystery Magazine, Alfred Hitchcock's Mystery Magazine, Mystery Weekly, Mystery Tribune, Sherlock Holmes Mystery Magazine,* and elsewhere, including the anthology *Under the Thumb: Stories of Police Oppression,* edited by S.A. Cosby.

About the Editors

Janet Hutchings has been the editor-in-chief of *Ellery Queen's Mystery Magazine* since 1991. She is a co-winner of the Mystery Writers of America's Ellery Queen Award and the Malice Domestic Convention's Poirot Award, and in 2003 she was honored by the Bouchercon World Mystery Convention for contributions to the field. Under her editorship *EQMM* was named Best Magazine/Review Publication by Bouchercon 27 and in 2017 was celebrated by Bouchercon 48 for Distinguished Contribution to the Genre. Her own short stories have appeared in anthologies from the Mystery Writers of America, Bouchercon, the New York chapter of Sisters in Crime, and elsewhere.

Jackie Sherbow is the Queens, New York-based senior managing editor of *Ellery Queen's Mystery Magazine* and *Alfred Hitchcock's Mystery Magazine*, the author of the poetry collection *Harbinger* (Finishing Line Press), the publisher at THRASH Press, and a short-story author whose work has appeared in *Mystery* magazine and several anthologies.

SOCIAL MEDIA HANDLES:
  Twitter: @eqmm
  Instagram: @elleryqueenmm
  Facebook: facebook.com/elleryqueenmm
  blog: www.somethingisgoingtohappen.net

EQMM WEBSITE:
  www.elleryqueenmysterymagazine.net

Also by Janet Hutchings and Jackie Sherbow

Terror at the Crossroads: Tales of Horror, Delusion, and the Unknown, edited by Emily Hockaday and Jackie Sherbow

The Crooked Road, Volume 1, edited by Janet Hutchings

The Crooked Road, Volume 2, edited by Janet Hutchings

The Crooked Road, Volume 3, edited by Janet Hutchings

Passport to Crime, edited by Janet Hutchings

The Deadliest Games, edited by Janet Hutchings

EQ Presents Great Mystery Novellas, edited by Janet Hutchings

Simply the Best Mysteries, edited by Janet Hutchings

Crème de la Crime, edited by Janet Hutchings

Murder Most British, edited by Janet Hutchings

Once Upon a Crime, Volume 1, edited by Janet Hutcings

Once Upon a Crime, Volume 2, edited by Janet Hutchings